PRAISE FOR *THE*

"Enthralling and highly imaginative. *The Surviving Sky* is a richly crafted story set in a fascinating world… I loved the protagonists and their relationship, fraught with tension and secrets, ambition and desire."

Sue Lynn Tan, bestselling author of *Daughter of the Moon Goddess*

"*The Surviving Sky* is a fast-paced, fascinating novel wrapped in philosophy and spirituality. Rao's debut will dazzle many."

Fantasy Hive

"Rao weaves a tale of broken love, redemption, and the Hindu concept of samsara in her magical and mind-bending debut… this heart-pounding cli-fi adventure will leave readers breathless."

Publishers Weekly starred review

"This Hindu-inspired sci-fi fantasy is a transcendent debut, full of cosmic magic and set in an exquisitely glorious and treacherous world. Such a daring ecological and metaphysical endeavor is perfect for fans of Wesley Chu and Brandon Sanderson."

Library Journal starred review

"Kritika H. Rao crafts an inventive and cerebral debut, reimagining South Asian culture in a wonderfully different world. A story about love, duty, power, as much as it is about fascinating lore and costly magic."

R. R. Virdi, bestselling author of *The First Binding*

"Breathtakingly inventive, *The Surviving Sky* is a twisty, cerebral journey. . . This is a book to get lost in."
TASHA SURI, AUTHOR OF THE BURNING KINGDOMS TRILOGY

"*The Surviving Sky* is a high-octane science fantasy with heady, cerebral ideas and a lushly imagined world, whose story centers on a 30s-ish married couple—very unusual for fantasy! There is nothing else out there which is quite like it!"
SUNYI DEAN, AUTHOR OF *THE BOOK EATERS*

"A reading experience that is incalculably enjoyable, creatively built, thoroughly immersive, and just like a majority of concepts in Hindu philosophy, thought-provoking and incredibly hard to distill."
FANTASY BOOK CRITIC

"A unique blend of sci-fi futurism, eco-fantasy mystery, and intriguing spirituality. . . truly unlike anything I've ever read. Extremely original and thought-provoking. . . I utterly loved it and couldn't put it down."
SHANNON CHAKRABORTY, INTERNATIONALLY BESTSELLING AUTHOR OF THE DAEVABAD TRILOGY

"Intensely imaginative and heartbreakingly human. . . Filled with both startling revelations and the intimate portrait of a struggling marriage, this is a story that is hard to put down."
ANDREA STEWART, AUTHOR OF *THE BONE SHARD DAUGHTER*

"*The Surviving Sky* weaves a compelling web of wounded hearts and warped duty. . . Fall from its floating city's edge into a storm of emotions!"
MELISSA CARUSO, AUTHOR OF *THE OBSIDIAN TOWER*

"*The Surviving Sky* is a prodigious gift best slowly unwrapped. Nakshar is an enigma of a city, as rooted and protective as its people; its stakes feel cosmic yet intimate… Rao has offered us a world like no other."
Suyi Davies Okungbowa, author of *Son of the Storm*

"This wildly imaginative book explores a fracturing world through the deeply painful lens of a fracturing human heart. At times brutal, often beautiful, *The Surviving Sky* offers a thrilling glimpse into a flawed society scrambling to survive… Don't miss it!"
Lucy Holland, author of *Sistersong*

"Sentient forests. Flying cities. Lost histories. Power, rivalry, love, and exile. *The Surviving Sky* is a cornucopia of wonders… Combining the best of Stanislaw Lem's *Solaris* and NK Jemisin's *The Broken Earth*, *The Surviving Sky* is an immersive and original epic fantasy."
Gautam Bhatia, author of *The Wall* and *The Horizon*

"*The Surviving Sky* is utterly creative, a heady and mysterious tapestry of love, duty, and discovery… Add in a slow-burn romance and Rao's exploration of human drive, desire, and consciousness—and *The Surviving Sky* is sure to stay with readers long after the final page."
H.M. Long, author of *Hall of Smoke*

"With lush prose, compelling characters, and a wonderfully built world, *The Surviving Sky* has everything I hope for in a novel. This is a book for anyone who has ever loved and longed for the natural world around them."
Joshua Phillip Johnson, author of *The Forever Sea*

"In this brilliant, gorgeous debut, Kritika H. Rao's *The Surviving Sky* weaves a kaleidoscopic environmental plot with relationships that feel very real indeed... This is a story unlike any I've read before, an epic adventure through fantastic landscapes and heartscapes."

Fran Wilde, double Nebula Award-winning author of *Updraft* and *Riverland*

"Brimming with fascinating lore and dangerous magic, *The Surviving Sky* is an evocative debut that will sink its roots—and thorns—into your heart."

Chelsea Abdullah, author of *The Stardust Thief*

"Immersive, inventive and intense, at once both universal and wholly South Asian, *The Surviving Sky* is a debut destined to live many lives. Let it grab your heart with its spiked, slithering vines!"

Samit Basu, author of *The City Inside*

"*The Surviving Sky* dares to imagine a boldly unique fantasy world and succeeds in spades. Lush and evocative, this flying jungle city will draw you in, and the characters anchoring the story will keep you reading to the very end."

Rowenna Miller, author of The Unraveled Kingdom trilogy

"*The Surviving Sky* has some of the most intricate and inventive worldbuilding I've ever had the pleasure to lose myself in, coupled with a story that both examines exactly what it means to be human while daring to ask: what if we were more?"

Anna Stephens, author of The Godblind Trilogy

"*The Surviving Sky*'s characters struggle passionately to balance communal survival and individual ambition, exposing the private strain on a marriage. Teeming with detailed world-building, this debut is perfect for fans of original science fantasy."
E.J. Beaton, author of *The Councillor*

"Some books reach right into your brain and give it a good shake, and this expansive science fantasy, with its wildly inventive worldbuilding and characters who feel desperately real, shook mine in the most delicious way. Highly recommended!"
Sam Hawke, author of The Poison Wars

"With worldbuilding and magical metaphysics as alive as the emotion on the page, *The Surviving Sky* devastates and resurges... The protagonists navigate the love and fury of a fraught marriage, class struggles, and layered secrets as thick as the jungle itself."
Essa Hansen, author of *Nophek Gloss*

"Daringly inventive and uncannily enthralling... While storms and strange ecology shape the world, the characters' personal cataclysms are grounded in the compelling struggles of the human heart."
Cass Morris, author of *From Unseen Fire*

"Precise, exquisite, and jaw-dropping. The world is rich and alien and wonderfully new, grounded by characters so familiar they ache. I loved every page."
Dan Wells, *New York Times* Bestselling Author

"A vivid, verdant fantasy world rife with ethereal magic."
M.J. Kuhn, author of *Among Thieves*

THE SURVIVING SKY

KRITIKA H. RAO

TITAN BOOKS

The Surviving Sky

Print edition ISBN: 9781803361246
E-book edition ISBN: 9781803361253

Published by Titan Books
A division of Titan Publishing Group Ltd.
144 Southwark Street, London SE1 0UP
www.titanbooks.com

First Titan edition: June 2023

10 9 8 7 6 5 4 3 2

This is a work of fiction. All of the characters, organizations, and events portrayed in this novel are either products of the author's imagination or are used fictitiously.

A CIP catalogue record for this title is available from the British Library.

Printed and bound in Great Britain by CPI Group Ltd.

For you, wonderful reader, of whom I first began dreaming when I knew writing books was what I wanted to do.

1

AHILYA

The bracken didn't react to Ahilya as it should have. She tried again, drawing her desire for the leaves to part to a single point. "Open. I want to see."

It was unnatural—eerie almost—how defiant the plants were. It was as if her limbs refused to move despite the command of her mind.

She stood alone on a wide curving terrace of her airborne city, Nakshar. An hour earlier, a dozen citizens had flocked to the promenade, seeking a final look at the open skies before Nakshar landed in the jungle. Ahilya had yearned for solitude, unwilling to conduct her study in front of them, but now she gazed at the empty bark benches, the shady trees, the soft moss floor. Everything looked the same. Then why did the bracken wall behave so differently? It had been waist-high earlier, a mere parapet, but now it towered over her, growing rapidly. Tendrils curled into tight, thorny balls. Branches squeezed together, twisting in intricate lattices. The entire structure hardened as though to deny her. And none of it responded to her desire to see beyond the city.

Ahilya jogged alongside the wall until she found a small gap in the leafy growth. There, below thick clouds within a twilit sky, waited the earth's surface. She unslung the satchel from her shoulder. Eyes on the gap, she rummaged until she found her telescope, then dropped the bag gently by her feet.

Ahilya pressed the telescope to her face so hard, it pinched her skin. The image focused just in time for her to see another dust explosion. Her breath quickened. There was a pattern to the dust, a shift she had theorized once. For the first time, she was viewing the *epicenter* of the fading storm. Her hands itched to take her tablet and stylus from the satchel to draw the patterns, but there was no time. The leaves on the city's wall were morphing too fast, she'd just have to commit the explosion to memory—

Dark green shuttered her vision. Ahilya lowered her telescope and peered through the foliage, but the wall was relentless again. "Come on," she muttered. "What is wrong with you? Open up a little bit, at least."

"Nakshar's plants won't respond to non-architects anymore," an amused voice called out.

Ahilya spun around.

Naila stepped off an ascending wooden pedestal that had emerged from a hole in the floor. She was dressed in her architect's uniform: an embroidered green kurta reaching her knees, flared over narrow, pleated trousers. Her long translucent robe wafted in the breeze. Thick black beads looped around Naila's neck; more beads—bracelets and rings—clinked around her wrists and fingers, held together by thin glassy optical fibers. The Junior Architect was perhaps twenty-five, nearly a decade younger than Ahilya, but the rudra beads indicated more responsibility for their flying city than Ahilya would ever be granted. All Ahilya owned was her obligatory citizen ring.

"Ordinary citizens no longer have any control over the architecture," Naila repeated, striding forward.

Ahilya forced a smile. "Great, you're here. I think I saw something—this incredible pattern of dust that might reveal the source of the instability down there. Will you open the wall for me? I want to sketch it."

"You want to draw… *dust*?"

"I want to draw dust during *landing*," Ahilya corrected. "It's the best way to understand earthrages."

"Oh, I can explain those to you," Naila said, flicking a lock of dark hair behind her. "They're cataclysmic storms—"

"Yes, thank you. I'm trying to understand why they happen at all."

"Because of a disruption of consciousness—"

"No, I meant, why did earthrages begin in the first place—"

"They've been around as long as we have—"

"How did—"

"Really, Ahilya," the Junior Architect said, sniffing. "These questions have already been answered. And these dust patterns you want to draw—the architects have studied those for years."

Ahilya turned back to the wall. She had asked the architects for their drawings, but they had summarily rejected her requests, citing their records as *privileged architect information*, a slap on the face she had never received before. "Right. Fine. Thanks for that," she said. "Could you open this, please? I might still be able to get a few rough sketches."

"I can't—"

"Sure you can. You're an architect, aren't you? The plants literally shift at your behest."

Naila gave her an unimpressed look. "That's very reductive. How can you be married to a *Senior* Architect and not know the intricacies of trajection?"

"We try not to talk about it, lest we begin arguing about how we see the world," Ahilya said. Her voice remained mild. The workings of plant manipulation had always been too esoteric for her, but the truth was that ever since her husband had been promoted to the council, the two had stopped talking about each other's pursuits altogether. Her fingers scrabbled at the leaves. "Please. You don't have to open it all—just enough for me to see."

"I can't," Naila said, exasperated, as though dealing with a child. "Now that there's *finally* another lull in the earthrages, and now that we're *finally* landing, the temple architects have enforced higher limits on the architecture. *That's* why non-architects don't have any control—"

"But you're—"

"Yes, I know, but I'm a *Junior* Architect. Anything that doesn't align with the temple's guidance is almost impossible to do, especially by me. And they're closing the city. Look around you. I'd be trying to fly against a windstream."

Ahilya released her hold on the wall. Loose leaves glided down onto the moss floor—but the floor wasn't moss anymore; it was transforming into bark. The benches and trees were gone. From all sides, thorny bushes rushed toward them, eating the curve of the terrace in their hungry approach. Even the bracken wall had extended, entrapping the terrace in a dome. Leaves and stems crisscrossed in a hundred different layers as the foliage tightened. Darkness would fall in seconds.

Ahilya's brows furrowed. Nakshar had always been a flat city flying in the sky. Its architect-formed hills, with massive trees that housed the library and schools and homes, usually spanned acres. Checkered fields grew on the edges, and rainwater was harvested in rocky pools and waterfalls. She had never heard of the architecture changing so completely.

"Relax," Naila said. "The council will release permissions beyond the temple again as soon as we land. Non-architects will be able to mold the architecture, and this part of the terrace will transform into an entry point close to the jungle. Shouldn't affect your expedition."

Ahilya frowned and stepped away from the wall, the dust patterns she'd wanted to study forgotten. There was something in Naila's casual words, a message she did not understand. She glanced at the unresponsive architecture, studied Naila's insouciant stance, thought about the easy assurances. A prickle of worry climbed the back of her neck.

She had lived in Nakshar all her life, but matters in the city had been changing recently. Hardly anyone paid attention, but Ahilya had kept track. First, it had been the suppression of the architects' records. Then the fight to get her expedition approved. Now this? Control was being taken away from the citizens slowly and subtly, one way or another; a dangerous pattern.

The weight of this realization grew, pressing her shoulders down. In the end, wasn't that what life in the flying cities was really about? The lack of autonomy she and others like her had over their own lives? Ahilya's expedition, her dealings with Dhruv, the vacant council seat she was eyeing—everything she had done all her life was to balance this inequity, but things were coming to a head now. She could feel it.

She cleared her throat and returned her attention to Naila. "Why was the design changed?"

"I told you. They've enforced higher limits—"

"Yes, but why?"

The Junior Architect tilted her head and studied her for a long second. Then she smiled.

"For architect reasons," she said coolly. "Why does a historian care to go into the jungle?" she added, asking her own question.

"Aren't there detailed accounts of our histories in the libraries?"

Ahilya flinched. The questions were calculated insults.

Naila knew Ahilya was an archeologist, not a historian. She knew any histories of the world were *her* histories, architect histories. She knew why Ahilya explored the jungle—life had begun there, and Ahilya's entire research was to find a way to return to it again, to find survival on land instead of in architect-dependent cities in the sky.

This was a deliberate attempt to bait her. Either that or Naila had learned nothing from the documents Ahilya had provided to prepare for the expedition. It was likely beneath the Junior Architect to take any instruction from a *non*-architect. Refusing to indulge either attempt to shame her, Ahilya snapped the telescope shut and dropped to her knees to place it back into her satchel.

If only they would *tell* her. Naila had mentioned the recent earthrage as a reason behind this new design, and based on that alone, Ahilya could have helped the architects, shared information about what she discovered, even studied something *for* them.

But she was a non-architect, a pretender. What use was an archeologist in a civilization that had only ever known flight? Ahilya had practically invented the term. They were not going to tell her anything. The Junior Architect was simply reminding her of her place.

Ahilya pushed aside her strain with an effort, closed her satchel, and rose to her feet. In the few seconds it had taken her to repack her instrument, the terrace had closed entirely, so that she and Naila stood face-to-face on a square of bark. Thorny bushes enveloped them from all sides, obscuring any view.

"So, where are Dhruv and Oam?" Ahilya asked, referring to the other two members of her team.

Naila tilted her head. "They're in the temple. With the rest of the citizens."

"Why? I told them to assemble here."

"Iravan-ve. He insisted the temple was the safest place until Nakshar had fully landed."

The respectful suffix attached to her husband as an architect, but never to Ahilya as an archeologist, grated on Ahilya. Her hand curled tightly around her satchel. Iravan had abandoned her for seven months, and now he thought to give orders to her team without her knowledge? All of her restrained irritation bubbled up, tightening her throat.

"And they listened?" she said. "Even Oam?"

"Oam tried to protest, saying you needed us here. And Dhruv—well, I don't think Dhruv wanted to go toe-to-toe with a councilor."

Oam was only as old as Naila. Iravan would have intimidated the boy with a glance. As for Dhruv—ever since his last few inventions had failed, the sungineer had become wary of disturbing the council. Ahilya's closest friend he might be, but Dhruv wouldn't openly oppose Senior Architect Iravan.

"I see," she said.

"Iravan-ve requested you go to the temple, too. That's why I'm here. I'm supposed to bring you there—"

"*Bring* me?"

"Escort you," Naila said. "Request you. He didn't demand it—"

"But he might as well have," Ahilya completed, her teeth gritted.

Naila shook her head in furious protest. "No, no, not like that. It's a matter of safety. No one should be out here."

Ahilya remained rooted. The dome above was a mere handbreadth away now. Sharp-pointed leaves reached so low, they tickled her ears, but the instant they made contact with her skin, the pinpoints shed themselves. Instead, the stem budded softer leaves. Ahilya smelt the warm, sticky sap of regeneration.

If she didn't move soon, she'd be entombed in a layer of foliage. Nakshar's living architecture would sheathe her in her own personal wooden armor. That had been Ahilya's plan, for her and her expeditionary team. *Rage* Iravan and his raging interference.

"I'm staying here," she said, voice cool. "You can tell Iravan-*ve* that."

Naila extended a robe-covered arm upward toward their cocoon. Her skin, like Ahilya's and most natives of Nakshar, was terra-cotta brown. Naila's veins, however, began to glow an iridescent green as she influenced the vegetation around them. A thousand tattooed vines and creepers grew on her arms underneath the translucent sleeves of her uniform's robe. Some of the leaves touching Ahilya retracted.

"Please, that is really not wise." The condescension had left Naila. "I know this design. It's ellipsoidal, like a sunflower seed. We're in the outermost shell. This is where the greatest impact will be. That's why everyone was asked—*requested*—to the temple, to Nakshar's core. You received the instruction through your citizen ring too, didn't you? I know you did."

Ahilya rubbed a thumb over her single rudra bead. "It flashed and rang a few hours ago. But I know the city will provide an alternative."

"At great cost. The architects in the temple will have to divert unnecessary trajection to keep you safe here. You're risking the reliability of the entire construction. Nakshar could crash into the jungle instead of landing safely." Naila jingled the rudra beads on her wrists as though to emphasize the burden of her responsibility.

Her words and actions were typical architect manipulation, but Ahilya had spent more than a decade married to a Senior Architect. "Is that really true, Naila?" she asked quietly. "Because I asked the temple about this. I was told I could wait here."

"That was before Iravan-ve altered the landing design. Your old permissions don't apply anymore."

Ahilya clutched her satchel. Of course. She should have guessed Iravan had been behind the design's change. Still, she could not help the abrupt anger and shock throbbing under her skin.

Iravan knew why it was important she leave right away. Without the data from the expedition, Ahilya could forget about being nominated to the council. But, of course, he had never fully thought her capable of being a councilor. Was that why he had done this? Because of the vacant council seat? Iravan was *on* the council but he had his own plan for the vacancy. One that involved Naila.

She studied the Junior Architect, the suddenly nervous gestures, the newly feigned concern, the barely veiled contempt. Naila had sounded logical with her warnings about safety, but there was more there, an undercurrent of unbending dogma lacing her words. Architects were so used to the world submitting to them, they could never see how terrible it was that civilization was designed to be architect-dependent in the first place.

Ahilya wouldn't have begrudged it so much right at this very instant if it weren't for everything else with Iravan. The beginnings of a headache formed behind her eyes, at the thought of giving in now, acquiescing to his silent call for obedience. His attempt at maneuvering her was so feeble, it was almost insulting. She felt suddenly tired, outrageously defeated.

"You should go," she said. "Go be safe."

"I can't abandon a citizen to potential danger," Naila said, her voice incensed. "If I leave you, it'll go on my record as endangering Nakshar. I'm a *Junior* Architect. I can't afford transgressions."

"Nice try," Ahilya shot back. "I know you're well on your way to becoming a Senior Architect one day. Wasn't that the real reason Iravan gave you a key to accompany my expedition? To add the jungle to your field of experiences so he can *nominate* you to the council? I hardly think he'll hold you accountable for my stubbornness."

True to her profession, Naila switched tactics at once. "Well, then, consider. I can't disobey a Senior Architect. If you don't come with me, Iravan-ve will question me. Perhaps even forbid me from accompanying the expedition altogether. And then where will you be? No architect, no expedition, remember?"

Ahilya stared at her. "They teach you how to influence people as an architect, too?"

Naila smiled, a tightness to her mouth. "No, we gather that on our own. Can't maneuver anything beyond a plant, but I suppose the principles of trajection remain the same."

Against her will, Ahilya felt a strange morbid amusement. It was almost impressive, how skilled Naila was. None of the other Junior Architects the council had provided to her for previous expeditions had displayed such an effective change of strategy so quickly. No wonder Iravan had picked her to be his protégée. In Naila's quick-thinking and casual arrogance, Ahilya detected glimmers of Iravan's own personality. She sighed and clutched her satchel close to her. Her nod was curt.

"Hold on," Naila murmured. She closed her eyes and opened her palms in front of her. Her veins flared again, the iridescence making Ahilya's eyes water. A dozen dizzying patterns of vines formed and died on the architect's skin.

For a long moment, they remained motionless.

"Well?" Ahilya said. "Are we going?"

"We *are* going," Naila said, cracking open an eye. "We're descending. Can't you tell?"

Ahilya blinked.

Their little nest looked no different. The canopy was still touching their heads, thorns on all sides, no wind of passage.

Were they falling downward toward the city's core? Or was Naila changing the plants around them, outside of their nest? Perhaps the nest wasn't passing through a tunnel; it was destroying and reconstructing itself, using the plants of the city to undulate them through the architecture.

Ahilya's head spun. Contrary to what she had said to the Junior Architect, she *did* know some things about trajection. The power was inborn; it could not be learned. Even though under ordinary circumstances, Ahilya could ask the city's plants to react to her desires, that was a charity provided by the architects who allowed their energy to flow through the foliage for the citizens to use. Ahilya had no *true* control. Only architects could directly influence a plant's consciousness, forcing it to change form.

Yet for Naila to do it this way, in such an invisible manner...

Either the Junior Architect was more skilled than Ahilya had credited her with, or the architects had learned new tricks in the time since Ahilya and Iravan had held a proper conversation.

"How are you doing this—" she began.

The nest jerked. Ahilya's knees buckled.

"Sorry," Naila panted, steadying her. "Rougher than I intended. Trajecting is harder outside the temple, this close to the landing."

"I suppose you could have brought me with you without waiting for my permission, and I wouldn't have known," Ahilya said reluctantly.

Naila threw her another amused look. "Architects aren't tyrants. This way."

Her fingers twitched, a waving gesture. The leaves in front of them separated to reveal a small courtyard. They stepped through and new bark closed behind them.

In the distance, vast tree trunks collapsed as though crushed by a giant hand. Foliage folded into itself, then tightened into stony bark. What had once been apartment complexes in trees—schools and playgrounds and homes—all changed as Nakshar coiled in on itself. When Ahilya glanced behind, bark chased her footsteps. Small florets became hard seeds. Supple ferns developed rough calluses. Needles and cones grew where a moment earlier there had been languorous sprays. The courtyard morphed in front of her eyes.

She had no idea where she was. Nakshar's architecture was called a maze for a reason. Even in ordinary flight, everything except for the city's fixed landmarks grew and changed. A path was provided for citizens by the trajection coursing through the plants—except Ahilya no longer had any influence over the architecture. She hurried after Naila's blue-green light. It was one thing to be cocooned on a terrace that would become the best entry point to the jungle; entirely another to be encased within an unknown layer of the city. Sweat coated her upper lip at the thought of how little power she had.

She had lost measure of how much distance they'd covered when they reached another wall and Naila's iridescence flared again. The wooden wall transformed into a doorway. They stepped into a narrow, shadowy passageway. Bark closed behind them.

Naila slowed, her breath releasing in a huff. The Junior Architect grinned and gestured for Ahilya to precede her.

First came the scent: the rich, heady smell of moist earth. Then the lilting sounds of excitement and laughter. Tiny sungineering glowglobes, like stars trapped in plants, emerged from the foliage to guide Ahilya's way as she strode farther in. Ahilya squinted as her eyes adjusted to the swelling brightness.

A narrow archway beckoned at the end of the passageway, from where tiny white buds hung down in curtains. Ahilya's breath caught in her throat. Jasmine was her favorite. Could that be Iravan's doing somehow? But no, not after the way they had left things the last time together, not if his punishing silence were any indication of his feelings. She was being foolish.

For a long moment, Ahilya hesitated, staring at the jasmine. Her heart hammered in her chest; she recalled his expression, how he'd walked away from her, how angry he'd been. All the dread and outrage and confused love she had nursed for seven long months bubbled within her.

Ahilya took a deep breath, parted the fronds, and stepped into the light.

2

AHILYA

She emerged onto a crowded narrow balcony, its wooden railing visible beyond congregating bodies. Most citizens were standing, but interspersed were healbranch chairs, specially made for those who needed them. Behind Ahilya, the archway transformed into bark in a telltale creak. Naila had deposited her in a gallery full of familiar faces, but hardly anyone noticed Ahilya's arrival. The Junior Architect had disappeared, likely to fulfill her role in the landing. Ahilya began to pick her way through the crowd, murmuring greetings to the families of other architects. Vihanan waved at her, a man with alluvial dark skin like Iravan's, indigenous to the city of Yeikshar. Reniya smiled, her toddler clutching her saree with a chubby fist. The woman's eyes ran down Ahilya's clothing, then grew wide.

They were dressed in their finest kurtas and sarees, no doubt in anticipation of greeting their architect spouses who had been on shift in the temple. Ahilya's attire, a harness over a kurta and tapered trousers, stuck out like a weed in a tulip field. With a headlamp perched over her hair, and a compass around her wrist instead of bangles, she was more suited to an expedition in the jungle than a long-awaited landing. Ahilya pasted a smile on her face, avoided their gazes, and wove her way through the crowd. Most of them had grown up in Nakshar with her, but over the years all had devolved into mere acquaintances. Her own fault, of course; her pursuits had made her an oddity. Ahilya swallowed her rising shame and averted her eyes to the rest of the temple, visible through the gaps in the bodies.

The temple was oval-shaped, with fifty balconies circling from the floor to the ceiling, each full of chattering citizens. At the very center rose the rudra tree. The trunk mushroomed as wide as twenty people standing shoulder to shoulder. Countless aerial roots, like slender branches, hung down to the floor. Iravan had often remarked on how Nakshar's core tree was worth years of study, and for a moment, Ahilya agreed. Ethereal blue-green light flickered and gleamed in the top stories, making the tree appear mystical.

She squeezed through the crowd until she found her sister Tariya fidgeting on her chair, right by the gnarled railing of the gallery.

"Finally!" Tariya said. "Where have you been?"

Ahilya's older sister was shorter than her and beautiful. Her raven-black hair tumbled down her shoulders in glossy curls. Her skin, though the same brown as Ahilya's, seemed to glow. Her big kohl-lined eyes were shining with happiness. Tariya shifted restlessly on her seat, her baby asleep in her arms. "Here, hold him," she said.

Ahilya found Arth thrust toward her. Her nephew's weight was awkward; she squirmed, trying to ease the position, shifting her elbow, then her shoulders.

"I can take him," a soft voice said. Tariya's older son Kush edged through the press, gathered Arth, then returned to where the other children stood together in a rumble of noise.

Tariya called out a caution, then glanced up at Ahilya. "What took you?" she asked. "Can you believe it? The ashram is finally landing." She straightened the pleats of her saree around her waist and readjusted the bindi on her forehead.

Nakshar, maze, city—there were many words to describe the airborne structure in which they lived, but none was as pretentious as *ashram*. The term meant a hermitage, but the architects had appropriated it to imply more—the city's community, its people, a shared sense of purpose. Ahilya had once found it charming, but over the years it had become just another architect manipulation. She had stopped using the term altogether, her arguments with Tariya about it another point of difference between them. Yet Tariya looked so radiant this evening, her happiness rare and precious. Now was not the time to correct her.

"You look lovely as ever," Ahilya said instead, smiling. "Bharavi won't be able to keep her eyes off you."

"She had better not. I've something in mind for the two of us to do every day, for as long as this lull lasts." Tariya finished adjusting her saree and reached up to give Ahilya a hug but stopped as though only now noticing her. Her sister groaned, and unfastened Ahilya's wrist-compass, uncaring of the fragility of the instrument. "Really, Ahilya. Does Iravan like you looking like this?"

Ahilya caught Tariya's hands before she could do more damage. "I like me looking like this."

"But don't you know what landing means?"

"I finally get to go into the jungle for my expedition?"

"Your architect husband gets to be off duty. You get uninterrupted time with him. You don't have to be stuck in the library anymore, studying something obscure—"

"I'm sure we'll see each other once I'm back," Ahilya said.

Her irritation bubbled close to the surface, but she had learned to contain it with Tariya. Fighting got them nowhere. Ahilya had to remind herself that it had not always been this way with her sister. Tariya's despair had developed ever since their parents had moved away to a different city. It had affected her more than she was willing to admit. Ahilya leaned over the railing, hoping to spot Oam or Dhruv, swallowing the scorn in Tariya's words. Amongst the thousand citizens, it was impossible to discern the only two people who had any faith in her research.

"I can't wait to see Bharavi," Tariya continued. "Her last visit was ages ago, and only for a week. The boys miss her. *I* miss her."

Ahilya drew back. "Bharavi came to you during the flight?"

"Of course. Why—didn't Iravan visit you?"

Ahilya shook her head. "Each time you said you spoke to her, I assumed it was through the ring."

Her finger rubbed her single rudra bead. Everyone in Nakshar owned a similar bead, provided as a sign of their citizenship. With it, architects could contact the city's population in times of need. With it, citizens could view Nakshar's morphing architecture to know which areas were safe, which under construction. Over the years, the citizen ring had been embedded with several permissions, but it had been created originally for its messaging capabilities, and that was still its primary function.

"I didn't realize Bharavi actually left the temple to visit," Ahilya said, frowning.

"Of course she did. Several times."

"I thought they were both on duty. That they were busy."

"They *were* busy, but Bharavi had her breaks, same as Iravan and all the other architects. He didn't visit you even once?"

Ahilya shook her head again.

"Did you speak to him at least, through your ring?"

Ahilya said nothing. Right after the earthrage was announced, she had transmitted a message saying she wanted to reconcile, but Iravan hadn't responded. For seven months, Ahilya had disconnected every other note she'd composed. She'd spent long nights in her library alcove, burying her pain and confusion in her work, returning home only to sleep, a home where everything reminded her of him. Each time Tariya had asked about Iravan, Ahilya had murmured a casual response and changed the subject. How could she explain her marriage to Tariya now without betraying herself and Iravan? She knew her husband; this was his way. They had been down this road before, with his angry silences as cutting and eloquent as his words.

Tariya touched Ahilya's elbow in concern. "Did you two have a figh—"

"It doesn't matter," Ahilya said.

"But—"

"Please, Tariya. I get enough of this from the rest of Nakshar—all of them watching my marriage, judging my research, whispering about my plans for the city."

"Maybe it's time to listen, then," Tariya replied, a tone of exasperation entering her voice. "Time to set aside your childish ambitions, especially if it's affecting your marriage. Ahilya, this thing you do—trying to change history—at what cost?"

Ahilya jerked her elbow away. The last time she had seen Iravan, spent after their intimacy, they had argued about her *childish ambitions* too. Oh, he had been too artistic to frame it like that. He had begun slow, propping himself up on an elbow, his fingers feather-soft on her stomach.

"Ahilya," he'd said. "We're ready, don't you think? We've been ready for a while, surely."

"Ready..." she'd murmured, too relaxed to probe.

When she could no longer sense his touch, she had opened her eyes to see Iravan sit up. Sunshine danced on his skin, bright then shadow-dark. He ran his hand through his salt-and-pepper hair. "I want a child, Ahilya," he said. "Someone to fill this growing chasm inside me..." He laughed bitterly, gazing down at his hand over his heart. "Don't you feel it? Don't you want one anymore? You did before."

Of course she wanted one. She had always wanted one.

"Why now?" she asked instead, sitting up. Her heart beat faster. They had avoided speaking of this, knowing it would end in an argument. For him to bring it up now, again, when they'd stolen a moment of peace—

"Why?" he asked. "Why *not*? What are we waiting for? Ahilya, we've been married eleven years." He reached forward to stroke her hair. "You can give this to me... to us. If it brings us happiness, why won't you make that choice?"

"Because happiness is not your reason for wanting a child, is it, Iravan? Not really."

His hand had fallen away from her. He'd stared at her as she scrambled for her clothes.

"There's more to this," she said. "This has to do with the demands of the council. With an architect's arbitrary *material* bonds. Is this about making a child for a child's sake?"

"If making a baby helps convince the others that my commitment to Nakshar is irrevocable, why is that so terrible?"

"I won't make a child to please the council, Iravan. You shouldn't want something so precious for *architect* reasons."

"Is that what you think? That it's the sole reason I'd want a family? Rages, Ahilya, I want to be a father. Why is that so hard to believe?"

Ahilya fumbled as she began clothing herself, disbelief making her movements inelegant. She had to admire his finesse. He had waited until she was satiated to bring this up. "Architects and children—" she said. "My parents—the way they were, with me and Tariya, but we weren't born with the ability to traject like them—we were never enough—her despair, because of them—she doesn't admit it, but it worsened—they could never accept—"

Iravan cut across her. "I don't think like them—"

"Maybe not right now. But how long before you resent the child for not being like you? Before you're disappointed that it's like *me*?"

"This is ridiculous," he snapped. "When have I ever indicated you're not my equal?"

"When you started keeping secrets from me," she said, rising to anger despite herself. "When you became a Senior Architect and councilor. It began five years ago, Iravan."

Iravan's voice became hard. "This isn't about me. This is about you. Everything you do is tied to your resentment because you weren't born with the ability to traject. Your research, your reluctance to have a child—and now you suspect my reasons simply because I'm an architect?"

"I'm not an idiot, Iravan. Do you seriously expect me to believe you have no other reasons for wanting a child? No pressures from the council?"

"You're projecting your own insecurities—"

"Yes or no?"

Iravan threw his hands up, his rudra beads chinking. "All architects abide by the directions of the council. If my profession bothers you so much, why did you agree to marry me at all?"

"Because I loved you," she said. "Because you loved me—"

"I still do!"

"And because you were different from other architects. You didn't think normal citizens any less worthy before. Our ideas of the world were the same. Iravan, you were supposed to do *better* by us. That was the plan. That's why we worked so hard for you to become a Senior Architect. So you could change things."

"Rages, I'm still like that, Ahilya."

"Are you?" she'd asked sadly, her anger melting all at once into weariness. "Then why is it that when there's a council seat available, you're angling to nominate Naila, a *Junior* Architect, instead of a regular citizen?"

"It's not that easy," he'd protested. "Only those who make a significant contribution to the survival of the ashram can be nominated to the council. And Naila is well on her way to that. It doesn't mean I think non-architects any less—"

"I think it does," she said, quietly. Her heart felt heavy. Now, after all the arguments, they had finally come to it. "You've changed since you became a Senior Architect, Iravan. Since you became a *part* of the council, with all its secrets and rationales, above the rest of us. You don't like to admit it, but now I embarrass you. You look down on me and the rest of us who can't traject—maybe you always have. Our stories, our lack of history, our very lives in this architect's world, those mean nothing to you. Perhaps you don't even think anything is wrong with the way our civilization exists. And I'm not about to make a child until you figure out what's right."

Iravan's eyes glittered. His handsome face darkened in dawning outrage.

He'd stood up then.

Snatched his clothes and walked away.

With the earthrage announced hours later, she hadn't seen him since.

Tariya was still throwing half-concerned, half-irritated glances toward her. Ahilya sighed, reached for her sister's hand, and squeezed. Tariya's lips twitched. She squeezed back.

In front of them, the rudra tree began to vibrate. The crowd *ooh*ed and *aah*ed; several people clapped and cheered. A large ring-shaped platform—the Architects' Disc—became visible on the tree's topmost stories. Atop it, the shapes of a hundred glowing Maze Architects grew distinct, revealing the source of the ethereal blue-green light. Tariya gripped Ahilya's hand in excitement. Somewhere on the Disc, along with the other two Senior Architects of Nakshar, Iravan and Bharavi orchestrated the Maze Architects. Ahilya tried not to look too closely.

With the appearance of the Disc, the temple became denser. The gallery Ahilya was on crept closer to the rudra tree. The city that had spanned acres in the sky during an earthrage shrank, became smaller, stronger.

Pressure built in her ears, but before it could hurt, she inhaled and worked her jaw. The sharp scent of healbranch entered her lungs. Green tendrils sprouted from the woody railing and wove themselves over and under her hands; roots twined between her legs, arms, and waist, over to her neck, holding her steady. Ahilya closed her eyes, imagining what Nakshar must look like from the outside, an oblong tangle of roots, leaves, and branches, tied and tightened in a hundred different layers, plummeting toward the jungle below. She could almost feel its controlled hurtle, the snap and break of the trees as it crashed through the jungle like a comet. She breathed deeply, fighting the sense of overwhelming vertigo and turbulence. The will of the city grew inside her, all the citizens, attuning their consciousness, to keep everyone safe, and then—

Stillness.

The city hovered briefly.

A moment of weightlessness.

Exhalation.

Nakshar dropped the last few feet gently, and Ahilya felt the *thud*. She opened her eyes. Dim green light burst through the foliage, as the bark carapace gave way to roots and leaves again. Nakshar began expanding, grounding, reknitting itself. Vines and shoots untangled, stretching and integrating with the city's new design. Ahilya inhaled deeply, relieved despite herself as all the vines holding her dissolved back into the railing.

The rudra tree in the center shot up, tall and slender now. The temple floor softened into a grassy courtyard with rock pools tinkling between bark benches. Chatting, smiling Maze Architects in their embroidered brown kurtas and trousers poured out of the Architects' Disc, shucking off their translucent robes, relief evident on their faces. Only a few Maze Architects remained on the Disc as it soared toward the canopy, high enough so even the blue-green light of trajection was no longer visible.

Ahilya opened her mouth to speak, but she was alone on the wide gallery. Along with Vihanan, Reniya and the rest, Tariya had already started down the winding ramp that now connected the gallery to the temple's new courtyard, her chair dissolving into the ground. An excited babble of conversation arose, then faded, as citizens created pathways beyond the bark walls to leave the temple. Now that they'd landed, the council had evidently allowed the plants to respond to everyone again.

Ahilya's neck prickled. She turned and dipped her chin.

There in the courtyard, looking up at her, stood her husband.

Her eyes met Iravan's over the distance. He'd divested himself of his translucent robe, but the rest of his Senior Architect uniform, a white shin-length kurta over tapered white trousers, shone amongst the brown of other ordinary Maze Architects. His sleeves were rolled back, a dozen rudra bead bracelets covering both wrists. She knew there were more beads underneath his clothes, necklaces and arm-bands, far more than other architects, each bead holding special permissions. Iravan's skin was too dark to tell any patterns from afar, but there was no concealing the blue-green light that pulsed on his sinewy arms and stony face. His entire body seemed bathed in light from within.

Ahilya stared at him, the way he held himself, tall and proud, his thick salt-and-pepper hair tangled, longer and grayer than it had been before, his jaw tightening the way it did when he was trying to control himself. Her husband's almost-black eyes glittered back at her. He made no move to climb the ramp. They stood for a long moment, staring at each other. Ahilya's chest tightened; she couldn't get a full breath.

A cough sounded behind her.

"Dhruv and Oam have left for the meeting point," Naila said. "Did you want to… I can tell them to wait if you want to visit—"

"No." Ahilya broke the gaze first. She turned to the Junior Architect. "Let's go."

3

IRAVAN

In the usual manner of trajection, Iravan's vision was split into two.

In the first, he stood in the growing courtyard, clenching and unclenching his jaw, staring after his wife as she walked away from him. His fingers twitched. His feet stirred. He breathed erratically, wanting to follow her, forgive her, submit to her. Iravan forced himself to stillness.

He had searched for her from the Architects' Disc. The instant the ashram had landed, he'd leapt off the Disc and hurried to where the Junior Architect had brought her. Seeing Ahilya had frozen him in his tracks. She was so beautiful, tendrils of hair escaping her knot, those big eyes glittering with fierce intelligence. He'd waited for a sign, a lift of her lips, a softening of her gaze, anything. He'd waited for her to take a step.

And she'd walked away.

His heart thudded in his chest. Longing warred with rage and regret. The courtyard filled with the welcoming families of other architects. Children sprinted past clustering adults to jump into their parents' waiting arms. Lovers spotted each other, faces breaking out into smiles; others embraced and kissed, voices laced with relief. Within his first vision, Iravan stood silent and alone.

Within his second vision, he existed as a dust mote suspended in an infinite universe.

Golden lights gleamed in every direction, endless and breathtaking.

The universe was the Moment: a motionless reality reflecting the consciousness of the plants that comprised the building blocks of Nakshar. Each frozen star in the Moment was a plant's possible state of being.

Infinite such states existed for every plant, yet Iravan knew each one as well as he knew himself. Within this star, the water lily existed as a fully ripened bloom, frozen forever. In a star farther away, the ironwood was suspended in eternal decay. Birth through death, countless potentials twinkled. Iravan drifted through the Moment, surrounded by life.

Nearly fifty dust motes inhabited the universe with him, each an architect fulfilling their duty to stabilize Nakshar.

As Iravan watched, some of the dust motes generated constellation lines and wove between the stars. The lines intersected and locked, connecting different stars. Nakshar's architecture unfolded around him in a complex maze.

Iravan smiled. This was something that non-architects could never understand. Nakshar's living architecture was more than just a maze of plants. It was the intersection of lives, of promises, of intent. It was elegance and beauty and harmony.

Here was the temple, shaped like a warren of corridors. Further ahead grew the library, its loops indicating private alcoves. Iravan meandered through the lines of the solar lab. He drifted beyond the spaces of the infirmary. He swooped over bridge renditions, ducked under gazebo arches, slid over shapes of playgrounds. In his second vision, there was peace. Peace and belonging.

In his first vision, he stood in the temple courtyard, staring at where Ahilya had disappeared.

"Iravan," a woman's musical voice called out. "Your landing design was successful. You can leave the Moment now. The architects on the Disc know what to do."

Bharavi strode toward him still enveloped in her translucent robe, though like the other architects assembled in the courtyard, her skin no longer glowed with the light of trajection. Her eyes were narrowed in displeasure. Off-duty architects hurriedly made way for her.

The Senior Architect stopped right in front of him and crossed her arms. A slim woman with dark chin-length hair and rosy brown skin, Bharavi was short, reaching only to Iravan's chest. Somehow that didn't deter her from looming over him. Closer, the wrinkles on her face were more pronounced, the shadows dark and heavy under the eyes. He probably looked much the same.

"Did you hear me?" she said. "You can stop now."

Iravan trajected.

As a dust mote, he sailed over the stars until he reached Nakshar's perimeter. The outer maze, where the ashram bordered the jungle, was a tangle of disconnected lines. Iravan watched a dozen dust motes hover there: the Maze Architects on duty, currently trajecting from the Architects' Disc. The motes generated fresh constellation lines, connecting disparate stars, but the lines shattered before they could snap together in place.

Iravan frowned. He recognized the dust motes, Megha and Gaurav and Kriya among them. His superior skill and ascension to the council had created a natural distance between him and them, but they had once been nominated to the same council seat he now occupied. Each was a competent Maze Architect. Then why were their constellation lines shattering? The lull in an earthrage, and the subsequent landing, should have made trajection easier.

He leapt into the fray, generating his own constellation lines, exerting the force of his desire to influence the plants of the ashram. Iravan connected the star containing the briar bush, looped around the redwood, and fastened his lines to a hundred other stars in a complex net-shaped pattern. A dozen dust motes reached toward him, extending their own simpler lines. His constellation lines vibrated almost to their breaking point, fighting him, denying his will. Iravan focused his entire being into the action. He spun and wove between the motes, twisting and turning—

The outline he'd created snapped into place. Several thousand stars connected. Another part of the maze unfolded and settled. The dust motes soared, cheer and gratitude in their zipping streaks.

Iravan grinned. Here was a place where he was needed, where he was necessary. His breathing eased. He left the hovering motes and began to drift within the Moment again.

In the temple courtyard, Bharavi drummed her foot. "You're not listening to me," she said.

"Trajection was hard this time, Bha," Iravan said. "Don't tell me you didn't feel it. The Disc needs all the help it can get."

"Your landing design was new. A period of adjustment for the Maze Architects is expected."

"My landing design was simple. And still our constellation lines kept crumbling. That wasn't because the Maze Architects weren't familiar with the design."

"Maybe everyone is just exhausted because of the terribly long earthrage we've had," she said.

Iravan gave her a level look.

Both knew the length of an earthrage didn't matter. The rationale behind strict shift duty was for an architect to never overextend themselves; it was so the ashram could sustain flight forever. The lull was a mere opportunity for Maze Architects to traject with ease.

During lulls, all plants of Nakshar became easier to traject, the closer they were to the jungle. It was why the council had decided to land.

"It wasn't exhaustion," he said flatly. "I've watched the Maze Architects since the time the earthrage was announced. Viana made so many mistakes I had to send her back to the Academy. Karn struggled with basic patterns to the point of tears. It's a sign. The plants—they aren't responding to us as they once did. Trajection is getting harder. The Disc needs my help."

He paused within his second vision.

He had been patrolling the outer maze, assisting the Maze Architects. But there, behind the glow of a gigantic star, hovered... something. He'd noticed it before, through all the months of living in the temple, hidden behind his every trajection. At first, he'd thought it a dust mote, just another architect whom he didn't know well enough to recognize in the Moment. Yet unlike other motes, the particle didn't spin around the stars. No constellation lines were attached to it. Instead, it undulated like mercury, silvery and molten, throbbing like a heart.

Iravan approached it. The particle pulsed, approaching closer.

He stopped. The particle stopped.

He darted to the left, and it darted, mirroring him.

What are you? he thought, startled.

Bharavi shifted her feet. "Iravan, are you saying you didn't leave the temple at all during the flight?"

He barely heard her. Slowly, very carefully, he drew closer. The particle lingered, pulsing. He saw himself in it, although it was not his face he saw, not within the Moment. Instead, he perceived his... *echo*. Like he had fallen into a mirror to see his own eye reflected a hundred times over, until any image became meaningless. It felt like a—

Resonance, he thought. He could find no other term for it.

"Bha," he said in a low voice. "There's something in the Moment. Something strange."

She uncrossed her arms and tapped at one of her rudra bracelets. A hologram arose over her wrist—Iravan's picture next to a roster of names. It hung there for an instant before it collapsed. Bharavi dropped her hand.

"I see you signed up for watchpost duty," she said. "Wasn't it Chaiyya's turn?"

He waved a hand to shush her.

The Resonance swayed in front of him, silvery, liquid. He retreated, and the Resonance retreated. He floated back another step, and the Resonance did the same.

Then, in rapid blinking flashes that made Iravan think of a wicked grin, the Resonance spun and darted away, shooting through the universe.

Bloody rages, he thought.

Iravan dashed through the Moment, trying to keep his sight on the undulating particle. They whirled through the lights, zooming past constellation lines, startling dust motes. He sped past an architect, felt their indignation. He attempted to cut the Resonance off, but the particle stopped short and streaked back the way it had come. Iravan cursed again and wheeled around, swooping over a star, leaping past long lines of the maze. There was a familiarity in the particle's movements, like he ought to know what it would do next.

He rounded a golden star and pulled up in front of the Resonance. It drew up, alarmed and amused.

Ha, Iravan thought. He hovered, waiting to see what it would do next.

Bharavi pressed a hand to his shoulder. "Tell me. When was the last time you saw Ahilya?"

The Resonance attacked.

Iravan had a horrified glimpse of fury rushing over its mirrored surface before the particle collided into him.

The stars of the Moment winked out.

He was tumbling through blackness.

He was falling endlessly.

In the temple courtyard, Iravan stumbled into Bharavi, his mouth dropping open. The universe wiped out, all stars gone, just the sensation of plummeting down a black hole. He opened and closed his mouth, trying to make words, staring at Bharavi. His stomach lurched, and he leaned over, heaving.

"What's wrong?" she said at once. "Did your Two Visions merge?" She gripped his shoulders, holding him up.

He choked, shaking his head. Shooting a glance around them, Bharavi steered him away from the bustle of the courtyard and closer to the base of the rudra tree, where there were no other architects.

In his second vision, Iravan jerked and came to a standstill within an infinite velvety black hole. He spun around in tight panicked circles, scanning for a light, any light, hunting for a dust mote, a star, the Resonance, anything—

The Resonance slammed into him.

With shocking pain, Iravan lurched back into the Moment. Stars twinkled again, familiar and comforting. Nakshar's maze reappeared, blue-green constellation lines crisscrossing. The floating sensation that always accompanied Iravan on entering the universe returned, but the Resonance flickered in front of his dust mote, still, as though it had not just attacked him. Innocence reverberated in its silvery flaps.

Iravan darted away from it so fast that he bounced into the closest star—lush green paddy—before he dashed back out to hover in the Moment. He spun around, lights whirling through his second vision, but the Resonance had disappeared.

Bharavi was still looking at him with concern, her hands bracing him against the rudra tree's broad trunk. Iravan straightened, sweating. He nodded his thanks, and Bharavi dropped her arms. She took a step back.

"What happened to you?" she repeated quietly. "Did your Visions merge?"

"No." His voice came out cracked. "Not that—something else."

As horrifying as the experience of tumbling down that black hole had been, at least Iravan had remained himself. If his Two Visions had merged, he would have lost himself within a trajected-upon star, lost himself in a frozen moment of a plant's consciousness. He'd have no knowledge of a way out, no memory of who he was. Once Two Visions merged, it was nearly impossible to reverse them. Only very skilled architects could lurch themselves back from it.

"Then what?" Bharavi persisted.

"I—I don't know." His voice was still ragged. "There was this thing—this shape. No, not a shape. Like a rhythm. An interference within the Moment. A—a kind of resonance."

Bharavi's frown deepened. Her hands opened and closed like a dreadbud bloom.

The panic of the experience rolled through Iravan in waves. Within the Moment, he dove toward the star belonging to a budding jasmine. He tied the star to itself in a simple trajection, then flew to the homes within Nakshar's architecture, and into his own home. There, he secured the constellation line to the lush ixora bush. The constellation lines glittered in the Moment and settled. A measure of control returned to him.

He coughed, steadying his voice. "Yes, a Resonance. An interference. It—it—" He rubbed a hand on his face, feeling his bristles. "Bha, I think it knocked me out of the Moment."

Bharavi glanced around the courtyard but Iravan had kept his voice low, and the nearest architects were several feet away. "That's not possible."

"I know what I felt."

"Iravan, you're *exhausted*. Do I need to explain what happens when an architect is exhausted?"

"Don't patronize me, Bharavi. I'm not your apprentice anymore; I'm a Senior Architect in my own right. I know what exhaustion in the Moment feels like. And this wasn't it."

She stared at him. Iravan rolled his shoulders and leaned his head back on the tree. He closed his eyes, breathing deeply. Exhausted architects could lose their connection with the Moment, sometimes unable to enter it at all. Iravan had no such difficulty. He hovered in his home, between gigantic stars, then flew back out to where Maze Architects placed finishing touches to other structures. Orchards bloomed. Boulevards widened. With the familiarity, Iravan's heartbeat eased. When he opened his eyes, Bharavi was still watching him.

He spoke before she could. "If this is interfering with trajection, then it could cause critical failure. We could plummet into the earthrage mid-flight next time."

Bharavi sighed. "You need to let the architects on the Disc take care of the maze. You need to rest—spend time with your wife."

Iravan shook his head. He pushed past her, back into the courtyard. The temple was starting to resemble an expansive cavern. The architects had flattened the ellipsoid of the landing architecture almost completely. Evening sunshine fell in thin shafts through fissures in a high root-encrusted ceiling. Water rippled from rockpools, adding its tinkle to the echoes bounding off the hardened walls. Off-duty architects made way for him, giving him a wide berth. Iravan tried to wipe the scowl off his face.

Bharavi kept pace with him. "Why did you sign up for watchpost duty?"

He grunted. "Do I need to explain how the watchpost works? I signed up because a Senior Architect is supposed to perform the duty."

"Don't give me that," she snapped. "It's Chaiyya's turn. Why did you switch it?"

"She's pregnant. I volunteered."

"How chivalrous. When was the last time you saw Ahilya?"

Bharavi was one of the few people in the ashram who could question him on his marriage, but Iravan's eyes narrowed in displeasure nevertheless. "Why do you ask?"

She waved a hand at the temple courtyard. "Ahilya's not here, is she? Every other Disc Architect's family has come to greet them."

"We've landed, haven't we? I'm sure all I will do this lull is see her."

"I know the number of shifts you took this time. Too many. Far too many."

"Yes, well, with so many architects struggling with basic trajection, it was the right thing to do."

"It's not healthy, Iravan. It's not safe."

Iravan held up a hand. "You can excoriate me further about my choices, Bha, or you can go to *your* wife. Tariya is waiting." He gestured past the shifting bodies in the crowd. Tariya was carefully climbing down the last foot of the ramp, her baby cradled in her arms, Kush by her side.

Bharavi's face softened. Perhaps knowing Iravan would follow, she began to weave through the clusters of people without another word. Iravan trailed more slowly. Seeing Tariya with her children made his chest spasm in sudden longing. A picture blinked at him, something he had created in his mind long before, of a boy and a girl, with his dark skin and Ahilya's fierce magnetic eyes. He forced the image away.

Bharavi reached her family, kissed Tariya, then gathered Arth into her arms. She murmured something to Kush that made the boy giggle. Tariya watched her fondly, then turned to Iravan. Her expression changed to annoyance, though he could tell it was not for him.

"Ahilya," she began.

"I saw her," he said shortly.

Tariya shrugged, an uncomfortable gesture. "I'm sorry. You know how willful she can get. She was prattling about her experiment and how she really had to leave."

"Her expedition," he corrected, at the same time as Bharavi said, "Leave for where?"

Tariya bit her lip.

"The jungle," Iravan said. "For her archeological study. She's studying the yakshas."

"I thought she'd give it up," Tariya said, grimacing. "That she'd grow out of it. It's like she's going out of her way to convince herself that her research will give her a shot at the council as though she were an architect herself. She can't see how misguided she is, and rages forbid you try to talk to her about it. Doesn't she see how it's affecting... well, you two?" Tariya shook her head in exasperation.

Iravan averted his gaze. Tariya was saying aloud what others in his company only dared to whisper. His demeanor didn't allow for more insult to Ahilya than that, or for such familiarity toward his marriage. But suddenly he couldn't bring himself to disagree with Tariya, let alone challenge her. By its very nature, Ahilya's ambition to the council was flawed. These jungle expeditions were useless—it was why the rest of the council had dithered on giving her permission to go at all, unwilling to raise false hopes. In the end, Iravan had made the decision, accepting her request, but he had done it for her, not her expedition. Had he truly bought into believing architects were better than non-architects?

Tariya studied Iravan for a long moment, waiting for a response. When he said nothing, she glanced at Bharavi. "Shall we go, my love?"

"A minute, if you don't mind, dear," Bharavi replied. She handed Arth back to her wife, and Tariya walked away a few paces, beckoning to Kush.

Bharavi grabbed Iravan's arm and pulled him away from the nearest architects, back into the recesses of the rudra tree. "I notice you didn't defend Ahilya."

"She's a grown woman. She's making her choices. She doesn't need me to defend her from her *sister* of all people."

"You fought with her, didn't you? That's what this is about."

Iravan jerked his arm away. "*She* fought with me, and I'm not going to apologize, if that's what you're going to say next. I didn't do anything wrong."

"Don't be childish. You know you need to fix it."

"I did. I gave her the council's permission to go. I even gave her a Junior Architect so she has someone to traject the jungle for her."

"That's hardly the same as making things right, Iravan."

"What else do you want me to do, Bharavi? Force my presence on her? She had a chance to come visit. She was there, standing right next to Tariya. Isn't it clear? She doesn't want to see me."

"You had a chance to go to her too. Did you? Even once during the seven-month flight?"

Iravan glanced away from her knowing gaze. "I was angry."

"What could she have done to make you this angry?"

He didn't answer. Each time he had thought to leave the temple, each time he had connected his citizen ring to reply to Ahilya's message, broken images from their last encounter had reignited his cold fury—Ahilya accusing him of secrets, Ahilya questioning his intent for fatherhood, Ahilya *never* understanding what the pressures of being a Senior Architect were. She had been right to fear the change his promotion had brought. He *had* changed, but it hadn't been wrong, had it? It had been necessary; he'd grown, he'd evolved, he'd kept the difficult secrets of his position—alone, without her support.

Bharavi read his silence correctly. "She didn't do *anything*? Rages, *seven* months, Iravan. You know she can't come to the temple during a flight, not without permission. It was your move to make. What kind of a sign are you sending her by not going to her at all?"

"Let it go, Bharavi," he growled. "This has always been our dynamic. Ahilya and I aren't like you and Tariya. We don't need to talk to each other every hour of every day."

"Are you serious? The subtleties of your marriage don't concern me, but something is wrong, so don't you dare try that. If you haven't seen Ahilya at all, maybe we need to begin vigilance again."

Iravan scowled. Senior Architects were not above the rules that Maze Architects obeyed, but both Iravan and Bharavi had lapsed into ignoring the vigilance they usually kept over each other's material bonds. For seven months, Iravan had logged his whereabouts in the most general terms, and Bharavi had attested it without looking too closely, just like he had attested hers, a sign of trust in each other and their positions. But as she crossed her arms over her chest now, her stance unmoving, he knew she was not joking about making him account for his every step again as though he were a Maze Architect.

He forced his features into calm. "It's not that serious. You're reading too much—"

"Am I?" Bharavi said. "I don't think so. I'm seeing a pattern. You've been in the temple all during the earthrage. You signed up for extra watchpost duty. You're clearly avoiding your wife. And even though you're not on the Disc anymore, *you are still trajecting*."

Iravan glanced at his arms. His skin gleamed as vines grew on it in a simple twining parallax. He had been interlocking more jasmine within his home—for Ahilya, he thought pathetically—just as he had in the entryway to the temple, for all the good it had done—but at Bharavi's words, Iravan collapsed the constellation lines and stopped trajecting. The blue-green tattoos on his arms receded.

"Very good," Bharavi said. "Now leave the Moment."

Iravan drew himself up to his full height. "You can't order me about, Bha."

"Consider it a professional suggestion, then. Leave the Moment."

Her voice brooked no argument. Equals though they were now, old habits died hard. Iravan let his second vision collapse. The blue-green glow under his skin disappeared. He blinked, now fully in the bustling courtyard. The floating sensation in his belly vanished as soon as he retreated from the Moment, and sudden exhaustion crashed into him, filling his limbs with dead weight.

"If I were running risks," Bharavi said in a hard voice, "I wouldn't do it in the temple, where the rest of the council is probably watching."

"What are you implying?"

"Would you like me to spell it out?" She closed the distance between them and poked a finger into his chest, stabbing him with every sentence. "It's dangerous for an architect to traject without a break, lest they lose touch with the material world. If they lose touch with the material world, they lose control over themselves. If they lose control over themselves, they begin to destroy architecture in the Moment instead of building it. They become an Ecstatic."

"Bha, I'm not becoming—"

"If the council *suspects* an architect of Ecstasy," she went on, speaking over him, "it can demand they take an Exam."

"That won't—"

"If an architect fails the Exam," Bharavi continued, her words a low snarl, her finger pressing his rudra beads into his chest over his kurta, "they are excised."

The word hung between them, dark, dangerous, malevolent.

Excision.

Free from the focus of trajecting, a picture conjured itself in Iravan's mind, of architects he had seen excised. Their grief had different expressions, but all of them had one thing in common. They had been cut away from their trajection. It was the ultimate punishment, reserved for Ecstatic Architects.

"Are you threatening me?" he said, his voice cold.

"I'm warning you."

"No, you're grasping at weeds. Last I checked, I was part of the council, a Senior Architect. And a Senior Architect can traject whenever they want."

"A Senior Architect knows the limits of trajection. A Senior Architect understands why a healthy family life is an indicator of tight material bonds. A Senior Architect is smarter. Or have you so quickly forgotten Manav?"

Manav had been a Senior Architect and councilor not five years earlier. Iravan had excised him personally, and Manav's position had lain vacant ever since. Iravan's babbling about the Resonance, his feud with Ahilya, his concern for the Maze Architects, all took on a darker note. He stared at Bharavi, and she stared back, relentless: his friend, his confidant, and, if he were ever so wretched, his executioner. She was too damned watchful for his own good.

"Are these lessons you need to relearn?" she said. "Because I could ask the rest of the council to vote on having you tested for Ecstasy right now. Is that what you want, Iravan?"

"No," he said. "No, I don't."

Bharavi's hand pressed into his arm again, the grip hard. "If I'm noticing these patterns, others are too. My responsibility is clear. Please don't give me a reason to tell them what I've observed. Whatever is going on with you and Ahilya, fix it." With a final cautionary glance, she swung around and joined her family.

Two paths opened in Iravan's mind between his brows, one toward Ahilya, and the other toward his own intuition. The call of the second path was almost too seductive to ignore, tempting him to return to the Moment, to seek the mysterious Resonance, *solve* it. Yet he could not bring himself to disregard a direct instruction from Bharavi. She had been his mentor; she had nominated him into the council; she was his most vocal supporter. Iravan thought of how Ahilya had walked away from him. He remembered how he had left her. The anger, the hurt, the outraged righteousness—they reverberated through him again, warring with the memory of the Resonance.

Is that what you want, Iravan?

With a sigh, he turned his back to the Architects' Disc and approached a wall. The philodendron opened, reacting to his desire. Clenching his jaw, Iravan guided the plant to weave him the fastest way to the outer maze and to his wife.

4

AHILYA

The others were already waiting by the time Ahilya and Naila arrived at the outer maze. The Junior Architect had trajected a path directly from the temple, yet the two had needed to stop for Naila to switch her uniform for attire more suitable to the jungle. She wore a shorter kurta now, much like Ahilya's own, and her long wavy hair was tied into a sensible knot. They hurried into the outer maze together, toward Dhruv and Oam, pushing past thick brambles.

What had earlier been a terrace of Nakshar now resembled a shady copse, complete with towering trees and soft, cushiony moss. Evening sunlight fell in translucent shafts of green. From high in the branches, the birds of the city twittered and squawked. It might have been peaceful, but Ahilya froze in her tracks, her heart throbbing in her throat, startled at its familiarity.

The clearing resembled far too much the very grove she and Iravan had fought in all those months before. For an instant, she remembered the jasmine curtain at the temple's entrance, the way he had stared at her, so cold and unyielding. Had he built the outer maze? It would be so like him, this wordless sign, this dark apology. Ahilya's breath grew quick and uneasy, as though she had unexpectedly come face-to-face with him. Guilt weighed her body down.

Material bonds were crucial to an architect's trajection, and a healthy marriage was a visible sign of those bonds. Ahilya had walked away from Iravan knowing that. It was an action born out of cold fury, but in her mind's eye, she could still see him snatch his clothes and leave after their argument. He'd punished her with silence for so long—what was her small rebellion compared to his? They went around in circles, each of them furious with the other. She couldn't remember anymore if things had always been this way. Her stomach churned in confusion and anger.

"Ahilya," Dhruv called out, breaking into her thoughts. "Over here."

She blinked and looked away from the thicket toward him. Tall and lanky, with wire-thin spectacles, Dhruv appeared the consummate sungineer. His yellow-striped kurta gleamed in the last shafts of sunlight. He pointed at the shiny devices in the bag by his feet.

Ahilya swallowed and approached him. Naila had already joined the group, turning this way and that, adjusting the harness Dhruv placed over her, but the last member of the expedition stood leaning against a tree, watching the proceedings with casual amusement, his own harness loose and hanging off him.

"Oam needs help," Dhruv said. "See to him, please, while I finish with the Junior Architect."

Ahilya took a deep shaky breath. The familiarity of the copse, the memory of her fight with Iravan, the growing twilight, all of it conspired to shape her misgivings. But she couldn't afford to be distracted. The expedition was what mattered now. She had waited too long, fought too hard.

She nodded at Dhruv and forced herself back to *this* thicket, to focus on seeing it for what it was, not what it reminded her of. Next to the sungineer, Oam greeted her approach with a wicked smile. Of a height with Ahilya and only as old as Naila, Oam spread his arms wide, as though inviting Ahilya to embrace him. He still wore his nurse's scrubs from the infirmary, but his braided curls were tied in a concession to the expedition. As Ahilya reached for his harness, his grin grew wider, too familiar to be respectful.

Ahilya bit back the creeping humiliation of her circumstance and returned a tight smile. She couldn't fool herself—Oam's eagerness with the expedition had more to do with his infatuation with her than her research. But in time, he would become her first true apprentice, Nakshar's second archeologist. Her work would continue beyond her lifetime. She ought to be grateful the council had allowed him to accompany her at all.

Oam dropped his arms as she tightened the harness around him. His fingers brushed against her satchel. Before Ahilya could react, he pulled out her solarnote, beginning to swipe through it.

Irritation bubbled within her, but she took a deep breath, calming herself. She had meant to give Oam the tablet in any case within the jungle; his entire job in this excursion was to sketch the elephant-yaksha they were tracking. Out of the corner of her eyes she saw the images on the glassy screen flicker, pictures she'd drawn herself on previous expeditions—the gorilla-yaksha's massive shoulders, the wolf-yaksha's menacing gaze, the tiger-yaksha lapping water from a pond.

"Are you ready?" she asked, buckling the straps on his shoulders tighter. "It ought to be exciting."

"I've never seen one before," Oam said by way of reply.

"Few people have," Ahilya murmured.

Yakshas had been a part of the world almost as long as humans, yet a regular citizen learned little about the creatures. All records glossed over the yakshas, mentioning them in happenstance, typical of architect histories that focused only on flight and matters of architect welfare. Even people who couldn't traject were rarely mentioned, except as bystanders, and then only to indicate how architects were superior in comparison.

She gestured for Oam to turn so she could adjust the clasps on the front. He obeyed, his brows slightly furrowed. This close, she could feel his barely contained nervousness hidden behind the bravado of youth, the twitch by his eyes, the fast breathing, the beads of sweat.

"It's all right to be scared, you know," she said softly. "It can be a disorienting experience."

"I'm not scared," he said at once, stiffening. Then, betraying his words, he added, "So, these yakshas. They're huge, aren't they? You ever see a small one?"

"No, they're always gigantic. The last time I saw the elephant-yaksha, it was twenty feet tall. The architects think that's how these creatures survive the earthrages, but of course, there's more there than that."

"My fathers said that a bird-yaksha nearly attacked the ashram when they were younger—"

"Not attack," Ahilya said, shaking her head. "Collided. I remember when that happened; the architects had to change the flight path of the city abruptly, and Nakshar ended up avoiding the collision. But it happened because these creatures don't notice us at all, not even our cities. Whatever plane of existence they are on, we have no part in it. In and of themselves, they're truly passive."

Oam bit his lip, nodding slowly.

"Don't worry," she said, her voice gentle. "I'll keep you safe."

"Maybe I'll keep *you* safe," he said, straightening. He winked at her, rolled his shoulders back, and returned his attention to the solarnote.

Ahilya didn't attempt any more placation. Oam had much to learn about personal boundaries, but she couldn't deny his knack for stumbling into practicalities. The only reason the council entertained her excursions was because she had convinced them of the benefits long before. With her data, they could avoid crashing into the aerial incarnations of the yakshas. They could judge changes in jungle plants after an earthrage. They could discover the best places to land during a lull.

Ahilya had urged Nakshar's council time and again to use her research for these very matters, but if their response to her latest requests was any indication, most of her reports were languishing in some unseen part of their communiques. They were losing patience with these trips to the jungle, she knew. This time, it was a last-minute concession. Next time, they might not allow her out of Nakshar at all. The urgency grew within her to leave the city already, to dawdle no longer. Her fingers worked faster, securing one clasp after another.

"It says here you didn't really expect these expeditions to work," Oam murmured.

Ahilya crouched and adjusted the brace along his waist. "There's always an element of uncertainty to these things."

"But this seems more than that," he said. "It says here you thought the expedition needed luck. That"—and he quoted—"*archeology is a joke. Until I present an alternative, everyone will be content to believe the architects' inadequate explanations.*"

"Their explanations *are* inadequate. The yakshas have adapted to the jungle somehow—beyond what the architects say. If we find out how, then our civilization will no longer need to fly. Our dependence on the architects could end."

Oam paused, a nervous laugh escaping him. "You really don't like the architects, do you?"

Ahilya glanced at him, meeting his uncertain gaze. "Architects are... necessary," she replied carefully. "I'd be foolish to deny that. We need them in the city and I need them in the jungle. Who else would traject a path outside?"

"But what you wrote here," he persisted in a low voice. "What did you mean?"

"I only meant there might be other ways to survive, Oam—better ways. And if you and I find them, then maybe we could change *something*."

"That's not our problem, though. Survival is the council's concern. Sungineers and architects, they can worry about that."

"We're part of the city too. Isn't it our concern as well? If we found something useful to contribute to survival, maybe one day an ordinary citizen like us could get a seat on the council."

"But people like us, we don't know anything about flight and architecture—"

"If we offered another solution, maybe we wouldn't need to—"

"But if architects bothered you so much," Oam said, his voice serious, "why did you marry one?"

The question was so innocent, so obvious, that Ahilya recoiled, momentarily stunned. She opened and closed her mouth, sudden hot tears burning the back of her eyes. *Because Iravan is different*, she thought, but couldn't bring herself to utter the words. Iravan *had* been different, once, a long time before. He'd been passionate about changing the old ways of the council. Arrived from Yeikshar at Nakshar, he had been willing to look at her and the world differently. But his promotion had changed him so much. Her throat tightened. Blood heated her face. In her mind's eye, she watched him walk away from her again.

Ahilya stepped back from Oam, tugging her solarnote back from his hands. "I think we're done here," she said quietly. "Your harness is ready."

She turned away from Oam's startled eyes and toward Dhruv.

"Are you finished? The yaksha could move away any minute."

"Not quite," Dhruv answered. "There are devices for both of you in here." He nudged the bag by his feet, and Ahilya strode toward it, Oam trailing her, an abashed look on his face.

The long days of loneliness following Iravan's silence had returned to her the minute Oam had asked his question. Her husband flickered in her mind, his face darkening in outrage as she questioned his integrity, precipitated his anger, but Ahilya pushed the image away, *violently*, and focused on the devices that glittered in the bag. Her hand encountered a diamond-shaped half-locket dangling from a glassy chain. Like most sungineering equipment, the locket was made of resilient bark and thin optical fibers connecting the circuitry inside. A low chiming sound emerged from it, muffled by Ahilya's fingers as she withdrew it.

She looked up, her eyebrows raised. The last time she'd used this tracker locket, it had been silent.

"I've made a few adjustments," Dhruv said, understanding her unspoken question. "The ringing will become faster the closer you get to the yaksha. It should help navigate your path."

"Thank you," she said, wearing the necklace.

The locket was heavy at her throat, its steady beat at odds with her racing pulse. Somewhere out in the jungle, the transmitter that formed the other half of the tracker waited for her.

Dhruv nodded, his eyes solemn behind his glasses. Some of Ahilya's tension receded with his steadying presence.

In all of the city, the sungineer alone remained her true companion. They had grown up together, discussing Nakshar's politics, angry and passionate, wanting to *do* something. Their choices had taken them in different directions, Dhruv toward the solar lab and her to archeology, but their separate careers had only drawn them closer. She and Dhruv had prepared for the nomination together, trying out their theories for survival, learning and quizzing each other about Nakshar's administration, analyzing and dissecting their competitors' theses. It was Dhruv who had come to her mere days earlier, babbling about how one of the trackers had transmitted a signal to his lab. Ahilya's mind had been on Iravan, but Dhruv had almost dragged her to the library's leafy walls.

"You don't have much time," he'd said. "You need to get your crew together."

"How can there be a signal at all?" she'd asked, unable to get her hopes up. "I thought all sungineering equipment ran on trajection."

Dhruv had nodded, an excited smile splitting his face. "Yes, yes, the tracker can only recharge if it's around a trajecting architect. But don't you see? Nakshar happens to be in its range for the first time during landing. All the trajection from the city must have kickstarted the transmitter. You can study the same yaksha you did before."

"But—"

"*Go!* I can explain all this later."

Ahilya hadn't asked any more questions. Dhruv had pushed her toward the walls, and she'd created paths first to the Academy to request an architect and then to Oam, to prepare for an expedition.

She watched him now as he bent next to her to withdraw more pieces of equipment identical to the ones she had in her satchel.

"You need to bring back every piece," he said severely as he handed those to Oam one by one. "Every piece. They're very expensive and I will hold you personally accountable for their care."

"Why don't you just come with us?" Oam muttered, turning the devices in his hands.

"Out in the jungle? No, thank you. I'm not designed to go outside a city, and neither is this equipment. All of this runs on trajection, so don't stray too far from Naila; she's your only source of energy out there."

"Don't stray too far from Naila, regardless," Naila urged, standing next to them. "The jungle is unpredictable, and trajection… It's a bit—There's something about it—Just stay close."

Oam frowned. In a world destroyed constantly and unpredictably by earthrages, where the only certainty was trajection, the architect's words didn't inspire any confidence.

Ahilya spoke before he could raise any objections. "We'll be fine. Won't we, Oam?"

A startled glance passed over Oam, perhaps at the unexpected warmth in her voice. He returned her smile, flicked a loose braided curl behind him, and stood up straighter.

"Right," Dhruv said briskly. "Inspect your equipment, both of you—and then double-check each other's gear. Ahilya, with me, please, while I do the same for you. These should be your final verifications."

Oam and Naila murmured, each of them asking the other to turn first. Ahilya followed Dhruv to the other side of the copse reluctantly. She knew why he had pulled her out of earshot, but time was running out.

She'd tagged the elephant-yaksha nearly five years before, yet for the first time in her life, she'd see the same creature more than once. The expedition could vindicate all her previous forays into the jungle; it could convince the council to take her seriously; it could even provide hard evidence for survival on land—something that could directly contribute to being nominated to the council. Based on what she found, today's expedition would either clear her path forever or dash all her expectations to the ground. She followed the sungineer, her mind on the comparisons she could make to her baseline readings.

Dhruv stopped and his voice dropped. "All right," he said, his businesslike manner vanishing now that they were alone. "Let's see the deathbox."

From her satchel, Ahilya pulled out an opaque glass cube larger than her fist, a dozen dials embedded into it. She twiddled the dials, and the cube opened. She flipped the dials again, and the deathbox closed.

"Good, good," Dhruv muttered. "I'll need a complete specimen this time, something with root and stem, preferably. The box should accommodate it."

"I know. I'll try."

"They're really pushing hard for the battery now," he said, and she knew he meant the council. "Kiana asked about my designs again, and I'm running out of options. She told the entire lab that the council is looking to transfer a sungineer in exchange for an architect next time we trade with the other cities." Dhruv's spectacles shook in his hand as he removed them.

Ahilya nodded, her mouth dry. All occupations had to serve the city in some way, and she herself was on thin ground with reports from her previous expeditions becoming increasingly useless. If her study didn't yield any results soon, the council could revoke her very profession, force her to become a historian who studied and exalted architect histories, just like it could transfer Dhruv. A weight settled in her stomach at the thought of failure.

Dhruv took a deep breath and glanced sheepishly at Ahilya. "Iravan didn't mention anything, did he?"

"You know we don't talk about the council."

"I think—" Dhruv looked at her awkwardly. "I think *he* asked for the battery."

She clenched her fists and swallowed the lump in her throat. Dhruv had never liked her husband, though since Iravan's rise to the council, Dhruv's forced politeness had verged on careful deference.

Iravan had known this, of course.

He had likely seen through it, had likely disdained it. Was his push for the battery simply an attempt to get rid of an exasperating irritant? Once, she would not have thought it possible, but the power her husband wielded now, the decision he had taken to change the architecture, his numerous subtle calls to obey him…

She met Dhruv's gaze. "I won't let him take you away."

"It's not that," Dhruv said, shaking his head. "The battery is not just a way to avoid the transfer; it is the *only* way for a sungineer to be nominated to that vacant council seat. Kiana said she can't nominate anyone from the lab unless they make progress with a battery. Iravan has clearly convinced her this is necessary." He removed his glasses in frustration. "This is the problem with architects. They don't understand sungineering and its methods. They think just because they can manipulate the world so easily on a whim, we can create devices to do the same thing. The battery is a bad idea for many reasons, but of course, no one listens to me."

Ahilya pressed his hand. "If you become a councilor, they'll have to."

He nodded distractedly and wiped his glasses. "Which depends on today. Just bring back the spiralweed, all right? And be careful. You can't be close to Naila when you're harvesting the spiralweed, but once you *are* beside her again, the forcefield will engage in the deathbox, ensuring the weed stays trapped inside. You do that, and I'll take care of the rest."

His warnings to be cautious were understandable, but in his words Ahilya detected an unwillingness to speak to the real matter.

She dropped her voice further, the pressure to leave momentarily forgotten in the face of Dhruv's hidden reluctance.

"Dhruv, listen," she said quietly. "I read about spiralweed. Doesn't it feed on trajection? If it gets loose in Nakshar, it could endanger everyone. And if we're found out, they could exile us both to some backwoods sister city."

The sungineer drew back in surprise. "Ahilya, we don't have much time. The council's nominations close in three months. We're up against architects for that position. We have to make a *significantly* better case than them just to be considered. If we don't do this—forget being nominated; we can wave our professions goodbye. The first thing a full council does is to look at everyone's professions and how they contribute to the welfare of the city."

"I know. I don't like it, though. Isn't there another plant that'll do instead?"

Dhruv replaced his glasses. "I'm not even sure spiralweed will do. I've already tried everything else, Ahilya—all the plants you've brought the previous times. This is my—our—last shot."

"It's just—this is so much more dangerous than anything else I've smuggled in. The others were manageable, but spiralweed, it's the highest level of contraband—"

"There are *two* layers of protection on the deathbox. Glass itself is the strongest material we have in the city, and the forcefield will block any interaction the spiralweed can have with the world outside the box. Both of those layers would have to stop working for anything to happen, and you'd have to be an utter idiot to willingly meddle with a working deathbox."

"But—"

"Look, if you find usable results outside with the yaksha, maybe we won't have to worry about any of this at all. *You'd* be our hope for the council seat. But Ahilya, you'd have to find incontrovertible proof of survival in the jungle today to beat the architects. That's... that's—"

"I know," she said shortly. "It's too long a shot."

In the silence that grew between them, Oam and Naila's murmurs sounded louder. A light breeze ruffled Ahilya's hair. Wordlessly, she returned the deathbox to her satchel.

Then Dhruv said, "I'm sorry."

Ahilya didn't reply. Her mind echoed with Tariya's voice, asking her to abandon her childish ambitions. Naila's condescension dripped from her tone as she explained to Ahilya what an *earthrage* was. The truth was there was precedence for sungineers on the council. Dhruv had been an ally—he had always been encouraging—but they both knew he had a better chance at the council seat than she did. Yet to be reminded of it now, in such stark terms—

She glanced away to the other two, not wanting to think about it. "Do you think they're done yet? We're burning the last of daylight."

Dhruv didn't follow her gaze. He squeezed her cheeks together and lifted her chin up as though she were a reticent ten-year-old again and he her constant cheerleader.

"You've come far, all right?" he said. "I shouldn't have said that. We both have an equal chance. A terrible chance, yes, but an equal one. Who knows what you'll find out there when you study the yaksha? Getting spiralweed back just doubles our—"

Dhruv froze.

His gaze went past Ahilya and his voice faltered. "I-Iravan," he said, and dropped his hand. "I didn't know you'd be joining us."

Ahilya spun around.

Through a curve in the copse, her husband stepped forward. Iravan brushed a few stray leaves from the cuffs of his kurta. His gaze went from Dhruv to Ahilya, an assessing look. Dhruv moved back.

Ahilya stared at her husband, her heart pounding. She gripped her satchel out of instinct, the instruments clinking together. How long had he been standing there? Had he heard them talk? Why was he there at all? Iravan smiled as though he had heard her last question. Ahilya had always hated that particular smile: dark, humorless, heavy with irony.

"I came to see my wife," he said to Dhruv, though his eyes held hers. "If it's all right with everyone here, of course."

Oam and Naila had stopped their chatter to stare at him. Iravan was not the tallest there, yet when he strode forward, his presence dwarfed the copse, making the others insignificant. On Dhruv's face Ahilya read her own alarm. Had Iravan heard them talk about the spiralweed? It didn't seem so, unless he was hiding his reaction. But why would he do that? She was being paranoid. Wasn't she? A hundred thoughts piled in her mind. Ahilya felt Dhruv leave her side.

Iravan wasn't trajecting anymore—there were no blue-green tattoos on his dark skin—but the copse became smaller the closer he came. He stopped a handbreadth away from her and inclined his head, a wry smile on his face.

Ahilya inhaled, trying to calm herself, but Iravan's scent assaulted her: firemint and eucalyptus, sharp and spicy. She could almost feel his stubble, like dry brush. She could distinguish the deep brown from the black in his eyes. The copse, the twilight, him—it unsettled her. In her mind, Dhruv and the others melted away, and she and Iravan stood there alone, as though transported back to seven months before. This was how they'd faced off, right before unclothing each other, their haste youthful, almost angry. She felt suddenly, desperately, a desire to cup his cheek, embrace his body, forget their feud. Yet panic paralyzed her.

"Hello, Ahilya," he murmured. "It's been a while, hasn't it? I was hoping we could talk."

"I can't right now. We're already late."

"We haven't seen each other in months—"

"That was your decision, Iravan. I sent you a message."

His face grew withdrawn. Iravan pressed a hand against the nape of his neck. "I—yes—that's true. But I'm here now, and we could—I don't know—sort it out. Perhaps your expedition can wait?"

"It can't," she said. "I'm tracking a tagged yaksha for the first time, and it might move any minute. We can talk when I'm free."

"Or I can accompany you. If you're heading into the jungle, you need an architect to traject your path outside."

"We have Naila," Ahilya said. "She is—"

"A Junior Architect," Iravan completed. "I know; I assigned her to your expedition."

"And I accept with gratitude. She'll do."

"Ahilya, please—trajection isn't as easy as it's always been. My skills can be helpful. And we can—I don't know—I've missed you."

"*No* means *no*, Iravan."

He drew back at that, shock on his face. They still stood close, and their voices were quiet, but in the tension of his neck Ahilya could sense his hurt and confusion. His eyes traveled to her throat to the tracker locket, then toward Dhruv and the others, and back again to the satchel she gripped.

She released her bag at once, but she knew it was a mistake even as she did it. Iravan knew her too well. Besides, he was an architect, a *Senior* Architect. No one could traject humans, but his entire job was to detect and maneuver latent states of being. He had *asked* the sungineers for a battery. How much did he know of Dhruv's desperation? How much had he guessed about their alliance? How much had he *heard*? She tried not to swallow.

Iravan's brows furrowed. "This is unlike you," he said, his voice becoming reflective. "Why are you being this way?"

"Maybe I'm tired of doing everything on your terms."

"*My* terms?" he began, sudden fury in his eyes, but then he breathed deeply and shook his head. "No, you're deflecting. You're hiding something. What is it?"

"Go back inside. We can talk later."

Iravan's veins blazed blue-green, and the grass by Ahilya turned to thorns. "Tell the truth, Ahilya. Why don't you want me out there with you?"

"Tell the truth, Iravan. Why didn't you visit me at all during the earthrage?"

He blinked. He hadn't expected that. The thorns by her feet receded.

"I was busy keeping the ashram in flight," he snapped. "There were complications which required the skills of a Senior Architect. It may surprise you, but terrible effort goes behind the comfort and safety you live in. If architects don't traject constantly, the city falls to the earthrage."

Ahilya's own anger rose. She stared at him, unable to believe he would throw her inability to traject in her face.

"Let me come with you—" he began again, but Ahilya stepped back a few paces, increasing the distance between them.

"I'm afraid I can't allow that," she said, and this time her voice was pitched loud enough for everyone to hear.

The other three paused their murmuring.

She took another step back. "I'm sorry, Iravan. You don't know our expedition, you have not been prepared, and frankly, I've no time to explain it to you. Naila is more than capable of trajecting out in the jungle. We can talk about this later. Leave."

For a moment, Iravan stayed unmoving. His face was calm, but his eyes shone with fury and humiliation. He would never create a public scene, she knew, not Senior Architect Iravan. Shameful triumph rose in Ahilya; *rage him* for forcing her to behave this way. She turned away, infuriated with the both of them, when from the corner of her eye she saw him cross his arms, straighten his back, and plant his feet firmer on the ground.

"Junior Architect," he called out. "I believe I gave you a key to the boundary?"

Naila glanced from Ahilya to him. "Yes, Iravan-ve," she whispered. She unlocked a rudra bead from her bracelet and hurried over to him.

Ahilya's breath caught in her chest. She stared at the key—it was more precious than any other rudra bead in the world, a means to go outside the city that she had begged and fought the council for. With necessary permissions embedded into it, the key was a physical approval for her expedition. Ahilya might be the expedition's leader, but the temple always gave the bead to her accompanying architect. She watched in rising horror as Naila's trembling hand placed it on Iravan's upturned palm.

Iravan's hand closed. He crushed it.

Woody flakes and glass circuitry fell gently to the earth.

Ahilya felt Iravan's cold gaze on her.

For a second, they stared at each other silently, the copse churning with the tension in their gaze.

Then Iravan turned back to Naila. "I have another engagement for you. Something better suited to your talent, I should imagine."

He withdrew one of his many rudra bead necklaces and detached a single black bead. It looked no different to Ahilya—perhaps a tad larger than most others—but Naila gasped. "I... I'm not ready," the Junior Architect said.

Over by his sungineering equipment, Dhruv frowned.

"If you're ready for the jungle, you're ready for this," Iravan replied, and smiled.

The kindness in his smile took years off his face. It cut through Ahilya like a knife. She stumbled back a step away from them. Iravan reserved those smiles for when he shared in other people's joys. When was the last time she'd received such a smile? She couldn't remember.

Iravan placed the rudra bead in Naila's palm. He closed his own palm over it, and a tight pattern of interlocking branches grew on their hands. After a moment, the blue-green light dissipated.

"Go," he said, releasing Naila. "They'll expect someone at the watchpost soon."

A smile of disbelief crept onto Naila's face. She attached the bead to one of her bracelets. Within minutes, she had shucked off the equipment Dhruv had given her. Without as much as an apologetic look, the Junior Architect disappeared the way Iravan had come, still riveted by whatever the rudra bead had meant.

In the silence that grew with her departure, Iravan turned to Ahilya. "It looks like you're short an architect."

Ahilya's heart beat a tattoo in her chest. She shook in cold fury. "You don't know what you've done. Without that key, we have no permission to leave the city. It'll be weeks before I find another Junior Architect. There would be no point to an expedition. The yaksha will have moved on by then."

"You might need someone who doesn't need permission to leave the ashram, then. A *Senior* Architect." Iravan spread his hands, the gesture unsympathetic. "As it happens, I'm quite free."

Ahilya glanced at the others by the knot of trees. Oam was glaring at Iravan, but Dhruv met her eyes unblinkingly. Sweat beaded the sungineer's forehead. His hands shook as he reached for his spectacles. In his nervousness Ahilya read her own anguish.

It would have been easy to smuggle the spiralweed in with Naila, but with Iravan? Dare they attempt it? Yet without the jungle plant to aid the battery he was building, Dhruv would be forced out of Nakshar's solar lab. Ahilya herself would have no chance at the council if she postponed the expedition. Her best friend, her research, her pride… with his one action, Iravan had threatened to take *everything* away.

Iravan's hands curled by his sides, clean of the rudra bead he had discarded. He stood emotionless, waiting for her to speak.

"Very well," Ahilya said coldly. "Dhruv will resize Naila's gear for you. And then we *leave*."

5

IRAVAN

Iravan fell in with Ahilya and Oam as they progressed through the outer maze. He didn't traject; there was no need to yet. All the plants here were still guided by the Disc Architects in the temple who dispersed their trajection energy for citizens to use.

Even so, he noticed the temperament of the foliage. The farther they continued from the ashram proper, the wilder the maze became. Tall, unkempt grass climbed up to his waist. Vines crept on the floor, reaching up to grab his ankles. At one point, Iravan had to physically stop a branch from whipping the headlamp off him. He remembered the trouble the Maze Architects had on the Disc. Perhaps they were still struggling with this part of the ashram.

Or perhaps, he considered, the plants were reacting to Ahilya's desire.

As the expedition's leader, she strode ahead of him, her posture mutinous, head held high, a path opening in front of her a few steps at a time. They walked in a single file, Iravan stumbling half a step behind her, Oam bringing up the rear. Iravan ducked as a misshapen rosewood shot out a branch. The plants were attacking him. *Ahilya* was attacking him. When he dared to glance behind, Oam seemed to have no trouble at all. The boy grinned at him maliciously, a smile with all teeth.

Iravan tightened his jaw. He didn't say anything, and he didn't traject to take control. The plants couldn't truly hurt him; the rudra tree was embedded with permissions to *protect* architects. Here, though, farther away from the tree, these near misses were to be expected. He even deserved it; he had behaved like a brute. Iravan slackened his headlamp, slid a finger under the wrist compass, and continued the march.

When the branches stopped startling him, it took him a moment to understand why. Ahilya had come to a standstill. Iravan drew up to her, but she paid him no mind. Instead, she stared at the dense snakeroot bush blocking their path. Her hands curled into tight fists. Her eyes narrowed. The snakeroot bush ran shoulder-height, its branches knotted together, unbreachable. A small gap in the brambles opened. One thin branch trembled, unfurled, then collapsed.

"Do you want me to take over?" Iravan asked quietly.

"You're accompanying us for a reason, aren't you?" she snapped. She moved aside and crossed her arms over her chest, without looking at him.

Iravan reached into the Moment.

He dove toward a golden star where the snakeroot lay curled tightly. Binding several constellation lines to it, he streaked past its other possibilities to the star where the bush had begun to decay. His dust mote tied the two stars together in a layered knot. The constellation lines shimmered and snapped together in a miniature maze.

The snakeroot bush uncurled. Clusters of tiny white flowers grew and fell at Ahilya's feet, straying all along the path that opened into the darkness.

All of it had taken Iravan less than a second, but it was a fraction too long. He could feel the difficulty of trajection that he had tried to explain to Bharavi. The exhaustion rippled in him, deep within his bones, past the floating sensation of the universe. Refusing to show his unease, Iravan extended a gallant hand into the widening pathway.

Ahilya looked at him, her eyes glittering. She made a brisk motion with her head, and Oam brushed past, his shoulder knocking into Iravan.

Iravan kept his gaze on his wife. He knew she could see it, what the tension between them was doing to her youthful protégé. The way she clenched and unclenched her fists—she wanted to punish Iravan but knew this was not the time. She wanted to go into the jungle but didn't want to need him. She was clearly hiding something, but *what*? It couldn't be Oam's infatuation. Iravan had seen at a glance she was using the boy. Besides, disloyalty wasn't her failing. Obstinacy was.

Iravan sighed. She would never make the first move.

When Ahilya stepped behind Oam, he widened the path so they could walk side by side.

"I'm sorry," he said. "I shouldn't have been—"

"Cruel? Selfish? An utter bastard?"

"So dramatic," he said, giving her a wan smile. "I shouldn't have been so dramatic."

Quiet though their voices were, they echoed within the bush's corridor. Oam could hear them, but there was nothing to be done about it. Besides, the young man had already heard the two of them fight; it couldn't be any worse to see them try and make peace.

Ahilya must have been thinking along the same lines. Iravan knew his wife too well to assume she had forgiven him so quickly, but despite the effort he knew it took her, she forced herself to speak now that they had begun.

"Why didn't the bush respond to me? We're still in the city, aren't we?"

"It's a matter of efficiency and priority. The closer we get to the briar wall at the boundary, the less flexibility Maze Architects inject into the plants of the outer maze."

"It's never been a problem before. All the previous times, the outer maze still obeyed me."

"It's been a bad earthrage, Ahilya. The architects need this lull more than you can imagine."

Ahilya's brow furrowed further. Oam turned with an uncertain look. The crunch of their footsteps echoed within the thick brush walls.

"You said this before," Ahilya said, still frowning. "What did you mean?"

Iravan pursed his lips. How to explain matters that he didn't understand himself, and which the council would not want him to air in front of citizens like Oam? Ahilya was his wife—she was an exception—but if ordinary citizens heard a Senior Architect mention that trajection was getting harder, the rumors and panic it could spread within Nakshar would be disastrous.

He would never have unlocked this channel of conversation had he thought for a moment of where it could lead. Bharavi had been right. He *was* tired. Overworked from all the months of the last earthrage.

"Nothing, really," he said, keeping his voice casual. "The previous lull only lasted fourteen days before we had to fly again. Lulls are becoming shorter and earthrages longer. It's easier to traject during lulls, but we just don't have as much of a break as we'd like between flights. It's why I didn't visit. I stayed on duty longer than I should have."

Ahilya's expression changed, from indignance into confusion. Iravan looked away to the unrolling path.

Strictly speaking, his statement was not entirely true. Trajection *had* become harder—he knew that, no matter what Bharavi said—but he'd been angry with Ahilya, too angry. He had chosen to live within the temple, ostensibly to assist the Disc Architects, when in fact the thought of going to his wife after the way they had left things had been too much.

Fury still rippled through him. Bharavi might have forced him to reassess his material bonds and reconcile with Ahilya for the benefit of the council, yet the two paths still blinked in his mind, as though every instant were a fork between choosing Ahilya and his own intuition. The memory of the Resonance, its familiarity and strangeness, beckoned him. Iravan crushed the need to seek it within the Moment.

Ahilya still watched, a question in her eyes, so he cleared his throat. "The council is considering we trade again with other ashrams," he said. "Maybe Reikshar or Kinshar, the next time we fly. We'll exchange some of our sungineers for one of their architects."

Ahilya's hands twitched, then stilled. "I thought the council was beginning to agree that sungineers were as vital to the city as architects."

Iravan snorted. "If the sungineers did enough, then maybe. But this earthrage showed us how little we can rely on them. It's one thing to create lightbulbs and power looms so citizens can live in convenience. But a sungineer's real purpose is to find us a better way to sustain flight. Some way where the architects don't drain themselves every earthrage."

It had been Iravan's exact argument at the last council meeting when Kiana, one of the Senior Sungineers of Nakshar's council, had tried to defend her team. The bespectacled woman, with her redwood skin and piercing gray eyes, had explained how the lab's latest inventions had assisted flight.

"With enhanced thrusters, we've avoided seven yaksha collisions," she'd said, tapping her cane on the wooden floor for emphasis. "And magnifiers will identify us a prime landing site. We no longer have to land arbitrarily and hope the architects can stabilize the ashram."

Her voice had been enthusiastic, but Iravan had leaned forward on the round mahogany table that had been grown for the meeting and rolled his eyes. "Correct me if I'm wrong, Kiana, but these machines—don't they rely on transformers that convert an architect's raw trajection into usable energy?"

"Well, yes."

"And these transformers—weren't they created—oh, I don't know—a hundred years before?"

Kiana had nodded tightly.

Iravan shook his head. "I don't believe it. Are you—a modern-day sungineer—still resting on those laurels?"

"Invention is not as linear as you'd like, Iravan," the Senior Sungineer said. "We are bound by whatever materials the ashram supplies to us. I'll admit the transformer was sungineering's last big invention, but we've made great advances in its application."

"But none of it works without an architect! Your transformers merely take an architect's energy and use it to power toys. What use is that for flight efficiency? How does that protect the architects from the efforts of trajection? From Ecstasy? How does that protect the ashram from falling into the earthrage if the architects stop trajecting?"

"What about the heat shields and the dust probes?" Kiana burst out. "What about the tools we've made for the citizens' infirmary? Think of how those have changed our lives."

"But all your machines are still architect-dependent," Iravan said, frustration making his voice louder than normal. "You aren't creating anything new at all; you're just trying to perfect the same old thing. We don't need gadgets; we need a battery that can replace the need for constant trajection. We need," he said, "to give architects a rest."

The other four councilors began to chime in. Mutters and raised voices had filled the temple as old arguments resurfaced. Nakshar's council oversaw many nuances of ashram life, but none was as much a source of controversy as flight architecture. Every plant that made the ashram, every sungineering project that was approved, how citizen homes contributed to an efficient maze, all of it returned at the heart to balancing *life* with *survival.*

The meeting had finally adjourned with Kiana and Senior Sungineer Laksiya grudgingly agreeing to prune their teams should there be no more progress from their lab.

"It's nothing to worry about," Iravan said now to Ahilya, although he said it more for Oam's benefit. "It's normal business for the council. We just have the impossible task of trying to find the best way for Nakshar to survive every earthrage." He gave them a mild smile and shrugged.

In a series of loud creaks and sighs, the snakeroot brush opened on the edge of a large pond that surrounded the ashram like a moat. Beyond it, from the other bank, a briar dome loomed in every direction, enclosing them within it. The dome was a thick, thorny wall allowing in light and air but keeping the ashram separate from the jungle; it was what Naila's key was encoded for.

Iravan trajected, reaching for the lilies in the water. Giant leaf pads emerged, their diameters expanding into an engorged circle large enough to hold the three of them. Iravan stepped onto a leaf and the others followed.

The lily pad bore them gently to the other side toward the briar wall. The gentle bobbing was almost soothing, but Ahilya looked troubled, her eyes unfocused. Her hand clutched her satchel, where she absently outlined a cubical piece of equipment over and over again.

"Enough of that," he said, dismissing the council's troubles with a wave of his hand. "Will you tell me about your study?"

"You know what my study is," she muttered. "Like you and the council, I'm trying to find out how best we can survive an earthrage."

"By looking for yaksha habitation in the jungle."

"It didn't seem like such a ludicrous idea to you before."

Iravan glanced at her. He knew about her standing agreement with the council, of course, even if Ahilya had made the deal before he had become councilor. A memory came back to him when as a Junior Architect he had newly arrived from Yeikshar. Early in their courtship, he and Ahilya had lain on their backs, limbs entangled, staring at the clouds over them, discussing their ideas on survival. Those conversations had been the food to nurture their relationship. She had propelled him toward becoming a Senior Architect, and he had encouraged her theories. On becoming a councilor, he had even tried to intervene on her behalf—but the others had shut him down without ceremony. Over the years, Iravan had learned too much to disagree with their decision. The changes Ahilya wanted to make in the ashram would be terrible for architects and for survival itself.

"It was never a bad theory," he said now. "But I think you'll find the records of early architects were right."

"What—that the sizes of the yakshas are their only defense against the earthrages? That they have no particular habitat?" Ahilya let out a derisive laugh. "Naila was skeptical too. You architects are all the same. You only think about evasion, not about survival, with your buildings in the sky."

"Evasion *is* survival."

"Not for the yakshas. They live in the jungle. They thrive here.

They must have a home, some kind of shelter, even if they burrow or… or grow shells. Studying them will reveal something."

"It'll reveal that nothing except them can survive an earthrage."

"The trees survive," Oam interrupted. "Clearly, all the plants of the jungle survive an earthrage, or there wouldn't be a jungle."

Iravan raised his eyebrow, studying the young man. Ahilya winced, embarrassed. She'd understood his expression, of course. Had this boy ever visited the jungle at all?

"Don't look like that, Iravan," Ahilya muttered, her voice low and pitched for his ears alone. "It's Oam's first time. I'm the only real archeologist Nakshar has, and you know as well as I do that no one cares about the jungle. Not when trajection and flying are the only truths we've known. None of our histories teach us about the jungle except to remark on how we escaped it."

Iravan shook his head in disbelief and raised his voice. "Jungle plants don't survive an earthrage. Nothing survives an earthrage. You've never seen its true devastation. Nakshar flies away before one truly erupts."

He himself had only seen an earthrage when Kiana had unveiled the magnifiers to the council a few years earlier. Iravan still remembered his shock and awe as he had peered through the magnifier window to study the view below. He had always known—*everyone* knew—how devastating the earthrages could be. The storms were tremors and quakes of massive proportions. They were tornadoes that eroded deep layers of the very soil. Yet to see one, to actually see the earth roiling, gigantic clouds of dust ballooning, boulders and tree trunks ricocheting and crumbling, endlessly, violently… He had left the magnifier trembling, terror and humility throbbing in him in equal parts.

"The violence wipes everything out," he said. "Jungle plants grow from seeds that are flung around every earthrage. The oldest tree you will see is only as old as when the last earthrage came to an end. You are about to walk into a jungle that is literally birthing itself in front of you."

"That depends on the length and ferocity of the earthrage," Ahilya muttered.

"Other animals," Oam began at the same time, then stopped.

Iravan nodded—at Ahilya; she was right, if pedantic. But Oam's knowledge of the world was appalling. He glanced at the boy and said, "You mean squirrels and birds and all those creatures we have in the ashram? You think those survived in the jungle?"

Ahilya winced once more, avoiding his gaze, but Iravan could read her mind perfectly.

Oam *should* have known better. If he had paid more attention to her research and less to flirting, he would have already known this. Iravan was almost impressed with how easily she had ensnared the young man. Ahilya would have made a magnificent architect if she'd had the ability.

Her voice was gentle when she spoke. "There are no such creatures in the jungle, Oam. It's only the yakshas and the jungle plants out there. Our species was land-dwelling once, and the jungle was our natural home, but a thousand years before, when earthrages grew in frequency and ferocity, the early architects took us to the skies along with any creatures that were lucky enough to be part of the first ashrams. The only remnants of jungle creatures now are the yakshas, and not all creatures evolved to become them."

"Only the yakshas survive here," Iravan said. "They might be dull, unable to sense us if we get close, but they're tough. There's no doubt their sheer sizes help their resilience. We can never hope to do what they do."

But Ahilya turned to him, her eyes flashing.

"You don't know that," she said. "Even if the architect records are right, even if there isn't any habitat down here for the yakshas, *even* if their sizes are the answer behind their survival—studying them will still give us information. It will give us clues for our own survival, if we ever need to return to the jungle."

"We are refugees," Iravan said flatly. "That is our history. Our identity. The jungle was our home, but it turned us away; it expelled us. That is why we fly. If the early architects had not discovered how to traject plants for flight, we'd be extinct like everything else. The architects found us a new home. They ensured the survival of our species. Returning to the jungle will never happen, not while there is sanctuary in the sky. Not while there are architects."

Oam scowled but didn't say anything. Ahilya stared at Iravan, her chin trembling. He stared back, a silent challenge in his gaze to refute his logic, but then, without warning, something within him stirred, breaking the seriousness of the moment. Iravan's lips twitched. He felt an abrupt desire to take her in his arms, breathe her in, tell her how much he had missed her and their conversation. He didn't want to fight anymore. He wanted to *spoil* her. The realization took him aback. Iravan blinked and looked away.

When the lily pad bobbed against the bank silently, it almost came as a surprise. The three stepped off. Above them, the wall of the briar dome glittered, thorns and spikes covering every inch.

Iravan stopped trajecting and tapped at one of his rudra beads. It was a similar one to the one he'd taken from Naila and crushed, except this one contained higher permissions granted only to Senior Architects. The key activated, and a subtle complex melody emerged, audible only to him.

For a moment, nothing happened.

Then the briar wall groaned. Wood unfurled, a painful sound like bones gnashing. The branches snapped one by one in agony.

A doorway appeared in the wall, but the movement seemed forced.

Iravan frowned. His key was working but there was a strange resistance. It was as though the ashram didn't want to let them out. He thought to speak a warning, but after his speech, such a caution would hardly reflect well on the architects. He couldn't call the mission off, either; at best, they'd think him a coward, and at worst, an imperious bastard. He gestured silently to Ahilya, but she ignored him.

Her eyes were trained on the doorway. Her hands trembled.

"What's wrong?" Iravan asked.

She toyed with the locket on her throat. It chimed softly. Underneath it he could see her pulse race.

"Is it the jungle?" he pressed. "We don't have to go. It might not be a bad idea."

"No. You won't understand."

"Try me."

She didn't bother to respond, fiddling with her locket.

Oam extended his hand and Ahilya gripped it. "It doesn't matter about our histories," the young man said. "You'll find something from the yaksha. It'll all be worth it."

Realization dawned on Iravan. All his talk of the architects and their importance, all his speech of their history—normal citizens had nothing of their own to relate to. The existing histories had practically erased them. His arguments about survival had been right—but all he had done was discourage Ahilya on the brink of her expedition. In this group of three, *he* was the interloper. The thought took him aback. He glanced at Ahilya, but what could he say? He'd only make it worse.

Iravan held his tongue. Leading the way, he stepped through the briar doorway into the jungle.

6

IRAVAN

The cry of the jungle slammed into Iravan first—breathless, feverish, ominous.

It pierced him like spikes under his veins. The rudra bead bracelet began to vibrate on his wrist, barely able to maintain its hold on the briar wall. The moment Oam emerged from the outer maze, Iravan tapped the bead again. The briar wall recoiled viciously and snapped away.

Iravan swallowed. The cry was a raga, a residue of trajection, a way nature harmonized an architect's workings with a plant's natural state. Architects interpreted ragas as melodies, but in all of his years, Iravan had never sensed anything like the jungle raga. It sounded like the last ravaging echoes of an ancient scream. The hairs on his neck rose.

The doorway they had entered through disappeared. Creepers and vines slithered over the briar, thickening. Above them, branches knit themselves together. The leaves on the trees were already ripening, plump white berries ready to burst. The grass at his feet was now up to his knees. The growth was astonishing, far more accelerated than he would have anticipated so soon after an earthrage. That there were trees here already—and laden with fruit, no less—it was unbelievable.

Ahilya's eyes were darting everywhere, from her satchel to the expanding white-beech trunk, to Oam, and finally to Iravan. When their gazes met, Iravan opened his mouth, but she strode over to where Oam stared at the jungle. She whispered something, and the two opened their satchels, digging through them and removing various pieces of equipment.

Iravan began trajecting and followed her. "You can feel it too, can't you?"

She eyed him warily. "Feel what?"

"The jungle. Something isn't right."

As always with trajection, his vision had split into two. In the first, he could see what Ahilya and Oam did, the bushes thickening, the rubber plant dripping sap, leaves and shoots unrolling in all directions at dizzying speeds.

In his second vision, existing as a dust mote, Iravan saw the jungle as a field littered with stars. It had been years since he had visited the jungle, but he did not remember its Moment being so sinister. He drifted through it, feeling the wildness, the dark casual cruelty as weeds and stems existed only in possibilities of violence, throttling each other for precious sunlight. The early architects must have contended with a Moment much like this when they flew the species to the skies for the first time, nearly a thousand years before.

Ahilya said nothing. She and Oam continued to unpack, pulling out their machetes, shaking and elongating the equipment with soft clicks, attaching things to their harnesses.

Non-architects could not hear ragas, but there was something furtive in Ahilya's manner, a nervousness in the way she moved.

Surely, she had seen the hostility of the jungle. Could she be so angry that she wouldn't validate his concern?

Iravan generated his constellation lines, tying together various stars in complicated patterns, but even as he did, his lines trembled violently.

"Is this normal, Ahilya?" he pressed. "Did any of the other architects during previous expeditions ever mention the jungle feeling strange?"

"All of them did," she said. "But it was always their first time in the jungle, so..."

She met his gaze and he could see her open appraisal. He knew what she was thinking; he had been thinking it too. Even if the jungle had disoriented a Junior Architect in previous expeditions, Iravan should have been above that.

"Do *you* feel any different?" he said. "Does the jungle feel different to you?"

"Not any more than usual. It *is*, technically, a new jungle each time." Ahilya slung her satchel over her shoulders again. She lifted a hand to her chiming locket, studied it for a moment, then began walking into the trees. "This way."

"Stay close," Iravan said. "You too, Oam."

The boy threw him a contemptuous look and scurried after Ahilya, hacking at the engorging creepers with his machete. The chopped pieces fell to the ground, writhing, before they slithered toward each other. Oam's eyes grew wide. He followed Ahilya, a mere step behind her.

Ahilya herself looked more comfortable than Iravan had ever seen her. His wife's eyes were trained on her locket, and she glided instinctively through the jungle. Unlike Oam, who seemed intent on decimating a path, Ahilya ducked under growing branches, swept away feathery leaves, and only used her own machete to split vines that reached for her. The vines changed direction instead of dropping and re-seeding themselves.

She knew this jungle. Better than Iravan did, despite his drifting in the Moment. When she disappeared from view for long moments, his heart raced—not, he realized, out of concern for her but with concern for himself. Oam looked panic-stricken, turning round and round in circles, slashing at the jungle in wild swings. Iravan trajected, harshly, to retract the plants from smothering the boy. He used his own machete, cutting a path to Oam. The two exchanged a nervous look. Iravan opened his mouth to shout for Ahilya, but before he could gather his breath, she emerged again, visible through the trees, settling her clothes with a satisfied smile.

"Don't do that again," Oam muttered as they caught up to her.

She merely grinned and waved them forward, confidence in her steps.

Iravan trajected a path, pushing back the itchweed on the forest floor. The weed resisted, and sweat broke out on his chest and neck with the effort. Instinctively, he reached for Ahilya.

"Talk to me," he blurted, his hand on her arm.

"What?" Distracted by the tracker, she brushed his hand away and kept moving.

"Tell me about the arrangements inside Nakshar. Can you hear the flight alarm past the briar wall?"

Ahilya gave him a quizzical glance, then returned to her tracker. "We've just landed, Iravan. It hasn't even been two hours. It'll be days, weeks, before we need to fly."

"Please, Ahilya, just tell me." Iravan was very aware of how there was nothing out there to protect them if his trajection failed, no other architect and no temple. The realization was chilling. "Can you hear the alarm from the ashram?"

Ahilya waggled her hand at him. "When the alarm goes off inside Nakshar for citizens to prepare for flight, it chimes through the citizen ring, just like it would if I was in the city. I've used it all the hundred times I've been on an expedition. I never wander too far from Nakshar, and we always return with hours to spare."

"And you've checked your ring? It'll work, no problem?"

"It'll work as long as you keep trajecting," she said dryly.

Her words gave Iravan no comfort. The jungle plants didn't like his trajection. His constellation lines quivered like spider webs in a storm. Any moment now, he expected the plants to force his Two Visions to merge. Could evolution change the innate consciousness of a species? Was the behavior of the jungle plants somehow affecting their counterparts in Nakshar? Was that why it had been so hard to traject during the last earthrage? He was so preoccupied that he bumped into Oam, who brusquely pushed him away.

The archeologists had stopped. A gigantic gray tree trunk lay in their path, the bark pebbled and rough. Iravan flew within the Moment to look for its star, but he couldn't see it; an oddity in the birthing jungle, for the plant to be invisible in any of its possibilities. There was only one reason for that.

"We'll have to go around," he said. "Whatever tree this is, it's dead. Fully, irreversibly dead. I can't traject it."

Ahilya stared at him, a dazed expression on her face. "This isn't a tree."

Oam's mouth fell open.

Iravan frowned and straightened. He turned back to the gray trunk. Ahilya left his side, reaching forward, pushing aside low branches, trying to create a clearing. Iravan trajected, sweat soaking his kurta, and the branches retracted. Vines and creepers scaled back. A shower of leaves fell on them.

And then through the gaps in the leaves, he glimpsed black bumps, gnarled like a boulder, and farther up, something blinked, a gleaming eye.

Iravan stumbled back. A yaksha. He was looking at a yaksha.

His mind reeled. Moisture coated his palms. All of the times while Nakshar had been in flight, he had glimpsed the aerial incarnations of the creatures from afar, flying like gigantic specks in the distance. He had never seen one so close.

The elephant-yaksha's size defied all reason. It rose at least twenty feet tall, its broad bony forehead like a small hill. Spiky ridges of vertebrae rolled down its gigantic back. The yaksha trumpeted, a shrieking, bloodcurdling sound that shook the trees and set Iravan's heart thumping. The creature moved its head, and Iravan saw two thick tusks curved on either side of its trunk, their edges sharp and lethal. Vines tightened on the tusks, but as the creature moved, the plants broke away and dropped to the jungle floor like writhing snakes. And Iravan saw, circled around one of the tusks, an identical locket to what Ahilya wore.

Yakshas were known to be placid, but to go seeking them out... Iravan couldn't wrap his mind around it. His shallow breath resonated in his ears. His trajection wavered. A stray thought came to him, that perhaps he should have fought the council harder, to give the expedition a chance, to give *Ahilya* a chance.

He glanced at her, seeing her clearly for the first time in a long time. Ahilya's eyes were trained on the elephant-yaksha. She was radiant, an amazing woman full of sheer guts and stubborn courage, a delighted laugh escaping her. Fearlessly, she pushed through the weeds, leaving Iravan humbled in her wake.

7

AHILYA

Ahilya laughed out loud. She felt dizzy. It was difficult to catch her breath.

Hello, old friend, she thought, but in the back of her archeologist mind, she was already recording her encounter for posterity.

Despite the passage of years and the numerous earthrages, the elephant-yaksha has hardly changed. The tusks have acquired more curls, but the animal is no larger than it was. Importantly, it shows no signs of injury, suggesting it must have had shelter during the many earthrages since it was last observed.

Her hands shook as she collapsed her hiking equipment. The yaksha's robust health, the lack of change in its size—this here was proof enough to build her hypotheses. All she had to do was take careful measurements, and she'd have a true chance at being nominated to the council seat. Ahilya squirmed in excitement, and the rope underneath her kurta chafed her bare skin. In those moments she had disappeared from Iravan and Oam's view, she had taken a terrible risk to find spiralweed for Dhruv, but the sungineer would no longer be their best chance for changing the circumstances of the city. *Ahilya* could understand survival in the jungle. *She* could be their hope. Her hand clutched and released her satchel in nervousness.

Next to her, Oam whooped, a sound edged with hysteria. "This is incredible," he said. "This is incredible!"

She grinned. "They take your breath away, don't they?"

"They're monstrous! How did you ever do this? It's incredible. *You're* incredible."

The elephant-yaksha exhaled, the vibrations shaking the surrounding trees. It moved, its gigantic feet eating the distance. Ahilya pushed the implications of finding the yaksha away from her mind. She started to jog, fumbling in her satchel, retrieving pieces of her sungineering equipment, handing Oam her solarnote.

"All right. Let's begin. Oam, you know what to do—"

"Sketches, yes," he said. "I can do more, Ahilya. Let me take the readings."

"No, we can't depend on Dhruv's instruments—our sketches and observations are all we can rely on until he invents something more enduring. And Iravan, I need to reach the tracker. Traject me up, please." She stepped forward to follow the yaksha and found herself on her knees, the breath knocked out of her.

In the moments she had paused, white grass had snaked up her thighs. She lay on the forest floor, half-crouched, half-sprawled, the grass growing over her arms and legs, holding her down. Oam was on all fours too. The apprentice's gaze went past Ahilya, behind her. He swore.

Ahilya moved her neck painfully against the hold on her limbs. Iravan stood exactly where he had been. He stared beyond her, tall, handsome and—Ahilya noted—utterly useless. His dark skin no longer radiated the blue-green light of trajection.

"Iravan," she snapped. "Are you trying to kill us?"

He grunted as though in sudden understanding. Without taking his eyes off the yaksha, he began to jog toward them. "I don't trust it."

"What?"

Next to her, Oam slashed awkwardly at the white grass with his machete. "Unbelievable. Is he trying to hijack this mission again?"

"I don't trust it," Iravan repeated. He stopped moving, the white grass trapping him as well. "Every living thing has consciousness that can be detected, even if it can't be trajected. But I'm testing it, and I don't detect consciousness in this creature."

Ahilya blinked. This was new information. "Are you sure?"

Iravan nodded, and a moment later, his skin lit up with trajection. The grass stopped curling at Ahilya's waist; it tightened, squeezing the breath from her. An icy chill went through her; Oam gasped. Then the grass snapped and dissolved into dust. Oam shook himself, arose, and followed the yaksha.

"No consciousness," Iravan said, catching up to Ahilya as she arose to her feet too, brushing white flakes off. "What do you think that means?"

"I don't know. I just assumed... I mean, how is it alive if it doesn't have consciousness?"

"Precisely. Consciousness exists on a spectrum of life activity. Dead beings and non living objects are the only things to have no consciousness. But this creature is clearly neither. No one else mentioned it?"

"Well, no... Their role was just to traject the plants here for our path, and I think they had enough to do with managing the jungle." Ahilya eyed Iravan. "How can you tell?"

"It's a quality of trajection. When architects traject, they see states of consciousness existing as stars in the Moment."

"Yes, I know. But I thought the Moment showed only plants."

"The Moment can show humans and other animals, too. But architects aren't taught to see any other consciousnesses except plants. It's dangerous to dwell in the Moment with beings more complex than plants, so we deliberately teach architects to blind their second vision lest they accidentally traject a complex being. Trajecting a complex being can—"

"Damage an architect's mind irrevocably. Yes, I know." Ahilya considered this. "But you can *see* animals and humans in the Moment? Even if you can't traject them?"

"*I* can," Iravan said. "If I try. I'm a Senior Architect. It's my job to enforce the limits of trajection, and I can't enforce what I don't understand. But even I rarely allow myself to expand my vision enough to see complex beings in the Moment."

"And you don't see the yaksha?"

Iravan licked his lips, his eyes still on the creature. "That's impossible, you know. It means that the yaksha doesn't exist. That it isn't alive."

"Maybe you're missing it. Making a mis—"

"I'm not making a mistake."

Ahilya frowned. The creature had stopped moving, its tusks entangled in rapidly curling vines. It trumpeted softly, shaking its gigantic head side to side. She glanced back at Iravan, wondering if she should ask him to elaborate. It would change her entire study. But he didn't meet her gaze. This close, she heard his rapid breathing. Sweat beaded his brow.

It took her a second to understand. He was scared. The realization took her aback.

All Junior Architects who had ever accompanied her in the jungle had shown nervousness when they'd encountered a yaksha. Some reacted with stunned silence, others with incessant swearing or nervous laughter. Ahilya had learned to ignore their reactions, but this was Iravan. He was always so self-possessed. Besides, he was Nakshar's expert on consciousness; it was how he'd gained his council seat in the first place. For him to sense no consciousness in this creature… what could it mean?

"I don't like it," he said again.

"Iravan, it's harmless. I've worked with it before, remember?"

"No, not that," he muttered, and swallowed. "Not only that. The trajection. The jungle. All of it. We shouldn't be here. We should be back in the ashram."

She touched his elbow lightly. "Exactly what are you afraid of?"

His gaze when it met hers was uncertain. "I don't know. It's instinct."

Ahilya had heard this before, too. The jungle always made architects nervous, but she had expected better from Iravan. She glanced at him and then back at the yaksha. As angry as she was with him, he was the most competent man she knew. Could she afford to dismiss him? *We don't have much time*, Dhruv said in her mind. *If we don't do this, we can wave our professions goodbye.*

Ahilya sighed, tugged at her harness, and pointed up at the yaksha, looming above them. "I need to get up there."

Her husband stared at her uncomprehendingly. Then the patterns of his tattoos changed. Plants grew over Ahilya, up her legs and her thighs. They tightened their grip, clasping her waist, curling around her harness. She began to rise. Her view twisted from Iravan's face to the foliage. Thick green leaves blocked her; branches slapped against arms that protected her head. Sticky sap dripped on her neck.

Then she emerged clear of the growing canopy.

She blinked, gray filling her vision. She was level with the yaksha's knee, then its shoulder, and finally its left tusk. The spiral stopped, and she hung there, suspended, feeling the plants grip her tighter. In front of her, the gigantic tusk shone a dull yellow. Curled around it—exactly where she had left it five years before—a tracker glinted gently.

Ahilya reached out and cut the fibers. The tracker dropped into her palm, heavy and familiar. Grinning, she attached it to her necklace, where the receiver and transmitter clicked together into a bulky pendant. She delved inside her satchel until she held the replacement tracker, and carefully attached it where the first one had been.

Oam called out her name, and Ahilya twisted her head to see him spiraling on the other side of the yaksha in his own tornado of foliage. The apprentice grinned, his expression exhilarated. He let out a soft whoop.

She grinned back. "Can you believe this? I never thought I'd see this creature again."

Oam watched her, his eyes wide. "You're incredible, you are."

Ahilya laughed, pulled out her skin-density scanner, and watched the readings. *The percentages are no different from a human's*, she thought, as though already writing in her solarnote. *But with true comparison, this can disprove the prevailing theory of yaksha survival, which relies on their sizes.* She replaced the scanner back in her bag—it would continue calculating as she took other readings—and turned to look down. Iravan had trajected a clear view for himself. He waited there, pacing back and forth, his eyes disturbed, a crease forming on his forehead.

"Higher," she called out. "I need some pupil readings and I need to scope its hearing."

He nodded, his golden headlamp and blue-green trajecting light bobbing. The vortex carried her upward, past the nubby fold from where the tusk grew, until she was at level with an eye. She saw herself reflected, life-size but warped.

Ahilya gasped.

There was a strange pattern glinting in the yaksha's eye, almost like it had developed more rings around the iris. Ahilya gripped her retinoscope. Powered by Iravan's trajection, the slim pen-sized machine buzzed in her hands. She waved it like a beacon in front of the pupil. The yaksha didn't blink.

"Ahilya," Iravan called out from below. "Something isn't right. I think I know why the jungle feels odd. Why it's fighting my trajection."

She glanced down but he had moved several feet away. Only his dim blue-green light was visible, moving in small circles through the weeds. Ahilya replaced the retinoscope with the eye refractor. She gripped the refractor and repeated the motion, waving it for several moments.

"These are the same species we use to test safety..." Iravan called out. "But why aren't they..." He trailed off, but the tension in his voice was palpable.

Ahilya stopped what she was doing and gazed down at him, frowning. "What do you mean—" she began, but then the spiral holding her dropped a few feet, knocking the breath out of her.

Her heart thumped loudly. She gripped the edge of the foliage spiral. Gasping, she looked down. She could see Iravan now, crouched among the weeds, far from her. His eyes were wide with horror.

And then the spiral collapsed under her, leaves and branches splitting in an explosion.

It seemed to Ahilya she was falling very slowly. She had plenty of time to observe Oam drop alongside her, his face terrified. She had time to note she was screaming. She had time to note Iravan cast his arms wide, time to see the green ground rushing up.

Then, through a shower of leaves and bark, Ahilya crashed onto something soft and bubbly. Her vision swam. Her left elbow twinged.

She arose slowly. She had landed on slippery moss.

Iravan stood several feet away, still blazing like a torch in the dimness of the jungle. His teeth were gritted in a snarl. His eyes bulged. He was waving his arms, but the movement seemed sluggish.

Oam had landed on his own pillow of moss. Ahilya stumbled to her knees, sliding on the moss, fury taking over her fear.

"What in bloody rages—" she began, but Iravan cut her off, his voice tight.

"Lost control."

"Are you fucking joking—"

"We need to leave," he snapped. "Both of you. Come to me *now*."

"*What?* We aren't leaving yet; we came here on a mission!"

"Bloody rages, Ahilya," Iravan said, turning toward her, still surrounded by the tall weeds. "You have to come back to me *now*. I'm doing all I can to contain this already." He jerked his head at the weeds. Each blade was rapidly growing several other needles, almost like arrowheads. "Look. This is magnaroot. The same species in the temple that tells us when we can't land. When there's danger, it's not limp. It's thorny. *Look* at it."

She stared back. What did he mean? Nakshar had landed, and she had set all precautions before going into the jungle.

Then the ground trembled through the moss. It reverberated like a thrum in her heart. Her eyes widened, her mouth still half-open.

Earthrage.

Oam moaned, a pitiful sound. He tried to get to his feet, the wet sounds of slipping and sliding.

"Impossible," Ahilya said, even as she started to crawl off the moss. "The alarm from Nakshar, it should have—"

Another tremor, this time louder and deeper, rumbled through the forest floor. The elephant-yaksha roared, the sound deafening this close. Her ears rang, the yaksha reared its head, thundered toward

Ahilya, she screamed and scrambled back, slipping, the creature barely missing the moss she was on. She felt the wind of its passage as it disappeared into the trees. Stumbling, she stood up, brushed her clothes instinctively. Her hand came up empty against her thigh. She blinked, not understanding, looking down at her hand.

Her satchel was missing.

Ahilya stared at her empty hand, as the tremor subsided.

"Ahilya, rage it, back to me, *now.*"

"I've lost my bag," she yelled back. She rolled off the moss, her eyes searching, spinning on her feet, kicking at brush and creepers; where was it, where *was* it?

"We don't have time. The earthrage is coming; those were the first tremors."

"It has all of Dhruv's sungineering equipment!" she screamed. "All the data I just collected. I can't leave it."

"I see it, I see it," Oam yelled. He changed direction and sprinted to where the yaksha had been. He swept the satchel into his hands and over his shoulders, and dashed back toward Iravan.

The jungle roiled.

Ahilya lost her footing. Her vision blurred.

"Ahilya, BACK HERE, *NOW.*"

Ahilya glanced down, to where bark had trapped her legs. She struggled but it didn't give.

Her eyes went to her husband. Iravan was a vision of blue-green. He had trajected an orb of branches around him and Oam, but they were nearly fifty feet away. Tears blurred her vision. The jungle snapped and heaved.

She could see then that she would never make it. They would die there because of her. She had promised Oam she'd protect him, but she'd failed as an expedition leader. Their voices came to her from far away, but all she could hear was Tariya disdaining her choices. Her sister had been right. This was what she'd wrought. Her fault.

"Go," she whispered.

"Get up," Iravan snarled. "Get up."

"Iravan, go. Please, just take him and go."

"Ahilya, come on," Oam shrilled. "Use your machete. Come on!"

Her hands trembling, Ahilya groped for the machete she had hung on her harness. She began hacking at the bark. It had slowed its growth; from the corner of her eye she saw Iravan extend a fist toward her. He was controlling the bark's growth, but the distraction cost him. A gigantic branch slammed like a spear into the nest. Oam shrieked, cowering, but the nest held.

"I won't make it," she rasped as the earth bucked underneath her. "Go, please; you have to go. Protect him. Just *go*."

"NO!" Iravan bellowed. "Get up, rage you."

The bark snapped. Ahilya kicked and jerked, shards piercing her skin. She crawled out and pushed through the churning wind, against the dust and the jungle. Iravan extended both fists toward her. He was blazing so brightly that Oam's eyes were shut against his light. The nest creaked, became smaller.

Ahead of Ahilya, a path opened, one step at a time. She swiped her knife with one hand, cutting and slashing at roots that grabbed her, at the vines that flew at her face. She was almost at the orb.

Then Oam reached his arm out. He hauled her in and she slammed into him. The two of them sprawled, limbs entangled, and the nest tightened. The ground shook, and this time the tremor was audible, a roar from deep within the earth.

The nest bucked high in the air. Ahilya flew, slammed against Oam, their heads knocking together, blinding pain, landed hard. Iravan, standing steady in the center of the nest, arms extended, yelled, "Brace."

A tree trunk filled Ahilya's vision through the gaps in the nest. It slammed against them, once, twice, thrice. Oam was screaming, she was screaming, and then.

Silence.

The nest floated down gently, back to the forest floor.

Ahilya's terror was reflected in Oam's eyes. The jungle had stilled. Every plant, every root, unmoving, as though dead.

Oam's breathing reverberated around them, panicked and shallow. "I… Is that it?"

"No," Iravan replied. "It's just beginning."

"N-Nakshar?" Ahilya gasped. "Is it still there? Are they still here?" She rubbed her citizen ring, but it was quiet, though her sungineering locket still chimed softly.

"I don't know," Iravan said. "But we have to believe they waited. It's our only chance." The trajecting light on his skin brightened. "Hold on. I'm going to roll us out of here."

Ahilya grabbed the branches and squeezed her eyes shut.

8

IRAVAN

Nothing happened. The magnaroot nest didn't move. It didn't roll away.

Iravan was suspended in a nightmare. The stillness was more chilling than anything he had experienced.

In his split vision, his constellation lines thrashed like snakes, refusing to lock in to the magnaroot. Iravan held on, bearing the weight of his existence on the star. It fought back, and for a second the force of their opposing desires made the nest *thrum* with agitation. Ahilya gasped, and Oam yelped, and then they were all screaming. Iravan's teeth burned; his bones shook through his skin. A stabbing pain reverberated through his arms and chest. The magnaroot whipped and fought, live-wire, red-hot pain, more alive than any plant he had ever trajected.

Iravan released a few constellation lines. The magnaroot nest shook one last time, then stilled, content to be shaped like a nest for now but to do little else.

"What was that?" Oam gasped.

Iravan's breath came out in short gasps. Trajection in the wild jungle was known to be harder than in a tame ashram, but he had never felt such opposition to his guidance before. It was as though the magnaroot were more than just a plant, like it had the sentient consciousness of a complex being.

Outside, trees began to shudder and wave.

Another tremor shook the nest. It rose jerkily into the air. Ahilya and Oam shrieked. Iravan's stomach lurched. They crashed into a massive tree trunk and bounced, vision skewed, upside down, bile rising, and then a gentle roll. The nest landed far from where it had been.

Hold on, Iravan tried to say, but he couldn't form the words. A bone-deep exhaustion weighed him down, but he flew through the Moment, frantically examining and discarding possibilities, even as the other two righted themselves. Should he release the magnaroot and search for teak or ironwood? No, too late; there was no time to look. Should he dissolve the nest and create armor? No, any armor would be crushed as soon as the first wave of the earthrage hit. His heart sank.

"What are you doing?" Oam squeaked. "Why are we just waiting here?"

Iravan tried again. In his first vision, he saw himself as Oam and Ahilya did, feet dug into the crisscross of the nest, fists gripping branches, head bent in exhaustion. His skin glowed blindingly as trajection tattoos articulated themselves in complex fractals.

In his second vision, he approached the magnaroot star, wielding his constellation lines like a hundred whips, hunting for an opening to latch them.

The star anticipated him before he could decide his move. It expanded in his second vision, crashing into his mind, leaving him no time even to gasp.

His Two Visions merged.

At that instant, Iravan felt true terror.

His skin began to crack and bleed. Spines grew on his back, in his neck, through his eyes. He opened his mouth, but only dust blew out, tiny gray-white seedlings rushing out of him. His gums rotted, spikes under his nails, twigs yanking his hair, and he thought, *Yes, good, rip, bleed, die, seed, survive*. He recognized a tiny battering interference—his own—as his trajecting dust mote tried to stop from ripping his plant self apart. He smiled through bloody teeth and pressed the pain deeper into himself. The agony was beautiful; he wept in its rapture—

Iravan blinked.

He wrenched himself free, tearing through the grip of the magnaroot. He scrambled away from the star in panic.

The visions separated, but Iravan continued to retreat through the Moment, whimpering, terrified. Dangerous, *dangerous* to have the Two Visions merge. An architect could lose himself and wither away, never to return into his own body. He emptied his stomach on the nest's floor. His trajection light faded.

The nest began to dissolve.

Thorns crumbled over their heads into dust, then a branch cracked and popped in shards. Ahilya whimpered, eyes frantic, as she watched their slim defense breaking.

"What is he doing?" Oam shrieked. "Is he crazy?"

Ahilya stared at him, hair disheveled, blood trickling down her forehead, beautiful and terrified. Her hands trembled as she tried to physically hold the nest together, as though anything she could do would make a difference.

Desperately, Iravan leaped back toward the magnaroot star. With no time for subtlety, he jammed his constellation lines, hundreds of them, into the star's depths in an inartistic, inelegant command. The nest stopped dissolving. It thrummed in fury again.

The constellation lines reared up, vibrating in his grip. The wrath of the magnaroot was almost too powerful. He was going to be sucked into it again, visions merging; he couldn't let that happen—

Abruptly, the nest stilled.

Iravan's heart soared, a brief moment of victory.

Too late he saw a boulder sail through the air toward them, a wrecking ball.

Desperately, Iravan flung up a hand, clawing his constellation lines to grip the outer filaments of the nest. He jammed the branches of the nest into each other, splintering the magnaroot, knitting it through itself.

The boulder crashed into the nest. They hurtled on the forest floor, tumbling, bodies crashing into him, but the orb held, *rages*, it held.

How had the magnaroot known the boulder would fly toward them? It was a plant, it wasn't a dust mote, it shouldn't have seen the possibilities—but there was no time.

Iravan steadied himself in the Moment, generating one constellation line after another, tying them to the nest, using as much of the magnaroot's desire to splinter itself as he could. Intent on destroying itself, the magnaroot leaped to obey him this time. Shoots ruptured into each other. The nest's crust became a crisscross of branches. It became tighter, denser, and a surge of hope, of triumph, shot through Iravan. He'd done it; he had found a way.

In the next instant, soft white seeds flew out of the fractures, filling the air.

The bright light from his body diffused, and now they were all coughing, wheezing, choking, even as they were flung around. Ahilya's eyes bulged, her hand on throat, and he knew he was killing her, he was killing all of them.

NO, he screamed soundlessly.

Through his trajection he could feel the magnaroot's ecstasy at the release.

There had to be a way out to safety. There had to be!

Iravan flailed around in the Moment, hunting, cursing. He tried it all again, trajecting constellation lines into the star to stop the plant from rupturing itself, but the nest thrummed and flung itself into the air. He changed the pattern to force the nest into stillness, but the magnaroot waited until a boulder or a tree trunk rammed into it, shaking them. He attacked it, using its own desire against it, but the nest filled with tiny white seedlings, choking them, and Ahilya was becoming purple. Again, and again, and again.

He couldn't outthink it. He couldn't do anything. There was no way out. He'd exhausted all possibilities, all combinations.

The magnaroot taunted him.

He stared at it, the corners of the Moment they were caught in.

To the rages with you, he thought. *I'll take you from the inside.* And he flung himself at the star, merging his Two Visions.

Blackness.

They tore into themselves.

The ecstasy made them weep.

They thought in horror of what they were doing, what they were becoming. But the horror was fleeting.

Veins ripped apart, leaves decaying into mulch, and the dispersion of precious, precious seeds. Dimly, they thought they had become the magnaroot for a purpose. But there was no other purpose except survival. Survival of their kind; for them, it meant death.

They smiled through bloody teeth. The consciousness of the jungle assaulted them. It rose under the earth like a crescendo, waves upon waves of destruction. A million screams erupted in their mind, faces warped in fright, rushing toward them, hungry eyes, regretful mouths.

They knew how they had been able to fight themselves so deftly.

The star wasn't just their state of being. It was the possibility of the jungle, the possibility of life. Each frozen star, each discrete state was an illusion. When an architect trajected, he only created images to comprehend and navigate the universe, but the Moment was not a motionless reality. It was a furious storm.

I am he, they realized. *I am an architect. Iravan.* For an instant, his Two Visions separated. They glimpsed him roaring in agony, Ahilya and Oam watching horrified, but then all was as it should be, and they were the magnaroot again.

Holding the line, merged irrevocably, they watched the Moment hurtle to them. It wasn't the existence of a single plant. It was the pause of the jungle, of the entire planet. The immensity of it... They felt it in every slap of a branch, in every tear of the bark. They were the jungle. And the jungle was poised toward one possibility, aimed at a single intent: annihilation.

They sobbed softly.

Embedded in the Moment, they could see what would happen. His right arm would be ripped off, head smashed in, and they'd be aware of his own death in horrified eternity. They could feel his panic and terror from the future, from far away.

Let it be over soon, he thought.

The Resonance flickered, silvery molten.

It flashed like mercury behind their eyes, and they jerked and reached for it.

The Moment winked out.

An eternal fall.

Then blindness.

Recognition.

He smelled flesh burning; it was his own. He was descending. *We did it*, he thought. And then, immediately, *This was a mistake.*

It was too late now. He had separated.

A call, like the rhythms of his own heart.

Drifting away to eternal loneliness.

Birth.

There was screaming, but it seemed far away.

His Two Visions separated, but not in the simultaneous way of trajection. Instead, his visions expanded, enhanced into something greater.

A terrifying sensitivity overwhelmed him. Iravan *saw* for the first time in his life. The magnaroot was a speck, and suddenly its desire to self-destruct was laughable in his power.

He reached into the Moment with precision and crushed the magnaroot star. The nest fell limp, ready to obey.

Why had it been so difficult before?

A part of him knew the horror of what he had done, the unreality, its implications. Then the horror disappeared. He was a mountain and these tiny consciousnesses were insignificant.

Iravan stopped screaming.

He stood up.

Outside, the storm picked up intensity, but he gathered the magnaroot in his mind and it responded, its will destroyed completely. Ahilya and Oam stood as far back from him as was possible. Oam stood in front of Ahilya, shielding her, but she stared at Iravan, reaching out a hand. Her eyes were wide in fear. Iravan watched them both dispassionately.

Beyond the now-stationary magnaroot nest, the earthrage

screamed and roared, dust and earth making it impossible to see too far.

He trajected, but it wasn't trajection, not really. He *desired* it, and the plant changed its form; it leaped to obey. Branches twined around the three of them, wrapping their legs, torso, arms. Thick wooden armors of magnaroot covered them. In seconds, the three stood completely shielded, facing each other. Through his armor's eye slit Iravan saw the churning dust.

Ahilya's voice came to him, muffled. "I-Iravan?"

"All right," he said quietly. "Let's try this again."

9

AHILYA

Ahilya's body shook uncontrollably. Goosebumps covered her skin.

Her heart thrashed in her ears. What could she do? How could she protect them? She was helpless. Her decisions had already cost them precious time.

She glanced at Iravan nervously. He stood a few feet in front of her, arms loose by his side. Trajecting light shone dimly through his own wooden armor. To be visible at all, she knew he had to be bathed in the power. Only a few moments before, he had been on his knees, close enough to ripping his hair out, his eyes feral, unearthly screams tearing through him. What had happened? She resisted the urge to touch him lest she disturb his concentration.

The nest dissolved. A whimper escaped her. Vines grew from her suit, anchoring her to the ground, but the fury of the storm was mere inches away. It pushed her heavily, pulled at her, and she gasped, trying to balance herself. Debris flew everywhere. Grit seeped in through the armor and she tasted wet earth. She couldn't see clearly past the blur of dust and her own terrified tears. Twice, something—a boulder, a tree trunk—split a handsbreadth above them. Clods of heavy earth and pieces of vines ricocheted off the armors. Luck that they had missed?

Iravan. He was trajecting the jungle, crushing boulders before they hit. They were standing in a small bubble of protection. Awe filled her. This power… Even with trajection, it should not have been possible.

Something nudged her: thick vines growing from the forest floor. They encircled her waist and tied her to Oam so the two stood back-to-back. She'd told him she'd keep him safe. What had she done? They should never have left the city.

Oam shouted something; she couldn't hear, but she could guess from his terrified voice. Where would they go? Was Nakshar still there? Her citizen ring was silent. Had Nakshar survived? What was Iravan doing?

Iravan stood there, his head tilted to a side.

He's listening. Did this armor amplify sound to him? What was he listening for? What could he even hear in this maelstrom? Ahilya swallowed, her breathing quick and shallow. She twisted her head to look at him. Iravan's gaze was directed to where the city had landed. Slowly his head moved, gazing up as though he could see something fly through the storm.

He barked something, a raw laugh. The vines tightened around them.

Ahilya burst through the obliterating jungle.

Tied to Oam, unable to move at all, she was flung into the air. Something grabbed the pair of them; they twisted, gasping, bangs echoing inside her armor, locket pealing wildly. Nausea gripped her. She squinted through the eye slit but only saw dust and gigantic tree-trunks flash by. Her body spun, changed directions. An abrupt lurch swirled deep in her stomach, and she saw in horror a gigantic piece of debris heading for her. *NO*, she cried. Her body turned at the last second, a narrow miss. Blue-green light leapt midair from boulder to tree. Iravan.

Ahilya burst through the canopy and soared into the air. Vines thickened around her legs, keeping them restrained to Oam's.

Tied together, the two of them surged through the debris, rotating and flipping. Branches and trees whipped past, only just missing them. Iravan ascended next to them in his own armor, a vortex of vines snapping and knitting underneath him, carrying him like a tornado from the jungle.

Ahilya's body spun and she saw. Less than a hundred feet away from them, hovering like a giant bark moon in the sky. Nakshar.

A sob of relief escaped her. They had waited. Iravan was going to save them.

Iravan wasn't looking at the city. He faced Ahilya and Oam, rising above them. His arms thrust out forcefully in front of his chest, and he rotated them like wheels.

Ahilya glanced down. Her mind spun. Boulders sailed through the jungle canopy, crashing into trees, churning in the wind. Giant balloons of dust mushroomed, exploded, collapsed. Rocks hit the vine vortex that carried her and Oam, but the vines knit themselves almost immediately. A state of unreality gripped her. Her muscles tensed.

Ahilya's neck whipped as her body twisted. Nakshar appeared in her view again. She moved her arms, bracing, reaching. So close.

The vines tying her to Oam split.

Her arms flailed. Her stomach plummeted. She spun head over heels in midair, too shocked even to scream, dropping. Glimpses came to her, Oam's vines untying, horror in his midair roll, the passage of wind, the writhing jungle becoming bigger.

Below—then above her—light exploded.

Something snatched her from midair. Her vision jerked horribly, then steadied. She was rising again, vines encircling her. Far away, Oam was rising too.

Ahilya craned her neck. High above, Iravan had stopped moving toward Nakshar. He shone like a miniature blue-green sun, but his own vortex was barely a raggedy vine. Furious beams shot out of his armor. She could see his face now, and she knew. The trajection was too much; he couldn't keep it all up. His armor split, cracking. He was directing all his ropes to Ahilya and Oam. He was sacrificing his safety for theirs. *No*, she thought in horror. *What are you doing? Save yourself. Save Oam.*

More bark peeled off him, she *felt* his desperation, his exhaustion, even as she arose. Debris punched at him, slapping his face, and he spun for a moment, losing balance. The straggly vine connecting him to the jungle tore.

Iravan flung an arm, a frantic gesture, and something surrounded Ahilya like a tentacle. In a whirlpool of wind, she was sucked toward the city at a dizzying speed. The last vine connecting her to Iravan snapped.

Then shocking pain smashed into her, vibrating through her feet, her knees, jarring her teeth. Air squeezed out of her. She was being chewed up, the magnaroot armor peeling off her, taking rips of clothing and skin with it.

Ahilya broke through Nakshar and slammed into something hard.

For a moment, she lay there, her ears roaring, spots in her vision. Her breath came out in heavy gasps. She rolled on her side and emptied her stomach. Her body was a mass of blood, a million cuts and scrapes, but there was no sign of the magnaroot. The city's bark had scraped it all off. Nakshar had let her in but not the jungle.

She staggered to her knees. Already the solid ground was growing soft grass. The walls became a tapestry of curling leaves.

A moment later, Iravan slammed through the foliage, sliding on the grass next to her. Ahilya sobbed in relief, scrambling over to clutch at him. He didn't move. His skin was dark again, no longer trajecting. Bruises and bloody scrapes covered his face and body. His breathing was shallow. She waited, one, two, three seconds but the wall didn't move anymore.

Ahilya released Iravan and staggered to her feet, her heart beating frantically. They were in a corridor, and it was empty save the two of them.

There was no sign of Oam.

10

AHILYA

She surged to the leafy wall, pounding it with her fists. "Open, rage you!" she screamed.

In response, thorns emerged out of the leaves. The thorns were too soft; they didn't hurt her, but they were a warning. The wall would not open.

She banged at it again in frustration. Why wouldn't it respond? She was in Nakshar; the plants ought to obey her now without the need for trajection. Was the city still on flight protocol?

"Open, rage you to death," she screamed, tearing at the leaves with bloody fingers. But the wall just grew back, denser than before. Why didn't it—

She was trying to go outside Nakshar. She wouldn't be able to, not without a maze key like the one Naila had, or a Senior—

Ahilya spun on her feet to where Iravan lay slumped on the floor. Grass had grown around him, cushioning him. Healbranch vines circled his chest, reacting to his deepest desire: rest. The pale white vines grew all around the city, boosting immunity and elevating strength. Ahilya hastened to him and dropped to her knees.

The scent of eucalyptus and firemint came to her. Iravan's scents—plants that healed him, specific to his body. Nakshar had already begun curing him, but he didn't move. Ahilya choked, clutching his hand. "Please be all right," she wept. "Please, Iravan, please be all right."

His eyelids fluttered open, "A-lya," he breathed. "You… safe."

"I'm safe," she whispered, tears streaming down her face.

He exhaled and collapsed deeper into his cushion of grass.

"But Oam," she said, her voice trembling. "Oam is still outside."

He moaned, a soft sound.

"Please," she whispered, sobbing. "He's just a child, Iravan. A foolish boy."

Iravan's eyes flickered underneath closed lids. His veins pulsed under her fingers, a brief spasm of blue-green, in and out, blue-green then dark, over and over again like he was malfunctioning.

Ahilya's vision blurred. "I'm so sorry, Iravan," she wept. "I'm so sorry. Please, I had a duty of care."

"No," he mumbled, his voice soft. "*I* did."

He tried to straighten, and she put her arms around his shoulders, but he felt like deadweight. Iravan gritted his teeth, eyes still closed, his breath coming out in shudders. His tattoos sputtered again. Sweaty hair lay limp on his forehead. Ahilya gazed at the wall outside, hoping.

He collapsed in her arms, unconscious.

She half-arose then, thinking of getting help, when she heard the crunch of footsteps. Ahilya spun toward the sound just as Bharavi appeared and pushed her aside. The short-haired woman fell to her knees next to Iravan, her face ashen. She pulled one of Iravan's eyes open. The capillaries were blue, the pupil rolled back.

Bharavi cursed. She tore the tattered remains of Iravan's kurta and lifted his bare arm to the sungineering bulb that appeared in the grass, supplied by Nakshar in response to her desire for light.

Illuminated by the golden beams, Ahilya saw what she hadn't before. Iravan's dark skin was crisscrossed with angry black welts. They looked like grotesque creepers, sharp and angry, burned as though permanently.

"He's overextended himself," Bharavi said, her tone clipped. "The trajection has left an afterimage. He needs help now, or his veins will incinerate."

Ahilya's heart skipped a beat. "The sanctum?" It was where architects were healed.

"This is beyond the sanctum." Bharavi stood up. "He needs to be connected to the rudra tree directly now."

She gestured for Ahilya to move away, and Ahilya scuttled back. Bharavi narrowed her eyes. Light exploded from her. Ahilya threw a hand up for shade, her eyes watering. When she lowered it, Iravan lay on a pale white healbranch platform, his head turned to a side. The waist-high platform began to skim forward. Bharavi swept past Ahilya, following it.

Ahilya struggled to keep up. "Will he be all right?"

"I don't know. He needs Chaiyya now."

Ahilya's heart pounded harder. She reached to touch Iravan's damp hair, but the platform moved too fast. Tears trickled down her face. Her mind couldn't comprehend what had happened. They had been safe. She'd gone on a hundred successful expeditions before. This was supposed to have been a routine excursion. The platform passed through darkness and light, sungineering glowglobes flashing through the corridor.

"Bha," Ahilya began, in a whisper. "My apprentice. Oam. He's still outside. Iravan had him, too—"

Bharavi's eyes were on Iravan. She cursed and trajected again, her veins sparkling. Underneath Ahilya, the ground firmed, and then she and Bharavi were skimming behind Iravan.

Ahilya swallowed back her questions. Oam had to be all right. He had to be. If Bharavi had known to come to the part of the city where she and Iravan had entered, then the temple—the council—had been watching their ascent from the jungle. Surely it meant Oam had made it safe. He must have entered Nakshar through another part. Maybe he was already at the infirmary, receiving healing. Ahilya opened and closed her mouth, wanting to confirm it, but hot tears choked her. She couldn't take a full breath.

At last, Bharavi put up a hand, blue-green with a simple curving pattern. The corridor ended in a wooden wall. Bark retracted. The platform skimmed forward, and the wall closed behind them again. They were back in the temple.

Unlike the expansive courtyard Ahilya had left, the temple now resembled a small dark cavern. The rudra tree stood at the center, shorter, and the Architects' Disc was only a few feet off the grassy floor. Maze Architects moved over it, as many as during the landing. Most wore their robes, but several wore ordinary kurtas and trousers. A nervous chatter hummed around them, sharp and anxious.

"He's here," someone shouted.

Instantly, Ahilya and Bharavi were surrounded by the other councilors. The rudra tree grew thicker, taller, carrying the Disc into its upper stories. Senior Architects Airav and Chaiyya trajected Iravan's platform away, and laid him at the tree's base. The temple transformed as rock walls expanded, pushed by writhing roots. Multiple levels formed, doorways materializing then disappearing, passageways lit by sparkling glowglobes before all became dim once more. Ahilya gazed up but saw the ceiling had risen too high.

With the ascension of the Disc, only the six councilors remained in the temple. Bharavi stood next to Ahilya, but the two Senior Sungineers Kiana and Laksiya strode away, heads together, voices indistinct. Lying at the base of the now-massive rudra tree, Iravan was a mere dark shape buried under wet earth. Chaiyya knelt by him, trajecting fiercely, and Airav's voice was raised in a lilting hum. Ahilya made to move, but vines had crept over her legs without her notice, up her arms and chest—healbranch and sandalwood, scabbing her wounds, sealing her cuts. She blinked, not fully understanding.

If the temple was changing, then they were no longer under flight protocol. It meant the rescue was over. Then where was Oam? She tapped her citizen ring, her heart beating hard. Nakshar's map hovered over her palm, the Architects' Academy, the architects' homes, the solar lab, all prioritized and under construction. Yet there was no infirmary where Oam could have been taken. Fingers trembling, she tapped at the ring again to compose a message to him, but the connection dissolved before she could complete it.

"Where's Oam?" she asked, her voice cracking. "Why isn't he receiving healing?"

Airav and Chaiyya didn't look up, continuing their healing of Iravan. Senior Sungineers Laksiya and Kiana in their glittering yellow kurtas exchanged wary glances.

Bharavi put her arm on Ahilya's shoulder. "I'm sorry. Oam never entered the ashram."

"No," Ahilya said, choking.

"Only you and Iravan returned."

"No."

"You know this already."

"No, I don't know," Ahilya said, tears streaming down her face. "I *don't* know. Please, Bha. He's out there, in the jungle. Iravan trajected the both of us. I saw him rise. Maybe he entered the city from a different part. Maybe he's in a different corridor. We have to look for him. We have to help him."

Bharavi merely shook her head.

"He's only a boy, Bha. Please. *Please*."

Bharavi's eyes were full of sorrow. She shook her head again. "I'm so sorry."

"Or he must still be in the jungle," Ahilya said, weeping. "Still held up by Iravan's vines. Iravan had him. He *had* him."

Bharavi pressed her shoulder, and the healbranch vines over Ahilya retracted. Ahilya let herself be led away. Behind them, Kiana and Laksiya's soft conversation returned. Bharavi stopped by a leafy wall, and the leaves separated to reveal a glass magnifier. The Senior Architect pinched her fingers and spread them apart. The view expanded.

Ahilya's words died away. There, underneath them, was the jungle.

In a way, from up high, the earthrage was even more terrifying. Ahilya heard it in her head, the gnashing of rocks, the rush of the storm, the whipping of the wind. The jungle appeared a dark, bestial creature, writhing and churning in its own madness, massive balloons of dust exploding into the earth. She wanted to look away, but she couldn't. How long had Oam lasted in his armor? Had he been in pain? She hoped there hadn't been pain.

"It all happened too fast," Bharavi said, her arm still around Ahilya. "The earthrage began nearly on the heels of the landing. Maybe minutes after you and your team left. I'm surprised Iravan was able to traject in the jungle at all. In here, it was chaos. All the Maze Architects who had been sent off duty had to be called back. We needed to take off immediately, but we didn't have enough architects ready. We didn't even have flight architecture in place—we had to reuse Iravan's landing design."

Thick tears clogged Ahilya's throat. She couldn't breathe properly. She'd told Oam she'd keep him safe. He'd been scared. *We shouldn't be here*, Iravan had said. *We should be back in the ashram*. What had she done? Had she killed her husband, too? She should have called the expedition off. She should never have allowed any of them to take such a risk.

Bharavi sighed. "This has never happened before. We didn't even know the earthrage was happening until the first tremors. At the very least, the lull lasts a few hours. The shortest ever recorded was seven hours. But this?"

Ahilya swallowed. Her face felt sticky. She brushed her fist to her eyes, her chin. She knew this about the length of earthrages, but she couldn't speak. Her chest hurt as she tried to draw in a breath.

"We thought you had returned," Bharavi continued. "By the time your sungineer friend—Dhruv?—was able to tell Kiana about your absence, it was too late. We couldn't risk waiting any longer, not in the jungle, at least. The best we could do was rearrange Nakshar's architecture so we could hover safely, but it was a slim hope. Nothing survives an earthrage. We didn't think..." Bharavi's voice shook. "We didn't think any of you would come back... ."

Ahilya turned her eyes away from the chaos below to gaze at the Senior Architect. No architect explained themselves unduly to a non-architect; even Iravan would have kept his words restrained. Why was Bharavi saying all this now? Merely to comfort Ahilya?

Bharavi's eyes were troubled. "Whatever Iravan was doing... I've never seen trajection like that before. None of us have. We didn't feel him in the Moment. We couldn't even keep track of all the plants he was trajecting. That... that's very bad."

Ahilya stared at her. "Wh-why didn't you help him?"

"It couldn't be risked. We can't allow any jungle plants inside Nakshar, and he—all of you—were covered in those contaminants. Only Iravan knew what those plants were. We couldn't, in good conscience, unlock the bark to help you."

"And if it had been three architects out there? Could you have helped then?"

Bharavi shook her head. "Ahilya, it's not about that. Our survival depends on such rules. We will always do what's best for the ashram."

But preserving *architects* was what was best for the ashram. That had *always* been the best for the ashram.

Ahilya turned away back to the magnifier, sickened and confused. She couldn't make a clear thought. Was she doubting Bharavi now? The woman was her family. This was her own fault. *She* had failed. She had been the mission's commander. She had let Oam die.

She blinked her tears back, trying to discern the jungle, but Nakshar had ascended too far now. Despite the magnifier's enlargement, all Ahilya could see of the earthrage was the dust. She had waited at the city's terrace only a few hours earlier, wanting to study these very dust patterns. Years had passed since then. Hysteria built in her, threatening to bubble out as incongruent laughter.

"So, it was Iravan who let us in?" she asked dully.

Bharavi shifted her weight. "Ahilya, it shouldn't have been possible. He trajected your entry while simultaneously stripping his trajection of the jungle. That's very advanced, even for a Senior Architect. He broke several known limits of trajection. But..." She drew a deep breath. "You're here. You're alive. And that's what matters."

Us, Ahilya thought. *But not Oam.*

The citizen ring felt heavy on her finger. She nudged the useless thing with a light hand, and Nakshar's map blinked over her palm again, showing her all the architect areas under construction, while the rest of the city lay dark.

"Whatever happens now," Bharavi said, "you have to remain calm. All right? Try and stay calm—"

"Why didn't the alarm go off?" Ahilya interrupted.

Bharavi frowned. She looked past Ahilya.

Ahilya turned around. She heard the scrape of bark, the magnifier closed, and they stood once again in a temple separate from the jungle.

Kiana and Laksiya stared at her. Her question had carried into the quiet temple. From near Iravan, Airav and Chaiyya arose. Iravan struggled to sit up on the chair that had grown under him. His eyes were open but unfocused. Shadows stood out despite his dark skin.

Ahilya lurched over to him. "Are you all right?" she asked.

She grabbed his hand and pressed it to her cracked lips. He raised his eyes to her and squeezed her fingers, so gently it was a mere hint. Ahilya breathed deeply. He was injured, but he was going to be fine. He had to be fine.

Chaiyya and Airav had moved away when she'd approached Iravan, but now Ahilya turned back to them, her gesture protective of her husband. The councilors all stood in a cluster, watching her.

"Why didn't the alarm go off?" she repeated, louder.

Kiana coughed and fidgeted with her wooden cane, leaning on it and straightening like she couldn't decide. "We don't know yet," she said at last.

"You don't know."

"I assure you we'll be looking into it closely—"

"Don't you dare," Ahilya said softly. "My apprentice is dead. Iravan and I nearly died. So, you will give me more than *I don't know.*"

Senior Sungineer Kiana pursed her lips.

Ahilya glanced from her to Bharavi. "Why didn't the alarm go off, Bha? I deserve an answer."

Bharavi cleared her throat. "It should have," she said slowly. "By our assessment."

"Then why didn't it?"

"It… it wasn't sounded on time," Bharavi replied. "We don't allow anyone but a Senior Architect at the watchpost, and—"

Ahilya swung back to face the council architects. "So, it was one of you. Which one? Who was at the watchpost?"

The councilors glanced at each other, but no one said a word. Then Airav made a gesture, and from behind the rudra tree, a figure walked forward, trembling.

For a moment, Ahilya didn't understand. "Naila," she said, seeing her shake from head to toe. "No, but you're no Senior Architect—you were supposed to be with me—"

She cut herself off. The muscles in her legs grew weak. It took a long time for her to turn to see Iravan straighten on his chair. Ahilya stared at him, feeling dizzy, horror and disbelief coursing through her. Her hand disengaged from his. Her feet staggered back.

Iravan locked gazes with her warily, shadows darkening on his face.

11

IRAVAN

The room spun. Iravan knew what was happening. He didn't have enough blood in his head. He tried to focus on Ahilya, the one thing he had tried his best to hold on to during the horror of the jungle. *She's here. She's safe.*

But Ahilya's expression changed as his gaze locked on hers. Her mouth fell open. Her fingers flexed, then tightened into fists.

He recognized those signs. He ought to know what they meant.

Iravan blinked. Something was escaping him. Something that had happened.

He gripped the arms of the healbranch chair with shaking hands, noticing the angry black welts burned into his skin. Trajection scars. That was bad. He had felt the rudra tree's healing presence through a daze. Why hadn't the scars receded? Oh, rages. His Two Visions had merged. He had become the magnaroot. He had tried to kill himself. Wrong, wrong, *wrong*.

They were all staring at him. The councilors looked watchful, wary. And Ahilya… She was backing away. He read fury in her stance… and something more, something he had never seen before, glittering in her beautiful eyes like an open wound, except darker, eviscerating—

Betrayal.

On the heels of the understanding came another. He was in danger, grave mortal danger.

But that was ridiculous; he was in the temple. His eyes slipped from Ahilya toward Bharavi and the other councilors, then back to his wife.

Pieces clicked in his mind, as though he had finally seen the obvious path to a difficult trajection. Images returned, of crushing Naila's rudra bead, entering the jungle despite his misgivings, someone he had left behind, so many mistakes he had made—

Oh, rages.

"Ahilya," he began, his voice hoarse. "Please, listen—"

"It was you. You sent her away—"

"I only wanted to spend some time with—"

"You threatened my expedition—"

"No," he said quickly. "That wasn't my—"

"You were supposed to be at the watchpost—"

"Yes, but—"

"*You killed Oam*," she sobbed.

Her accusation hit him like a physical blow. Iravan recoiled.

I killed him. She was right. He remembered it now. He'd torn his own magnaroot armor off. He'd unraveled his own vortex of jungle plants. But in the end, in that moment of choice, he had chosen to save himself. He'd pushed himself and Ahilya into Nakshar with the last of his energy and let go—he'd *let go*—of Oam.

Iravan's hands shook and tears blurred his vision. He blinked them back.

"I—I," he began, but then he glanced at Bharavi, who shook her head emphatically. "I saved you," he said.

Bharavi's nod was nearly imperceptible.

Iravan tried to remember. He'd made the choice, between himself and Oam. That was right, wasn't it? It's what the council would say. He had followed protocol. Each person embodied the potential of an ashram, but the life of a Senior Architect was worth much more than any citizen. A Senior Architect sustained the ashram. Had there been another architect out there instead of Ahilya, Iravan would have had to save *them*. That was *protocol*.

"I saved you," he choked out, trying to believe it. "If I hadn't been out in the jungle, you wouldn't have made it back to Nakshar—"

"This wouldn't have happened if you had stayed in Nakshar in the first place! If you'd been here to sound the alarm!"

Iravan's vision edged with crimson. The pounding in his head worsened. Bharavi's face was inscrutable, but to him there was almost entirely too much expression there. She wanted him to say something.

"This is not about the alarm," he mumbled. "This is about trajection. About interference. This is bigger than what happened in the jungle."

Chaiyya drew in a breath.

Bharavi frowned.

Iravan regretted the words the moment he uttered them.

"How dare you?" Ahilya spat. "He's dead, Iravan. He was just a foolish boy with a harmless infatuation. Were you jealous? Was that it?"

Iravan blinked at her. This was wrong. They shouldn't be fighting. Not in front of these people. Not at all.

"Ahilya," he began, but she cut him off.

"If you'd been at the watchpost, where you were supposed to be, none of this would have happened. If you'd sounded the alarm, we'd all have returned in time."

Iravan stared at her. Her reaction, it was natural, *obvious*. Why hadn't he predicted it? He opened his mouth, trying again, but Chaiyya beat him to a response.

"You're right," the Senior Architect said quietly. "You're right, Ahilya. Please, calm. Calm." The Nakshar-native woman, her long hair caught in a braid, held up her hands. "This is a grave error. You will have your justice. You have my word."

"The word of a Senior Architect?" Ahilya said. "Regarding a *non*-architect's life? I'm no starry-eyed girl, Chaiyya. I know how this world works."

Chaiyya flinched. Ahilya pushed past her and strode away to the closest leafy wall, her body shaking.

The temple didn't react to her. Like Nakshar itself, the temple could only be accessed by a Senior Architect or a key unless permissions were changed. Iravan prepared to traject—the thought made him nauseous—but the other architects flared blue-green underneath their robes, and the wall in front of Ahilya unfurled in a creak of branches and twigs.

Without a glance toward him, Ahilya marched away into the darkness.

In the wake of her departure, Naila hurried forward nervously. "Please, councilors, I have something to say—"

"Leave, Junior Architect," Airav said. "This doesn't concern you."

"But I can explain what happened at the watchpost—"

"And you will. But this is a council matter for now." Airav made a gesture, and the Junior Architect shot Iravan an anxious glance and hurried away, following Ahilya out the same wall. The trajecting light died out from the architects. Leaves curled closed behind the two women.

With them gone, something in the room changed.

A heavy silence descended over the temple.

All the councilors turned to look at Iravan as one. He collapsed in his chair, and his hands trembled as he lifted them to his head. The marks from the headlamp throbbed under his fingers. Someone had removed the broken sungineering equipment from him. All his rudra beads were gone too, his bracelets and necklaces, his citizen ring, everything that had marked him as the bearer of responsibility. Even an ordinary citizen wore more than he did right now. The only jewelry they'd left him was the bone-white healbranch bracelet he'd received on graduating to Maze Architect, and that perhaps because they couldn't remove it.

Behind closed eyes, the images attacked him again. He felt the magnaroot piercing his skin, the yearning of death when his Two Visions had merged. Ahilya's anger, the council's reaction. It would ruin him, he needed her, oh fuck, what had he done—

A hand squeezed his shoulder. Iravan gasped, nauseous, and opened his eyes.

Chaiyya's round face peered at him in concern. Plump and mild, the Senior Architect had always been motherly. She had been the one to formally induct him into Nakshar's council five years before. She leaned in, asking him the same question she had asked then.

"Iravan," she said gently. "Are things well with your marriage?"

Iravan was anticipating the question, but it still made him wince.

"E-everything is fine. But the last earthrage—it was so long. It's been difficult for Ahilya. For the both of us. And now, for this to have happened..." He pressed the heels of his hands to his eyes. "It shouldn't have happened."

He felt more than heard the others walk up and join Chaiyya around him.

When he glanced up, he faced all five of them. Seats grew under them in a circle.

Bharavi was the only one left standing. "This can wait," she said. "Look at him. Hasn't he been through enough?"

The others said nothing, merely stared at her. For a long second, Bharavi stared back, defiant.

Then she reluctantly lowered herself onto her fragrant rosewood chair, behind the others, directly opposite Iravan. He watched them, naked without his rudra beads.

Chaiyya rested a hand on her bulging stomach. "To be clear, are you accepting responsibility for all that has happened?"

The images came to him again, the boy's panicked tumble as Iravan let go, how Iravan had been so dispassionate, how easy the decision had been. In that moment of choice, he had been fully aware of his actions. There was no escaping it. He had done it. He had killed Oam. The horror threatened to consume him. Iravan couldn't breathe.

He opened his mouth to acknowledge his guilt, glancing at Bharavi, but her eyes burned like hot coals. A small gray ice rose sprouted between her fingers, barely visible, resting on her rosewood chair—

And Iravan hesitated.

Chaiyya raised an eyebrow, waiting for his response.

The ice rose. It meant something.

Iravan inhaled deeply, his breath ragged in his chest. Arbitrary thoughts chased each other. Why hadn't Chaiyya chosen a more comfortable chair? The way she was sitting—squirming—And Airav, so unsmiling. How often had he laughed with Iravan after their council meetings? For Airav to show no concern right now, for all of them to be so aloof—

Iravan's shoulders straightened as it hit him.

He stared at them, and they stared back, his friends—no, not his friends, councilors. Those rosewood chairs weren't ordinary chairs.

They were high-backed council seats. This was not an informal gathering. This was a council assembly—impromptu, formal, significant. Iravan's heart began to race. The rudra beads felt heavy in their absence.

"Iravan?" Chaiyya pressed.

Bharavi still played with the ice rose. What was it? What did she mean?

The image came to him in a flash. A private ward in the sanctum, its floor entirely laced with those gray flowers. Manav's ward, where Bharavi often worked. Iravan had visited it once.

He stared at the ice rose. Manav had been a Senior Architect and councilor five years earlier—the last time Nakshar had possessed a full council of seven—when Iravan himself had ascended to the position. The man had turned out to be an Ecstatic only weeks after Iravan's own rise. Iravan had personally excised him, and ever since then, Manav's seat had lain vacant.

Why did Bharavi want him thinking of him? Something to do with the vacant council seat? The one that Ahilya was eyeing; the one the rest of the council had to make a decision on in three months? Each councilor had to place their nominations for discussion, and Bharavi had never been fully supportive of Naila's nomination, not recognizing the talent in her. And Naila had been at the watchpost. Was this Bharavi's way of telling him the Junior Architect wasn't worthy? Why talk about that now, at this critical moment?

"You were asked a question," Airav said.

Unable to see the snares, Iravan answered slowly. "I—I'm not taking responsibility for anyone's death. Nor for the alarm's failure. I'm accepting responsibility for sending Naila to the watchpost."

"And you sincerely believe that's the only wrong you did here?" Chaiyya asked.

Bharavi didn't move, but Iravan could almost see her nod. She still held the ice rose between her fingers.

"Yes," Iravan said, swallowing. "That's the only weight I choose to bear."

Chaiyya exchanged glances with Airav.

Airav's penetrating stare lanced through Iravan, and Iravan stopped himself from recoiling. Airav was the seniormost councilor. His arms were covered with rudra beads up to the elbow, a sign of his tenure and responsibility.

"I'm afraid your wife is right," Airav said in his slow, rumbling voice. "This fine distinction you're making isn't reasonable. Your failure at the watchpost was the failure of the alarm. It killed a citizen. It endangered the life of a Senior Architect—"

"My life—"

"Not yours. Your life belongs to the ashram first and foremost. That's what it means to be an architect. Especially a Senior Architect."

The reprimand seared through Iravan. He forced himself to meet Airav's gaze.

"Your actions nearly annihilated Nakshar," Airav continued. "You risked everything for a selfish motive."

Iravan rubbed his empty wrist with a shaking hand. "No. Please. You know the watchpost duty isn't hard. Naila should have been able to do it. She's good enough—you know this. You *know* this."

Chaiyya glanced at Airav, troubled. "He's right."

"He still shouldn't have assigned it to her. That was an action calculated to keep his own needs in mind, not the welfare of the ashram."

"You're right," Iravan said, desperate. "But please—you have to see. Even if I had been at the watchpost, the alarm would've failed. Three people would have died. I—I saved two."

"This is conjecture at best," Airav said. "You're suggesting there's a higher reason the alarm failed. You have no evidence of that."

"Unless you're implying something went wrong with the sungineers in the lab?" Kiana asked. The Senior Sungineer, her cane across her knees, frowned at the possibility of it being her team's error. She was Iravan's greatest rival on the council, but she'd seconded Bharavi's nomination allowing Iravan a chance at the council in the first place. Now as she looked at him, her face was grave.

"No, that's not—not what I mean," he said, tripping over his words. "But it's a pattern. This has to be the shortest lull in our recorded history. And earthrages are getting longer. Whatever happened with Naila—it's a part of this. These are symptoms of a greater problem."

"What do you mean?" Kiana asked, pushing her spectacles up.

Bharavi shook her head, but Iravan forged ahead anyway, stumbling through an explanation of the Resonance—how it had knocked him out of the Moment, how it had chased him, the manner in which it had overtaken him in the jungle. "It's an interference in the Moment," he ended, looking from one face to another. "I've—I've sensed it."

Airav drew in a breath. "You're condemning yourself with your own words. This Resonance—this is something an Ecstatic would say. Is it not?" The bald man turned to Bharavi, asking for confirmation.

Iravan's heart sank. Too late, he understood Bharavi's warning. Manav's Ecstasy had shocked all of them. To have an architect with such incredible power lose control of trajection? It would have destroyed Nakshar. No wonder the councilors were wary now. They were scared of him.

He stared at her, silently pleading. With her work in the sanctum, Bharavi was the council's expert on Ecstasy. She hadn't believed him about the Resonance earlier, but she had to now. She had to.

Bharavi's voice was careful. "Detecting Ecstasy is as obscure as it has always been. I can't speak about this Resonance specifically."

Senior Sungineer Laksiya cleared her throat. Iravan had been dreading her. Laksiya was always the last to speak in any council meeting, with a habit of cutting straight to the matter at heart. Her manner was cold to everyone, but she didn't even look at him now, as though his being there was a presumption.

"We don't need an expert's opinion on this," she said. "I think the situation is quite clear. I did say he was too young to be a part of the council."

"We don't induct people into the council based on their age," Airav said reprovingly. "We induct them based on their expert skill. Their independent thinking. Their contribution to the survival of the ashram. Iravan fulfilled those criteria when we chose him."

"Yes," Laksiya said. "But look what those demands have done. If he were an ordinary Maze Architect, he'd have an opportunity for a healthier life. As Senior Architect, he's burning out. He's at greater risk of Ecstasy than any ordinary architect."

"You're jumping to conclusions," Bharavi said. "Detecting an Ecstatic isn't straightforward. Three separate conditions must simultaneously fail before we determine if an architect is at risk."

"Yes," Laksiya replied. "And hasn't Iravan failed all three? His material bonds are loosening, as is obvious with his marriage to Ahilya. He has been flirting with the limits of trajection—he admitted to taking on more duties, we all saw his incredible escape from the jungle, and now he tells us about a mysterious Resonance that only he can sense? That's two out of three. Add the fact that he chose to send a Junior Architect to the watchpost, knowing full well such an action would endanger Nakshar's safety? That's three on three."

"The last one is hardly on the same scale," Bharavi began, but Laksiya shook her head.

Her withering gaze swept them all in it. "He has always been reckless, and his position has made him more so. And now because of your decision to have him perform as a Senior Architect, he must lay himself bare for all of us."

Bharavi jerked in her chair. "What are you saying?"

Laksiya transferred her cold gaze to Bharavi. "I vote that we put Senior Architect Iravan through the Examination of Ecstasy immediately."

Iravan started to shake. His vision blurred. His throat grew thick.

A vote. A formal vote. This couldn't be happening. It couldn't. Bile rose in him and he resisted the urge to vomit.

"You can't be serious," Bharavi sputtered. "You want to Examine him now? Look at him—he can barely sit in his chair. The Exam is the last step in checking an architect for Ecstasy. We never administer it unless there's great proof—"

"How much more proof—"

"It strips away self-esteem," Bharavi continued, speaking over Laksiya. "Even healthy architects take time to recover. He's in no condition to be tested. You might as well excise him without the farce of an Examination."

Laksiya remained unmoved. "If he truly is an Ecstatic, then it's more dangerous for the ashram to wait until he is over his ordeal. What would you do—wait until he has tried to sabotage the rudra tree like Manav did? Wait until he trajects a person? Place your vote, Senior Architect Bharavi, and consider whether your reasoning isn't biased because of your personal affiliation with him."

Iravan's stomach roiled. His gut hardened with a need to escape. He wouldn't survive the Exam. He knew this as certainly as he knew his own name. Bharavi appeared to him as though from afar.

"I vote no," she said to Laksiya, eyes flashing. "In order to do the Exam, he needs to enter the Moment, and I don't think him capable of doing that—not right now. He'll fail the Exam on those grounds alone. It would be a false positive. I vote no."

"The Exam isn't meant to be a trap," Airav put in, his deep voice rumbling over them. "It's a pass-fail test. The goal is not to traumatize him. It's for him to sift his mind for the truth." Airav glanced at Iravan. "I'm sorry, my friend. But Laksiya is right. The trajection we saw you do should not have been possible. I vote yes."

Iravan clenched his fists, hard. His head threatened to explode like an overripe melon.

Two yesses. All it would take was one more, and he'd be forced to crawl through his mind. He'd have to examine every grievous breach of trajection's limits, every regrettable decision that had jeopardized the ashram, every perverse thought about his material connections, all to prove he was not an Ecstatic. He'd be forced to relive it all, how he had crushed the magnaroot. How he had let go of Oam. How he had failed Ahilya.

A small moan escaped him. He tried not to gag.

Chaiyya studied him. Her round face was disturbed, wrinkles heavy on her forehead. "I think Iravan is in danger of Ecstasy. But to test him now—we'll be testing his will, not his intent. He could spiral out of control. The Exam itself would fail. It's wiser to wait until he has recovered. I vote no."

They all turned to Kiana. The Senior Sungineer frowned into her hands. Her fingers moved in the manner of weighing the pros and cons of each side. Oh, rages, what if she decided against him now? Iravan had opposed her so many times. When they'd argued about the battery, Kiana had walked away from the meeting before Iravan could smooth things over. They were still friends, surely, but when it came to the ashram's safety, Kiana would not relent.

She looked up at Iravan. "There's merit to your arguments. Maybe there's a pattern to what you say. I wonder if by putting you to the test, we might not be premature. And if Naila is as good as we've been led to believe, then why didn't she sound the alarm? I vote no."

A dry sob escaped Iravan.

"Th-thank you," he whispered.

"There's still the question of punishing your transgressions," Airav said. He turned to the others. "He's still guilty of abandoning his post. That's actively endangering the ashram. That alone is grounds to ask for a vote of no confidence."

"That's rule-bending, Airav," Bharavi snapped. "We've all done something similar. He needs a slap on the wrist, not to be disgraced and returned to Maze Architect. The punishment needs to fit the crime."

"It resulted in a citizen's death—"

"You can't decide that in isolation," Bharavi said. "The measure of Iravan's guilt regarding the watchpost depends on whether there is value to his arguments about the interference. What if he's right? Are you going to demote him for saving two lives? You agreed that Naila should have been able to sound the alarm."

"I did. Which means we'll need to investigate this claim."

"I can do that," Kiana volunteered.

"No, let me," Iravan burst out, voice scratchy.

"No," Airav said. "It can't be one of us, Kiana—we have to sit in judgement of his arguments. And it certainly can't be you, Iravan. That would be a conflict of interest."

"It's not," Iravan protested. He cleared his throat. "Please, it's the best use of my resources. I'm not going back on the Disc this flight, not after what I've been through. I'm most invested in clearing my name. And I'm the only one to feel the Resonance. Let me do this."

"It would still be a biased report—"

"It won't—Please—"

"Let him do it," Chaiyya interrupted, putting a hand on Airav's arm. "Biased or not, we have to sit in judgement. If we're not convinced, it's all the same."

Airav frowned. "We'll have to make a healbranch vow. It's the only way for us to be impartial to his findings. But you can't make such a promise, Chaiyya. If you break it, the ashram's healbranch won't respond to you anymore."

"I'm still going to."

"It will poison you instead of healing you."

"I know, Airav."

"You'd waste away, Chaiyya."

Chaiyya's round face twisted in a sardonic smile. "It'd be the same for any one of us if we broke a healbranch vow."

"The rest of us aren't pregnant," Airav pointed out. "How do you think your wife will react if you tell her you endangered yourself?"

"Not well," she admitted, tiredly. "But would you let me judge Iravan if I didn't take the vow?"

Airav shook his head, disturbed.

"Precisely," Chaiyya said. "I won't recuse myself, Airav. Word the terms and conditions as you see fit, but let Iravan investigate and let us be about it."

For a moment, everything hung in balance. Iravan watched them, Laksiya's expressionless face, Airav's sonorous breathing, Bharavi's grim eyes. Then Airav nodded, and one by one the others did.

A simple twining pattern began to grow on Airav's arms. Between the chairs, a thin white stem emerged, then split into five branches that reached for the councilors. All of them extended their hands, and the branches twirled around their wrists forming wooden bracelets.

"In three weeks," Airav said, "I vow to render judgement on Iravan's findings about his theory of interference in trajection."

Iravan tucked his trembling hands under his arms. Three weeks. The shortest standard duration for any investigation. Airav must think him a lost cause already. The trial was not merely about the results of the investigation; it was about becoming worthy of the council again. A deep shame rose in Iravan.

"I vow to pervert neither my interpretation," Airav continued, "nor my understanding of Iravan's findings. I vow to base my judgement not on my friendship or kinship with Iravan, neither on hostility or rancor, but on Nakshar's preservation, first and alone. If his claims are insufficient, I vow to enforce appropriate punishment as dictated by Nakshar's laws, my conscience, and the rest of the council."

"Agreed," the others murmured.

The branches snapped away and retreated into the floor. A white bracelet gleamed on each of their wrists along with their rudra beads.

"Well," Laksiya grunted. "I suppose now we're all in for it. The judgement will be as much of us as it would be of him."

Chaiyya rose ponderously. "Make your best case to us, Iravan. We're on your side. If there's logic to your theory regarding this Resonance, then you have nothing to worry about."

Airav rose too, digging into the pockets of his white kurta. He withdrew a tangle of rudra bead necklaces and bracelets and handed them back to Iravan. Iravan gripped them hard, breathing in their scent before looping them around his neck and wrists.

"For what it's worth," Airav said, "you're still a councilor and a Senior Architect. It's time to act like it, my friend."

A woman of few words, Laksiya merely nodded at Iravan. She walked away with Airav and Chaiyya, their chairs melting behind them.

Kiana stood up, her chair dissolving as well. Her eyes looked wary behind her spectacles. Her cane tapped on the ground soundlessly. "I'll alert the sungineers' lab that you may be around to ask questions, shall I?"

"Thank you, Kiana."

She gave Iravan a long look. "Annoying as you are, I'd hate to see you leave the council." She pressed his shoulder, strode away to a wall, activated her key, and disappeared.

In the end, only Bharavi remained.

Iravan dropped his head into his hands. "What do I do, Bha?"

He felt Bharavi's tread, then she was kneeling by him, lifting his head up. "You understand what you're up against," she said grimly. "Why do you think Airav gave you back your beads?"

"I… I'm still a Senior Architect."

"A Senior Architect with full privileges," Bharavi said. "He gave you vine to see if you would crawl out of this pit or hang yourself. They're going to watch you, Iravan. If there are signs, any at all, another indication of a failed marriage, the slightest rule-bending, even if it's your due as a Senior Architect—an Examination could happen. You don't have three weeks; you have until your next mistake."

"I—I won't make a mistake."

"See that you don't. They could vote for an Exam again, tomorrow, day after, as soon as you're healed. And next time, I won't be able to protect you. If I see a sign of you becoming an Ecstatic—"

"I kn-know. You'll have to ask for an Examination yourself."

She nodded.

"Then I'm doomed," Iravan said, his voice hollow. "If I make a mistake, you'll vote for an Exam. If I don't prove my theory, you'll vote for an Exam. I could pass the Exam and still be demoted, and if I fail it"—he shuddered—"my life in Nakshar is over. There's no path out of this."

"There's always a path. You need to find a way to prove your theory *and* veer the council away from the risks of Ecstasy. Start with something tangible, visible. Something that cements your material bonds."

"You mean—"

"Yes," Bharavi said, standing up. "Start with Ahilya."

12

AHILYA

In a silent corner of the library, Ahilya sat alone, trying not to shatter.

Her eyes were closed. She held herself very still. Any sudden movement could crack the fragile wall she had built inside herself.

Her hands fiddled with the silent tracker locket from the expedition. Oam had clutched her, in excitement, and in fear, when they'd come upon the elephant-yaksha. He had been so afraid in the nest; he'd been safe, she'd *seen* him be safe. He'd only left her sight for a moment. He'd—He'd—

No, not that, not again. She opened her eyes but her vision was blurred. *Focus.*

Ahilya blinked back hot tears. The locket lay limp and heavy in her hands, no longer chiming. It was supposed to work on trajection, but the last time Ahilya had heard it chime had been through their escape. Now it was likely broken, the data likely distorted, certainly not valid enough to make any conclusive argument that would help her with a nomination. In her head, Oam screamed again, flipping in the air, panicked. He fell through the sky, away from her. Did a council seat matter? Ahilya closed her eyes. It didn't matter.

A week had passed since the city had flown away. Messages had gone out from the lab, flashing through the citizen rings every day. *Not all systems are functioning. Thank you for your patience. Everything will be back to normal soon.* Ahilya had wandered the streets, watched the children play, heard other citizens wonder why so much of the city was still under construction. No one knew about the expedition, about Oam—

He screamed at her to cut herself loose. He urged her on and ran to retrieve her satchel. He did it for her, he'd been so brave, *Don't worry, I'll keep you safe, I'll keep you safe*—

Ahilya choked, unable to breathe. Her throat clogged. She was going to suffocate on her own tears. Long green leaves grew around her, over her lap and arms, enveloping her. The moss seat she sat on transformed into thermogenic lily. Ahilya rocked herself, back and forth, a low keen escaping her. If they hadn't entered the jungle, if she'd left the satchel behind, if only, if only. Iravan flashed in her head, his head bowed, expression defeated. He pressed her to cancel the expedition; he yelled at her to rush to the nest. Whose fault had it been? Hers? His? They were catastrophic together. They'd let Oam die so easily. Anger and grief built inside her in a rising wave, and her fingers curled in on themselves as she fought to breathe, fought not to go under.

She didn't know how long she sat there, held by the plants of the city, breathing in and out in short bursts, but eventually a knock sounded on the wall of her alcove. She tapped at her citizen ring and Dhruv was there, sitting next to her, patting her back, and saying, "I'm sorry, I'm so sorry. I came as soon as I could."

"I—I asked him to go," Ahilya got out between spasming sobs.

"I know."

"He—he was studying the mind—He was going to impact everyone's lives."

"I know." Dhruv's arm tightened around her.

"He was there—because—because of me."

Dhruv sighed. He held out a clay cup of water to her lips. Ahilya choked, trying to drink. She hadn't even brought back a body. Oam's fathers had nothing to give back to Nakshar, nothing to put into the reclamation chamber, nothing that would take root and flower again as a symbolic continuation of Oam's life. In the end, the two men had offered Oam's clothes to the soil. His funeral had been brief and unceremonious. Ahilya hoped he'd be reborn in better circumstances.

She wiped her face with a sleeve. The grief settled in her mind, a constant companion, and she sank a little under its weight. It would be patient, she knew. It would strike when she wasn't looking. Her sobs grew sparser, subsided into hiccups. A vast emptiness replaced them.

"My messages—You didn't reply—" Dhruv began after some time. "Have you been alone all this while?"

Ahilya shook her head. She'd seen those messages but there was nothing she could say. Tariya had come to her every day with Arth and Kush, refusing to leave until Ahilya had begged her. Had Bharavi told her what had happened in the temple? Of what Iravan had done? Ahilya hadn't the energy to probe.

"Is this your alcove now?" Dhruv asked. "Where you work from?"

She nodded.

"It's a good pick." Dhruv reached out a hand. Responding to his desire, a window unfurled in the wall revealing a muddy field. "That's where one of the playgrounds will appear. You can watch it grow. It's from an archival plan, replicated from designs from years ago."

Ahilya knew this. She had recognized this alcove the minute it had appeared. Once, she'd spent many hours in an identical alcove, sketching out her theories of the earthrage. How long ago was that? She had been a different person then; she had lived a different life.

Dhruv dropped his hand and the leaves grew back, closing the window. "It's been chaos in the lab. All our systems are slow. We had to power the critical buildings first—the sanctum and the Architects' Academy and their homes. The architects are in a state. They lost a lot of vital plants that need to be grown from scratch. But we ought to begin powering citizen spaces soon."

He drew his arm away and cleared his throat. Ahilya glanced at him warily, the grief in her mind spiking.

"I'm sorry," he said awkwardly. "I hate to ask you, but I need to know. Did you lose my equipment in the jungle?"

Ahilya pressed the heels of her palms to her eyes. She had wasted precious seconds diving for her satchel. Oam had swung it around himself. He'd risked himself for her. Her chances at a councilorship were gone with the bag, but none of it mattered. She hadn't been smart; she hadn't *thought*. She didn't say anything, but Dhruv understood.

"Oh, rages," the sungineer swore, removing his spectacles and pinching the bridge of his nose.

Ahilya trembled, her shoulders drawing into herself. Sungineers weren't allowed to invent on a whim. Sungineering materials were precious, and every invention had to serve the city. Dhruv had taken personal responsibility for the equipment he'd loaned her. One wrong expedition—and they had lost so much.

"What will happen?" she whispered.

"I don't know," he said, looking up from massaging his nose. "We need every bit of spare parts to return Nakshar to the status it was in before the accident. The Disc had to take off without preparations. A lot of our instruments were smashed. Kiana has asked for an inventory."

"Maybe you can lie. Say that the equipment was crushed in the flight."

Dhruv started to polish his spectacles. "Kiana knows I lent you those devices. I only got permission to make them because I said it'd help us perfect machines in Nakshar—and to get that permission was hard enough. If I had the equipment to return now, she wouldn't care. But to return nothing? She can't let that go."

"She would blame *you* for that loss in the jungle?"

"Not for that alone, no, not Kiana. But it is another event in a long line of what the rest of the council is, no doubt, considering my sungineering failures. Kiana might have no choice."

"What will she do?"

Dhruv gave her a small smile. "If she needs to make a cut from the lab… I've just made myself… notable."

"I'm sorry," Ahilya whispered.

"It's not your fault. I suppose the deathbox, that's gone too?"

Ahilya extended her hand to the wall on the right. It split open and a glass cube secreted out, pushed by the leaves. She pulled it to her and handed it to Dhruv. He drew in a shocked breath.

"You didn't," he said in disbelief. "But how—"

"I was nervous—Iravan being out there with me. With us." Tears filled her eyes, but she forced them away. "When we were out in the jungle, I took the box out of my bag and tied it underneath my clothes with a rope. It's inside. The spiralweed."

She could remember it, how panicked Oam had been that she'd left them in the jungle for long moments, how panicked *Iravan* had been. She had been too focused on her husband, on getting the sample without him noticing. She had been too vindicated in her success. And she'd left Oam to gather the specimen; she'd left him again—to his death the next time.

"It doesn't look like the forcefield is activated," Dhruv said, examining the glass cube.

Ahilya's voice was toneless. "It's only a single source leaf. The forcefield is inside the box. It's the best I could do. Maybe you can still make the battery. You won't be transferred."

The sungineer shook his head. He had wanted a complete specimen, but did it matter? The spiralweed had been difficult to procure, and the cost had been too high. Ahilya closed her eyes, forcing the tears back. What had all of it been worth? They could do nothing with it—she had already lost, and Dhruv—all she had brought back was one tiny leaf. They should never have left the city. She should never have gone to the jungle.

She opened her eyes to see Dhruv continue to roll the deathbox in his hands over and over again, horror and wonder in his face in equal measures.

"Keep it," he said, thrusting it back to her. "I can't store it in the lab. Kiana said that whoever is conducting the investigation into the alarm has full access to the lab. It's too dangerous to hold it there. Keep it hidden until I ask for it."

Ahilya nodded mutely. She reached back to the wall. A thin branch crept out and encircled the deathbox, storing it in her personal archives. Dhruv still had a chance, perhaps a small one, at least enough to stave off an ignominious transfer to some far-flung city. But archeology was finished in Nakshar. The council would not forget Ahilya's culpability in the failed expedition. Perhaps they were merely waiting for matters to return to normal before they informed her of her change in profession. She'd become a historian at best, forced to revere architect culture. All those months of planning, all those dangerous expeditions in the jungle, all the humiliation she had endured—it was ultimately for nothing. Everyone would know her for a failure. Perhaps that was what she deserved.

Dhruv replaced his spectacles. "Do you know who is investigating?"

It took her a moment to realize he was still talking about the flight alarm.

"No," she said dully. "Why would I?"

"I thought—maybe—" Dhruv cut himself off.

He thought Iravan would have told her.

Ahilya hadn't seen Iravan, not since the temple. Had he come home? She herself had been home only briefly, the beautiful three-story apartment lonely and empty. It was identical to the apartment she and Iravan had owned many earthrages before, pulled from an archival design like the playground and the library. They had been happy in that house once. Why hadn't he come to her? Had he been punished for a loosening of his material bonds? There was no other way the council could have interpreted her screams in the temple. Anger and grief flared in her mind again, making her chest tighten. They had corrupted him, and he had *allowed* it. He had been *weak*. How could he have forgotten himself so easily?

She and Dhruv sat in silence. Once or twice, Dhruv opened his mouth to speak, but then he glanced at her and began wiping his spectacles instead. She thought she should tell him about the yaksha, but she couldn't make the words. Guilt weighed her shoulders down, in her failure as a mission commander, in her failure as a wife.

When the wall behind them split open in a loud creak of branches, both Ahilya and Dhruv turned.

Iravan sat on a wheelchair of pale white wood, his fist raised. He wore one of his spotless white kurtas again, but the shirt hung off him, a few sizes too big. His hair was grayer in the week since they'd returned from the jungle. He dropped his hand.

"I meant to knock," Iravan said. "But I suppose the privacy controls to the ashram haven't been restored yet."

"They've been restored," Dhruv said. "This alcove must be tuned to your permissions."

Iravan skimmed himself inside and the wall closed behind him again.

With his entry into the alcove, the foliage began to change. Jasmine buds peeked out, the moss grew lusher, and phosphorescence twinkled through the walls in tiny sparkles of blue. Ahilya's heart pounded in her chest. Iravan was not trajecting—it was nothing he was doing—but archival designs of the city had memory. This alcove was the exact replica of the one they had spent so much time together in once, studying and exploring, teaching each other about their research, planting the seeds for their marriage. The alcove had been the path to their courtship. With him there, Nakshar remembered.

Dhruv stood up and offered Iravan an awkward smile. "I'm glad to see you're up. Kiana said you were recovering at the sanctum."

"For what it's been worth," Iravan said, smiling back. He looked at Ahilya and his smile faltered. "How are you?"

Ahilya stared at him, not replying. Closer, the shadows under Iravan's eyes were deeper. His dark skin, normally so healthy, appeared ashy. *He's had a haircut*, she thought arbitrarily. Iravan was impeccably groomed as always, but if anything, it made him look worse than ever, as though the clothes and hair were just more half-truths and deceptions from the council. She trembled, wanting to go to him, touch him, see if he was all right. Relief and anger warred with each other.

"Is that permanent?" Dhruv asked quietly, gesturing at the wheelchair.

"No," Iravan said, tearing his gaze from her. "Maybe a week. The architects in the sanctum will decide. It's made of healbranch so—"

"Why are you here?" Ahilya blurted out.

Iravan flinched like she had struck him, but his hurt was gone in a flash, replaced by cold dispassion. "Can we talk alone?" he asked.

"No," she said.

"Sure," Dhruv said at the same time.

"No," she said again, grabbing Dhruv's arm.

Her friend extricated himself gently, his expression uncomfortable. "Ahilya, I don't mind."

"I mind. Stay."

The sungineer threw Iravan a helpless, apologetic look. The alcove continued to grow smaller, more intimate. The scent of jasmine filled her. Ahilya needed to think, to keep her mind clear, but in that instant, it was as though the alcove was conspiring to cloud her mind, *Nakshar* was conspiring to make her give in to Iravan. She didn't trust herself with him alone. She didn't know what she wanted, what she needed, and the wave of grief and anger within her reared its head again, making her tremble.

"It's all right, Dhruv," Iravan said. "But I'd appreciate it if you—"

"I won't say a word."

Iravan nodded. His gaze locked on Ahilya. "First, I brought you this," he said, and withdrew two small bark-bound books from his pocket, offering them to her. "I know you lost your research in the jungle. These are... historical records of earthrage patterns and yaksha encounters from the architects' archives. I thought they would help."

Ahilya stared at him. Dhruv's eyebrows shot up. The both of them knew Iravan was giving her privileged architect records, ones that she had struggled to access for months. He had acknowledged the loss of her research—so, then, was this pity? She studied him, the fullness of his mouth, the watchfulness of his gaze, the manner in which his jaw tightened and released.

No, this was a trap.

Iravan wanted something in return.

Her fingers twitched, but Ahilya didn't move to take those books.

Iravan didn't drop his hand either. They regarded each other, the both of them waiting to see who would relent first; and she thought abstractedly, *How long will you hold your hand out for me? You owe me so much more than this.* Iravan blinked as though he had heard her thought, but otherwise remained still, the two of them suspended in this silent battle.

In the end, it was Dhruv who accepted the books from her husband. The sungineer placed them on a shelf quietly and took a step back.

Iravan glanced at him and nodded his thanks. His gaze returned to Ahilya.

"Second," he said, as though nothing was amiss, "I wanted to ask if you'd like to be a part of the investigation. The one being conducted to look into the failure of the flight alarm."

Ahilya blinked, taken aback. She had expected words about the flight alarm, certainly, as soon as he had skimmed in, but she'd thought Iravan would remind her of her obligations as his wife, that he'd demand she say nothing to Dhruv or Tariya or anyone else about his part in what had happened. She had expected him to apologize, or demand an apology. *He was just a boy*, she'd screamed. *Were you jealous?* Ahilya frowned, trying to understand.

Her silence confused him. Iravan looked from her to Dhruv. "You do know about the investigation, don't you?"

"Only what was transmitted over the citizen rings," Dhruv answered.

The announcement had flashed through the rings for days after the earthrage. *The delay in the flight alarm caused the death of one citizen. The council is undertaking a formal investigation. Please be patient while we resolve the matter.* Buried between the announcements about what parts of Nakshar were functioning and what permissions pending, Oam's death had barely been noticed. The citizens had moved on quickly.

"What exactly is the investigation?" Dhruv asked.

"Another farce from the council?" Ahilya said, before Iravan could answer. "Because it seems pretty clear why the alarm failed. A Senior Architect didn't do their job."

Iravan didn't wince, not visibly, but she could see behind his dark eyes the ghost of a shadow. "I think there's more to it," he said, frowning.

Ahilya laughed, a scornful sound. "They put *you* in charge?"

"I volunteered. I thought," he bit out, speaking over her as she opened her mouth, "that if I'm not on shift, it might give us time to spend together. Seeing as how we've been apart for so long and don't trust each other. A bad way for a marriage to be, don't you think?"

Dhruv shifted his feet and turned his gaze to the ceiling.

Ahilya's cheeks burned. Iravan had always been good at turning her own weapons against her. She had pushed him to it, but he had provoked her too, and they continued to spiral, round and round endlessly. How had they fallen this far? When had they become like this? Did they even have a marriage now? The grief and anger thrust higher; suddenly, she couldn't think clearly. In her mind, she saw him sprawled on the grass again, flickering as though malfunctioning, returned from the earthrage. She saw him strip himself of his vine, redirect it toward herself and Oam. *I had a duty of care*, she had whimpered. *No*, he'd replied. *I did.*

"I'm trying," Iravan said, "to reconcile, Ahilya."

She studied him, still not speaking. Vaguely, she wondered if she was being too unforgiving, not allowing him to explain, to rest.

But this was Iravan. Iravan who had held her expedition hostage. Who hadn't owned up to his fault with the alarm. Who had chastened her with detachment for *seven* months because of a stupid fight. She wasn't being *nearly* harsh enough, and the anger returned to her, for his words now, for his attempts at *reconciliation*.

Ahilya looked away to the sparkling phosphorescence on the walls, transported back to eleven years before, when Iravan had asked her to wed him, when they'd taken their vows in the temple and promised to go on a path together or not at all. There was no interest in each other's work now, no common journey in life, no shared dreams about the future. Iravan's promotion to the council had ripped the bark off the tree that was their marriage. The last few months had hollowed the wood, and the sap of shared experiences that had coupled them so tightly had separated. All that remained was the seed of affection nearly dead.

Was there any point in reconciliation? She should end it now, before it became any worse. She should free them both, leave Iravan to dwell in his duties, and her to her powerless guilt.

Ahilya opened her mouth to speak the words, but Iravan anticipated her, reading her as only he could, the shadows behind his face becoming deeper.

"Think of it this way," he said, giving her a watery smile. "You telling me how wrong I am, arguing constant opposition, will help the objectivity of the investigation. If we find out why the alarm failed, the perpetrator would be punished harshly. You'd get justice for Oam."

Ahilya froze.

The perpetrator would be punished harshly. *Iravan* would be punished harshly.

They would demote him. For all she knew, they could excise him, cut him away from the most precious thing in his life, his trajection. It would be justice, but more than that—it would be absolution from her relentless guilt.

Her gaze darted around the alcove, the lowering canopy, the blooming jasmines, the blue-green twinkles in the foliage. Once, she had encouraged Iravan to be his best and pursue his dreams, but as long as he was a Senior Architect, there would be no going back to the way things had been. Yet in one stroke, Iravan was offering her the chance to vindicate Oam and rebuild their marriage even at the cost of his title. All she had to do was say yes. The word dangled in front of her like a ripe fruit, tempting, delicious, poisonous.

Ahilya's gaze locked on her husband. He sat on his wheelchair, clenching and unclenching his jaw. He wanted her to join him, badly, *desperately*, but why? What did he have to gain?

Iravan was no fool; he had seen an advantage, something he wasn't telling her, some way to keep it all, his position, his reputation, his marriage. She could join him on the investigation like he so clearly wanted, but if her reasons were different, were they allies? So often, even on the same path, the fulfillment of one's desire had been the ruin of the other's. Perhaps, then, they were adversaries. The thought summed up their marriage so succinctly, so perversely, that Ahilya almost laughed out loud.

Iravan stared at her. "Will you come with me? Please?"

After all the traps, and all the machinations, it came down to one simple question: did she love Iravan enough to attempt reconciliation?

"Please?" Iravan asked again.

Was he—was their marriage—worth saving?

"Yes," she said, surprising herself. Iravan's chest dropped in deep relief. She glanced at Dhruv, but he only looked curious. The wave of grief and anger in her mind retreated slightly, to be replaced by something else. Opportunity. Opportunity for happiness—perhaps, if they were lucky—but certainly for more. "I'll help you," Ahilya said, her palms sweating. "But on one condition. You nominate one of us to the council seat."

Iravan recoiled. Shock, admiration, and calculation flickered in his eyes in rapid succession. "With you, me and Bharavi," he said at once, "it would practically be nepotism."

"I said one of us," Ahilya said coldly. She gestured to Dhruv, whose mouth had fallen open. "I leave that up to you."

Iravan glanced from her to Dhruv, then back at her. Her words were simple enough, but all three of them knew what she was asking.

Nomination was no easy affair of a councilor picking a name from the candidates who applied. Each councilor could nominate only one person and, in doing so, became their candidate's most vocal champion, placing their own reputation on the line. Iravan had taught Naila, wanting to raise a *Junior* Architect, so he may prove himself. In nominating Dhruv or Ahilya, a floundering sungineer and a misfit archeologist, he'd be sabotaging his own career. Yet for Ahilya and Dhruv, a nomination would be clemency. Even if they didn't win the council seat, Kiana could hardly transfer Dhruv after such an honor, and Ahilya, for all her recent failures, would be allowed to remain an archeologist.

Iravan's face was inscrutable but he was thinking rapidly, looking for a way out. "It's not that simple," he said. "I have an obligation to nominate a candidate who is best for the ashram. This is why the council waits five years before making such a decision—it is to give a fair chance to anyone who wishes to join it, for candidates to mature their ideas on Nakshar's survival and present them to a councilor—"

"We know this. We have been working on our ideas far longer—"

"They have to be likely ideas. Serious ideas. With a high probability of success. You'd still have to present your theses for survival. Without those, I wouldn't be *allowed* to nominate you—"

"Then perhaps you should consider helping us," she said coldly. "Those books are a good beginning. Sharing more records would be to your benefit."

A slight crease formed on Iravan's forehead.

And all of a sudden, Ahilya could remember every argument the both of them had ever had about the vacant councilor position. Airav, Bharavi, and Chaiyya would nominate their own candidates, each of them an architect. Laksiya and Kiana would undoubtedly pick sungineers from the lab. Ahilya and Dhruv already knew the names of their most likely competitors—but with what Ahilya proposed right now, she was not merely taking away a nomination from Junior Architect Naila. She was taking it away from an *architect*.

For the first time in Nakshar's history, the decision would equate the number of architects and non-architects up for a vacant council seat. It would create shockwaves, marking a change in the city's administration. It would show a Senior Architect's willingness to have a civilian occupy an architect's position, a serious relinquishing of control, if there ever was one, which would have repercussions for future nominations. Even if Ahilya and Dhruv did not win the councilorship—and they most likely wouldn't—Ahilya was asking for a change in the city's future, immediately.

She knew Iravan could see all this. But she'd trapped him in his own game. The very people he scorned—he'd have to uphold them in all his eloquence, a greater challenge than he'd anticipated.

Ahilya held her breath, watching these very thoughts fly through Iravan. Grudging approval settled on his handsome face.

"Help me solve this," he murmured, "and we have a bargain."

"Agreed," she said at once.

Dhruv exhaled audibly. Iravan nodded and skimmed his wheelchair around.

For an instant, Ahilya couldn't believe what she had done. Her heart throbbed in her chest like she had been running. This had been a coup, and she'd won, against a Senior Architect, against *Iravan.* Disbelief made her lightheaded; laughter formed on the edge of hysteria, and she blinked once or twice to clear her head.

Iravan was already leaving the alcove. Dhruv raised a hand in farewell. Still enveloped in a haze of unreality, Ahilya nodded to the sungineer and followed her husband out the library alcove, her heart pounding rapidly.

13
IRAVAN

Iravan shifted as the thick, knotted branch that formed the landing firmed under his wheelchair. Ahilya followed and the alcove closed in a whisk of bark. Their shared alcove had been grown in one of the highest boughs of the fig tree that formed Nakshar's library. Three stories below, in the heart of the tree, the main hall appeared through gaps in the long leaves. Citizens clustered by the rock pool at the center, filling their clay jugs with crystal water and bringing them back to the smaller branches that were shaped as benches. Iravan considered descending through the fig tree's depths, past the open-air hall and the public spaces of the lowermost tiers. Bharavi would have recommended it; Nakshar would see him and Ahilya together.

But then he glanced at his wife, at her trembling shoulders and unseeing eyes.

Iravan swallowed and took the branch that spiraled outside the tree.

Neither of them said a word. Ahilya brushed a strand of her long black hair behind an ear. Iravan breathed deeply as the rich scent of sandalwood wafted to him. Once, there had been comfort in that soft scent: home, security, *Ahilya*. Now a yearning seized him, and with it a challenge.

He had not thought his state on the wheelchair would move his wife into forgiveness—she knew him far too well for that. Yet her maneuver with the nomination had been so ingenious, it was almost *diabolical*.

Nomination was not merely a test of the nominee; it was a test of the councilor. Power in the council came from fruitful decisions, from gambles one took that paid off in the long run—it was why Iravan had selected Naila to be his protégée; to have her rise to councilor from a Junior Architect would have given him more sway than an increment of small decisions. But nominating Ahilya or Dhruv? The two had contributed nothing to Nakshar's survival. The nomination was doomed to fail; it would deplete his carefully built goodwill, irrevocably weaken his position.

Besides, was it *right*? A stable council directly impacted the solidity of a city. Councilors made most decisions together, either by majority vote or by unanimity. Ultimately, a council maintained a delicate alignment between the trajection of architects and the desires of non-architects—an alignment that flight and survival itself depended on.

Which meant that more than anything else, the councilorship was about *fit*. Both Ahilya and Dhruv had shown only disdain for architects throughout their careers. The sungineer at least was a safer choice; sungineers by their very nature *had* to work with architects. But Ahilya? Her entire research was to make architects redundant. Would it be fair to Nakshar to nominate either of them? Were they capable of hard decisions to keep the ashram in flight?

Iravan pressed a hand to his neck to assuage the sharp pain that had settled there. Under him, the massive, gnarled branch smoothened into a ramp, then grew creakily into wide steps for Ahilya. The design was old, inefficient. Why hadn't the Disc Architects created permanent stairs? Or, better yet, replaced all stairs within the ashram with ramps? Nakshar lay flat, spanning acres. With so much space, inclines would be easy, and trajection could be conserved instead of being wasted back and forth on conversion. This was what it meant to be on the council: thinking of minute decisions that affected their world. Were Ahilya and Dhruv capable of factoring such things into the implications of their own research?

To Iravan's surprise, Ahilya frowned at the branch and stepped beside him to share the ramp. She couldn't know about matters of architectural efficiency—perhaps, then, this action was a small sign of forgiveness. He studied her but said nothing. Together, they descended the tree's thick limbs.

Finally, Iravan's wheelchair sank into the earth.

They'd emerged onto the very playground their shared alcove overlooked. Wispy white clouds scudded above them. The playground was smaller than any in Nakshar's latest designs. In a few hours, grass would cover the field, swings and bars would rise between trees, and slides spiral in gentle loops. The children would find it before the day was done, but the structure was a compromise, easy, nondescript, created so architects didn't tire themselves to maintain its constellation lines. Iravan opened his mouth to tell Ahilya this, but she shambled next to him, her shoulders slumped, hair a dark curtain that hid her face. Her eyes had looked swollen in the library, the tear tracks clear on her cheeks.

Iravan stopped the wheelchair. *What am I doing?* he thought abruptly. The nomination, the investigation, even Nakshar's architectural designs, those were *his* games. *She* needed comfort. A stab of self-loathing cut through him, making him flinch. He lifted a hand toward her, but she kept walking.

Iravan sighed and scrubbed his face instead.

Ahead of him, Ahilya paused and turned slightly, her eyes dull.

"I'm sorry," he said. "This is not how I wanted to do this. I can't seem to get it right. With you. With us. If you don't want to come, that's—that's fine. The judgement of the council will still be fair. They made a healbranch promise." He clenched his fists so she wouldn't see his trembling hands. *If there are signs, any at all, another indication of a failed marriage, an Examination could happen.* "Are things forever broken between us?"

Ahilya was silent for so long, turned slightly, gazing at him, that he was afraid she hadn't heard him. "I don't know," she said at last. "You abandoned me for seven months."

Iravan winced. "I… I was wrong to do that. It… shouldn't have happened."

The apology rang hollow. Iravan clutched the nape of his neck where a sharp pain had settled. For seven months, his anger had felt right, it had felt *honest*, yet Ahilya's feelings had become collateral damage to an action born out of neither logic nor love. What kind of a man did that make him? What kind of a *husband*? The two paths opened behind his brows again, ever present, relentless, one toward his wife and the other toward this hateful person he was revealing himself to be.

"You should have saved Oam before you saved me," she said, her voice cracking.

"I wasn't going to leave you to die, Ahilya."

"This guilt. Nothing is worth it."

"What of my guilt?"

"You should have left when I told you to," she said.

"You should have returned when I asked you to," he answered.

They stared at each other. For a second, he saw the both of them the way they had been once, laughing together on their wedding day. Ahilya's eyes had danced as she'd placed the marriage garland around his neck. He had swept in and kissed her, claiming her for himself forever. They had been happy once; they had touched each other endlessly, their hands entwined, the constant nudges and embraces. His fingers twitched now, wanting to feel her, to comfort her, but her naked pain stabbed his heart, and Iravan broke the gaze first. He skimmed forward on his wheelchair and Ahilya started to walk again.

"Oam's fathers," he began, awkwardly.

She swallowed and pressed the heels of her hands to her eyes. "They want to move to a different city. Kinshar or Reikshar."

"I should have gone to them," he said, his head hurting.

He had told Bharavi as much, during all the last week of recovery, when she had come to visit him, but the Senior Architect had settled herself on the edge of his bed in the sanctum and set her mouth in a hard line.

"No one needs to know an architect was out there in the jungle," she'd said pointedly when he'd raised the idea of making a personal apology.

Iravan had sat up despite his aching limbs. He had not been able to shake the image of what he'd done—of how he'd let go of Oam, how he'd pushed himself into Nakshar with the last of his energy. The guilt was too much—it was affecting his recovery, he knew.

"This isn't about the *reputation* of the architects, Bha," he'd said. "It's about the right thing to do. I had a duty of care."

"What do you think will happen, Iravan?" Bharavi shot back. "You think broadcasting your role in this will relieve your guilt? No one knows except the council and Naila—"

"So, your solution is to let Ahilya carry this burden alone? To let the boy's parents think his death is her fault? *That's* your advice?"

"Airav gave you three weeks," Bharavi said, unfazed. "You've spent one of those recovering, and let's not overestimate the progress you can make in the other two. Laksiya will provide the council's condolences to Oam's fathers. You need to forget what happened in the jungle and focus on your investigation."

They had argued for nearly an hour, the both of them becoming more and more agitated. The guilt had grown in Iravan, along with a fury at himself and Bharavi and all the council, but Bharavi had been relentless. Eventually, Iravan had grown tired, his will to fight her depleted. He had reluctantly agreed to her demands, but his headache had become much worse, and the burden on his chest had only grown heavier.

"Your being there would have helped," Ahilya said quietly now, glancing at him. "Perhaps his fathers would not choose to leave Nakshar."

"I—I concur. But for now, the fewer people who know about the investigation and the expedition, the better it is for... the both of us."

She scoffed, a soft sound. "Is this where you cleverly ask for my silence?"

"Rages, Ahilya—I'm not—That's not—" Iravan took a deep breath to calm himself. A dull fury throbbed in him. "You can only do what you think is right. I'm trying the best I can, to make things better between us, but I can't do it alone. And I can't do it if you suspect everything I say."

She studied him for a long moment. "It won't be easy. We're angry with each other."

"Anger is honest, at least. But suspicion? That gives me—it gives *us*—no chance."

"We might find a limit to the effort."

"Or maybe we'll find that's how we are. We've always returned to each other no matter what. Ahilya, we've always *returned*."

Her eyes grew thoughtful. Perhaps she was remembering those other times they'd argued, how they had become stronger for it.

Rages, he hoped she was remembering it like he did. He hadn't trajected for a week, his mind bereft of the comfort of the Moment—but at least trajection was available to him now, if not advisable. With the Examination of Ecstasy—with *excision*—

Iravan gripped the arms of his wheelchair, breathing hard. They'd cut him away from the Moment completely, denying him his natural state within a second vision, denying him any power, leaving him to be less than ordinary. He watched Ahilya, his breathing shallow. *If there are signs, any at all, another indication of a failed marriage—*

Ahilya glanced at him, then nodded once. Iravan trembled slightly, exhaling, and released his chair.

The field narrowed into a tunnel of rose bushes, then opened into one of Nakshar's main thoroughfares. Iravan had taken the same path toward the library, but where there had been emptiness only an hour before, a bazaar had now emerged. Tall, multistoried trees stretched in all directions, thin and weak-looking. Simple wooden bridges connected the heights of one tree to another. Vendors and artisans had arranged their wares on flat branches and between roots, shouting about sarees and carvings and pottery.

In the tight, narrow clusters of the stalls and the weak selection of the plant species, Iravan recognized Airav's hand. The man had compromised space for efficiency, security for architect welfare, but had not taken into account the effect it would have on the citizens. Shopkeepers hailed Iravan, calling out questions regarding room for their wares, for stronger wood to balance on.

He waved but didn't stop, his helplessness rising. He could hardly tell them trajection was becoming difficult. Even the youngest architect knew what the combined panic of the ashram could do to the architecture. Trajection tapped into the desires of consciousness: without the desire of the non-architects to sustain the power, constellation lines could grow weaker; the ashram could lose its very structure and cohesion—a dangerous consequence in flight that could affect everyone's survival.

Already, this structure was flawed. Undoubtedly, the citizens' unease would only weaken the construction, sending the architecture into an infinite loop of destruction. It was another thing the council had to navigate carefully so as not to jeopardize the design, but this, here, now—Airav's decision to use *these* plants for citizen spaces would only antagonize the citizens, change their desire for safety into one of resentment. It would give rise to a hundred Ahilyas; it would *contribute* to the difficulty in trajection. What was the man playing at?

Iravan pursed his lips, frowning. He could already see what his absence in the council was doing to the architecture—this was exactly the kind of design he would have opposed vehemently. He ran a hand through his hair in silent frustration. He and Ahilya zigzagged through the chaos, their silence loud in the clamor.

Finally, Ahilya broke the silence between them, her voice toneless. "Where are we going?"

Iravan glanced at her. "The Architects' Academy. To speak to Naila."

"You think this is her fault?"

"No. The trajection required to sound the alarm is extremely simple. Even a beginner architect should have been able to do it."

Ahilya nodded at a vendor selling sarees. "Why don't you just traject a direct path to the Academy instead of going through the city?"

"An architect isn't supposed to traject when off duty."

She glanced at him, opened her mouth, then closed it again. In his mind's eye, Iravan saw Bharavi, warning him of the consequences of too much trajection.

"I know you're thinking it," he muttered. "You might as well say it."

A startled laugh escaped Ahilya. "I'm trying to trust you."

Iravan sighed. "Yes, architects aren't supposed to traject when off duty. No, it didn't stop me before. As a Senior Architect, I'm exempt from certain rules, but I shouldn't have done it regardless, not without just cause."

The trajection scars on his skin still burned, looking like welts. The rudra tree had done nothing to heal them. Iravan resisted the urge to feel them below his kurta. It was bad enough he could still see the scars so clearly, warped around his forearms and elbows as though seared permanently. He was no healer, but even he knew for this to occur, the injury was too serious. He might never recover from it, no matter how long he remained at the sanctum. The implications of this thought made him nervous.

"That reminds me," he said, swallowing. He removed a bracelet with a single black rudra bead from his wrist. "This is for you."

A corner of Ahilya's lips lifted in irony. "A little too late to be giving me jewelry, don't you think?"

He returned a small smile. "Guess I have to start making up somehow."

When her fingers grazed his palm to pick up the bracelet, it was all Iravan could do to not grasp them. He dropped his hand. Tingles ran up and down his skin.

"So, what is this?" she said, dangling the bracelet on a finger.

"It's a key. It'll let you anywhere within the ashram—all architect-reserved spaces, the sanctum and the orchard, everywhere I can go as a Senior Architect."

Ahilya's head lifted sharply. "And the rest of the council? They're fine with you giving me this? A key so precious?"

"They don't know," Iravan replied, holding her gaze.

He had calculated the risk carefully. He didn't need the bracelet, he could use his other beads in combination, but sharing his permissions was rule-breaking, something Bharavi had warned him against. Yet matters had deteriorated far too much between him and Ahilya. A few books from the architects' archives were not going to cut it; she was too clever; she could see right through him. He needed to go beyond his boundaries, a real indication of remorse for his mistakes. None of this was truly swaying her, Iravan knew, but he did not have the luxury of time and subtlety. He gripped his wheelchair, then forced himself to release it.

"I know you're thinking it," Ahilya said, a ghost of a smile on her face. "You might as well say it."

He didn't smile back. "You're trying to trust me. The least I can do is return it."

Ahilya didn't take her eyes off the bracelet as she donned it and tucked it beneath her kurta sleeve. "I'll be discreet, Iravan."

He breathed in relief again and nodded his thanks. They crossed a wooden bridge, away from the forest bazaar, down another ramp, this one toward areas frequented by architects.

At once, the architecture changed. The ramp circled into a spacious clearing, where a tall sungineered waterfall gushed into a glistening stream. Flowers grew in abundance, lilies, tulips, even cherry blossoms, which took special effort to grow beyond their trees. Each bush was meticulously pruned, caressed into aesthetic shapes. Iravan could almost see the complex constellation lines that were being maintained to keep the design intact. A few Junior Architects in their green kurtas bustled past, bowing at him hurriedly. Then he and Ahilya were alone, facing an archway of thick, golden leaves over a wide bark wall.

Ahilya froze, her hand on her wrist, staring at the archway.

For an instant, Iravan did not understand her hesitation.

But then he was transported back to the days he had been in training. Fresh from Yeikshar, as a Junior Architect of twenty, he'd seen Ahilya for the first time when she'd visited the Academy as part of a citizen tour. Iravan had become so bewitched by her intelligent eyes and her sardonic smile that he'd fumbled his trajection and been knocked off his feet by a whiplashing root. He had sought her out the next day.

He had thought the story romantic; all the men, women, and many others he had ever been with, no one had affected him in such a way before. But it had taken Ahilya's constant early rejections of him to fully acknowledge his incomplete perception of the event. The tour had been calculated to show citizens what they'd never have. It was meant to cement admiration for the architects. A young Iravan had been confused and aghast.

"Tap the bracelet," he said to her now quietly. "Focus your desire on the Academy."

Ahilya's gaze moved to him, wondering, slow. She tapped the bracelet silently, her finger trembling.

The bark in front of them creaked open, but Ahilya didn't move, the tear tracks shocking in her chalky face. Shame throbbed in Iravan. This was the same woman who had been fearless in the jungle, fearless with the yaksha. What had he and Nakshar—an ashram *he* counseled—done to her? The weight in his chest grew heavier. Silently, he whisked his wheelchair forward and preceded her into the Academy.

14

AHILYA

Iravan's bracelet felt warm on her wrist. Ahilya fidgeted with it, rolling it back, pushing it forward, incredulous still that she wore it. Iravan had handed over, quite literally, the power of Nakshar's council. Discomfort nagged at her, like a thorn under her skin. She had not earned this yet; she didn't deserve it. Ahilya tugged the rudra bead again, feeling its unfamiliar weight.

Then she realized she was gathering attention.

The archway had led into a wide indoor courtyard shaped like a quadrangle. Multiple levels in burnished gold wood overlooked the courtyard as though Ahilya were in a hollow, square tower. Robe-covered students in their green and gray kurta-trouser uniforms milled about in clusters, and leaned over the balconies. Several called out to Iravan, who waved, but as their eyes fell on Ahilya, curiosity and contempt replaced the admiration. Whispered giggles broke out in muted derision. Ahilya's cheeks burned.

Even though Iravan wore no translucent architect robes, he was *Iravan*, Senior Architect and one of the most admired councilors of Nakshar. Ahilya was a nobody, and that was apparent at a glance.

She felt like a child again, appraised by her own parents and their friends for being born without the ability to traject. More and more people had been born with the power recently, yet *she* had not, and a buried shame gripped her; she could not help its rise under her skin.

But she could help her response.

Ahilya dropped her wrist, stood up straighter, and stared boldly back at the architects. *You're doing this for Oam*, she reminded herself. *For Oam and Dhruv and a nomination that will force the architects to rethink their disdain.* Gritting her teeth, she followed Iravan to one of the wide corridors lining the quadrangle.

Unlike the other parts of the city that had appeared cramped, the Architects' Academy was exquisite. Not a single tree was gnarled; instead, all of the trunks along the courtyard were evenly spaced and symmetrical. Sunlight danced through the foliage, showers of delicate blossoms drifting down from the canopy. The floor was no ordinary grass; gold and blue flowers grew in a lush mosaic, and soft moss cushioned Ahilya's boots. Even the railings along the corridors were delicate. Patterns winked out of wood carved by artistic trajection.

Iravan stopped outside a dimly lit classroom. Inside, young beginner architects in their gray uniforms stood in a circle around tall thorny weeds. He moved discreetly to a side of the doorway, but Naila, who was teaching the class, noticed them, and then everyone was bowing. Some of the boys and girls twittered and nudged each other. Iravan smiled and waved at them to carry on.

"They like you," Ahilya observed.

"They're infatuated," he muttered. "Some of them."

"But they like you. All of them do. You haven't taught here for so long, but I suppose it doesn't wear off."

"It hasn't *been* so long," he said, his voice guarded. "I was here briefly, during the last earthrage, when I..."

When he hadn't visited *her*.

Ahilya's chest tightened in anger and hurt, but she said nothing. Those seven months were not the first time she and Iravan had been so distant after an argument. Once, long before, they'd had a similar fight that had kept them away from each other.

They'd been courting a full year then, and Nakshar had made history by opening its council to sungineers for the first time. The city had been decorated lavishly, flower bursts at every corner and glowglobes twinkling within every bush. The two of them had celebrated with Iravan's last bottle of rasa from Yeikshar, but afterward, Iravan had turned to Ahilya and suggested she become a sungineer.

"It's become a promising career," he'd said, throwing his arm out lazily, his head on her lap. "Perhaps you should consider it. You could change the world."

Ahilya had frozen, midway through detangling his hair. Somewhere, a lightcracker exploded, filling the sky with pinpricks of radiance. "I'll change the world with archeology," she'd said carefully. "It will have its time."

"Yes, but look to where the seeds are flying. Ahilya, if you gazed forward instead of back, you could do so much!"

The statement had been so callous that Ahilya had abruptly pushed him off her, maddened. "Why are we talking about me?"

"I'm just—"

"I want to change things *this* way. *My* way. Why don't you believe in me?"

Irritation had flashed on Iravan's features. "I believe in you, but you make things harder for yourself as an archeologist. Why not try a better—"

"*Better?* Iravan, why is sungineering *better* simply because the architects have finally deemed it so? Why would you think archeology is lesser? You're supposed to be on my side."

They'd both been so furious with each other, they'd spent the next two months apart. Then Ahilya had returned home one day to see her walls full of jasmines. A contrite Iravan had been waiting with a rare book from the architects' archives that had helped her with expanding her theories.

She glanced at her husband now, her anger wavering. Iravan's apology for abandoning her now had hardly been better than the one all those years back, but did she *want* a false apology? They had always been able to disagree. It was what made them strong, to be themselves and still be *them*, to always return. What had happened? She couldn't see back to when things had deteriorated, but she knew that at the heart of it was both their pride. Yet Iravan had come to her today, no matter his reasons. He was trying, despite his feelings, despite his obligations to the council. Ahilya turned back to the classroom, attempting to focus.

One by one, the children in the classroom began to glow blue-green, their skins lighting up. As Naila called out more instructions, some students stopped glowing while others blazed brighter.

"What are they doing?" Ahilya asked.

"They're learning to enter the Moment," Iravan said. "It's when—"

"I know what it is," she said, then offered a small smile to take the heat out of her voice. "I *have* been married to a Senior Architect for over ten years."

"I didn't think you'd remember."

"Not all our memories are bad."

"N-no," Iravan said, glancing at her, stammering in his surprise. "Not all."

Ahilya nodded her head toward the children, feeling the flush rise in her as he watched her, still surprised. "It seems pretty easy."

"It is. It's the easiest part of trajecting. It's the first thing we teach beginners, and we teach it for months, no matter how talented the child is, because it's the most important thing for architects to learn."

"Is this relevant to the investigation?"

Iravan gestured into the classroom. "See those plants in the middle?"

Ahilya squinted. The thorny weeds waved around, their leaves shaped like arrowheads. An image flashed in her mind, of Iravan screaming for her to return, and Oam whimpering. "Is that—" she said. "Is that—magnaroot?"

"Yes, it's—" Iravan cut himself off.

Ahilya stumbled away from the doorway, her body trembling. She leaned against the wall opposite the classroom. A bench grew on the floor and Ahilya collapsed onto it, hugging herself.

Iravan cursed. He slid his wheelchair toward her, but Ahilya barely registered him. She was back in the earthrage, in the nest, and Oam was screaming. She knew what was going to happen next. He was going to die. She was going to leave him behind. Her breath emerged in shallow gasps. Ahilya closed her eyes, and Oam urged her on; he ran to retrieve her satchel. She began to rock, shaking her head, trying to force the images away before they returned to that fatal point.

Iravan's fingers grazed against her hand. Ahilya gripped him tightly, and he squeezed hard, as though trying to pour into her his strength.

"I'm sorry," he said quietly. "Maybe we shouldn't do this."

"I'm all right," she said. She wrenched her eyes open and the images abruptly dissipated. Ahilya let go of his hand and avoided his gaze. "Thank you."

Iravan cleared his throat. His fingers stretched in and out. "Did you go to the infirmary? For medicines and healing?"

"I can't," she whispered. "That's where Oam—He was—"

Raw emotions flashed across her husband's face, guilt and shame and consideration. *Were you jealous?* she had screamed in the temple, and she knew he was remembering it too, but incongruous laughter built in her at the memory. Imagining Iravan jealous was like imagining a yaksha speak. Whatever his faults, her husband was not the man to feel such a petty emotion. Iravan opened his mouth, perhaps to offer more comfort, but Ahilya shook her head, guilt searing her.

"So," she said quickly. "The magnaroot, huh?"

He hesitated, but she stared at him, pleading silently for him to change the subject. She couldn't take his kindness, not his. It would shatter her remaining strength.

Iravan's eyes flickered in understanding. He turned back to the classroom. "Yes," he said, his voice hollow. "Magnaroot is one of the most sensitive species of plants in the ashram. Inside the Moment, those children are surrounded by magnaroot stars. And that's exactly what someone at the watchpost does."

Ahilya took a deep breath, her mind still gripped by the earthrage. "They enter the Moment?"

"They enter the Moment surrounded by magnaroot. The watchpost chamber is full of uncontaminated magnaroot. The plant is unique—it responds hours before an earthrage occurs. Any ordinary citizen should be able to see the plant change, but being in the Moment allows an architect precious hours of warning. When an earthrage is imminent, all the stars of the magnaroot turn toward a singular possibility—for it to become thorny. The experience is quite surreal."

"You're saying it's impossible to get wrong."

"For someone like Naila? It *is* impossible. The magnaroot in *here* is harder to traject than the one at the watchpost; this one here is accustomed to trajection. But the one at the watchpost is grown from seed every landing. It's untouched, pristine."

Ahilya shook her head, not understanding. "Then how could the flight alarm have failed?"

Iravan gave her a lopsided smile. "Exactly. The way the alarm works—when an architect sees the magnaroot's possibilities turn thorny in the Moment, they send a signal through their watchpost key to the Architects' Disc. The Disc begins to prepare the ashram for flight, and the trajection releases the flight raga, which is amplified by sungineers in the lab. That's what we ought to have heard in the jungle. But the Disc didn't receive a signal from Naila at all."

"Maybe someone tampered with the magnaroot in the watchpost before Naila went in."

"There's only one way in and out of the watchpost. It's the rudra key I gave her. No one can get into the watchpost without it. Not even me—which is why I needed it in the first place."

"So, maybe someone tampered with the key."

"Not that, either," Iravan said, shaking his head. "All four Senior Architects embed multiple labyrinths within the watchpost key, and the key is then tuned to the architect on duty. When I gave it to Naila, I aligned it to her, which meant only *she* could get into the watchpost. We checked it, to be certain, and it's not tampered with." He paused and looked at Ahilya. "You can ask the others—Bharavi or Chaiyya. If you don't believe me."

"I don't think you're lying, if that's what you're suggesting."

"Thank—"

"You make excuses, and you avoid the truth, and I don't think I know anyone else with the ability to phrase their words so deftly that someone is led to a wholly untrue interpretation. But," Ahilya said, heavily, "I don't think you lie outright."

Iravan grunted. "As turbulent as that was, I appreciate it."

His lips lifted, but Ahilya didn't return the smile. In her mind, she saw the way Iravan had walked into the copse, the way he had demanded she take him on her expedition. "I don't understand you, Iravan," she said meditatively. "You know how many measures the council takes to protect the watchpost key, yet you just handed it over to Naila?"

He held her gaze. "Maybe I'm not as dedicated to the ashram as a councilor ought to be."

"Maybe not," she agreed.

"A fact unmissed by the rest of the council," he said. He turned away back to the classroom, uncomfortable.

Ahilya continued to study him. What Iravan had done with the key and then with the bracelet—it was typical of him. Her husband behaved recklessly often for his own reasons. He had come to her, twice now; there had been a concealed motive both times—this was Iravan, after all—but did that make it any less sincere? These mysteries he held close, it was who he was. She had known this when she'd married him. She had reveled in it. In the past, when he'd finally shared his mind, it had been that much sweeter for the wait. Maybe she owed him more trust than she was giving. Ahilya shook her head, trying to focus on the investigation.

"Perhaps," she said, throwing a shot in the dark, "the plants at the watchpost didn't work."

Iravan gave her a long look. "What do you mean?"

"I don't know. I don't understand your architectural sorcery. Maybe the plants in the watchpost didn't grow the way they were supposed to."

Iravan sighed. "That's not something our *sorcery* can control. The watchpost plants grow as a permanent feature of the ashram. No amount of trajection can change that."

Ahilya raised an eyebrow. "I thought trajection could change everything."

"Not the rudra tree. The rudra tree is such a sentient tree on the consciousness spectrum that it might as well be a complex being. It's as old as Nakshar itself, and it was cultivated to have some unalterable desires. Like healbranch growing. Like the ashram protecting an architect at any cost. Like magnaroot sprouting without interference at the watchpost. Whoever the original architects of Nakshar were, this is how they encoded the tree when they first grew it from a sapling. Not even a Senior Architect can interfere with that."

Ahilya slumped forward, her elbows on her knees. Iravan's tone was not patronizing, but he had clearly already considered all the points she was making. Did he even need her help? "So, it's not sabotage, it's not the key, and it's not the magnaroot," she said.

"You see what I mean? The system is designed to be foolproof. It cannot fail."

"It did, though."

"Yes. It did. And the only logical way it could is because of human error."

Iravan paused as a low bell chimed through the Academy. In the classroom, Naila called a halt. The children picked up their bags from the floor and began to file out. Iravan nodded to them, waited until they had all passed from earshot, then led Ahilya inside the now-empty classroom where Naila waited, looking apprehensive.

The Junior Architect began speaking before they had fully approached. "I'm sorry, Iravan-ve," she stammered. "I tried to stay, but Airav-ve—"

"It's all right, Naila," he said gently.

"I didn't mean for you to get into trouble—"

"You didn't. We just have a few questions."

Naila's gaze ran over Ahilya. Her eyebrows climbed her forehead. Her mouth quirked in amusement.

"Both of you?" she asked mildly.

Ahilya stiffened. Heat pooled in her stomach, and Oam said, *People like us, we don't know anything about flight and architecture.* Her skin itched beneath Iravan's rudra bead bracelet, and in her mind's eye, she saw herself and Naila standing on one of Nakshar's terraces before the landing. She heard the condescension in the woman's voice as she explained to Ahilya—to an *archeologist*—what a damned earthrage was.

Iravan's eyes glinted at Naila's presumption. "Junior Architect?" he said, dangerously.

"I—" Naila laughed in quick embarrassment. "I meant no offense. It was a poor joke. We just don't get too many non-architects in the Academy."

"Perhaps that's because you don't allow citizens in these privileged spaces," Ahilya said, her fingers curling.

Iravan looked from one to another.

For a moment, Ahilya thought he'd say something more, that he'd chastise Naila like he had chastised her at the copse before the expedition—perversely, she almost wished it. But then he sighed and shook his head. "Naila, what happened after I sent you away with the key?"

The Junior Architect twirled a lock of her hair on a finger and turned her attention to him. "I went to the temple, past the root labyrinths of the rudra tree. The key worked fine, and the watchpost was full of fresh magnaroot this high—" Naila lifted a hand to her waist and dropped it. "I entered the Moment like I was supposed to, but I didn't traject. It was rather boring."

Iravan snorted. "And the Moment? What did you notice there?"

"Nothing. The magnaroot stars didn't become thorny. Nothing happened at all, and I wasn't expecting it to, either, was I? After all, we'd just landed. It would have to be days, *weeks*, before another earthrage occurred."

"So, you didn't signal the Disc?" Ahilya asked, crossing her arms over her chest.

"No," Naila said, barely glancing at her. "I only knew something was wrong when my own citizen ring began chiming. The Disc must have realized on its own that the earthrage was happening and begun flight procedure, prompting my ring to chime. But I didn't feel a change in the magnaroot or see it become thorny in either my first vision or the second."

Iravan exhaled deeply. "All right. You may go, Naila."

For an instant, the Junior Architect lingered. Her gaze flickered between Iravan and Ahilya, and she opened her mouth as if to say something more.

Then, changing her mind, she hurriedly bowed to Iravan and left the classroom, gathering up her own bag from the floor. Ahilya strode over to the bench and sat down where Naila had been. She raised an eyebrow at her husband.

Iravan grinned, his sincere smile cutting through her. "So, that's that."

"You believe her that easily? She's nervous. Maybe she's lying."

"She couldn't have." Iravan gestured at the black, velvety, teardrop-shaped leaves peeking out on the walls around them. "See those plants? They're veristem. Veristem is part of the Psychephyta of plants, created by architects for specific purposes."

"Such as?"

"Detecting lies," he said simply. "Veristem blooms into white flowers when someone around it is lying. It doesn't just bloom when a person is deliberately lying; it blooms when a person is lying to *themselves.* It doesn't depend on interpretation; it's not bound by literal intent or subjective perception. It bypasses the individual and goes down to the truth, to *facts.*"

Ahilya drew in a sharp breath, remembering the spiralweed hidden in the library, the lethal plants she'd repeatedly brought Dhruv for his battery, the lies the sungineer had undoubtedly told to supply her with her archeological equipment.

"That," she said quietly, "is a dangerous plant."

"It is extremely dangerous," Iravan agreed. "Its use is heavily regulated by the council. The Academy is the only place it's grown so abundantly. Young architects lie about being overworked, or about testing trajection's limits, so they're carefully watched during training. But you see what it means?"

"Naila wasn't lying. Not to herself or to us."

"She wasn't even *accidentally* lying. She did everything she was supposed to do. Everything *I* would have. And if she didn't sense the magnaroot change, I wouldn't have, either."

"Then how could the alarm have failed?" Ahilya asked, rubbing her forehead tiredly.

"There's only one explanation," Iravan said in grim satisfaction. "An interference in the Moment caused it. The Resonance I've been feeling."

He explained what he had said to the council a week before, about the patterns he had seen in the length of earthrages, and the mysterious Resonance. Ahilya listened silently as he told her about the silvery particle throwing him out of the Moment, how it had danced in front of him with a vague familiarity, and the many times he had noticed it throughout his seven months in the temple. Her husband was as eloquent as ever, yet Ahilya shook her head when he finished.

"I don't think this is right," she said, finally understanding what had been nagging at her. "The alarm might have failed when we were out in the jungle, but Naila said the trajection of the Disc Architects released the flight raga."

"All trajection releases a raga," Iravan said. "Ragas are residues, byproducts of trajection, audible as melodies to architects and indiscernible usually to non-architects. It's a matter of consciousness sensitivity, but unlike other ragas, everyone needs to hear the flight raga. That's why the solar lab amplifies it as the flight alarm during take-off—"

"Right," Ahilya said, frowning. "So, one way or another, everyone in the city *heard* the alarm. Naila's own citizen ring was chiming. If everyone heard the alarm, why didn't we? You were trajecting the entire time in the jungle, powering our rings. I saw you."

Iravan frowned, his excitement waning. "Yes. I see."

"Do you think our rings are flawed?"

"All of ours? All three at the same time? No, I don't think that's possible. But I think you're right. We're no longer investigating the alarm. We're investigating why the magnaroot didn't respond in the Moment and why our citizen rings didn't work. One is related to trajection and the other to sungineering."

Iravan stared in front of him, clearly thinking hard. His wheelchair skimmed around, back toward the courtyard, but he stopped past the doorway again, his face pensive. As Ahilya joined him, the leafy doorway closed in soft creaks, the classroom shuttering now that it was no longer in use. She watched him closely, the tightening of his jaw, the fingers curling on the wheelchair, the tap-tap of his foot.

"When we returned from the jungle," she said, "Bharavi mentioned your trajection was something like she'd never seen. Does this have to do with Ecstasy?"

"It has nothing to do with Ecstasy," Iravan snapped. Ahilya

recoiled, but his expression softened instantly. "I'm sorry—but it has nothing to do with Ecstasy. Bharavi shouldn't have said that."

"Is there more to Ecstasy than I know?"

"What makes you say that?"

Ahilya shrugged. "The way you architects fear it..."

Iravan took a deep breath. "Ecstasy is a state of uncontrollable trajecting power," he said. "It's a danger to the ashram and to the architect. That's why we fear it. There are ways to prevent it, but there are no ways to cure it. Excision is the only solution."

"And excision—it's what, exactly?"

Iravan was silent for a long moment. "It's a punishment. The Ecstatic Architect is cut away from their trajection."

Ahilya nodded slowly. Everyone in Nakshar knew this, and Iravan did not lie. Still, she couldn't shake away the feeling that he was hiding something. Would he be excised if he failed the investigation? She had a sudden image of him: all his vitality gone, humbled and weak. Even if it meant justice for Oam, could she lead him to that? *It's the only way*, Dhruv said. *Or we can wave our professions goodbye.* Dhruv would tell her to press her advantage; he would remind her of their position and ask her to learn as much as she could about the council and its secrets. But Iravan had given her trust. He was trying to reconcile. Ahilya was no longer sure what her role in this investigation was.

"I promise you," he said, reaching out a hand. "I'm not in danger of Ecstasy."

She wavered, but he didn't drop his hand, waiting, so she reached out and squeezed it.

Iravan didn't let go. Very slowly, with enough time for her to withdraw, he brushed his lips against her fingers. A jolt of warmth shot through Ahilya. She tried to still the fluttering in her stomach. "Will you come home tonight?" she found herself whispering.

She had surprised herself with the question, but not as much as Iravan. His eyes grew darker, a heat gathering in them. Ahilya detected fury and passion and regret before he masked his expression. Iravan shook his head. "The sanctum architects. They want me there longer."

Another bell chimed through the Academy. Iravan and Ahilya released their hands, blinking. Heat climbed high in Ahilya's cheeks, and she took a step away from him, suddenly brought back into the present.

"We better go," Iravan said as chatting students poured into the courtyard from adjoining classrooms. "The Academy is adjourning for the day."

He skimmed forward, and they followed the bustle of architects out of the Academy. Once outside, Iravan paused near the waterfall. Ahilya tensed, the brush of his lips still lingering on her skin. The weight of unsaid things grew heavy between them. She thought of the both of them at home together, what she'd have done if he had said yes; how they would have *been*, with everything that had happened. Neither of them moved to leave, glancing at each other awkwardly, half-oblivious of the crowd of chatting architects.

When she heard a familiar voice, Ahilya finally tore her eyes away from her husband and looked toward the ramp they had taken before. Reniya, Vihanan, and other citizens she didn't recognize descended the slope together. Among them was Ahilya's sister, easily the most beautiful, her laugh high and clear. Ahilya's brows creased. Tariya had no more business at the Academy than Ahilya herself did, but Ahilya had been invited, at the very least.

"They have children in the Academy," Iravan offered. He'd followed her gaze, understood her unspoken question.

Tariya's older son, Kush, couldn't traject, but had her sister accompanied her friends in the hope that Arth one day would?

Was that why she was there? Ahilya knew the Academy regularly conducted meetings with citizen-parents, informing them of the likelihood of their child's trajection abilities. Snatches of conversation came to her, confirming her suspicions.

"—truly serve the ashram—"

"—worthy one day—"

Tension rose in Ahilya's shoulders. Iravan's mouth became a hard line. He had heard, he had *remembered* the fight that had precipitated his absence for seven months: their argument about making children of their own, Ahilya's misgivings about a non-trajecting child. She made to move, to bid him goodbye, to get away from there before they fought again, but Iravan extended a hand.

"Wait," he said. "Please—"

She paused, glanced over her shoulder.

But Iravan's eyes were growing wide in shock, the expression familiar from the jungle before the earthrage. He opened his mouth—

The ground under Ahilya's feet *cracked* in an explosion of noise.

Her heart jumped in her throat.

She had a moment's horrified glimpse of her husband's lips forming her name—

Ahilya screamed as she fell.

15

IRAVAN

"*AHILYA!*" Iravan bellowed as the clearing around him erupted into chaos.

The ground cracked, dust swirling, cries and coughs echoing in the air. Iravan's wheelchair skimmed away from the widening hole without his command. Almost he entered the Moment—for a chilling second, he thought he had, as the silvery Resonance blinked behind his eyes. Then he wrenched himself away from the urge. Iravan coughed, searching frantically for Ahilya through the eddying dust.

A small hole gaped where she had been. Balloons of earth rose and fell. Dust climbed his nose, settled in the back of his throat. Student architects were clambering back from other holes, cries of shock and consternation rising from them. Some of the older ones pulled the younger ones away. The smallest were in tears, and even Junior Architects looked shaken, their translucent robes layered in thick dust.

Yet all of them seemed unhurt.

And there was no trace of the other citizens.

No, Iravan thought, his heart sinking. *No, no, no.*

The ground moved again. More cries rang through the broken clearing as architects jumped back. The dozen small holes undulated like waves toward the center, snaking past the architects, who watched stunned. The holes turned into a bowl of depressed earth. Water splashed into the crater, filling it, as though the ashram was trying to fix this error before it was noticed.

Cries of wonder and shock echoed through the crowd. Several children wept, shivering as they watched.

"Gather yourselves," Iravan commanded sharply. "You are architects of Nakshar."

His words rang loud, cutting through the clamor.

The students quieted, staring at him with wide eyes.

Iravan searched the crowd, and his eyes settled on Naila as she pushed her way to him. "You'll have to direct them," he said curtly. "We have to pull up the earth—"

"The Academy," she gasped at the same time. "It must all be in shambles—"

"Rage the Academy," Iravan said. He pointed at the bowl. "There are citizens trapped there."

"But sir! The architects in the Academy are our priority!"

"Your priority is what I fucking tell you, Junior Architect," Iravan snarled, his hands balling into fists.

She recoiled in shock. The others exchanged nervous glances. They had never seen him this furious; he had always been patient with the children. His eyes ran over them, his heart pounding; he had no time to explain, but all of them had been taught how architects preserved the ashram, how architect lives mattered more. Iravan's wrath coiled in him, for what he had been forced to teach them, for the fact that Naila made more sense to them now than he did.

He took a deep breath, trying to calm himself. "I don't care if the Academy is under," he said loudly. "The Academy is *empty*. But every citizen trapped in there embodies the potential of the ashram."

The children shifted on their feet. Exchanged nervous glances.

"Even if the Academy isn't empty," he went on, meeting as many gazes as he could, "all architects are protected by the permissions of the rudra tree. It's why none of you were sucked in." It was why his healbranch chair had retracted on its own, sensing the danger.

"But the citizens there are in peril. They can't traject. So, *you* need to do your duty."

The children murmured. Some of the older ones stood up straighter.

Naila's face grew considering. "What do we do, sir?"

"Follow my instruction," he said, gazing at them, this army of children, the youngest perhaps eight and the oldest barely a decade more. "Naila, arrange them in order of skill. Quickly, now; we don't have much time."

Naila moved away, calling out names. Grim but confident children strode forward, rolling the sleeves of their dusty robes back, readying for battle.

Iravan gripped his chair to keep from shaking.

The sungineered waterfall was filling the bowl quickly. The water was likely trickling down through crevices. Why weren't the Maze Architects responding to this? They ought to have seen the accident in the Moment. He tapped one of his bracelets, fighting dizziness, but the message didn't connect to Ahilya.

Sweat broke out over him. *This is normal*, Iravan told himself. *It's normal.* Rudra beads weren't directly connected to the Moment; they were a combination of sungineering technology and trajection, the first casualty if active trajection failed. And no architect had fallen inside the crater to sustain trajection. It was to be expected.

His fingers shaking, Iravan connected a message to the temple administrators, and to all the councilors. Why hadn't they reacted yet? Maze Architects ought to have been swarming the Academy—

"We're ready," Naila said, returning to his side.

"Enter the Moment," Iravan commanded. "Find the stars of the Academy."

All around him, the skins of nearly fifty children lit up. The Resonance flickered at Iravan—for a terrible second, he thought he had obeyed his own command, his visions split—then the feeling subsided, and Iravan panted, winded.

"What do you see, Naila?" he asked, gritting his teeth.

"The constellation lines," she gasped. "They're all broken."

"Maze Architects?"

"There are none here, sir. I—I don't see any other dust motes, at—at least not near the Academy stars."

Iravan swallowed. He had known this already. The citizens had been sucked in, but no architects were hurt, because the rudra tree had reverted to its base permissions. Until there were strong, active, unbroken constellation lines, the citizens would not be able to mold the architecture to their desire. Ordinarily, Disc Architects would have been patrolling the maze, repairing old constellation lines. The fact that this accident had happened at all—it indicated the absence of those architects.

"All right," he said, jaw tightening. "You're going to rebuild."

Shocked cries echoed around him. The children gazed at each other, flustered. They had never done anything as complex, not outside the protection of the practice Academy, not without careful supervision.

"Sir," Naila said quietly. "Won't you help?"

A deep shame seized Iravan. He imagined the Resonance flapping behind his eyes, terrifying. He saw himself tumble through the Moment, watched his Two Visions merge, watched as he trajected better than ever before with an ability that was *dangerous*.

Naila's question carried among the crowd. Scared faces regarded Iravan. They were so young. Some had their eyes closed; they had to have their eyes *closed* to focus on their second vision. That's how untrained they were.

I could do it, he thought desperately. *I could rebuild it alone without breaking a sweat.* The two paths opened behind his brows again, wavering in and out of each other for the first time, like they had been a single path all along. His hands trembled. *You don't have three weeks*, Bharavi said. *You have until your next mistake.*

"I'm right here," he said, swallowing. "You can do this. You're gifted and brave, and I'm counting on you."

Some of them stood up straighter. They nodded at each other.

"Ready, architects," Naila called out, pushing back her sleeves.

Iravan shifted his attention to the Moment. He didn't enter it—he didn't have to—he knew Nakshar's universe intimately.

"Generate your constellation lines. Don't traject them into any stars yet, but be ready. Naila," he added in a quieter voice. "Some of them won't be able to traject more than short lines. Make sure those are strong, then bind them together and wait for my command."

She nodded grimly. Simple vines grew over the brown skins of all the children collected.

In his mind, Iravan floated in the Moment. Citizens lay buried underground, potentially injured. He'd have to build around them without knowing where they were, a blind trajection liable to go awry. He'd have to brace the earth first, interlace roots bottom to top, lest all of the debris come crashing down. What if the plants attacked the citizens under his instruction as he did this? He was using untrained architects. Their constellation lines would not be as strong as a Maze Architect's. Even if the citizens used their desire to keep themselves safe, there was no telling if the roots would respond, not with weak constellation lines. It would take a concerted strength of will by the citizens to aid this amateur trajection.

The architects were waiting. Water pooled deeper into the crater.

"All right," Iravan said, taking a deep breath. "Naila, find the rudra star. Thirty-five degrees right ascension; the banyan exists in a state of tangled roots. Tie the first lines to it in a half-hitch pattern, but leave at least nine ends open."

She nodded, the tattoos on her arms articulating. Iravan tensed as a thick root grew from the edges of the bowl. His breath resounded in his ears, but curt instructions continued to pour out of his mouth.

16

AHILYA

Ahilya screamed, tumbling through darkness, but came to rest almost immediately. She gasped, and a paroxysm of coughing gripped her. Dust blinded her, entered her nose. Debris fell from above, hit her shoulder; she spasmed in pain and squeezed her eyes shut, throwing her arms over her head. Someone cried out; she heard more debris fall. She was back in the earthrage. She was going to die. This was her punishment for leaving Oam. The ground shifted under her, undulating, and she curled into herself, whimpering.

Eventually—it seemed hours—the sounds settled.

Ahilya wrenched open her eyes.

The dust had thinned. Far above them, an earth roof blocked any chance of escape. Others had tumbled in, most of them the citizens she had seen climbing down the ramp to the Academy, all coated in dust, coughing and sneezing. She had been far from them aboveground, but somehow the cave-in had rearranged itself. Now they crouched only a few feet from her.

"Is—is everyone all right?" Ahilya coughed, her tongue thick with dust.

They nodded in shock. Some said yes. A trickle of blood ran down Vihanan's forehead. A person Ahilya didn't know touched their scalp gingerly. Undoubtedly, they were all bruised—Ahilya's own elbow twinged, but there seemed to be no large injuries. Heart pounding, Ahilya searched Tariya's face. Her sister looked stricken though unhurt.

"Are there any architects with us?" Vihanan called out.

They all listened, their ears straining.

"I think we're alone," Ahilya said at last.

In the abrupt silence, the creaky writhing of thick black roots over the debris walls sounded unnaturally loud. The others began murmuring. Some tapped their citizen rings, their faces anxious.

"The architects will save us," Reniya said, hugging herself tightly.

Ahilya's eyes remained on the roots. Dread formed a leaden weight in her stomach. The way the roots moved, curling and writhing, reminded her of the jungle. In her mind's eye she saw again the way the bracken wall had disobeyed her. The delayed permission for her expedition, the protocol Iravan had followed in leaving Oam behind, and now this—

She and the others were safe, but how long would that last? Her stomach churned in growing terror.

Then something chilling seeped through her bamboo boots.

"We just have to wait," Reniya said, nodding to the others. "They are probably attempting rescue already."

Water.

"We can't wait," Ahilya cut in sharply. "We have to get ourselves out."

"Not now, Ahilya," Tariya began, frowning.

"We can't wait," Ahilya said louder. "Listen to me—"

"She's right," Vihanan said suddenly, sounding alarmed. He

stepped back and stared down. "Water. It's the waterfall. It'll fill this hole right up."

"It already is," the person with the scalp injury said in terror.

"We can't traject—" Reniya began, her eyes wide.

Her voice cut off. She started to choke.

For one bizarre moment, Ahilya thought she saw fingers curled around Reniya's throat.

Then she realized—not fingers. *Roots.*

The others froze, stunned.

Ahilya reacted first. "*NO!*" she screamed, and jumped forward.

She scrabbled at the roots even as Reniya choked, turning blue. *No*, Ahilya thought. *Not again. Not again.* Tears filled her eyes as Reniya gasped. Ahilya's fingers became bloodied. Oam flashed in her head, grinning wickedly. *Don't worry. I'll keep you safe. I'll keep you safe.*

The others began pulling at the root. Vihanan climbed a rocky ledge for better reach. Reniya's eyes fluttered and closed.

"NO," Ahilya screamed again. "Retract, damn you! Retract!"

To her shock, the root obeyed.

Instantly, it retracted, letting go of Reniya. The woman collapsed in Ahilya's arms, wheezing. The others stared.

Then Tariya scurried forward and pulled Reniya to her, making soothing sounds, cupping her hand to the rock where water flowed.

"How could this be happening?" Vihanan said, sounding shaken. "The ashram is designed not to hurt us."

Not us, Ahilya thought. *The architects.*

Iravan had admitted as much when he'd told her how Nakshar's original architects had coded the rudra tree. All those other times the city had protected citizens—the *Maze* Architects had done that. No architects had fallen in with them now—it meant the rudra tree had reverted to its original permissions. Ahilya didn't know as much about the core tree as Iravan did, but her husband had talked of it often: the rudra only reverted to its base state in case of failed trajection. *Trajection isn't as easy as it's always been*, Iravan said in her head. *There's an interference in the Moment.*

His bracelet weighed her wrist down. Ahilya took in the nervousness around her. She couldn't tell them what she knew. The city functioned on the desires of its people—to tell them trajection was failing would only result in panic; it would worsen their situation.

Another root reached across the citizens. They screamed and ducked as the root knit itself to the other side.

"What do we do?" Tariya said, panicked, as more roots whipped around them, hair-thin.

The water rose to their ankles.

A great powerlessness swept over Ahilya. She saw herself trying to hold the magnaroot nest together with her fingers. She saw herself on Nakshar's terrace, facing the bracken wall. She saw herself pound at the barrier, crying for Oam. None of it had mattered. In the back of her mind, she remembered how she and Dhruv had once been caught in a cave-in much like this when they had been little.

A thick root crept slowly toward them as though managed by a more skillful hand. It wove between Ahilya and the others, bracing itself to the far rock. Tariya steadied Reniya, tears sparkling in her eyes. Ahilya had saved the woman only to let her die again. She'd broken the roots only to—

"There is a way," she gasped out.

The others turned to her.

"We can't do anything about the water," Ahilya said, her voice louder. "But we *can* do something about the roots. These roots aren't trying to hurt us; they're trying to build a way out. That means the architects are rebuilding their constellation lines, just like Reniya said. They're trying to rescue us. We have to help them."

"What do we do?" Tariya asked again, her face worried.

"Focus your desire," Ahilya replied. "Focus it on one thing and one thing alone, for the roots to not hurt us."

Understanding flickered in their eyes. These people were not architects, but all of them were likely married to one; they had family who were architects. They knew how the city worked. What Ahilya had suggested—it was akin to landing protocol, when the combined desires of Nakshar's citizens had provided a catalyst to the Disc's trajection. The consciousness of the ashram, directed toward a singular purpose, had guided Nakshar to safety hundreds of times before. She and these people would have to do the same for themselves.

Around Ahilya, one by one, the citizens blinked their eyes closed, their faces frowning in concentration, even as thick roots wove between them. Ahilya closed her own eyes, her heart hammering. The water reached her shins, and her trousers stuck to her. She heard everyone's panicked breathing. A root touched her cheek and she flinched. Ahilya battled down her fear, her shame, her terrible helplessness.

There were many ways to endure, but all of them began at the same place. Desire. Heart beating fast, Ahilya focused her mind into a singular possibility. Survival.

17

IRAVAN

Under Iravan's instruction, the young architects of Nakshar reconstructed the maze.

Long minutes ticked by. Too long.

Terrifying thoughts circled him.

What was happening below in that cave-in? What if the citizens were injured? What if *Ahilya* was injured? Had he killed someone again with his actions? Had he killed *Ahilya*? Oam flipped in the air again, and Iravan watched himself let go of the boy. He watched himself ignore the call of his instinct to not enter the jungle.

Around him, the children shook like leaves in a storm. Iravan gestured to Naila to take the weakest off the Moment. His army was depleting. The children were tiring. None of them would last very long, and then everything they had built would collapse, burying the citizens if they weren't buried already.

The Resonance—or perhaps its memory—danced behind his eyes, tempting him. Iravan tensed. He'd have to do it. He'd have to enter the Moment. Nausea rose in him. He braced himself, gathering the shreds of his courage and judgement—

"They're here," Naila gasped. "Other dust motes. The Maze Architects."

Iravan's eyes widened.

Someone had seen his message—either the councilors or the administrating team at the temple. "Get these children out," he said at once, sitting up.

One by one, the little bodies around him relaxed, their lights winking out, their trajection vines disappearing. A few teetered to their knees. All of them appeared breathless and shaken.

"Naila, stay in the Moment," Iravan ordered. "Tell me what's happening."

The Junior Architect frowned and stared in front of her. "Looks like they're turning the roots we engaged into a platform. They're raising it, sir."

Relief so powerful burst through Iravan that he became lightheaded for a second.

The Maze Architects, with their resources in the temple, had directed his roots perfectly. They had repowered the citizen rings of those below, seen where the people waited, seen the broken architecture with sungineering holograms. They would be able to build around the citizens, ensuring they were safe, ensuring *Ahilya* was safe.

The waterfall in front of them drained to a trickle, confirming Iravan's suspicions.

The earth groaned and cracked open, chunks rendered apart like waves that undulated and lapped at his wheelchair. A chasm opened on the far end of the bowl and rippled in the beginning of a staircase, and Iravan thought abstractedly with a kind of dull anger, *Stairs. It is always fucking stairs.*

He skimmed his wheelchair forward carefully, the rocks under him flattening because of his desire.

Heart thundering, Iravan waited for Ahilya to emerge.

18

AHILYA

It was the hardest thing Ahilya had done.

Her mind slid from the task, unable to hold her desire steady. Hair-thin roots swept across her face, terrifying her. Once or twice, the whorls curled around her neck, almost lovingly, before moving on as though condescending to her broken will. Her helpless fear darted in her mind, trapped. Sweat dripped down her back.

Water rose to their knees, then their chests.

Ahilya opened her eyes, saw the panicked faces around her, heard their shallow breaths. Reniya swayed, as though about to slip below. Someone gulped, and the sound echoed around them. Vihanan began to cry softly. *I'm sorry*, Ahilya thought. *I couldn't save you after all.* Her heart weighed her down, obliterating her desire. In her mind, she saw Oam fall from the sky, heard his panicked voice asking what Iravan was doing.

Time slowed down. Ahilya lifted her trembling hand to her mouth, noticing the drip-drip in the cavern, the sweat that drenched her hair, the water level that kept rising. Eyes blurring, she reached for her sister, moving sluggishly through the cave.

The ground shook, ripples of water cascading.

Tariya cried out. Ahilya lurched—

Then the ground rose.

Ahilya staggered as the floor moved upward. The water level lowered, to her waist, her hips, her knees. Above them, roots parted and earth broke open, thin showers of debris raining down. She heard someone weep in relief; Ahilya nearly wept too. Her hand clutched her sister's tightly. Tariya trembled, and Ahilya drew her close, murmuring soothing sounds. More of the roof cleared, and then—

Blessed sunlight.

Steps formed along the edge. The others rushed for them at once. Ahilya waited, her eyes checking and rechecking every crevice. Was she leaving anyone behind? Did everyone survive? She counted them as they went past her, one, then three, then seven.

Tariya pulled her through at last, and the two emerged into the sunlight and collapsed on the grass next to each other, gasping. Ahilya covered her face with a trembling hand. Her other hand still clutched Tariya. She knew she should calm her sister down, but her entire body shook uncontrollably. Ahilya had trouble breathing herself.

It took her a long time to realize that both her citizen ring and Iravan's bracelet on her wrist were chiming insistently.

Ahilya rolled over and sat up. She had emerged at the lip of a bowl; it was all that remained of the clearing that had led into the Architects' Academy. The waterfall had stopped. On the far bank, Iravan leaned forward in his wheelchair, his posture tense. He waved and tapped at his wrist.

She tapped at her citizen ring, answering it. Iravan's face hovered over her palm.

"Thank rages," he rasped. "Are you all right?"

"I'm all right. We're fine—for the most part."

His hologram trembled; she didn't know if it was him or her own palm shaking.

Ahilya glanced around her, wondering if they *were* all fine. Tariya had sat up too. Her sister shook, and Ahilya could hear her nephew's soft voice. Tariya was speaking to Kush on the citizen ring, not Bharavi—why? Was the Senior Architect busy? Bharavi had never been too busy for Tariya before, and *this*—this ordeal—it would take a toll on her sister. Tariya was likely to lash out. She would need help.

It was as though Iravan had heard this thought.

"I'm sending architects over to you," he said. "To take you to the infirmary. To heal and counsel."

"What happened, how did this—"

"The trajection," he said. "It must have—I'm coming to you. I'll explain."

Ahilya glanced around her. The others were recovering too. Reniya had stood up and was massaging her throat. Vihanan was attending to the person with the injured scalp. Tariya had finished speaking with Kush and was looking over at Ahilya, her face withdrawn. Except for her sister, the rest were all married to mere Maze Architects. How much of what Iravan had told Ahilya was privy to them?

"No," she said, looking back to him. "I think—you should speak to the council first."

"Ahilya, no! I'm coming to *you*—"

"Iravan, please." She took a deep breath. "You know I'm right."

"But—"

"I'm unhurt. Trust me."

For a long moment, her husband's face was still, his jaw clenching and unclenching in indecision.

Then he nodded reluctantly.

"I'll return as soon as I can." His voice became quiet. "Ahilya, take care—trajection isn't—"

"I know," she said hurriedly, aware of the listening ears. "I know, Iravan."

He ran his hand through his hair; she glanced up to see the action across the crater. Iravan waved at her. Then the message disconnected and he was turning away in his wheelchair.

Ahilya looked away from her citizen ring to where Maze Architects in their brown kurtas and translucent robes hurried down a staircase. The temple—or perhaps Iravan himself—had already sent people to manage this crisis. The rest of her group rose on shaky feet, a couple of them limping. Tariya gestured to Ahilya and they joined the others.

"—was lucky," one of the Maze Architects was saying. "Had you not focused your desire at the same time as the architects were rebuilding, you would not have made it out safely. Whose idea was it to do that?"

The others turned to Ahilya.

The architect, a short man with a thin mustache, nodded, impressed. "I did not think a non-architect could be so astute about these matters."

"She's Iravan-ve's wife," Reniya muttered.

"Ah! That explains it." He turned away, gesturing to the other architects.

Irritation bubbled in Ahilya. After everything she and the others had endured because of an architect-made mistake, the casual insult of the statement burned her. She opened her mouth but Tariya placed a hand on her arm. "No, forget him. Look at what you just did—with all of us—"

"Look how little it mattered."

"It mattered," Tariya said flatly. "You saved us. Have you considered you're stronger when you want the same things as everyone else? That the ashram is stronger when we all want the same things?"

Stunned, Ahilya stared at her sister, momentarily robbed of speech. *People like us*, Oam said, *we don't know anything about flight and architecture. Survival is the council's business.*

Her mind spun. A thousand objections rose to her lips, about the council wanting the wrong things, about the justice *she* had always wanted for people like her, those who couldn't traject. That was what all her work was for. But, in the face of death, did any of Ahilya's ambitions matter? She had always dismissed Tariya's perspective before—the two of them had never seen things the same way—but was Tariya right? They all knew the power of their own desire, even Tariya—*especially* Tariya—who had struggles even Ahilya barely understood. Ahilya blinked and said nothing.

"Come," Tariya said. "Let's go to the infirmary." She grabbed her hand and followed the Maze Architects up the stairs.

Silently, Ahilya let herself be led away.

19

IRAVAN

The wheelchair impeded his speed, he wasn't allowed to traject, and the ashram was not back at full capacity.

All in all, it took Iravan nearly two hours to return to the temple. He noticed the passing scenery in flashes—the drying grass, the decaying trees, the popping bark that indicated just how poorly Nakshar was being maintained. Relief and anger throbbed in his head. He had been so close to trajecting. Even now, when he was not in the Moment, he could almost see the Resonance, familiar and tempting. What if Ahilya had not emerged? Would Iravan have let her die, rather than enter the Moment? Shame coursed through him; he was sickened with himself. If their positions were reversed, Ahilya would have damned the consequences and come to save him, no matter what.

Iravan entered the temple's extensive main chamber and immediately skimmed toward one of its honeycomb corridors, away from the rudra tree. He tapped at his bracelet and a wall opened to reveal a lush green elevator. The temple had recognized him; the elevator was already attuning itself to Iravan's preferred design, with bark opening to let in sunlight and a view of the open sky. How much trajection was being used to maintain this? Iravan saw again the earth cracking open near the Academy and Ahilya slipping through his grasp. His jaw tightened in anger at this magnificent waste. He emerged into a plumeria-lined corridor and skimmed to the council chamber.

Grown in the highest levels of the temple, the council chamber was a large, luxurious room with a massive mahogany table at its center. Thick, sweet-smelling moss layered the floor, and the walls were a tessellation of dark flowers. No windows were open—the councilors on their high-backed rosewood chairs had clearly been discussing sensitive matters—and a hologram hovered on the table: Manav smiling, a picture from before his excision. And beside him, Iravan's own face.

Airav smoothly waved the holograms away, and all five councilors turned to Iravan as he entered. Laksiya, who had been leaning forward, closed her mouth and sat back.

For one disoriented moment, Iravan saw himself sitting with them, in his own rosewood chair. He had once looked at Manav with the same expression the others had now, as though considering a dangerous animal.

Then Chaiyya spoke. "Iravan—what happ—"

"I take it you know what occurred at the Academy?" he asked, cutting in.

The others exchanged a guarded look across the table.

"We're aware," Airav said slowly. "The reports are back, and the affected citizens have all received healing. We intend to speak to them further, eventually." Airav's voice grew milder. "You were at the Academy at the time, weren't you?"

Iravan didn't bother to answer. They had been tracking his citizen ring since the investigation began; they must have seen him with

Ahilya, two dots on their map of citizens. Besides, he had sent them a message asking for reinforcements. They had certainly been involved in the reconstruction. Naila didn't know their dust motes in the Moment, but Iravan had recognized all three Senior Architects in the movement of the earth, the build of the platform, the way stonenut had created edges along the crater.

What would have happened had he been in the Moment himself? If he had trajected? *If there's any indication at all, the slightest rule-bending—*

Airav tilted his bald head, his eyes piercing behind his glasses, waiting for a response.

"How could this have happened?" Iravan asked. "Where were the Disc Architects?"

Airav tapped at his wrist and swept a hand so a map of the city hovered over the table. Several portions were yet under construction, with little access to water, sungineering light, or moving architecture. They were all citizen spaces, to be sure; architect spaces stood lush and complete—and anger stabbed Iravan's chest—at himself and Ahilya and the council, and the fact that this imbalance was not the fight he could fight right now.

"The Disc Architects are exhausted," Airav said, by way of explanation. "Their constellation lines are becoming weaker, and they're making mistakes. They've been taking shortcuts, unable to patrol the Moment as they should. This is to be expected. We wasted a lot of trajection energy with landing and taking off."

"Shift duty," Iravan began.

"—is a precaution; it's not a guarantee of rest—"

"—negates the possibility of architects becoming exhausted," Iravan completed, the same thing he'd said to Bharavi not two weeks earlier, when they'd landed in the jungle. "This is happening because trajection is getting harder. Because of an interference."

"You keep saying that," Airav said solidly. "Yet all three of us have examined the Moment and haven't found this *Resonance*."

"You might not believe my theory, Airav, but this is not about me anymore. If trajection fails, we'll crash into the earthrage. *We will all die*. It's an end to civilization."

"Calm yourself, Iravan," Chaiyya put in tiredly. "We're aware of the consequences—"

"Then take me off this ridiculous trial, and let me help."

"You *are* helping," Airav said coolly. "By investigating your theory."

Iravan's sarcastic laugh echoed around the luxurious chamber. "Without trajecting? Without examining the Moment?"

"No one," Airav replied carefully, "is stopping you from trajecting."

A charged silence greeted his words.

Iravan stared at the others. Kiana frowned, and Laksiya looked mildly curious as though waiting to see what he'd do next. But Bharavi—his closest friend and mentor—remained deadpan, her fingers tracing the notebook in front of her.

He could see in her face a warning. This was a trap, though an unsubtle one. *He gave you vine to see if you would crawl out of this pit or hang yourself.* Iravan's heartbeat grew faster. He licked his suddenly-dry lips. With an effort, he controlled himself.

"I misspoke," he said, inhaling deeply. "I only meant I shouldn't traject in my condition."

They continued to stare at him. Chaiyya shook her head at Airav, a secret message. The two had always been close, their relationship much like Iravan's own with Bharavi. Chaiyya would decide what Airav would. They would not listen.

Iravan turned to Kiana. "Did any of the other ashrams land during the lull?"

Senior Sungineer Kiana frowned and pushed up her glasses. "We haven't tracked that; it would take too much power. But I can show you *our* landing data."

She tapped at her own rudra bead bracelets and replaced Airav's hologram with a record of dust patterns in the jungle and the use of trajection during the last earthrage. Unlike flight, a command given by the uncontrollable earthrage—a command that every ashram obeyed—landing was a cost-benefit analysis. It was contingent on each ashram's architecture, its core trees, how much energy their Discs expended in landing and taking off again. Nakshar had chosen to land the last time because its architects had needed a reprieve.

"Exactly what is your idea here?" Kiana asked from across the table.

"I think the Resonance interfered with the magnaroot watchpost," Iravan said at once. "I want to know how many other ashrams registered the same."

Airav turned to Bharavi. "You were at the watchpost before landing. Did the magnaroot behave unexpectedly to you?"

"It relaxed like it should have when the earthrage stopped," Bharavi said, shaking her head. "It's why I called for landing."

"But it didn't sharpen for Naila," Iravan said, frustrated. In quick words, he told them what Naila had reported to him, about the stars of the magnaroot remaining unchanged, the very plant remaining still even after the flight alarm went out. "The Resonance is the only explanation—" he ended.

"It's not," Airav interrupted.

There was another silence, this one deeper.

Iravan frowned, glancing from one to another. Kiana blinked and looked away, rolling her cane in her lap. Laksiya cleared her throat, and her gaze trailed to Manav's empty seat.

And the full implications of Airav's words hit Iravan.

The holograms he had entered to see, Airav's unyielding demeanor, Bharavi's calculating silence—

He had told Ahilya that no one could interfere with the magnaroot at the watchpost, but the truth was an Ecstatic Architect could manipulate the rudra tree's permissions—it's what made Ecstasy so dangerous. The architect wouldn't even do so consciously. In Manav's case, less than five years before, a newly raised Iravan had caught Manav in the Moment, lashing a dozen constellation lines to the rudra star. Manav had held a whole conversation with Iravan in his first vision, clearly oblivious to what he was doing in his second.

It had been a tiny, unconscious slip.

That was the way of Ecstasy.

Until one day the slip became destruction and endangered all life in the ashrams.

Iravan's heart raced under Airav's scrutiny. His palms grew sweaty and he resisted the urge to wipe them on his kurta. His eyes fell on Kiana, the only person in the room who had any interest in believing him.

"Kiana, please," he said, his voice cracking. "Please—think about what I said."

Bharavi frowned. Airav merely shook his head.

But Senior Sungineer Kiana nodded again. "The next communication to all the sister ashrams is scheduled in a few days. I'll ask about their landing and flight logs."

"In the meantime," Chaiyya murmured. "Perhaps you should not overexert yourself, Iravan. You need to recover. That's the best thing you can do right now."

Iravan said nothing, his hands shaking. This was dismissal as clear as it could be.

The anger rose in him, sudden and sharp, tightening his throat.

Almost he retorted that he was still a Senior Architect, but before he could form the words, Bharavi stood up. "I call to adjourn this meeting," she said.

Airav looked from Bharavi to Iravan, then shrugged his acquiescence. The others nodded, and Kiana pushed back from her chair, steadying her cane.

Bharavi picked up the notebook in front of her and approached Iravan. *Come with me*, her lack of regard said. *I'll explain.*

For a second, Iravan didn't move. He wanted to shake them, force them to understand the Resonance, see the danger that he could see. But everyone except Kiana was muttering about other matters, Iravan clearly forgotten. Bharavi was already out the door; there was nothing else in there for him.

With a final, desperate glance at the Senior Sungineer, Iravan turned his wheelchair around and followed Bharavi out.

20

IRAVAN

"They've already decided my guilt." Iravan scowled outside the council chambers as they descended in the elevator.

"Yes." Bharavi nodded thoughtfully, studying her notebook. "I'm afraid so. You being at the Academy when that accident happened didn't help—"

"That's outrageous. I had nothing to do with that."

"Consider how it looks. Your first action after the event was to come here. Ahilya was one of those trapped citizens, wasn't she? Did you even stop to check if she was fine?"

"Tariya was one, too. Did *you* check on her, Bharavi?"

"Don't lash out at me, Iravan. I am not the one on trial for ignoring my material bonds. I spoke to *my* wife, and she said she saw you wheel away from yours."

"What else can I do to convince them?" he snarled. "Haven't I paraded around with Ahilya enough?"

Bharavi's eyes narrowed at his tone. "She's your wife. It shouldn't be hard. Don't you love her anymore?"

Iravan winced. "I—No—That's not what I—"

"Well?"

"Rages, Bha, of course I love her. I love her more than I can handle."

"Then why is it so hard for you to be with her?"

It's because you've taken away my choice, Iravan thought. That, in the end, was why he had stayed away from Ahilya for seven months. He'd been angry with her, yes, but it was more than simply that—it was a rebellion of his feelings, precipitated by the uncertainty of knowing whether his entire marriage had been a sham in the service of material bonds, or if he and Ahilya had only lost their way together. The need to preserve the bonds itched at him, like shackles around his neck. Questioning the bonds was unconscionable—they were the oldest architectural tradition. Yet as the two roads opened behind his brows, he knew the one that led away from Ahilya led to freedom, to clarity, to the discovery of the Resonance and all that lay unanswered.

He could never tell any of this to Bharavi.

Friends though they were, she still held a vote in the council. In rebelling against material bonds, Iravan would fail a condition of Ecstasy immediately.

Bharavi reached low and gripped his arm. "What is the problem, Iravan?" she persisted. "This isn't a rhetorical question."

"This farce—it isn't easy, all right?" he deflected.

"If you love her as much as you say, then where is the farce?"

"Loyalty is precious to Ahilya, and she'll stand by those who are hers through a hundred earthrages, even at the expense of everything else. You saw what she was like after Oam."

"And that's terrible because?"

"Because I can never measure up! Because I can never love her how she wants to be loved."

"Why in rages not, Iravan?"

"Oh, I don't know," he said scathingly. "Maybe it's because I must keep *so many raging secrets* from her all the time."

At this, Bharavi drew back, snapping her notebook shut. She stared at him, her expression grim, readying to chastise.

"She needs to know what excision truly is," Iravan said, before she could speak. "She needs to know the secrets I'm burdened with as a Senior Architect."

"No. You haven't earned the right to tell her that. The true nature of excision is deliberately shared with a select few. You'd be degrading every architect's dignity."

"Rages, Bha, she already knows there's more there than I'm telling her. She point-blank asked me. These half-truths and almost-lies—you don't know what it's doing to me."

Bharavi shook her head. "You haven't earned the right. Not yet. You made a healbranch promise when you became a Maze Architect, and you don't get to break it."

Iravan clenched his fists. "How many Maze Architects are in my position, Bharavi? How many of them are childless? You don't understand the burden of this—you, Chaiyya, Airav, all of you with children and the ability to share your burden with your spouses. My creative ways to love Ahilya mean nothing if I can't be honest with her."

"Don't make this about the conditions of the council, Iravan. Have you considered that if things were strong between you two, Ahilya would agree to a child?"

"Have you considered that the reason things aren't strong is because I have so many bloody secrets from her?" The image flashed in his head again, of himself and Ahilya, with two children who looked so much like her. Iravan's heart ached in sudden longing, but he waved a hand irritably. He had redirected Bharavi successfully, but this was not the conversation he'd wanted to have either, not right now. "I don't have the time for this," he said. "I have to convince the council I'm not an Ecstatic."

"I'm not sure you can," Bharavi said, observing him. "And I'm not sure you should."

Iravan recoiled, momentarily stunned.

The elevator came to rest, and Bharavi strode out toward a corridor that led to the sanctum. Disturbed, Iravan followed her, unspeaking.

The sanctum was a series of meandering corridors grown in the shade of a gigantic neem tree. Healbranch bushes, their white bones visible, flourished along the paths. As Iravan skimmed past, firemint and eucalyptus appeared and disappeared on the walls, his own personal healers. He had expected Bharavi to turn to his own suite; instead, she picked a path Iravan had visited only once, five years before. The Ecstatic ward.

He sped up, heart in his throat, as the healbranch bushes gave way to great glass windows. Beyond the glass grew individual chambers where excised architects... lived, Iravan supposed, though he would never choose that if it came to his own life. A dozen questions filled his mind. Why had she brought him there? What did she mean, saying what she had? He guarded his doubts, unsure what voicing them would mean, while Bharavi walked half a step ahead of him. They emerged into a circular terrace where an architect awaited them, accompanying a man on a wheelchair. The architect bowed, and then Bharavi and Iravan were alone, facing the wheelchaired man.

Iravan's throat filled with heat as he stared at the man who represented his greatest shame.

Manav was thin and short, and only slightly older than Iravan himself. His overlarge eyes blinked rapidly, and he rocked himself, holding a pale blue ice rose, a tremulous smile on his mouth. With premature gray hair, his dark brown skin lined and ashen, the excised architect looked disconcertingly like Iravan. Even their wheelchairs were the same.

"Why are you doing this?" Iravan burst out, unable to control himself.

Bharavi flipped open her notebook and glanced at him. "Ever since your trial, I've been working with Manav, trying to find you a better argument with the council. Do you recall what he was studying?"

Manav had been a poet-scholar fascinated with the idea of Ecstasy before he'd succumbed to it himself. It had been the man's specialization, one that had led to many advancements in the understanding and care of excised architects. Toward the end, before he was discovered as an Ecstatic, his poetry had become cryptic, and Bharavi had overtaken his research. She and Iravan had discussed the intersections with consciousness several times, but to bring it up now, at this time—

"What—" Iravan began, gripping his chair.

"It's not about the ashram or Ahilya," Bharavi said. "Those are not the conditions the council is assessing. The true reason they don't believe you regarding the Resonance is because of the third condition of Ecstasy—breaking the safe limits of trajection."

Of the three conditions of Ecstasy, the one concerning the limits of trajection was the hardest to detect. How could you distinguish real talent in the Moment from the dangerous overreach of an Ecstatic Architect? The rules architects abided by—trajecting only on duty, taking frequent breaks, adhering to shift schedules—all were designed as strict controls, but the truth was each architect was different, each with their own affinity to the Moment. An action that was safe for one was wildly dangerous for another. Even Senior Architects had little understanding of the limits of trajection. Iravan had always felt that the council's rules regarding safe trajection were like attempts to catch air with silk nets.

"What are you trying to say?" he asked, swallowing.

"You need to find the connection between your Resonance and Ecstasy."

Iravan's heart skipped a beat. "There *is* no connection between the Resonance and Ecstasy. You'd have me make a connection and prove to the council that I should be excised?"

"Everyone in the council already thinks you're in danger of Ecstasy," Bharavi said. "What you did while ascending the jungle was a clear indication that you're breaking the limits of trajection. The key to getting through this unscathed is not to ignore that but to spin it to your advantage."

Iravan opened his mouth to argue, but Bharavi was already facing Manav. She sat down on a bench that grew next to him.

"Manav, this is Iravan. Do you remember him? I've brought him here to join our conversations."

Manav said nothing but continued to smile. His eyes didn't even flick toward Iravan.

Undeterred, Bharavi opened her notebook, cleared her throat, and recited. "*A leaf contains a life / Paths form in wilderness / Two roads in sleep, and yet / I rouse to many / Balance is an unheard rhythm / Awakening occurs beyond time / We continue to live / In undying separate illusions.*"

"Dangerous," Manav whispered, and Iravan started. He had not expected the man to speak.

"*Two roads in sleep*," Bharavi repeated. "You meant the Two Visions, certainly. But what did you mean by *awakening beyond time*? Did you mean ahead of *our* time?"

Still smiling, Manav stretched a thin arm, his nails scrabbling for the book, but Bharavi placed it out of reach. Manav's hands continued to move; he made a tearing motion with his fingers, the action distorted and agitated, the smile still fixed on his face.

Iravan's flesh crawled. He tried not to stare.

"Shall I tell you what I think?" Bharavi said in the same gentle tone. "I think you were suggesting that it's possible to hold on to material reality while being in the state of Ecstasy."

"Bharavi," Iravan began warningly, but she held up a hand to shush him.

Of course, the theory of balance had always been postulated, but despite the ambiguous nature of Ecstasy, some things had been proved and proved again. Ecstasy was unbridled power; no architect could retain control over material reality while consumed by Ecstasy.

It was why the three conditions of Ecstasy existed, in the first place. Flawed though the conditions were, they were a council's best defense. Material bonds, dedication to the safety of the ashram, respect for the limits of trajection—these weren't moral endeavors; they were practical indicators of an architect's hold over reality. Without those, an architect was a ticking explosion, vulnerable to Ecstasy, intent on destroying architecture.

Bharavi trajected, and blue-green vines crept over her skin. A black, teardrop-shaped leaf appeared in the grass beside her, and she plucked it to hold in her hand. Veristem.

She leaned in closer to the excised architect. "Manav," she said. "When you wrote this… were you in Ecstasy?"

Despite himself, Iravan watched the other man intently.

Manav's fingers continued to scrabble toward Bharavi. He began to rock himself. Then, in a whisper, almost too soft to hear, he said, "Yes."

The veristem in Bharavi's hand remained still, unflowered.

Iravan stared at her in shock but saw only triumph in her eyes. Manav was telling the truth.

"Were you retaining control over your material world *while* in Ecstasy?" she asked, confirming.

Manav nodded but rocked himself back and forth harder.

"Why didn't you stay in that state?"

"Difficult, difficult," the man said. His fingers had fallen to his lap, and he began tearing the pale ice rose into shreds.

"Why is it difficult?" Bharavi asked.

But Manav didn't reply. He began to moan.

"Why is it difficult, Manav?" Bharavi asked again.

"The choices," Manav moaned. The ice rose in his lap was in pieces; the man grabbed his hair, appearing almost deranged. "*Incompletion—!*"

"Bharavi, stop," Iravan said, troubled. "He can't—Look at him—"

She glanced at Iravan, and for a fleeting moment he thought she looked furious at his interruption, but when she turned back to Manav, her face was gentler than Iravan had seen.

Bharavi dropped the veristem to the ground, where it was absorbed again by the ashram. She trajected, and the patch of grass they sat on bloomed with a hundred more ice roses.

Manav stopped moaning, his eyes wide. A smile wavered on his face. Bharavi began to speak about the ice roses then, their color and shape, their fragrance and their feel. Finally, she tapped at her rudra beads and summoned an architect on duty. A young man took Manav away.

Iravan waited until they were alone again, then turned imploringly to Bharavi. "Bha," he said, his heart pounding. "I'm not in danger of Ecstasy. You have to believe me."

She said nothing, merely stared at him.

"Out there in the jungle," he said, speaking faster, "when I was trajecting so brilliantly, I was thinking of Ahilya. I made the armor first for her; I created a path for her safety first, hers and Oam's, *before* I did for myself. I can't be an Ecstatic; I'd have lost my material connections if I were. I'd have forgotten Ahilya."

"Or maybe," she said, "you were doing what Manav did. You were holding on to your material reality while exercising the Ecstatic powers of trajection."

Iravan started to sweat. His skin grew clammy. A breeze flicked his hair slightly but he hardly felt it.

"It's only a matter of time before you're called to the Examination," Bharavi said. "And you're going to fail, Iravan. Because you *are* an Ecstatic. They will *excise* you."

Her matter-of-fact tone, more than her words, sent a chill down Iravan's spine.

"You have to give me more time," he said, his voice breaking. "I have another week."

Bharavi shook her head irritably. "You can protest all you like, but the council saw your amazing trajection in the jungle. The way to convince them is not to deny that you're close to Ecstasy but to show them that Ecstasy is not as bad as they think it is."

Iravan's eyes met hers. Was this a test?

"How can you say that?" he rasped. "You of all people, you who have studied Ecstasy."

"It's because I've studied it that I'm advising this," she said, sounding impatient now. "Look at what Manav just told us. This is something you can prove, unlike your theory of interference. I've been laying the seeds for this idea already with the rest of the council for years—you know this. Why won't you attack the problem from a different angle?"

"Because I'm already reaching for an unlikely explanation, trying to convince them there's an interference in the Moment. You want me to convince them that Ecstasy is desirable? They'll excise me without an Exam!"

"If you convince them of this, there won't *be* an Exam," she said, looking at him pointedly. "Controlling Ecstatic powers of trajection could be the answer we so desperately need. We wouldn't need sungineers to make a battery; with that much power, every architect would be a constant sustainable source of energy to the ashram. Think of the implications, Iravan. Our trajection would no longer be limited. Architects would become a race of superbeings. You could change the very definition of Ecstasy. You could show the council how Ecstasy is beneficial."

Iravan's head spun. "What you're suggesting is impossible," he sputtered. "When architects push the three conditions, it always, *always* results in uncontrollable power that damages the ashram. All our histories tell us this, and we've seen *evidence* of it."

"What you did in the jungle—"

"It wasn't Ecstasy—it was just exceptional trajection. I'm a talented architect, Bharavi. That's all it was."

"It shouldn't have been possible, and you know it. You're stating the same closed-minded drivel that everyone does, about Ecstasy being terrible—"

"Ecstasy *is* terrible," Iravan said. "It's the worst thing that can happen to an architect. Every beginner architect knows this."

"For fuck's sake, Iravan." Bharavi stood up and began pacing the terrace; Iravan had never seen her so angry, so scared. "You're not a beginner anymore; you're a Senior Architect, a councilor of Nakshar. You're meant to *define* the rules, to *create* them. Your independent thinking above all else is why you were promoted to the office. You want to escape excision *and* demotion? This is the only way. I'm trying to save you. Why won't you listen?"

Iravan ran his hands through his hair, clutching at his locks.

"A week ago, you said I had to be careful, and now you're saying I should break the rules. You said you'll call me to an Exam at the slightest provocation, and now you tell me that Ecstasy isn't bad after all. What are you trying to tell me, Bharavi?"

"I'm trying to tell you that you need to listen to your own moral intuition," Bharavi said. "That, above all, is what it means to be a Senior Architect. It's a balance between the individual good and the greater good. It's deep, unerring trust in the judgement of your own conscience. It's understanding the costs and consequences of power."

"I don't have the luxury of introspection. I'm on a clock!"

"You're missing the point—"

"No, I'm not," Iravan said, slamming his fists into the arms of his wheelchair. "You stand there, telling me to listen to my moral intuition, making it sound so easy, but it's not. All my life, it seems my role should have been clear. Born with the ability to traject, so become an architect, protect the ashram, be a good husband. Well, I let myself be guided by these truths, but the harder I try, the more I lose. No matter what I do, it doesn't feel right, and I can't see a path!"

Bharavi stopped next to him and sank down on the bench that had grown for her. "All architects are expected to pay a price—*that* is the cost of survival—the charge of power—"

"It's too huge—It never ends—I've already lost so much."

"What have you lost?"

"I don't know," he said, his hold on his hair painful. "I thought you'd help me—"

"Answer the question, Iravan. Is it Ahilya? Your clarity as a Senior Architect? The balance you need to maintain?"

"Yes, those, but no—"

"Then what?"

"I don't—"

"What have you lost?"

"I know what you're trying; it won't work—"

"*What have you lost, Iravan?*"

Iravan hurled himself into the Moment; his visions split and he trajected harshly.

"*I've lost myself*," he roared.

The grass around them shot up, converting into spiky, thorny cacti, a forest of lethal spines barely missing the two of them. Iravan breathed heavily, his chest ragged, the peace of the Moment sullied by his turbulent emotions.

Bharavi froze, staring at him, at the glowing vines over his skin.

He stared back, his heart thumping in his chest.

In the Moment, the Resonance fluttered in front of him, mirror-like, mercurial, waiting.

Slowly, very slowly, without taking his eyes off Bharavi, Iravan released his trajection. He departed the Moment.

The Resonance disappeared. The blue-green light winked out of him. On the terrace, the trees retreated with a slick whisking sound and became grass again.

Horrified by what he'd said, by what he'd done, Iravan sank his head into his hands. The two paths glimmered in his mind—paths that he now knew had haunted him all his life. He had found himself on that fork at every step, at every instant, and never picked correctly even though the paths had come again and again. What was he becoming? What was he *doing*? There was no absolution.

"This person who I am," he whispered. "This… *Iravan*. I don't know who I am anymore—I don't know what I'm supposed to be. I look inside me, and all I see is an eternal fall in a place where the rest of me ought to be. I try to fill that hole, with being an architect, a husband, a councilor, but it only grows wider, insatiable. The truth is, I don't care about the ashram, I don't care about Ahilya, and a part of me is convinced that caring about any of this is pointless until I understand who I really am."

The horror of what he was admitting sank into him, but he couldn't stop.

"You're asking me to balance known impossibilities," he whispered, "but I'm struggling to balance even my simplest identities."

His chest heaved up and down. He was aware of how he had laid himself bare for Bharavi, given her all the ammunition she needed to excise him and leave him to be worse than Manav. His entire body trembled in terror and release.

When Bharavi touched his shoulder, Iravan flinched like she had struck him.

Bharavi didn't say a word. She stroked his back in gentle, soothing rhythms, over and over again like he was a child.

They sat together on the terrace in the falling dusk, letting the silence grow between them.

21

AHILYA

Dawn broke outside the window, carrying the scent of cool air through cracks in the wood frame. Inside the library alcove, Ahilya bent over one of Iravan's books, brushing sleep from her eyes, fighting to focus on the minuscule words.

The books were old, likely some of the oldest in the architects' records. The paper was hard bark, with each word etched onto it through some ancient carving tool. Dark ink still glistened as though it had only just been calligraphed. How had they done that? There was some mixture of resin in the ink to retain its substance, but architects no longer used those methods, not with sungineering tools so easily available.

Ahilya rubbed her face tiredly. Her mind was wandering. She had spent the last three nights poring over these books. With the end of Iravan's investigation looming, there was no telling how long the records would remain in her possession. One way or another, the result of the investigation would decide Iravan's fate, and with it her own. If he were demoted, Ahilya and Dhruv's nomination would be forgotten, their very professions in peril. If he was not, the two still needed to present their theories, and Ahilya, more than Dhruv, had to make up for lost resources.

She turned over a heavy page, squinting in the dim light of the phosphorescence. A large sketch covered the center leaf of the book, inks of various colors glittering over the bark. Ahilya drew back, her eyes narrowing in thought.

The drawing depicted the jungle during a lull—yet this was no ordinary jungle rebirthing itself. Instead, it flourished and thickened, with lush trees rising and impenetrable bushes curling in all directions. Every now and then, a clearing grew between the trees—early ashrams with tiny stick-figure people within them.

Ahilya's eyes absorbed the image, for a moment seeing it for only its beauty. The picture was like frozen trajection. In the image, Ahilya could very nearly see movement itself, a herd of rhinos crossing a river, a pack of hyenas scavenging deer, carrion birds leaping for the kill, and leopards lolling in the mud. Other images emerged under the tracing of her fingers: a giant tiger-yaksha creeping toward an ashram, barely visible in the foliage; a lone elephant-yaksha as tall as the tree it uprooted; a massive falcon-yaksha circling the skies.

This picture was proof of an era when earthrages had been few and far in between. An era when there must hardly have been rages at all—instead, mere quakes and tremors, barely different from a lull, allowing for ashram life in the jungle. Yet knowing that, what had Ahilya really learned?

Everyone in the cities knew that life had originated in the jungle, that flight had been a necessary invention, a miracle brought about by the architects to save humankind from the ever-increasing earthrages.

Certainly, the picture showed scores of jungle creatures alongside yakshas, but that was likely creative license. Ahilya had always considered the yakshas to have *evolved* from the jungle creatures;

the similarities were far too many to ignore. But evolution took generations, *lifetimes*. It was a slow maturation where the yakshas would have been in their early form instead of this representation that showed them fully grown alongside their immediate ancestors. Valuable though the book was, it answered nothing. How had the yakshas survived? How many were there now? How were they related to their now-extinct ancestors? How long did they live? Iravan had helped her, but she was no closer to resolving any of the questions she had set out to.

Her husband had come home every night for the last three nights ever since the incident at the Academy, bearing more records from the architects' archives. They'd discussed the investigation and her nomination, yet Iravan had scrubbed his face with his hand last evening and stopped theorizing to blurt out an apology.

"Ahilya—" he'd said abruptly. "Our fight—I shouldn't have walked away. I shouldn't have *stayed* away. I… I've lost sight of who I want to be."

Ahilya had been so shocked, she hadn't replied. She had known this already; there was almost no need for the explanation. They'd sat in silence while phosphorescence sparkled around them and firemint flourished, its scent intoxicating.

Iravan had finally looked up from staring at his unsteady hands. He'd kissed her knuckles and bid her complete her thesis quickly, then returned once again to the sanctum.

Ahilya could almost feel his lips on her hand now. Her trembling fingers brushed over the page. She leaned forward, forcing herself to banish the image of him and study the picture instead. Her eyes focused on the early ashrams. Vines curled around trees, with giant fences cordoning the ashrams away from the jungle proper. She studied the postures of the stick-people as they went about their lives, backs turned to the jungle.

There was something here, in the manner in which the artist had depicted the ashrams....

According to the book, architects had been forbidden from entering the jungle. It had been because of the yakshas, but the creatures had barely been mentioned, all information about them condensed into one telling passage. Ahilya had read it so many times, she knew it by heart.

Deathlike, the yakshas' consciousness is unbreachable; unnatural creatures who must be avoided. Trajection is unviable; destruction, inevitable. Never would an architect remain themselves; desire overwrought. The jungle remains forever treacherous. For greater a consciousness, greater the danger; and in Ahilya's head, the text merged with Iravan's voice. *I don't detect consciousness in this creature. That's impossible, you know. It means that the yaksha doesn't exist. That it isn't alive.*

She drew back, staring outside the window.

Dawn had converted into a rainy day, drops of water plinking against the glass window. The alcove transformed, more heat-bearing plants appearing, and outside, children in their wet-cloaks had arrived to shriek and jump in pools of mud.

Ahilya watched them unseeingly, her fingers tap-tapping against the bark book. In her mind, she was back in the jungle, sketching the wolf-yaksha's fangs, drawing the large eyes of the gorilla-yaksha, tying the new tracker around the elephant-yaksha.

The text was typical of an architect record that went little beyond trajection and its uses, but Iravan had been unnerved on coming face-to-face with the elephant-yaksha. His fear had clearly mirrored the very fear that poured through these pages. Was there a deeper reason the architects had feared the yakshas? Had the creatures been once hunted, sought after and destroyed?

The senseless injunction in the book, the calculated indifference to the jungle, Iravan's reaction, all of it was linked somehow to a hidden truth. Ahilya could feel it in her gut. The yakshas had been erased almost as thoroughly as the non-architects. Yet knowing this, she was no closer to the council seat than she had been before. There was nothing in these texts about a habitat—the one thing that counted, the *only* thing that counted, which would indicate survival in the jungle.

Besides, even if she found proof of habitat, it would be no easy task.

If this was what the architects had been taught—if this was what they believed—then flight must have come as more than a simple miracle of survival for them. It would have been a means to escape the fearsome jungle, once and for all. Ahilya's attempts went against ancient architect values, a reason why she had been denied the records, why her expedition had not been approved until the last minute. She had always known she had been fighting against great odds, but to see the depth of it, the sheer magnitude of resistance... *This thing you're trying to do*, Tariya said. *Change history... at what cost?*

Ahilya slouched back on her chair, her heart sinking. If she had any hope of building her thesis for the council seat, she needed Iravan. She was certain he had the missing piece to this story. Their fates had become unexpectedly intertwined ever since their bargain, but Iravan had genuinely been curious each time he'd visited and discussed her archeological ideas. It had reminded her of their years of courtship, and she glanced around the library alcove now, her memory flooding with warm days of lying together, other lovers and concerns forgotten, limbs entangled, books spread over the floor.

The books now had proven too obscure—but perhaps she could try her luck with Dhruv. Her hand spread out, and the wall opened in response to her desire. Ahilya withdrew the broken tracker locket from the expedition, then stood up, stretched, and exited the alcove.

The day had broken, gloomy and cold, and dressed only in her thin kurta and trousers, Ahilya hurried down the stairs toward the main hall of the fig-tree library. With the weather being the way it was, the library was already full, with beginner architects in their gray uniforms slowly ascending the shelves, non-architect citizens arriving with their children in the play area, and competitors for the council seat, Umit and Shreya and Rana, bent over their own research.

Ahilya reached the main floor, tapped at Iravan's rudra bead bracelet, then wove a path toward the solar lab. In minutes, she had emerged onto a wide-open terrace, rain now falling steadily.

For a second, she stood, confused.

Then a wall on the far end of the terrace opened in a creak of bark, golden light glinting from within it. Ahilya hurried to it, and the wall closed behind her as soon as she entered.

Despite years of friendship with Dhruv, Ahilya had never been inside the solar lab. A vast open hall with cloudy sunshine streaming in through vaulted glass ceilings, the solar lab had always been restricted. If it weren't for Iravan's rudra bead bracelet, she'd never have found it now.

The lab was astonishing. Giant blue holograms floated everywhere in approximations of wheels, funnels, and tubes. Sungineers clustered around them, expanding and minimizing the images, studying them from different angles, chatting about how matters in the ashram had not yet returned to normal. More sungineers sat at windows, but as Ahilya looked closer, she noticed those weren't windows. They were bio-nodes: massive devices of which Dhruv often spoke, diagrams flickering on their glassy screens. Like gigantic versions of the solarnote tablets, the bio-nodes gleamed and hummed. Rays of dim sunlight ricocheted off them through the lab.

None of the sungineers paid Ahilya any mind as she strode in. Iravan had assured her of that yesterday, when she had asked about visiting the lab. "They tend to bury themselves in their work and forget their surroundings," he'd said. "Keep an eye out for Laksiya, though. I don't want her to know you have the bracelet."

Discreetly, Ahilya crossed the main hall and climbed a winding staircase. Each floor floated on its own, unsupported by the one below, like leaves on a plant, with smaller staircases branching out like stems. Ahilya checked Iravan's bracelet for Dhruv's whereabouts and found him on the highest floor. Her oldest friend sat hunched alone in a vast chamber, staring at a bio-node. Unlike the other chambers, Dhruv's office was covered with gray slabs of stone interspersed within the grass. A dozen bio-nodes whirred and clicked along the walls, no sungineers attending them. Barren and dreary, the chamber seemed like it was not a part of Nakshar at all.

"Go away, Umit," Dhruv called out irritably. "I've reserved this chamber today."

"I could go away," Ahilya offered. "But I'm not Umit."

Dhruv turned in surprise. "How in rages did you get in?" he asked by way of greeting.

Ahilya approached closer and sat down next to him. She pulled back her kurta and showed him the rudra bead bracelet.

Dhruv's eyes grew wide. "That's a Senior Architect's—Wait, *Iravan* gave this to you?" He whooped in sudden glee, leaning forward to examine the bead. "Was this because you told him he needed to help us? Ahilya, you mad, wonderful thing. I can't believe you did this."

"You can't say a word to anyone. He could get into trouble."

The sungineer waved her warnings away with a hand. "This is amazing. Think of what you can do with this. Access the architects' archives, all their historical records, all the secrets they keep even from sungineers. I had to *fight* to reserve the invention chamber today—damned Umit nearly stole it, saying he needed it to chart communication with Kinshar—but with a Senior Architect's permissions—"

"Dhruv," Ahilya interrupted. "You heard about the incident at the Academy, didn't you?"

"Yes—it was to be expected—the Maze Architects are exhausted, and there have been other incidents since then of architecture not working as it should—" The sungineer glanced at her face, then cut himself off. "Rages, Ahilya, you weren't *there* when it happened, surely?"

Ahilya searched herself for lingering anguish. Her hands didn't shake. Her heart beat steadily. It had been the same ever since the event at the Academy, ever since she had finally gone to the infirmary and faced the place where she had first met Oam. *I feel better*, she thought in wonder. How had that happened? It was as though she had redeemed herself by nearly drowning. *You saved us*, Tariya said in her mind. *Look what you did.*

Dhruv was still watching her in concern, and Ahilya's brow creased at the solicitousness.

Iravan had known when to withdraw his sympathy.

In all the three days of visiting her, her husband had never once forced his kindness on her. Instead, he had distracted her as she'd needed to be; he had remembered that she was more than her pain. In the end, that had healed her.

"Iravan thinks it wasn't exhaustion that caused the failure at the Academy," she said, ignoring Dhruv's question. "He thinks something interfered with trajection, the same thing that disrupted the flight alarm. Could this have anything to do with the spiralweed?" The plant was dangerous to trajection; for all Ahilya knew, it could break constellation lines in the Moment, too.

Dhruv shook his head. "It's not possible. The timings don't coincide with the alarm. Besides, the spiralweed is still in the deathbox, right?"

"Yes, in my archives within the library. What does that have to do with it?"

"A deathbox traps consciousness. Deathboxes create a barrier around the Moment, essentially creating a separate pocket Moment. When the forcefield is activated, then anything inside the deathbox doesn't show up in the normal Moment and only responds to trajection *inside* the box. I don't see how the weed could affect what happened in the Academy."

Ahilya frowned deeper. "How do you intend to get it out, then?"

Dhruv circled his pen around. "The inventions room is one giant deathbox—just without the glass boundaries. It's a death*chamber*. It's where we test all our battery experiments—we need to be certain the batteries don't depend on trajection. I haven't activated the forcefield yet; that's why the bio-nodes still work in here."

Ahilya considered this. She could not have borne it, she knew, if her actions jeopardized the ashram; the thought had haunted her for days, ever since Iravan had spoken of the interference in the Moment. What else could interfere with the universe but the possibilities of another plant, uninvited and unseen? The spiralweed was still dangerous, but if sungineering worked the way it did, then perhaps the plants she had brought back for Dhruv were not to blame, not for the difficulty in trajection.

She withdrew the broken tracker locket from her pocket—the real reason she had come there—and dangled it between her fingers. "Can you see—" she began.

"Do you think you can extend my permissions?" Dhruv asked at the same time, leaning forward, his eyes still on Ahilya's bracelet. "A few more days in the invention chamber, and I should have enough to satisfy Kiana about the beginnings of a battery to ward off a transfer."

Ahilya shook out her sleeve, covering the rudra bead. "Are we just going to make a habit of breaking rules now?"

"He gave it to you to use, didn't he?" Dhruv retorted.

Ahilya wasn't so sure. Iravan had given her the bracelet as a challenge and an invitation, to meet him halfway in their attempts at reconciliation. His action was tied somehow to the nomination he had agreed to; her husband did not do anything with a singular purpose. This bracelet was no ordinary gift. It was a test of trust. It was a measure to see how Ahilya would treat her power, how well she deserved the council seat.

"Can you see if anything on the tracker survived?" she asked, trying to change the subject. "I think it was damaged in the escape—it's no longer chiming."

Dhruv plucked the tracker locket from her. He connected one end to his bio-node and another to a spare solarnote tablet lying on the desk. "It's your bead," he said, ignoring her question. "But if you're unwilling to use it for our work, maybe Iravan has already seduced you."

Ahilya recoiled. "How can you say that?"

"Have you even noticed," Dhruv said, meeting her eyes, "that you've started to use the word *ashram*?"

Stunned, Ahilya said nothing. He was right. After years of resisting it, she had unconsciously incorporated the word back into her lexicon. When had that happened? Was it because of Iravan? Her husband had grown in her mind, a presence at the back of every thought, every private conversation; he had *returned* to the days when they had been together, and he had done it so quickly, without her notice.

Her eyes met Dhruv, and her friend shook his head. "I know you're thinking of forgiving him," he said.

"I—He's trying, Dhruv. I haven't decided—"

The sungineer snorted. "Don't take too long or he'll decide for you. He's a charmer, Ahilya."

"I know."

"You vowed never to associate with an architect because of your parents, you could have wed any of your other lovers, Eskayra or Amna or Jai but you still ended up marrying him—"

"I *know*, Dhruv."

"Then stop lying to yourself," he said. "You were clever, attaching our nomination to your condition for helping him—but Ahilya, both you and I know your real motivation was to save him from the council."

Shock rippled through Ahilya. "How do you—"

"I worked it out," Dhruv said dryly. "I recognized the rudra bead he gave to Naila. The rest was obvious. It's his head on the line personally, isn't it? Tied to the investigation? They think it is his failure."

Ahilya stared at him. Dhruv was her oldest friend, they'd grown up together, but he had never fully taken to Iravan. For him to have such sensitive information on her husband…

"Rages, Ahilya," Dhruv said tiredly. "I won't tell anyone. But you're becoming like him, for all that you want him demoted."

"I don't want him to be demoted," she said, still reeling. "I want him to get his priorities right. The council has confused him—there was a time when he'd choose his beliefs against the rest of the world, everything else be damned. But all he's done since his promotion is forget himself, forget who he is."

"As you say," Dhruv said, turning back to the bio-node where Ahilya's data appeared. "Just remember—demotion is as likely as excision, and neither is likely when it's Iravan. Either of those would be an embarrassment to the council."

He was right, she knew. Iravan was popular—too popular. His career trajectory was nothing short of inspirational. When it took most Maze Architects a decade to even be considered for a position in the council, Iravan had been inducted after a mere four years of service. Besides, the council would not easily relinquish an *architect*. Twenty years before, there had been no sungineers on the council at all. The architects may have agreed to non-architect representation, but Ahilya did not think their magnanimity would extend into excising one of their own so easily.

The solarnote Dhruv had attached to her tracker locket blinked. He disconnected it, muttered, "Looks like the data survived," and handed it over to her without another word.

Ahilya bent her head to study the information. The solarnote hummed, a newer model than the one she had lost in the earthrage. She swiped at the glassy screen and frowned. The tracker had stopped chiming in the jungle; she had expected it to be broken—but this, what she was seeing now—

"I think the data is warped," she said.

"It's not. I checked."

"But it doesn't make any sense."

Dhruv looked up. He took the solarnote from her, adjusting his spectacles. He frowned too, swiping at the glass. Then his eyes met hers, the excitement and shock startling in them.

They'd both observed the same thing. The data was continuous without break during the last five years. But no sungineering equipment could work without trajecting energy. If the tracker hadn't been around trajection for a decade, then what—out there in the deadly jungle—had been powering the sungineering device?

"H-how is this possible?" Ahilya stuttered.

"I think—I think it has to do with the tracker..."

"But it didn't chime—"

"The chiming was only an enhancement—It's no surprise it broke—"

"But—"

"Don't you see?" Dhruv said. "The tracker didn't just feed off Nakshar's energy; it fed off the energy of all the other hundreds of ashrams too." He stood up, abruptly energized, and pulled Ahilya to her feet, clearing a space. "Watch."

Clutching the tracker locket, Dhruv tapped at his bio-node, then waved the data toward the floor. A hologram flickered: flight orbits of nearly five hundred ashrams, and a line indicating the elephant-yaksha. Dhruv expanded the view, and he and Ahilya stood within the hologram, surrounded by elliptical lines. Ahilya turned her head to watch a miniature Reikshar float past her.

"You see?" Dhruv asked, pointing. "There's always some city above the path the yaksha traveled. At any given point, the tracker was charged by a city's energy."

Ahilya studied the intersections he indicated. He was right. Multiple nodes connected the yaksha's path and the ashrams' flight trajectory. The tracker could have charged itself at each node, never running out of power. It seemed like amazing luck. And that made Ahilya suspicious.

"We flew above the yaksha too, about two years ago." She pointed at the hologram, where Nakshar intersected with the yaksha's path. "If we charged its tracker, why didn't we sense the signal from the tracker? Why did we only hear it a couple of days before the expedition?"

"That," Dhruv said, pushing up his glasses, "is an excellent question."

He stared at the silent locket in his hands, his face brooding.

"Besides," she continued, "why did only this tracker transmit? Why didn't any of the others—from the tiger-yaksha and the gorilla-yaksha?"

"I think it has to do with this little beauty," Dhruv said, tossing the tracker lightly in his palms. "No two trackers out there are identical. Each time you took one outside, I made enhancements. I'd need to deconstruct this gem to see what exactly it is capable of."

"You don't know what your own inventions do?"

Dhruv shrugged. "Inventions are rarely in our control. We put things together and they take a life of their own. Did you know that sungineering's original purpose was to somehow use the sun's energy to replace trajection in flight? Instead, we ended up finding a way to *harness* trajection. Our entire occupational history is a series of accidents."

He fell silent and sat back down, still studying the tracker in his hands.

Ahilya turned to the hologram. Tiny shapes floated around her, each ashram on its own trajectory. The data was all there. For the first time, she'd be able to study patterns in the yaksha's movements—but even at a glance, she could tell this would only lead away from her hypothesis. If this data was accurate—and she was not certain it was—then it indicated that the elephant-yaksha had moved during the storm; it had survived the earthrage not because of shelter or a habitat of some kind, like she had hoped, but because of its sheer size. She had remembered how the elephant-yaksha had thundered past her during the earthrage; it had been headed somewhere—toward a habitat, she had hoped, but this data did not corroborate *her* theories; it only confirmed what the architects had believed for so long. She turned to Dhruv so he might deny this deduction, so he might offer another viewpoint; but the sungineer still studied the tracker locket, an expression of reverence on his face.

Ahilya cleared her throat.

Dhruv jumped. He had forgotten her presence, but now he smiled widely. "This tracker is incredible, Ahilya, even if I say so myself.

Our current sungineering technology isn't equipped for long-range recharging using other ashrams' trajection. But somehow, this little beauty was able to charge itself using the ashrams' energy from the *jungle*? If it has such a long range, then there's a way to extract that technology."

"And use it for a battery?"

"More than that," he said. "It could change the economics of our world. All ashrams share trajection by transferring architects based on trade agreements. But if sungineers replicated the way this tracker charges, there'd be no need to physically transfer people at all. We could charge our equipment remotely. We could buy and sell trajection. Trajection could become an amazing commodity."

"It's already an amazing commodity," Ahilya said softly, but she could see the implications of what Dhruv said. Trajection was scarce and rare. In transferring architects, ashrams shared it because they had to, not because they wanted to. "This could change the world."

"Precisely," Dhruv said, his eyes bright. "Sungineers would never be forced to replace a transferring architect; we'd be able to figure out the best way to use trajection while remaining in our own cities. If I follow this lead, I might not need to worry about making a battery at all. I might not even have to use the spiralweed."

Ahilya raised her brows. She'd known the spiralweed was a desperate attempt. The weed fed off trajection, which indicated it had an inherent way to store trajection, but Ahilya had seen how dangerous such a technology could be. Despite Iravan's push for it in the council, a battery was risky; it opened too many possibilities of having architects just to farm them, a couple of dangerous steps from enslaving architects altogether. If Dhruv made his case for the nomination by denying the battery and using this warning, he'd stand an even greater chance at the council seat—especially with any technology that made long range communication possible.

She turned back to the hologram, to the evidence of her own diminishing efforts at the council seat. Outside the lab, rain pounded harder, the steady patter combining with the whirrs and hums of the unattended bio-nodes. Her fingers lightly touched the hologram and it flickered, ready to respond to her shaping. Ahilya molded it idly, her heart heavy. The data indicated her own failure, one she could not afford to ignore.

Could the architects be right about everything? Ahilya had nothing substantial to support her habitat theory—it had always been a shot in the dark, constructed out of wishful ideas and reading between the lines. Some of the records she had seen, both from architect and non-architect histories, had indicated a time right before the discovery of flight of abandoned attempts to survive in the jungle. In the end, that was all Ahilya had to go on, the merest whispers, so obscure that she could suddenly, startlingly see why everyone had thought it impossible.

It was never a bad theory, Iravan said quietly in her mind. *But I think you'll find the records of the early architects are right.*

Was it true? Had her life's pursuit simply been a fool's errand? Ahilya's cheeks heated in embarrassment, in how flimsy the roots of her research really were. She had always thought there was more there, a reason the non-architects and their histories had been so thoroughly erased, but perhaps those histories had failed to endure because of their inherent irrelevance to survival. Not an active erasure but a quiet one, brought about by their own worthlessness. She stared at the hologram, her stomach dropping in dread. The hologram flickered under her wandering fingers, rearranging itself.

Ahilya blinked.

"Dhruv," she said softly. "There are gaps in the tracker's information. Look. What are those?"

"It's when nothing was charging the tracker," he replied, distractedly.

"No, see here. Other ashrams were above the elephant-yaksha. Yet somehow, the tracker didn't charge. Why did that happen?"

Dhruv shrugged. "It *is* experimental. Maybe it died or took time to restart."

"I don't think so. There seems to be a pattern."

The sungineer said nothing, still too taken by his own invention. Ahilya pushed him out of the way and began to rearrange the hologram with her hands. She compared the yaksha's movement with the length of the earthrage. She ran calculations from Nakshar's distance. She even moved the image upside-down, hoping for an epiphany, but apart from making her feel foolish, the image did nothing.

This was the worst part of being an archeologist. It was the implicit loneliness of the work, the inability to make anyone else care. Ahilya's heart ached in dull pain. If only she had Oam with her. The boy had an uncanny knack for seeing patterns. She should never have taken him into the jungle, the architects had been right to fear it; it had only brought her grief that had settled deep and true, and she thought again of the image she had seen only a few hours before, of the jungle laid out in the book, once glorious, now treacherous—

Ahilya straightened suddenly, her heart pounding. The image in the book flashed in her head again, and her eyes widened. She extended a hand, pawing the air. There was a method she hadn't considered at all. How could she have been so blind?

Dhruv set down the tracker and looked over at her.

"There's a pattern here," she said, her voice breathless. "All along, we've been looking at the yaksha's trajectory from Nakshar's perspective in flight."

"It's the only way to measure anything—we always know where *we* are. We are our own point of reference."

"Yes, but what if we looked at it from the jungle's perspective? Do you have any maps of the jungle?"

"Not really," Dhruv replied. "The jungle changes all the time, and our lives are in the sky. But the sungineers did divide the planet into latitudes and longitudes to record our landing sites. It's an archaic method. We don't use it for anything else."

"Can you layer that into this image?"

Dhruv pocketed the tracker and fiddled with the glassy screen of the bio-node for several minutes. Then, in a series of waving gestures, he superimposed the jungle's data onto the hologram floating on the floor. The gaps in the elephant-yaksha's path blinked and settled.

"Hm," Dhruv said. "You're right. These gaps where the tracker was uncharged are too uniform. I wonder if..."

He trailed off and sharpened the image for clarity. He reduced the flight orbits of the ashrams. He dissected the yaksha's movements so that multiple lines blossomed over the image.

Finally, he stepped back, his eyes wide behind his glasses.

"Bloody rages," he swore.

The hologram charted the elephant-yaksha's path all over the jungle planet. Yet all the gaps in the tracker converged on a single point. Each time the elephant-yaksha had traveled to a specific area in the jungle, the tracker had stopped charging despite a trajecting ashram hovering above it.

Ahilya stared at the hologram, her heart pounding in her chest. "Something in the jungle blocked trajection from reaching the tracker," she breathed. "Something *interfered*."

She turned to stare at Dhruv, and she could see her own astonishment and understanding mirrored in his face.

Iravan was right about his theory of interference.

Ahilya was right about her yaksha habitat.

And they had just found proof.

22

IRAVAN

Iravan stretched his legs, jogged on the spot, then stretched his legs again. "This will do," he said, appreciatively.

The two healer architects on duty, Geet and Raksha, nodded silently. They were Chaiyya's wards, Maze Architects in competition with each other for the vacant council seat. Chaiyya had undoubtedly assigned them to Iravan's recovery to test how they would restore even the worst trajection injuries. As far as Iravan was concerned, each of them deserved to win. It was too bad Ahilya was going to get that position—if he had anything to do about it.

"Take care, Iravan-ve," Geet said softly. "Any overexertion might bring you back to the sanctum."

The words were laden; for a second, Iravan wondered how much of his investigation and the looming threat of the Examination of Ecstasy was really a secret from Maze Architects. But there was no ill intent in Geet's face, nothing to indicate duplicity. He nodded, bade them return his things to his temple suite, and made his way out of the sanctum on a slow jog.

His legs still felt wobbly. He had started the morning on his healbranch chair, but several hours later, Geet and Raksha had finally pronounced him ready. As he picked up his stride, the strength returned to his muscles and lungs. What would the council make of his recovery? Chaiyya would receive immediate reports, that was certainly what Geet's comment had been about, but Iravan hadn't seen any of the other councilors for three days, not even Bharavi.

A part of him still froze in terror when he remembered what he'd said, what he'd done in the Ecstatic ward. Had Bharavi told the others of his uncontrolled trajection? Had they voted for an Examination? As the Examinee, Iravan's presence was unnecessary to their vote, but so far, none of his rudra beads had flashed, commanding him to the architects' orchard. He had been careful not to traject ever since then. He hadn't even entered the Moment. Apart from what the action would indicate to the council, it horrified him to think of how the Resonance had been waiting for him. Iravan still remembered how it had flung him outside the Moment; how merging with it had allowed him to ascend from the jungle. The memory sent a chill down his spine.

He lengthened his stride as the temple gave way to one of Nakshar's wide tree-lined boulevards. His recovery in the sanctum, the outburst in the Ecstatic ward, even the failure of trajection in the Academy—all of these were distractions. Iravan had mere days before his presentation to Airav about his theory of interference, a presentation that would decide his future as a Senior Architect. He had collected as much information as he'd needed, from Naila and the sungineers, but now it was time to assimilate what he had, and for that he needed Ahilya.

A smile tugged at his lips as he thought of his wife, the sheer intelligence of her, the uncanny manner in which she could piece together disparate data. Last night's apology had hardly been adequate, but something had healed between them. A deep desire to be with Ahilya, to hold her and kiss her, filled Iravan. He dashed through the city in the gray drizzle, past the forest bazaar, and the rose bushes. Ahilya was likely in their library alcove, either there or the solar lab. He would wait for her. He would ask permission to return home. She had suggested it that day in the Academy, and they would mirror the days they had once lost, find the happiness they had once inhabited.

Rain had begun to pour in earnest by the time Iravan reached the library. Iravan sprinted through it, his clothes soaked with heavy droplets. He took the stairs up the fig tree two at a time. The library's main hall had covered itself with bark to keep out the deluge. Iravan strode past children building patterns out of the foliage, past beginner architects hunched over wooden desks, and non-architects thumbing through shelves, all the way to the heights of the tree. He found a young woman pacing the short platform outside his alcove, wringing her hands nervously.

"Naila," Iravan said, startled. "What are you doing here? Why aren't you at the Academy?"

The Junior Architect jumped and turned. "I was hoping to talk to you, sir."

Iravan tapped his citizen ring and waved a hand in front of the doorway. The wall parted. "Come in, then."

Ahilya wasn't in their shared alcove, but the chamber had retained its low ceilings and sparkling phosphorescence, appearing terribly intimate. Iravan willed the architecture to change.

As Naila followed, the ceiling grew higher. A window opened overlooking the rainy playground, and a carved wooden desk grew in the center with loud cracks. Iravan circled the desk and sat down behind it. He gestured Naila to the seat on the other side and fixed her with an enquiring look. Was the Junior Architect there to speak about the council seat he had trained her for? Iravan hadn't voiced his intention to nominate Ahilya yet, not even to Ahilya herself. Yet the grapevine flourished in architect circles. He studied Naila, unsure of how to break the news to her, how she would take it, how it could affect her trajection.

The Junior Architect came straight to the point. "I wanted to thank you, sir. You saved my life."

Surprised, Iravan tilted his head.

"I know I did the right thing at the watchpost," she continued. "Everything worked how it should have. And I saw how you trajected from the jungle. It was an accident with Oam. You tried to save their lives. Just like you did at the Academy."

Not knowing how to answer this declaration, Iravan remained silent. He had spent months mentoring Naila, yet this was the most personal she had ever been. Besides, he didn't deserve the gratitude. He'd let go of Oam. His dispassion at the time still frightened him.

Naila shivered, evidently remembering. "I could never have done that kind of trajection. Trajection was hard for me *inside* the ashram."

Iravan leaned forward. "Trajection was hard for you? When did that begin?"

"It feels like forever. At first, I thought it was just me, but then the last earthrage…"

Iravan considered this. Here was proof, incontrovertible and firsthand. Would Airav believe him? If Iravan asked Naila to report on his behalf, would the man think it underhanded? Bharavi had already stressed how little his theories mattered, and Kiana had confirmed that only proof from other ashrams would suffice. What discussions were occurring between the councilors? After the last time, Iravan hadn't dared set foot in the council chambers, angry and humiliated. Even if he passed the Examination of Ecstasy, would he ever earn back their respect?

He looked up to see Naila watching him. He had forgotten her. "Thank you," he said. "Is there anything else?"

The Junior Architect fiddled with her rudra beads. She had grown very quiet, perhaps feeling his anxiety.

"Naila?" Iravan asked gently.

"That wasn't the only reason I'm here, Iravan-ve." The Junior Architect glanced up, held his gaze, then dropped her eyes back down.

"Yes?"

"The thing is... Right before you arrived before the expedition, I'd mentioned to Ahilya that trajection was becoming harder. But I don't think she understood the implication. Pardon me for saying this, Iravan-ve, but she doesn't appreciate architects very much, and I don't think she understands your position."

Iravan's entire body stiffened. Was this rivalry? If Naila had somehow learned he was planning to nominate Ahilya to the council seat, perhaps this was her way of ensuring he didn't carry his plan through. Still, regardless of her motivation, if Naila thought it was appropriate to seek him out and utter these criticisms about his *wife*, he had been a far worse husband to Ahilya than he'd feared.

The Junior Architect blinked at his silence.

"It's just that I don't think she understands how difficult it must have been for you," she continued earnestly. "Out there in the jungle. You must have been doing your best."

Iravan's jaw clenched. A bitter taste entered his mouth. It took all of his control to not bunch his palms into fists, but he could do nothing about the thickness in his throat.

He had only himself to blame. Naila was a mere Junior Architect, a *child*. She had seen him crush Ahilya's authority along with the rudra bead key before the expedition. She had seen their fight in the temple. Resentment pooled in his stomach like acid, but it wasn't directed at Naila for what she was saying; it was directed at himself and the council for what they had made him, for what he had become.

Naila seemed to wilt under his hardening gaze. Her voice became desperate. "I don't mean to say it's just her. It's non-architects in general. Ever since the council opened up to sungineers, it seems everyone has been questioning us. We work very hard, and normal citizens don't understand."

Still Iravan said nothing. He felt deeply a wish to be somewhere else, away from this girl revealing to him the kind of man he had become, the kind of *Senior Architect*. Was she a symptom of what was occurring in the Academy? Each councilor provided a specific expertise that dictated the manner of life in the ashram, a specific direction that impacted the manner of civilization. Bharavi studied Ecstasy. Airav watched the influence of tradition. Chaiyya oversaw an architect's health. And Iravan—he had studied consciousness. A subject he had picked while he had still been in the Academy. It was why he'd *asked* for the responsibility to preserve the Academy; he had wanted to nurture young architect minds like he had once been nurtured.

In that—as in so many other things—he had failed.

The weight of fatigue settled heavy on his shoulders. The silence grew between them.

Finally, Naila shuffled her feet and dropped her gaze.

"Sorry," she muttered. "I suppose I shouldn't have said all that."

"No," Iravan agreed quietly. "You shouldn't have."

The Junior Architect said nothing. Her shoulders grew stiff, her posture sullen.

Iravan sighed. "Naila. Look at me."

She glanced up, her eyes defiant and mutinous.

"I need you to understand something," Iravan said. "I should have said it sooner. What I did—by taking your place in the expedition—it was disrespectful to you, it was disrespectful to Dhruv and Oam. But it was *especially* disrespectful to Ahilya."

"You saved my life," she said. "If I had gone—"

"You probably wouldn't have survived; that's true. But it doesn't excuse what I did. A citizen refused to give me what I wanted, so I took it by force. I know you're on a career trajectory to becoming a Senior Architect one day, but that's not how any architect is supposed to behave, least of all one in my position."

"Our protocol tells us to preserve architects before non-architects—"

"Yes, but your conscience must guide *when*. That protocol was designed—well, it was designed for many reasons, not all of them good. If you're to one day become a Senior Architect, you need to understand that the position is a sharp balance. The fact remains—being born with the ability to traject doesn't make us better than the citizens."

Naila stared at him.

A slow smirk grew on her face, rich with familiarity.

"With respect, Iravan-ve," she said in a low voice, holding his gaze. "I'm not sure that's true. Are those really *your* words, and *your* way of thinking? I'm not sure you believe all this yourself."

"Then perhaps you need to spend more time in the Academy as a student and not as a teacher. Do not presume to *know* me, Junior Architect." Iravan stood up sharply, not bothering to keep the anger out of his face. The wall behind Naila unfurled into a doorway. He gestured toward it. "I accept your gratitude. Next time we chat, you'd do well to work on a better apology. You may go now."

Naila didn't move, still seated in her chair and fiddling with her bracelets.

Iravan raised an eyebrow.

"There was something else, too," the Junior Architect mumbled. "Something I thought would help you. For your investigation."

Despite himself, Iravan paused. He sat down slowly. "What did you find?"

She glanced up at him furtively. "It's regarding the basic equation."

Iravan gestured brusquely for her to go on. The basic equation indicated how a plant's existing state of consciousness converted into a new state of consciousness with the release of a raga. Naila had been studying the mathematics of energy conversion in an attempt at the council's nomination.

"I think the basic equation is wrong," she blurted out.

He resisted the urge to shrug. "I thought I taught you that the equation is imperfect. It's impossible to measure the loss of consciousness."

Naila shook her head. "Pardon, sir, but it's not impossible. I've checked and rechecked the mathematics. Every trajection releases not just a new consciousness and a raga but an unknown by-product. I've been calling it Nakshar's Constant."

"Very dedicated, I'm sure."

"I'm an architect of Nakshar, first and foremost, sir," Naila replied stiffly.

"A valuable identity, and one requiring more exploration, if you don't mind me saying. You can confirm that every trajection releases this… Nakshar's Constant?"

Naila nodded. "I've checked it with individual architects. Three things happen when an architect trajects. A plant changes. A raga emerges. And so does Nakshar's Constant. I thought," she said, adding tentatively, "that Nakshar's Constant might be the Resonance you're seeking?"

Iravan considered her words. He had only felt the Resonance recently. If this Nakshar's Constant *was* a constant, why hadn't he or anyone else noticed it before? He studied Naila impassively, the way she sat poised on the edge of her seat, her youthful face full of eager anticipation and hope. He noticed now what he hadn't before: Naila's lips slightly parted, her hands squeezing her forearms, her fingers trailing to her hair every now and then.

And he remembered the tension he'd sensed between her and Ahilya in the Academy.

A jolt of shock ran through Iravan. He couldn't believe how blind he'd been.

"Thank you for telling me," he said quietly. "I'm going to transfer your mentorship to either Airav or Chaiyya. I suggest from here on you bring your ideas to them."

Naila blinked in shock. Recognizing the dismissal at last, she stood up and hurried out of the alcove. Behind her, the wall closed.

The moment she disappeared, Iravan buried his head in his hands, shaking. The Junior Architect hadn't come to the library to thank him or share information about her convenient new discovery. She hadn't come because of a rivalry brought about by the council seat. She had come there to proposition him.

He had a sudden, bizarre need to laugh, but even as he smothered it, he knew it was edged with hysteria. Shame so great engulfed him that Iravan felt sick in his stomach. This was how the ashram saw him, then. This was how far he had fallen. Architects were trained to see opportunity, and Iravan was used to ambitious Maze Architects flirting with him, but to be so brazen? Naila had presumed to do so, despite his long marriage to Ahilya, despite his position, because she had identified a possibility of success. His morality, his scruples, all things that defined him had vanished in light of his treatment of Ahilya. *He* had wrought this behavior. *He* had created it. What a fool he had been.

A great revulsion for himself grew within Iravan. Ahilya had been right all along. He had been blind to his faults. His secrets, his machinations… He had failed his wife utterly, deeply, by opening up even the possibility for such an action, no matter how inadvertent. His body began to tremble. His vision blurred. The sheer weight of self-loathing threatened to bury him.

The two paths opened in front of him again, but he was trapped on the fork, never knowing if the choice he was making was right. *Release me*, Iravan thought desperately, a plea he knew not to whom. *Release me from this imprisonment.*

For a long time, he sat by the desk, holding his head, trying to contain his shivering.

Finally, Iravan took a deep breath and straightened. The alcove had changed again, back to the model he and Ahilya shared, with its low ceiling and jasmine buds on the walls. He gazed at it, his heart beating fast. Archival designs of the ashram retained memory, but memory was a matter of strength and endurance; ashram plants transformed based on a citizen's desire.

If the ashram remembered the happiness he and Ahilya had once shared, if it was so relentlessly portraying it in the library, then it meant only one thing. Despite their troubles, both he and Ahilya wanted to reconcile. *We're not done*, Iravan thought. *Not yet.*

He turned to the wall behind him, testing. How much did Ahilya trust him? Had she rescinded his permissions?

The foliage separated to reveal a cubbyhole. Iravan's heart began to race, some of the weight lifting from his shoulders. He still had access to Ahilya's personal inventory. She hadn't changed it; she hadn't forsaken him. Relief burst through his chest like a bird in flight. He gathered his wife's notebooks and sungineering equipment in his hands, feeling the smooth bark, the rustling pages, these things she valued and trusted him with. How could he have doubted her competence as a potential councilor? She *cared* about Nakshar. In picking Naila, all Iravan had cared for was his own reputation.

A white cube, smaller than his fist, clinked together with the rest of her paraphernalia. Iravan paused, dropping the other pieces back into the cubbyhole. He turned the opaque glass cube in his hand curiously.

A deathbox. Why did Ahilya own a deathbox?

The dials were positioned at being activated, but he couldn't see the golden shimmering forcefield. Either the box was damaged, or whatever was inside was small enough to warrant a very tiny forcefield.

On an impulse, Iravan flicked the dials to deactivation. He opened the deathbox.

He had a moment's glimpse of a leaf shaped like a bubble no larger than the digit of his thumb.

The next second, the plant exploded, expanding to a hundred times its size, overtaking the library alcove.

Iravan's eyes widened in shock.

Spiralweed.

23

IRAVAN

The alcove reacted instantly.

The window overlooking the playground shuttered into stony bark. The walls, ceiling, and floor hardened. Leaves, phosphorescence, and delicate jasmines disappeared along with the tiny glowglobes; the alcove became armor-like. Iravan was plunged into immediate gloom. He jumped to his feet in fright.

His mind raced. A dozen thoughts chased each other.

This was spiralweed. It wasn't allowed in the ashram. A single leaf could destroy Nakshar. Sabotage? Same as the Resonance? What could he do? He wasn't supposed to traject. Trajection would worsen the situation. Spiralweed *gorged* on trajection. It first attacked where the power was weakest. That's why the sungineering lights had disappeared. The next would be the rudra bea—

Iravan gasped. He reached to tap at his bracelets to alert the Disc, but a thin vein had whipped out of the bubbling mass to wrap around his arms before he could move. More cords darted out, binding his legs, his feet, climbing up his chest, strangling his neck.

He choked, his eyes bulging. The spiralweed lifted him clean off the floor. His body arched, the cords pulling him back.

His panicked eyes darted around the alcove. The spiralweed had grown monstrous, its thick tentacles writhing all over the alcove's walls and ceiling. It would break through the alcove's paltry defense in seconds. *The children*, Iravan thought in horror. *The children in the library.* In the Moment, the stars were surely winking out. Destroyed forever like he had destroyed the magnaroot. Why weren't the Maze Architects doing anything? What *could* they do?

Choking, he flexed his forearms and twitched his fingers, trying to tap on a rudra bead bracelet or his citizen ring, but the vine only tightened and jerked him back, throttling him. No one heard his muffled cry of agony.

One by one, thin tentacles reached underneath his kurta to his rudra beads, snapping the bracelets and necklaces and ring. Black beads fell to the floor, snatched up by the weed.

No, he thought, tears in his eyes, whether for the beads, the ashram, or his life, he couldn't say.

The spiralweed smashed against the alcove's cage. He watched, unable to scream, unable to thrash. This was how he'd die, then, paralyzed because of indecision, failing to protect the ashram, estranged from Ahilya. Screams of hysterical laughter echoed in his head.

His vision started to blur.

Iravan began to grow woozy.

It wasn't even that painful anymore.

He drifted and remembered.

The feel of Ahilya's skin, her eyes, her smile, her touch. Their wedding day, as he placed a flower garland around her neck; overcome with emotion as he kissed her; the feeling of rightness as he vowed to traverse together with her or not at all. His delight at receiving his rudra beads, each bead a promise. His fathers and mother, alive in Yeikshar, so proud when he was picked for a transfer, an honor for one from his native ashram. On and on they came, and he thought in wonderment, *Look at that. Life does flash before death.* His mind roared in laughter.

Still the memories came. Iravan a toddler, stumbling as he ran. Iravan kicking in the womb asleep, unborn. Iravan a woman in the jungle, screaming for her friends to take cover as another earthrage hit. Iravan, a man again, shorter and lighter-skinned, making ashrams fly for the first time in history. On and on, the lives he'd lived.

He was a boy. He was a woman. He was a father, a sister, a mother. He was born, he lived, he died. Each time the ability to traject manifested itself, sometimes used, sometimes untrained. He died in an earthrage, he died in strange ashrams, he died surrounded by family; each time, he died unlearned, alone. He loved freely, looking for completion. He lived a thousand lives, more, many more. At the end of all, he failed, his separation a chasm, because he—they?—had made an irrevocable mistake. Lives rushed through him, and in between—

He floated, surrounded by the silvery-molten mirrors of the Resonance.

Ever present, it engulfed him, reflecting all his births, all his deaths.

Ever patient, it waited; each time, he returned.

Eons passed in the winged echo.

He didn't reach, and the Resonance didn't either, yet both came closer with every life.

When they touched, it was in homecoming.

Their vision opened; *see*, they thought, and he saw

himself in the library alcove, trapped in frozen animation, rudra beads crumbling, spiralweed grabbing splinters

Nakshar, a flat city in the sky, innocent of its doom, existing in ignorance

the earthrage below, annihilating everything, unseen, misjudged, unwatched

and beyond

themselves in their true form *s-h-a-t-t-e-r-i-n-g*; and Iravan screamed in useless sorrow; a warning, a lament, a wail.

He cleaved open their heart.

The Resonance cradled him in its winged flaps.

His vision focused as all his lives, all his memories, drew down to *this* point in time. He screamed in rebellion, in fury and agony, and the spiralweed choking him in the library exploded into tiny shards.

Iravan dropped to the alcove floor on his knees.

Power surged through him—not the power of trajection—this was something else, familiar, intoxicating.

He looked up at the spiralweed, his teeth bloody. Light had returned to the alcove, but it was light *he* generated, his skin glowing blue-green.

The spiralweed changed its shape.

In a blink, its bubbling monstrous mass retracted. A thick trunk shot up from floor to ceiling as though the weed was bracing itself against the smashed alcove. The spiralweed hardened. Sharp, flat leaves grew over its trunk like lethal blades.

A part of Iravan watched in shock; he had never seen a plant change its form so completely. Another part registered in grimness: the weed was preparing to attack, only now truly, and *he* was fragile, *he* would not live.

The spiralweed trunk spun, unwrapping.

A bladed leaf shot out at Iravan, missed him by inches, and embedded in the wall behind.

Iravan moved, unaware he was moving, as more blades shot out from the trunk, axe-like, whipping past his hair, slashing his kurta, narrowly missing his skin. He smashed into a wall, then ducked and spun, falling on all fours.

The power still surged through him, but he didn't know how to use it, and a roar of anger sounded in his mind.

Help me, he growled, and the fury intensified.

His limbs reacted of their own accord. His body lifted, off the floor again, but this time as though invisible wings were trying to fly him. His legs kicked; he heard the enraged roar again. Iravan stiffened, his heart thundered, and his body flipped in midair, avoiding another bladed leaf. Trapped within himself, he watched as whatever had roared spun him, *flew* him, inelegantly, avoiding the slicing blades.

He couldn't do this forever.

Iravan reached to enter the Moment, to traject, the only power he knew.

Instead, he realized that he was outside the Moment.

He hadn't noticed, but his second vision had been an infinite velvety blackness, and the entire universe of the Moment had become a tiny, starry, undulating sphere. He gathered the strange energy coursing through him, patterns of blue-green tattoos lighting his skin, and he screamed, unleashing the power into the globe of the Moment, to destroy the spiralweed, destroy the Moment, destroy it all—

A third power knocked him aside before he could release it.

His stomach dropped.

He spun in the blackness of the non-Moment.

The third presence radiated next to him—not the Resonance—something else entirely—its shape rearing, making ready to kick.

A stream of golden light emerged from the third presence, shooting past Iravan into the globe of the Moment, and Iravan knew instinctively, this thing, this *ally*, had been fighting the spiralweed all this while. This was why the Disc Architects hadn't reacted yet, why the stars of the Moment hadn't winked out, why no one in the ashram knew of the attack. This ally had been forming the lone line of defense.

He imitated it, concentrating his power into a similar stream of golden light, merging with the ally's. The two streams connected, thickened, their combined power shocking—and enough.

In the library alcove, the spiralweed exploded into minuscule shards, scraping Iravan's skin like a million paper cuts.

He fell to the floor.

The ally spun and crashed into him, thrusting him out of the non-Moment. The scream of fury in his mind changed to one of betrayal; he glimpsed the Resonance flapping angrily in the darkness—

Then the Resonance and the scream were both gone.

Iravan's mind returned fully to the library alcove; all but his normal vision collapsed.

He lay facedown on the floor, a ringing in his ears. His face was wet. His throat had thickened with emotion.

He knew he had separated again, and a wave of regret and loneliness washed over him. He didn't bother to stop the tears that still wet his cheeks. He tried not to think.

A long time after, he scrambled himself to a seated position.

His tears had dried, but nausea gripped him. He cradled himself, his eyes closed, his heart thundering so loud, he could almost feel the cloth of his ripped kurta vibrate with every beat.

Broken images returned—senseless images. The spiralweed blades attacking, him leaping—and then before all that began, something, *something*. Iravan sat there, shivering. How long had that lasted? Minutes. It had to be minutes. No more than five since he'd unlocked the deathbox.

He opened his eyes. The library alcove had returned to the archival design. He was bleeding through his cuts—but no, healbranch had sealed his wounds. The threat had passed, unnoticed. No one would have heard the battle, not with the hardening of the room before. The Maze Architects were oblivious too, he was sure. Iravan crawled toward the center where the last of the spiralweed flickered, its single source leaf charred and blackened but still alive.

Trembling, he reached into the Moment and trajected a complex permission that was ordinarily stored in his rudra beads. He extended a shaking hand to the wall, and the ashram reacted; the wall secreted a new deathbox, and he grabbed the white glass cube as it emerged out of the foliage.

Iravan snatched the still-alive spiralweed from the floor. He thrust it into the deathbox, twisted the dials to activate the forcefield, then sat back against the wall, his chest heaving.

He lifted his arms and they were bare as though he had never worn any rudra beads. He only saw the deep welts from the trajection in the jungle. For the first time, Iravan considered those scars looked not like vines but something else…

He dropped his head into his hands. He had never before felt such a sense of rightness, of certainty, as he had on uniting with the Resonance. The power, whatever it was, must work like trajection, Moment to non-Moment, trajection to… some kind of… *super*trajection.

It hurt to think. He stopped.

For a long time, he sat with his back against the wall, his knees drawn up to his chest, the deathbox on his lap, his body trembling.

Finally, after what seemed like years, Iravan straightened.

He picked up the deathbox. He commanded the ashram, and a path opened straight from the alcove down to the playground, where furious rain still cascaded. Gathering himself, Iravan walked slowly toward the solar lab.

24

AHILYA

"I can't believe you're even considering this," Ahilya said, throwing her hands up. "Are you suggesting we don't tell Iravan we've found proof for his theory of interference?"

"I'm saying we think about it," Dhruv answered. "What do we know of his reaction to this?"

"You might as well ask what do we know of Iravan and whether we trust him."

Dhruv gave her a meaningful look. "Do we? Trust him?"

Ahilya sputtered in indignation. Almost she said, "He's my husband!" but after all that had happened, the argument rang untrue in her own head.

She and Dhruv were both on their feet. Dhruv had collapsed the hologram from the expedition and was now setting up the equipment for his battery. Wooden desks grew in the hall, a jumble of optical fibers and rudra beads on them. A dozen strange plants appeared on glass petri dishes. Ahilya recognized wormroot, poison ivy, and firethorn, plants she had brought into the ashram during previous expeditions, now harmless and heavily sedated, appearing little like they had before. Dhruv strode over to the corners of the room, fiddling with something in the close-cropped grass. A golden forcefield shimmered, then disappeared above and below the invention chamber, creating a deathchamber larger than the room.

Ahilya tried to make her tone pacifying. "What do you think is going to happen? What do you think Iravan will do if we tell him?"

"It's not about what he'll do, Ahilya. It's about opening a door." Dhruv arose from the last corner, brushed his clothes, and began pacing. "You're inviting him into your research—*our* research. The minute you tell him about this, he'll want to see the technology we're using; he'll want to examine the expeditionary equipment. How long before he finds the illegal plants we've been smuggling into Nakshar?"

"That's a bit far-fetched—"

"It's dangerous. He's a Senior Architect. The reason I wanted you to keep the spiralweed hidden was so he didn't find it in the lab. Now you want to lead him to it?"

Ahilya shook her head. "It won't affect what you're doing, Dhruv, this is *archeology* we're talking about. We don't have to tell him about the battery, but he has missing pieces that can help me—knowledge about the fear of the jungle, and similarities between the extinct creatures and the yakshas, and now with this interference—it could change my entire study. This has nothing to do with you. The spiralweed and the tracker aren't connected. One does not implicate the other."

Dhruv threw up his hands. "Of course they're connected. We can't just flagrantly walk in and announce our discovery. We have to cover our bases; we have to make sure everything illegal we've ever done is buried. Most of all, we have to destroy the spiralweed before the nomination."

"Who knows when we'll have the chance to do all this, Dhruv!"

"Ahilya, if we tell him about this now, it will be *his* victory. But if we wait until official nomination, then we'd receive the credit, we'd outdo all other candidates. That's what we set out to do. That was our goal!"

"So, you want to wait for *three months*?"

"Why aren't you more excited for *us*? We both have a chance now—I with long-range communication and you with your yaksha habitat. Rages, we have such a fantastic chance now at that council seat, we might as well be in competition with *each other*. This is a victory for all non-architects. Why won't you see that?"

"Because Iravan is on a clock. What happens if we don't tell him and he never discovers this? Or if we wait until after his trial? Suppose they demote him? Suppose they *excise* him?"

"So?" the sungineer challenged. "I thought that's what you wanted. You've had a problem with him being a Senior Architect, being an architect at all. Might it not help your marriage if he's just a regular person? Isn't that why you agreed to help his investigation?"

"No—That's never—No—"

Dhruv gave her a pitying look. Ahilya knew what he was thinking: that Iravan had already charmed her. A heaviness settled in her stomach. Disturbed, she closed her mouth.

Iravan *was* a charmer; she could see what he'd done with the invitation to the investigation and the unasked gift of the rudra bead. He had seduced her, manipulated her—but was that wrong? It was who Iravan was. He didn't do it to be deceitful; he did it to be efficient. His ability to maneuver his circumstances was what made him such a talented architect. He literally shaped the world around him to fit himself.

Yet underneath it—at his most relaxed—her husband was a blunt man. In the company of an elite few, his layers shed themselves; his honesty became thorn-sharp, almost hurtful. *That* was who he was around her. Dhruv could not understand. Where was her loyalty if someone like him could so easily question her marriage?

Outside the solar lab, the gentle rain became a furious downpour. Dhruv returned to a desk, flipping through his notes, but there was something in his manner, a hostility she had never noticed before, in the set of his shoulders and the grimness of his face.

Dhruv had never shown such opposition to her methods before. He had been *unhappy* when they'd discovered the habitat on the tracker locket. They'd begun arguing about Iravan at once, but for the first time, Ahilya had a true chance at the council seat, the only thing standing between her and it, the pieces that Iravan could provide. Yet Dhruv did not want her to involve her husband. Could it have more to do with *her* than Iravan? Could it be that, for the first time, her friend was seeing her as a threat—a mere archeologist becoming a councilor over a sungineer, a woman with no precedence, no support, no allies?

The thought made her sick to the stomach, in thinking it and the seed of truth behind it. A wave of loneliness washed over Ahilya, and she felt sullied, as though she had done something wrong, but it had been justified in some insidious way. What was happening to her? She had suspected Bharavi, Iravan, now Dhruv. *I can't go on like this*, she thought, dangerously close to tears. *Not without Iravan. I need him.*

She blinked back her distress and strode up to the sungineer. "Dhruv, listen to me. We can't keep this to ourselves; you know we can't. Even if we take Iravan out of the equation, suppose we never tell anyone we found an interference with trajection. Suppose the interference ruins Nakshar's architecture. We're dooming the ashram with our silence. You can bear to do that?"

The sungineer turned away from his notes and grabbed her shoulders. "Ahilya, we don't even know what this is. This thing in the jungle, it's blocking trajection going *down* to the jungle—we don't necessarily know it's blocking trajection *inside* the city—"

"You're arguing semantics—"

"I'm not," he said, releasing her and beginning to pace. "I'm being careful. You can't lie to me, Ahilya—I know it's not Nakshar you care about. You want to help Iravan do whatever he's convinced you to do."

"Rages, Dhruv, of course I want to help him. He's my husband! You say it like it's a bad thing."

"Because you're not *thinking*. What happens if we tell him and it's not related to his investigation at all? He'll realize we've been making side deals, smuggling plants in. He'll have to report us. You want that to happen?"

"He might not report us," she protested. "He might see why we chose to smuggle plants, especially if we tell him it was to make a battery."

Dhruv rolled his eyes. "Please. You want to appeal to his better nature? You've seen how he speaks about the sungineers. You know he thinks we don't do enough. Besides, he's a Senior Architect. He'll be duty-bound to punish us. What do you think he'll choose, between saving Nakshar and saving us?"

"It's not as simple as that," she said, shaking her head. "Iravan will do what he thinks is right. He'll stand by us if we convince him; he'll be our greatest ally through this. He's coming around to our side, Dhruv; he gave us his nomination already, he gave us *resources*—"

"A decision he made under duress because you forced his hand. If you give him this information, you think he will still support us? When he has power over us again? What if he's in a position where two of his beliefs go to war with each other? What will he choose then?"

"He will—"

Ahilya stopped talking. Both she and Dhruv turned toward the doorway, where the wall split open to reveal Iravan.

Her husband stood there, soaked. His damp white kurta clung to his skin. His salt-and-pepper hair was spiky from the rain, and his eyes glittered, either wet or too bright. Iravan strode in right through the forcefield of the deathchamber, unstopped. The forcefield wouldn't have blocked anything as substantial as a human body, but it was as though he had brought in a thundercloud with him.

"Iravan," Dhruv said. "You're out of the wheelchair."

"We were just talking about you," she began, deciding to tell him everything.

"Were you?" Iravan replied coldly.

His skin lit up with the light of trajection. The windows in the invention chamber boarded shut. Dhruv closed his notebook, a wary look in his eyes. With his glowing light, Iravan was the brightest thing in the room, and Ahilya noticed what she hadn't before. Iravan's clothes were full of tiny cuts, threads fraying from the edges, dark red stains on the collar and sleeves. Blood.

She closed the distance between them and lifted his arm, feeling his cold skin.

"What happened to you?" she asked, concern making her heart beat faster. "And your rudra beads—they're gone—"

Iravan glanced at her hand on his arm. Then he looked up at her, meeting her gaze. His dark eyes were filled with so much derision, so much *contempt*, that his gaze felt like a slap.

Ahilya instantly dropped her hand and staggered back.

He had never looked at her like that. Not once.

The rain outside sounded like a drum beat.

"I-Iravan?" she stuttered.

He reached into his pocket and extracted a white cube smaller than his fist. "Care to explain this?"

Ahilya stared at the offending deathbox, lost for words. "I—I—"

"Why don't I tell you what happened?" he snapped. "The two of you have been scheming up here in the solar lab, behind my back, behind everyone's back, sabotaging the ashram because of your petty resentments against the architects. This is why you didn't want me to accompany you into the jungle. You didn't want a Senior Architect watching you."

"You don't understand," Dhruv began.

"Iravan," she said at the same time.

"How long has this been going on?" he asked, speaking over them. "What else have you smuggled in?"

Ahilya exchanged a guilty look with Dhruv. Dhruv's eyes darted over to the desks where his petri dishes held samples of the plants she had brought in.

Iravan let out a cruel laugh. "I see. Well, this ends now."

One of the desks holding Dhruv's equipment flattened, the wood turning into grass, and the grass opening up into a yawning hole. Stormy clouds rumbled through the abyss. Dhruv's equipment went flying out of sight, whipped away by the wind. Ahilya's heart hammered in her chest as Iravan opened more gulfs in the deathchamber.

Dhruv lunged for the nearest cavity in the floor, hands outstretched. "NO!"

He stopped short, his hands gripping the edge, staring down at the endless sky.

"Iravan," Ahilya said, breathing fast. "Please listen. We were stupid and reckless, but it wasn't because of a grudge. Dhruv is using the plants to make a battery—just like the council wanted. Like *you* wanted. We're on your side."

Her husband ignored her. Iravan was a vision of blue and green vines, standing tall amidst the churning wind that sluiced through the invention chamber. His eyes were trained down at the turbulent sky, furious and glittering.

More holes opened up, one right next to Ahilya. She backed away, panicked. The wind tugged at her clothes and her hair, whipping them around her. The gap grew wider, all the holes joining together into a gigantic breach in the floor. Petri dishes, rudra beads, optical fibers fell away out of sight. Iravan stood a few feet from her, uncaring, but beyond them on the other side of the chasm, Dhruv was on his knees, staring at his life's work disappearing.

He looked up, his glasses askew, his normally placid face almost deranged with anguish. "You left us no choice," he screamed. "You don't understand the pressure to build a battery—"

Iravan's head jerked toward him. "*I* don't understand? I'm a Senior Architect—no one understands better than I do. But there are rules for a reason. Your irresponsibility nearly destroyed the ashram. It could have killed *everyone*."

"Iravan—stop," Ahilya gasped, but the wind took her words away. She retreated as far as she could, but still the void continued to grow. Dizziness gripped her as great gray-black clouds foamed underneath, their streaks climbing the void, then whipping away. Sharp flecks of wind-churned rain cut her like jagged knives.

"I hate this dependency on architects," Dhruv yelled back. "Sungineers can't do *anything* without it benefiting your kind."

"How dare you?" Iravan's eyes flashed. "You survive because of the sacrifices we make. You have no idea what we're put through."

Ahilya stared down, her hair lashing around her, feeling the emptiness below. The edge was so close. Her breath came out quick and panicked.

"You think being born with the ability to traject is a gift?" Iravan spat out, glaring at Dhruv. "It's not—it's a burden, and we have to do it for squabbling ingrates like you."

Ahilya's body swayed. Her fingernails sank into the foliage of the wall behind her.

"Iravan," she said again, choking. "Stop."

But consumed by his anger, he didn't seem to hear her. His face was twisted in cold fury, still turned toward Dhruv.

"You should be down on your knees, thanking the architects, all the children out there who are raised like lambs to slaughter for your benefit—"

The shrieking wind pulled at Ahilya. She trembled, too afraid to move.

"Iravan," she cried, panic breaking her voice. "Please."

"But why should you care—All you see are the glories—You see none of the costs—"

She was going to die there. Her body would tumble down through the stormy clouds and the yawning sky and smash into the earthrage.

Ahilya reached a trembling hand. "Please, Iravan," she begged. "*Please stop.*"

He jerked, looking at her arm extended toward him. His eyes grew wide as he took in their position. The patterns of vines on his skin changed into tighter leaves. The chasm closed immediately, thick roots and branches interlocking swiftly until the entire floor had reknit itself.

The sudden silence was shocking, almost as harrowing as the wind.

For a moment, the three of them stared at each other, all of them breathing heavily. Ahilya's legs trembled. Her chest heaved, her body still at the edges of nausea. She bit the inside of her cheeks to keep from whimpering.

Then into the silence, the rudra bracelet Iravan had given her began to chime. Ahilya glanced at it, disoriented, confused, then looked up at her husband. His face had turned ashen. He stared at Ahilya's wrist, where the bracelet still chimed, horror-stricken. His hands rubbed against his own empty wrists; she saw recognition and fear. Whatever the chiming signal meant, it terrified Iravan. Without a word, he turned on his heel and strode out of the invention chamber.

At the other end of the hall, Dhruv slumped down on the floor with a moan, his features numb with despair.

25

IRAVAN

The chiming on the rudra bead key was a call to the Examination of Ecstasy. Iravan had recognized its notes even before it fully finished ringing on Ahilya's wrist.

He ran through the rain toward the temple, fear gripping his heart. The council had voted. They were calling him to an Exam. He wasn't ready. He had lost his temper so furiously. He had thought to confront Dhruv and Ahilya, but to lose control like that—to lose *himself*? He'd almost grasped the Resonance again.

The councilors must have made the decision only minutes before. Iravan couldn't believe his stupidity. That incident in the library—and now in the solar lab—of course they had watched for him in the Moment. But the deathchamber had been activated in the lab; he had been trajecting in a pocket Moment. And the library—that was—that was—Bile churned in his stomach. Had that been *Ecstatic* trajection?

He arrived breathless and soaking at the entrance to the temple. Bharavi waited for him, wearing her full uniform, her translucent robe as still as her expressionless face.

"I—I can explain," Iravan stammered.

"It's too late for that," she replied, turning. She trajected, and a doorway opened in the wall. Iravan followed her in and the wall sealed itself behind him.

Within the temple, the rudra tree stood tall and imposing, blue-green light spilling from the unseen Architects' Disc hidden in the tree's highest boughs. Bharavi strode along the curving wall and trajected again to open another doorway. She climbed down to the architects' orchard.

Iravan hurried after her. Sungineering glowglobes grew on the leafy walls of the descending staircase, illuminating their steps one at a time. Iravan wrung out his damp kurta as much as he could but couldn't stop his shivering. He shook out his wet hair, splattering Bharavi.

She glanced back but said nothing. Iravan grabbed her arm, forcing her to look at him.

"Please, Bha," he said again in desperation. "You have to believe me. I'm not an Ecstatic. There is an interference in the Moment. Naila—she had some kind of proof—mathematical proof—"

"I told you before. This isn't about proving the theory; this is about proving your innocence."

"Why now? Because of what happened in the library? The lab?"

Bharavi's gaze was unreadable. "Did something happen in the library *and* the lab?"

"I—No—I mean—"

"Regardless. This is because you've healed. I told you an Exam was forthcoming one way or another. And we've voted."

She gently released his hold on her and continued down the staircase. The walls closed in on Iravan. He shook his head, trying to clear his vision. His hands trembled violently. He ran them through his hair, brushing out the water droplets. He tried to take in a full breath.

They reached the end of the staircase, and Bharavi trajected again. Another doorway materialized with creaks of wood. The architect's orchard formed a good portion of the ashram's underbelly, but the path Bharavi had picked led directly to the veristem garden. Iravan's stomach lurched. He had been inside the veristem garden many times but never like this, never because of this.

His gaze darted around. Velvety black leaves shaped like teardrops grew all over the ceiling, floor, and walls. Light glimmered from dispersed sungineering glowglobes, but veristem soaked it up hungrily. The councilors waited inside. The missing rudra beads weighed heavier than ever before on Iravan. It hit him then: he was there, he was with his friends, but he wasn't one of the council. For the first time, he realized how menacing the veristem garden was. The plant was a distorted window, intent on showing everyone nothing but the horrifying truth.

Bharavi turned to look at him. Iravan swallowed, tasting sourness in his mouth.

"I'm not ready for this," he said, his voice cracking. "Please. You have to intervene."

A part of him knew how futile his words were. How many times had he heard similar words from other architects he had tested? The Examination of Ecstasy didn't always result in excising an architect, but it forever stripped away an architect's dignity. The Exam forced an architect to see themselves for who they were, in all their shame, all their degradation.

Bharavi's hands gripped his shoulders, and she pulled him down to look into her eyes.

"I won't survive this, Bha," Iravan whispered. "Please."

"Remember who you are," she replied fiercely, her eyes glinting in anger.

And then she was walking away inside the chamber to join the other councilors. Iravan saw their shapes. He heard their mutters. They turned and looked into the stairwell where he hid, but there was no place to hide. He tried to straighten his shoulders, but the effort was too much. So, this was how the architects who were tested felt. He had only seen Manav's Exam face-to-face, but he had never fully understood the desperation. He had never appreciated the blinding terror.

For a split second, Iravan had the mad urge to turn and run, but that would be as good as admitting his guilt. A sense of cold unreality descended over him. He walked in slowly, but it was like someone else's feet trod on the black leaves. Someone else was hearing the doorway creak close behind him.

Airav and Bharavi watched his approach impassively, but Chaiyya's round face was awash in naked pity. The Senior Architect was holding back tears. Unexpectedly, anger rushed through Iravan. Bharavi's words rang in his ears, *Remember who you are.* Iravan straightened his back, lifted his chin, and closed the last few feet between them.

"I'm here," he said.

His voice sounded cold even to himself.

No one replied. None of the other three Senior Architects had entered the Moment, he could see. Confrontation with such a high concentration of truth-plants in the Moment could be a harrowing experience.

It was what awaited him.

Iravan was going to annihilate his own mind.

He tried to hold on to the indignation that had arisen at Chaiyya's pity, but already the feeling was dissipating. These people—they were his friends, his colleagues, his mentors; they would take no joy from the Exam. He had been in their position before. Iravan stared at them, not trusting himself to speak.

A golden light shimmered above him. Laksiya and Kiana rose from the corners of the veristem garden, dusting their hands. They'd activated the deathchamber. The glowglobes inside the deathchamber cut out, instantly pushing them all into dimness, emphasizing the stark darkness of the garden. The only light came from the sungineering devices far in the stairwell. Iravan's heart began to beat harder. Sweat drenched him, soaking his already-damp clothes. The two Senior Sungineers joined the others.

This was happening.

It was beginning.

Iravan's knees began to shake as Laksiya turned her penetrating gaze on him.

"You're summoned here, Iravan, because the council of Nakshar believes you are at risk of Ecstasy. We believe you are an active threat to the ashram which if left unchecked will result in Nakshar's destruction. It is only the safety of the ashram that dictates the necessity of this Exam. Let the veristem be testament to my words and our intent."

None of the plants in the deathchamber bloomed white. Iravan hadn't expected them to. She was telling the truth.

Airav nodded and Laksiya and Kiana moved away, out of sight, to stand behind Iravan. The other three spread apart as well, Bharavi right in front of him, Airav and Chaiyya on either side, enclosing him in a small circle.

Bharavi's voice echoed in his mind, *Remember who you are*, and he thought, in sudden despair, *Who am I?* He was about to find out.

"Keep your eyes on me," she said softly. With no trajection allowed inside the Exam's deathchamber, only primitive methods of checking an architect's health functioned. Bharavi would watch for the dilation of his eyes, for abnormal tics and strains. The others stood ready to intervene if seizures occurred.

"You will be tested on adhering to the limits of trajection," Laksiya called out from behind him. "Prepare yourself."

Iravan thought of the Resonance and his escape from the jungle. The deathbox containing the spiralweed dug into him through his kurta; he had pocketed it, not knowing. He had broken the limits of trajection so many times.

"You'll be tested on your commitment to the safety of the ashram," Laksiya continued. "Prepare yourself."

The memory of crushing Naila's rudra bead flashed in his head. He'd sent her away to the watchpost. He'd endangered the entire ashram. Consumed by his anger, he'd nearly killed Ahilya and Dhruv in the solar lab. He swallowed. He was going to fail. They would excise him.

"You'll be tested on your material bonds," Laksiya said. "Prepare yourself."

Iravan looked at Bharavi. She gazed back, unblinkingly, and he thought of her and Tariya, and their boys Kush and Arth. He thought of his parents in Yeikshar and how he looked so much like one of his fathers.

And Ahilya burst into his head, ahead of all of them; her smile and her beauty; trembling as he trajected in the solar lab, walking away from him after landing, holding him in relief after their escape from the jungle. *Don't you love her anymore?* Bharavi asked; and all the rage and confusion and turbulent devotion Iravan felt for Ahilya coursed through him like fire in his veins. If he failed, he would never see her again, not *him*.

"Remember," Laksiya said. "You are not to traject. That is immediate grounds for excision. Are you ready?"

Iravan nodded, his heart hammering in his chest. Trajecting now would show a terrible lack of control, disregarding all three conditions. He gripped his courage, but cold sweat bathed his skin and his teeth chattered lightly against his will.

"I need a verbal response, Iravan."

"Yes," he croaked.

"You may enter the Moment."

Iravan obeyed, and his vision split into two.

The effect was immediate.

The confrontation with pure, uncontaminated veristem smashed into him with the force of a dozen walls. Iravan staggered and fell to his knees with a grunt. Airav and Chaiyya exchanged a glance. Bharavi looked furious.

Iravan took a deep shaky breath. He pushed himself off the floor to stand upright again.

In the pocket Moment, infinite gigantic stars loomed in every direction. Uncontaminated veristem stars had no viewable states of their own; they were cultivated to reflect infinite interpretations of the same situation. The stars blinked golden and opaque.

Laksiya began to speak. Iravan tightened his jaw, and a view opened into his own memories.

26

IRAVAN

"Did you break the limits of trajection?" Laksiya called out.

In the pocket Moment, the golden stars glittered and shifted, like windows opening. Iravan glimpsed himself on every side.

In one star, he chased the mysterious Resonance after the landing. In another, he trajected three vortexes out of the jungle during the earthrage. He was on his knees, screaming and screaming, as his Two Visions merged. He was in the library, fighting the spiralweed.

Iravan drifted as a dust mote, examining his own actions.

And a window opened up to show him what he had been dreading.

He saw himself, a force outside of the Moment, reveling in his own power as he let go of Oam.

No, he thought, recoiling. *Not that. I don't want to remember that.*

In answer, the stars glimmered.

Around him every one of them opened a window to reveal his action in the vortex. Iravan zipped through the pocket Moment in alarm, but in every one of the stars, he saw a different interpretation of the incident.

He was formidable, drenched in power, uncaring of the boy's life. He was mad, gloating in his skill, and these tiny consciousnesses were no match for his own. He was a monster, flaying all of existence; the world existed for his entertainment, and he was a cruel god.

Iravan stared into Bharavi's eyes, and his breath came out in short, heavy pants.

"No," he said aloud, his voice hoarse, knowing it to be a lie. "No, I didn't break the limits of trajection."

In the veristem garden, the velvety black teardrop leaves began to unfurl. White buds emerged on the walls, floor, and ceiling. The five councilors stood in the humiliating white chamber, Iravan's blatant lie unfolding in front of them. Overwhelming shame filled Iravan. The pain of it was almost unbearable, like he was standing naked in a storm, whipped from every direction. He closed his eyes in a long blink and swallowed.

"A lie," Laksiya confirmed. "He broke the limits of trajection. Condition failed."

Bharavi's brown eyes reflected his own disgrace. She didn't blink. She didn't move. The white buds around them closed, preparing for the next question, and Iravan was submerged within the glinting darkness of unbloomed veristem again.

"Did you endanger Nakshar and its people with your trajection?" Laksiya called out.

The stars in the Moment shifted as the scenes within them changed.

The shame crept deeper in. Iravan started to hyperventilate. He saw Bharavi's eyes widen a fraction in alarm before his own eyes closed.

In the Moment, a window opened within a star. He saw himself traject within the solar lab. Ahilya cried out at him, but he paid no heed, opening one hole in the floor after another. She begged him, trembling, and he heard her say *Iravan, stop, please!* He laughed cruelly, glorying in his power; he crushed Naila's rudra bead, and the intoxicating control gratified him. In their escape from the jungle, he looked into Oam's eyes, coldly, as he let go of the boy.

Iravan whimpered in the veristem garden, lifting his arms above his head in protection. The memories battered him, pounding him wherever he looked. There was no way out. "I didn't..." he gasped. "I'm sorry... I should have..."

"He's spiraling." Bharavi's urgent voice washed over him. "Move to the next question."

"Can't—" Laksiya's voice. "—a wave!"

The scene in the star changed, and he watched himself become a Senior Architect; in the acceptance of his rudra beads he detected greed and hunger. Iravan fled within the pocket Moment, but there was no place to flee. Each star showed his own excuses, his self-deceptions, his brutalities. The light attacked him, laying him naked, and he couldn't avert his gaze. This is who he was. This is who he had been.

"Memories—*morphing*—lose him—"

"Ride out—hasn't confronted—"

Iravan fell to his knees. Again and again he saw himself crush Naila's bead and let go of Oam. Ahilya begged him, tears down her face, to stop, but he reveled in her terror, her fear the sweetest aphrodisiac. He saw himself in the library with the spiralweed, and he reached for the rudra beads too late. He walked away from Ahilya in anger because she had been right; after all his machinations, all his deflections, he was a ruthless beast, a power-hungry, petty little man with pretensions of grandeur.

"Stop," Iravan moaned. "Please stop... I'm sorry... I'm sorry."

Laksiya's voice cracked like a whip. "Iravan, did you endanger Nakshar?"

"I don't... I don't know..."

Tears fell from his closed eyes as he knelt in the veristem garden, spiraling deeper into despair. Ahilya looked at him accusingly and cried, *You killed Oam! If you had only stayed at the watchpost!* The deathbox pressed into his pocket, and he saw how he hadn't reached for his rudra beads, deliberately too late. Naila came to him, speaking of how architects were better, and deep inside him he knew he agreed. Oam screamed, just a child, and Ahilya said, *Please, Iravan, I had a duty of care*, and he replied, *No,* I *did.* He had failed. It was his fault. All his fault.

"I'm sorry," he wept. "I'm so sorry."

"Answer the question, Iravan! Did you endanger Nakshar with your trajection?"

"Yes," he cried. "I did, rages help me."

He heard a collective gasp around the garden. Iravan opened his blurry eyes, and everything had turned white around him again.

"Another lie," Airav breathed.

"He didn't endanger the ashram," Laksiya said, sounding stunned. "Condition passed."

Iravan turned his head. Airav looked shaken but relieved. Chaiyya had tears streaming down her face.

"That's enough," Bharavi said. "That's enough, Laksiya. He's passed the second question. All conditions must fail for an architect to be declared Ecstatic."

"No," Laksiya snapped. "We need better evidence. We are deciding whether to let him walk free or to excise him. Neither of those can be taken lightly. We continue."

"This is torture!"

"It's a test, and we have his consent. I pity him too, as I do all of us witnessing this, but he's wavering. If we don't continue, we'll be doing this again in a couple of weeks. Is that what you want?"

Bharavi cursed as Laksiya's voice called out again.

"Iravan. Do your material bonds tether you to your consciousness?"

I love Ahilya, he thought desperately. *It has to be true. Rages help me, it has to.*

For the third time the stars in the Moment changed.

And Iravan finally saw himself for the kind of husband he was.

He and Ahilya stood in the temple, exchanging flower garlands on their wedding day. Ahilya was beautiful, her eyes bright with unrestrained joy, but *his* eyes burned maliciously. He walked away from her, and her face crumpled in anguish, and his heart soared at inflicting the pain. He looked her over as she extended a hand to ask about his missing rudra beads. His contempt of her was a dagger through her heart.

"No..." Iravan wept in the veristem garden. "No... I wasn't... It wasn't... No, please."

Again and again, he saw as he made a vow to hold her as his highest ideal, as he promised to travel with her on a path or not at all. And Iravan watched as his words and his actions scorched her.

"No," he gasped. "Please, *please*."

He saw himself insult her as she ordered him away from the expedition. He saw as he laughed at her futile fury. He saw himself manipulate his wife as she grieved for her dead friend.

"Make it stop," he screamed, holding his head. "Please, oh, rages, please."

"Answer the question, Iravan," Laksiya's voice whipped out. "Do your material connections—"

He put his hands over his ears, still on his knees, and rocked himself back and forth.

"Iravan!"

Ahilya held out a pleading hand to him in the solar lab, but he continued to traject, and she trembled in fear; he saw himself, staring in satisfaction as she balked at his supremacy.

"No," he sobbed. "That's not me… It's not me… Please."

He abandoned her, over and over again, punishing her with his silence, and there was a sick vindication in the action. Her face trembled as he spoke about the architects; she would never be one of them, she would never understand.

Iravan's hands dug into his hair, the nails scratching his scalp. Uncontrollable sobs rocked his body. *I'm sorry*, he thought. *I'm so sorry*. Had he ever loved her? He had vowed to keep her at the center of his universe, and he had failed. This wasn't love. This wasn't *love*. He was a monster. A horrible weight pushed at him, and he grew smaller, disappearing.

"*Iravan, answer the question!*"

"No," he wept. "Release me. *Excise* me. I didn't… I haven't… Not tethered… I'm not tethered."

Through the tears blurring his sight, Iravan saw the veristem garden bloom again as every leaf budded a white flower.

"A lie," Chaiyya whispered, her voice choked.

"Material connections," Laksiya said, sounding surprised. "Confirmed and still holding. Third condition passed."

A silence greeted her words, broken only by Iravan's soft sobs.

"Leave the Moment, Iravan," Laksiya said quietly.

He obeyed, but the memories filled his mind, haunting him, shaming him. He was on all fours, his body shaking like a leaf in a wind, his head bent, tears relentlessly pouring down his face. He felt more than heard as the others clustered around and knelt by him.

Someone touched him—Bharavi—and he flinched as though she had hit him. Bharavi gently pushed at him until he was sitting back on his knees. Iravan put a forearm over his face, unable to meet her gaze. Her touch was gentle but insistent. She forced him to meet her eyes.

"It's done," she said. "You've passed."

"This time," Laksiya added in an undertone, but Iravan glanced up to see Kiana touch Laksiya's knee with her cane and shake her head. He looked away, unable to gaze upon them any longer.

"You need to rest." Chaiyya's voice quavered. "You've been through a traumatic experience."

"The veristem," Iravan whispered. "What I saw… it wasn't a lie. That is… that is who I am."

Chaiyya exchanged a worried glance with Airav. "Veristem doesn't account for the truth of your interpretation, Iravan," she said. "It's meant to sieve through your memories, past intent and desire, to objective fact. The flowers responded to the questions we asked. They're no guarantee of the accuracy of the feeling or the visions you saw in the Moment."

Iravan shook his head. There was no redemption.

"You spiraled, my friend," Airav said. "You hadn't confronted your own truths in a while, and in the Moment, they must have warped into their worst versions. It doesn't mean those memories, those *interpretations*, were true."

"They were true," Iravan rasped. "I can't lie anymore."

"You're being too hard on yourself," Kiana muttered.

"You need to rest," Chaiyya added. "You'll feel differently in the coming days."

Iravan shook his head again. Bharavi put a hand under his arm, and he staggered to his feet. His tears were drying, but a crushing weight settled on his shoulders. The others gave way. Kiana stumbled away to a corner, no doubt to turn off the forcefield of the deathchamber.

"We're done here," Bharavi said, holding Iravan, her arm around his waist.

Underneath her translucent robe, her arms turned blue-green. She trajected and some of the black veristem in the chamber disappeared to be replaced by green grass. A white healbranch bush pushed through the floor, and a gnarled rosewood tree began to take shape from stem.

Airav, Chaiyya, and Laksiya froze.

Bharavi started to lead Iravan away, but Airav said, "How did you do that?" and she stopped.

"You—you bypassed the deathchamber," Chaiyya blurted out. "That—that shouldn't have been possible."

"Don't be ridiculous," Bharavi snapped. "There's no force—"

She cut herself off as her eyes flickered around them. Iravan followed her gaze. The golden forcefield still shimmered. Bharavi's grip around Iravan slackened. He frowned, his mind slow. It was impossible to bypass the deathchamber's forcefield. If Bharavi had done it, she was breaking the limits of trajection. If she was breaking the limits of trajection, she was…

His eyes widened. His muscles drained of what little strength they had remaining. He threw her a startled sidelong glance. *No.*

Bharavi was staring at the plants around them as though unable to speak. Then she looked up at Airav, the corners of her lips lifting ruefully.

"Well," she said. "I guess there's no point in denying it now. Would you like me to bring back the veristem, or will my word suffice toward any truth?"

Airav, Chaiyya, and Laksiya seemed unable to move. Laksiya opened her mouth, but Iravan spoke over her before she could say anything.

"This is ridiculous," he wheezed out, his chest hurting. "You—all of you—you're targeting the both of us."

"Don't you dare be that much of an idiot," Kiana said, and he saw that she had not even made it to the deathchamber's controls in the grass. "You saw what she just did. Deathchambers are supposed to be impenetrable."

"Then your technology is flawed," Iravan rasped. "Bharavi is not an Ecstatic. You're not, are you?" he added, turning to her.

Bharavi shrugged, still smiling.

"No," Iravan said, stumbling back from her. "No."

Laksiya cleared her throat. "I vote we put Senior Architect Bharavi through the Examination of—"

"NO," Iravan shouted, his voice cracking, as the others began to nod. "No one should be put through the Examination without adequate evidence."

"She broke a blatant limit of trajection," Chaiyya said, her face drained of color. "There's no getting around that."

"You made an exception for me when I returned from the jungle. Make it for her. Give her time to defend herself."

"We made an exception for you because you had been through an ordeal," Airav said, in his deep slow rumble. "You needed time to recover. Bharavi is healthy. The Examination can happen right away."

"I'm afraid," Bharavi interrupted, "you can vote all you like, but there won't be an Examination."

Airav and Chaiyya glanced at each other, naked fear on their faces.

Iravan's eyes widened. "Bharavi. What are you saying?"

"I don't intend to undergo the humiliation you just did, Iravan," she said, her voice calm. "You were supposed to convince the council of the true nature of Ecstasy, but the truth is, this council isn't fit to decide my guilt. None of you are."

Out of the corner of his eyes, Iravan saw Kiana move slowly, her fingers twitching, reaching almost casually toward the deathchamber's controls.

"Don't be foolish, Kiana," Bharavi said. "I trajected *through* a forcefield. Do you really think you'll be limiting me if you took it away?"

A subtle blue-green glow permeated Airav and Chaiyya; they had entered the pocket Moment. Vines crept up their dark skins in intricate patterns. The grass Bharavi had impossibly trajected within the garden grew into tight, thick creepers and reached toward her, binding her arms to her sides, trapping her legs. She glanced down at her limbs, immobilized.

Then her dark skin lit up like a blue sun, ethereal.

Iravan lifted his hand against the fierce glare. Chaiyya and Airav screamed in agony, flickering like they were malfunctioning. The blue-green light winked out of them.

The plants binding Bharavi burst into tiny fragments, spraying all of them with leaves and twigs.

Chaiyya whimpered, her fingers touching the bloody scratches on her skin. Airav stumbled over to her and put an arm over her shoulders, his eyes terrified.

Bharavi emerged out of her bindings, shaking out her translucent robe.

"Bha," Iravan whispered. "No."

She reached and patted his cheek.

"Now," she said. "Let me show you what Ecstasy truly is."

27

IRAVAN

Bharavi raised her arms in exultation.

Her skin glowed with the blue-green light of trajection, but so close, Iravan saw what he hadn't seen before. The tattoos growing on her arms and face didn't resemble vines anymore. They appeared like delicately carved boulders, too square, too angular. There was an eerie familiarity to them, although he had never seen such a thing before.

He had no more time to wonder.

The next instant, the ceiling split open.

He looked up in confusion and horror. An upward tunnel grew in the ceiling, expanding, extending, revealing the thunderstorm. Great gray clouds billowed in through the hole. The walls of the chamber started to shake. The earth roiled, and Iravan lurched on his feet with a grunt. Gravity pulled at him, and his muscles trembled. The air seemed to push him down. His mouth fell open in disbelief.

This wasn't possible. The veristem garden was in the ashram's underbelly. Bharavi was raising it to the roof, ascending part of the architects' orchard, *through* the temple. To change the architecture so completely—she had to be trajecting against *all* the Disc Architects. The damage to the ashram would be incalculable. Iravan imagined he could hear screams all over Nakshar as architecture collapsed, as trees crushed citizens, as Maze Architects scrambled on the Disc in fear.

"Bharavi," he bellowed. "What are you doing?"

"This is the power that awaits architects, Iravan," she shouted over the din, her eyes triumphant. "This is who we are."

The ceiling continued to grow apart until there was no ceiling at all. Gigantic clouds churned above them, gray and thunderous, completely eclipsing the sun. Stabbing rain fell inside the open chamber, and boughs stripped from the redwood tree in the gale, whipping in every direction.

Iravan winced as lightning flashed above his eyes. Distantly, he heard the two Senior Sungineers scream. He forced his eyes open to a squint and saw Chaiyya and Airav pushed to a corner. The two flickered blue-green then dark again, trying and failing to enter the Moment.

"She—knocking—Moment," Airav cried, the wind whipping his words away. "Knocking—out—"

"Bharavi, release them," Iravan shouted. "Whatever you're doing, stop."

Caught in her Ecstasy, Bharavi didn't hear him. The storm raged around her. Swollen tentacle-like roots emerged from the floor, flinging boulders and dust everywhere. A thick branch, almost as tall as Iravan, slammed into him, hurling him several feet back. He landed with a painful thud, his vision swimming. The branch rolled off him in the gale, but gasping, Iravan gripped it and rammed it into the earth to totter upright onto his feet, barely maintaining his balance.

Grit entered his mouth. His eyes stung. He gripped the heavy branch with both his hands, trembling, as the squall pushed against him.

Bharavi stood where she was, her head tipped up to the open sky. Her arms raised in embrace. Fury rained down, lashes of lightning crackling over them.

"Bharavi!"

"We are more," Bharavi called out, her voice terrible and beautiful. "So much more than we know. So much more than we remember. This is what we need to become, Iravan. For all of us, for Nakshar. It's the only way."

Iravan crouched down against the thrusting wind. In one corner, Airav shielded Chaiyya, his body flickering in and out, still attempting to enter the Moment. In another corner, Laksiya and Kiana huddled together, their faces drawn down against the gale, their postures terrified.

"Bharavi!"

Arms still wide, she turned to face him. Deep in her eyes Iravan saw the blue-green light of trajection glowing like a kindled flame. Trajection didn't change a person's features, not like this, but she stared at him, inhuman, terrifying, magnificent.

"You don't want to do this, Bha," he choked out. "Think of Tariya. Think of Kush and Arth."

Her expression spasmed briefly into one of deep, profound anguish before it was replaced again with her rapture. Underneath him, the ground roiled again, tremors rumbling like in an earthrage.

Iravan threw a horrified glance at Airav and Chaiyya. He could see his own cold realization reflected in their eyes. The Maze Architects were fighting Bharavi back; they had to be. Airav lifted a hand and made a swift cutting motion, and Iravan knew what he meant. Bharavi and the Maze Architects would rupture the rudra tree in their battle. The tree would splinter in half. The ashram would plummet from the sky.

Iravan turned back to Bharavi. Twigs gouged his skin. Dust and water scoured him. He closed his eyes, moving forward by instinct alone, supporting himself on the heavy branch he had picked up. It shook underneath him, it was all he could do to grip it, but Iravan pressed against her immense power, one shuddering step at a time. He reached ever closer, opening his eyes despite his tears.

"Bharavi," he croaked. "Come back to us. Please. Come back to *me.*"

Radiant, she turned to him and smiled. She held out a hand, her gesture imperious.

"Remember who you are, Iravan," she said, still in that unearthly terrible voice. "Let me show you. Manav was right. There is a choice—"

Iravan whipped the branch he held at her.

Shock flickered in her eyes; the branch collided with her head with a sickening crunch.

For a moment, she swayed there, the light fading from her.

The scourging wind stopped as the ceiling knit itself together. Airav and Chaiyya lit up with the light of trajection. Kiana and Laksiya unwrapped their arms from their heads, their gazes horrified, disbelieving.

Then Bharavi collapsed slowly, gracefully, almost like a feather, into Iravan's waiting arms.

They stumbled down to the grassy floor together, her chest rising and falling, still alive.

Sobbing, Iravan gathered Bharavi to him and wept in horror of himself and of her, and the path they were condemned to follow.

28

AHILYA

It took Ahilya nearly twenty minutes to stop shivering after Iravan left. Dhruv had quieted but hadn't risen from the floor, staring unseeingly in front of him.

"Listen to me," she said, approaching him. "I'll fix this, all right? I'll fix this."

The sungineer said nothing. He buried his head in his knees, beginning to shake. Dhruv had never screamed at Iravan in this manner; the two men had always been civil to each other, forced though their civility had been. Ahilya knew any chance of being nominated to the council had disappeared now for both her and Dhruv, but Iravan could ruin Dhruv's career forever. Dhruv would be transferred to another city—and once there, would be shunned. The sungineer trembled on the floor now, knowing this as well as she did, his hands clutched around the tracker locket. They had both come so close—now, they had lost it all. Ahilya tried to rouse him, but he just shook his head and sank deeper into himself. In the end, she brushed a hand over his head, grabbed her solarnote, and walked away from the lab.

This was all a mistake. She had to find Iravan. She had to explain. She and Dhruv had been wrong to bring in the spiralweed. Of course they'd been wrong. Her body still shuddered in remembered terror of almost being swallowed by the hole in the floor, but Iravan had looked like he had been in battle, his clothes ripped in a thousand places, blood on his sleeves and collar. Was that why he had lost his control? Had the spiralweed *attacked* him? She needed to apologize. She needed to tell him about her discovery of the interference in the jungle. Despite his outburst, her husband was a reasonable man, but his actions, what he'd done, how he'd lost himself—

Ahilya shivered. Everything had become so convoluted. She and Iravan had once spent countless days reveling in each other's passions. How was it that today, on the day of her most important discovery, the two were estranged?

She took the long way to the temple. Rain thudded on the bark hedges and pathways of the ashram. The city morphed, thick foliage growing overhead in open-air spaces, but the movement was pained. Wind sluiced through the struggling leaves, sending chills through Ahilya. By the time she arrived at the temple, she was drenched and the storm outside had worsened. Ahilya flashed Iravan's bracelet at a leafy wall. The bark cracked open. Cautiously, she strode in.

There was no one around. The tall rudra tree in the center obscured the Architects' Disc in its boughs, but blue-green light shone down, dappling the chamber. Endless corridors radiated from the epicenter. Ahilya craned her neck, and a dozen dizzying levels overlooked her, rising in a circle, with lush vines curling down carved railings. The temple was a maze in itself. How would she find Iravan? Perhaps he was in a council meeting. He could be telling the other councilors about the spiralweed even now. She had just decided to enter one of the corridors when bells began chiming through the temple.

Trajection light grew brighter, dispelling the shadows of the chamber. As Ahilya watched, the Architects' Disc descended halfway down the rudra tree. A ramp formed and chatting Maze Architects climbed down, their translucent robes flitting like gauzy wings over their brown kurtas and trousers. Another door opened beside Ahilya, and other Maze Architects entered, nearly twenty of them, making their way to the Disc. She was watching a change of shifts.

One woman, with a swaying gait and long wavy hair, detached herself from the group exiting the temple. Ahilya recognized her at once. Megha had been one of the Maze Architects who had vied for the very council seat Iravan now occupied. Once Iravan and Ahilya had spent hours discussing her skills, the competition she had brought to him.

"You there," Megha began. "How did you get in—" The woman stopped and her heart-shaped face grew startled in recognition. "Oh, you're—Oh. I'm sorry. I didn't mean any disrespect to Iravan-ve—"

Ahilya frowned, noticing then dismissing the insult.

"What are you doing here?" Megha asked.

Ahilya nodded to the Disc that was ascending again, taking its new batch of architects. The change of shifts had been swift; the bark closed behind the last off-duty architect. She and Megha stood alone in the temple courtyard.

"Iravan. Is he up there?"

"No, none of the Senior Architects are. Have you contacted him on his citizen ring?"

Ahilya shook her head. Iravan had been missing his rudra beads. That seemed like a bad sign. Perhaps the council had stripped him of it for some reason. Perhaps her being there now—using his bracelet—was only going to get him further into trouble. Unwilling to worsen the situation, Ahilya opened her mouth to thank Megha and leave, but before she could form the words, the temple floor began to vibrate.

Megha shot out an arm, clutching Ahilya.

Sounds of consternation spilled from the Architects' Disc. Megha's skin lit up. The patterns on her skin flickered. Her grip on Ahilya's arm became painful.

"What's happening?" Ahilya asked.

"Ecstasy," the woman replied, through grit teeth, and Ahilya could tell she was tamping down on her terror. "An architect is in Ecstasy. It's the only explanation."

Iravan, Ahilya thought at once, her pulse racing. *What has he done? What have I forced him into?* "Let me go," she said, but the architect's grip grew tighter.

"You must know the dangers of Ecstasy! You're practically an architect yourself—"

The light from the Disc sputtered, shrieks reverberating. Wind churned through the temple, as though the courtyard was exposed to the storm outside. Leaves rustled in the sudden gale. Wood cracked and bark peeled.

The next instant, the rudra tree *screamed*.

The high-pitched whine pierced through Ahilya like needles in her ears. She clutched Megha and the architect *flickered*, tears running down her face, mouth dropping in a small O. The scream went on and on, the single most chilling sound of Ahilya's entire life. She could see her terror reflected in Megha.

Shouts ricocheted off the Disc, and the ground in front of Ahilya rose like a mountain forming. Megha staggered back, pulling Ahilya with her. A jagged mound of earth shot up in the sky, raining down soil and roots, covering the both of them in dust. The temple shook, and for one horrifying instant, the light of the Architects' Disc disappeared as though extinguished; they were submerged in total blackness.

Then trajecting light flickered again. The incongruous column of earth reared next to the rudra tree, like a monstrous pillar reaching from floor to ceiling.

"I have to find Iravan," Ahilya cried, trying to shake Megha off. "Let me *go*!"

"There's nothing you can do right now. There's barely anything *we* can do."

Megha's grip became vise-like and a wave of powerlessness washed over Ahilya. She was useless; she was worse than useless without the ability to traject. What was happening? What were the architects doing?

She must have asked the last question out loud. Megha shook her head. "We're trying to contain it. But the Ecstatic Architect is too powerful. The tree is going to shatter."

The rudra tree trembled in front of them, a blackness pouring out from it like thick smoke. Its scream echoed in Ahilya's mind. Something burned; it smelt like flesh. Megha began to swear, a torrent of filthy words, but the patterns on her skin grew more furious.

The rudra tree arched like a spasming body, and—

Stilled.

The chilling whine silenced like someone had cut the scream from its source. Ahilya glanced at Megha, seeing her own fear and confusion there.

"The Ecstatic Architect," Megha breathed. "They've stopped. It's stopped."

Terror clawed up Ahilya's throat. This was Iravan's doing. He had unleashed this destruction. She had forced him to it. She was sure of it.

The column of earth near the tree descended; it disappeared back into the floor that reknit itself. The wall next to Ahilya burst open and nearly a hundred Maze Architects rushed into the temple, some in their uniforms, most dressed casually. The Architects' Disc descended again, and architects stumbled out and sank to their knees, retching. Others poured into the Disc, shouting instructions. Ahilya realized she was standing all alone, trembling; Megha had left her. Disjointed voices came to her. Everything seemed to happen in slow motion.

"—citizens' infirmary is fine—but the residences—"

"—the Academy has collapsed—there's *children* buried underneath—"

"—Gaurav, Megha, report to the Academy. I'll bring the other healers—"

Ahilya caught a glimpse through the doorway out of the temple. The corridors leading to the temple had completely disappeared. Great swathes of foliage had ripped apart like broken limbs. A tree trunk lay across a teetering bridge. In the distance, an unchecked fire burned, a horrifying sight in the leafy ashram. Ahilya took a step forward, wanting to help, wanting to do *something.*

Another doorway opened in the temple wall. Senior Sungineers Kiana and Laksiya hurried out, followed by Chaiyya, who rushed despite her advanced pregnancy. Airav and Bharavi were nowhere to be seen, but a familiar shape—*Iravan*—stood in the darkness. His head leaned back against the wall. His eyes were closed. His clothes were ripped, blood smeared his face and his arms, and his hair was filled with earth and dust, but he was fine, he was *alive.*

Ahilya stumbled to him, and he must have sensed her, for his eyes flickered open and surprise flashed through them. Iravan straightened.

"Ahilya—What are you—Are you all right?"

"A-Are you—Ecstasy—?" she stammered at the same time.

"No," Iravan said, shaking his head. "Not me. Bharavi."

Such a powerful wave of relief crashed over Ahilya that for an instant she felt unmoored. Sorrow followed, but before she could untangle it, Iravan shuddered and crumpled to the floor like the last of his strength had left him. His head dropped on his knees. Great big sobs wracked his body.

And in that moment, Ahilya forgot everything else.

She forgot what she had come to say to him. She forgot all that had happened between them. She forgot the chaos behind her, the damage to the ashram, the bustling architects. All she knew was he was Iravan, he was *hers*, and he was in pain.

She dropped to her knees next to him and wrapped her arms around him.

His body stiffened, but then his arms came up to surround her and his face buried in her shoulder. Crushing her to his chest, her husband wept like she had never seen him weep before.

Ahilya didn't speak, didn't say anything, didn't question. She ran her fingers through his damp, grit-filled hair, tears streaming down her face as well. She stroked his back, his neck, his shoulders as shudders passed through his entire body.

"I'm sorry," he said, his voice muffled.

"I'm sorry too," she whispered.

"I frightened you."

"I lied to you."

He pulled back, shaking his head, protesting her apologies, and their lips met. He tasted of dust and loneliness and heartbreak, but he gripped her tightly, as though the ground underneath them was still roiling and she was his only lifeline.

When he pulled back, Ahilya leaned in to close the gap, but Iravan shook his head again and tipped her chin up with a knuckle. He gave her a watery smile.

"We have so much to talk about," he said.

"Damn right we do," she replied softly, but his eyes ran past her and his expression changed, and Ahilya stopped talking.

Pushing her back gently, Iravan stood up. His eyes were red from the weeping, but something in him had closed. She rose too and turned to see the three women councilors approach the stairwell.

Ahilya gripped his arm. "What happened? In there—with Bharavi?"

Iravan glanced down at her. "You need to go to Tariya. Tell her... about Bharavi. It'll be better coming from you."

"I'm not leaving you."

"You have to. Please. You're not allowed where I'm going—I'm sorry—"

Ahilya made to argue, but Iravan's eyes grew pained again. He cupped her cheek with his callused hand. His touch was delicate like he was afraid of hurting her.

"Trust me," he said, and she could tell he was at the end of his courage.

Reluctantly, Ahilya drew back and nodded.

She slipped out of the stairwell, back into the main temple courtyard, as the three women of the council entered and began climbing down. Iravan straightened his rumpled and dirty clothes. His eyes became hard—he seemed to come to some decision. His glance fluttered up to Ahilya, but he didn't smile. He studied her face, but Ahilya got the sense that he was really seeing someone else. Then the bark closed on the stairwell and Ahilya was alone in the chaotic temple again.

Her fingers touched her lips. She wavered as Iravan's sobs echoed in her ears. He had looked so desperate, so *alone*, examining her face like it was a stranger's. She knew what she had to do; she had made up her mind already.

Ahilya counted slowly to twenty. Then, glancing behind her, she waved the rudra bead bracelet Iravan had given her, and the bark slid open to reveal the staircase again. Silently, she climbed down, following the muffled voices of the councilors.

29
AHILYA

Their voices drifted up to Ahilya almost instantly.

"—given instructions," Kiana said. "The lab is gathering reports from the rest of the ashram."

"Thank rages you stopped her when you did, Iravan." Chaiyya's voice sounded heavy. "A few more minutes and the rudra tree would have split."

There was a tense silence. Ahilya pressed herself back to the wall. She had climbed down to the last step. Carefully, she peered around the corner and saw four shadowy shapes, illuminated by sungineering glowglobes. The councilors stood in what looked like a curving corridor. As Ahilya watched, another shape joined them.

"She's asleep," Airav said, and he sounded exhausted. "But she will have to be excised tonight. She trajected *through* a deathchamber. I don't know how well even the deathcage will hold her, despite the layered forcefields. I have at least a dozen architects maintaining those in a chamber below the garden. I dare not have them guarding her face-to-face lest she find a way to traject them. I've never seen so much power."

"Her family," Chaiyya said, clearing her throat. "We should send for them. Tariya and the boys—and Ahilya—"

"No." Iravan's voice was quiet. Hard.

"They're Bharavi's family," Chaiyya protested, horrified. "They have a right to see her before her excision, to comfort her."

"I am her family," Iravan replied. "I will comfort her."

There was another deep silence. Ahilya's heart clawed up her throat. In her mind's eye, she imagined Iravan staring at the others, silent and still, unwilling to move.

"The excision," Chaiyya began. "Who will perform—"

"I will," Iravan said.

"You don't have the strength in the Moment," Airav said. "Not after—"

"Don't test me, Airav," Iravan cut in softly. "Not tonight."

The silence that greeted his words was tenser than any before. Ahilya shivered despite herself. Iravan's voice had been calm. He'd said his words without anger or rancor, but there was a naked threat underlying his tone. The man who had wept at Ahilya's shoulder only minutes before had disappeared.

One, two, three heartbeats passed.

Then Airav said, "Very well."

A note of finality and regret steeped the Senior Architect's voice. Sweat broke out over Ahilya. A bitter taste entered her mouth.

The shadows moved, coming back toward her. Panicked, she slipped out of the stairwell and ran on light feet in the opposite direction. The bark closed behind her, but she had no way of knowing: Were they going back into the temple proper? Would they come down the corridor? A few feet away, she pressed herself against the leafy wall. Tendrils reached over her slowly, then faster, responding to her petrified desire to hide. In seconds, Ahilya was covered in soft, thick leaves.

Two shapes came toward her, murmuring in low voices.

"—pact, maybe for the best," Airav was saying. "We won't know until later."

"A pact is *never* for the best." Chaiyya sounded troubled. "There are other ways, better ways. And for him to carry it out, the way he is? Laksiya is right—he's still a danger—"

"We will just have to keep an eye—"

"But if it's true? We've lost Bharavi already. We can't lose him too, Airav. We just *can't*."

Then the two passed Ahilya, their footsteps fading, voices receding.

Ahilya broke through her leaf cover and jogged in the direction they had come from, toward Iravan. The two Senior Sungineers must have left for the main courtyard of the temple, for there was no sign of them. Keeping to the wall, Ahilya hurried forward. She glimpsed the white of Iravan's kurta disappear into another stairwell, then bark closed behind him.

Once again, Ahilya began her count. She made it to five before impatience and nervousness got the better of her. Using the rudra bead bracelet, she opened the wall again.

This time, the staircase led upward, curving over and over. Ahilya could hear Iravan's tread above her. As quietly as she could, she followed, keeping to the wall. Her husband was alone, but all her instinct told her to be silent. There had been something in his voice—in his face—And his words… Why send Ahilya to Tariya but refuse Tariya from comforting Bharavi before she was stripped away from her trajection? Why send Ahilya at all, when it should have been one of the councilors to break the news of Bharavi's Ecstasy to her family? No, that had been a distraction. A way to get rid of Ahilya, no questions asked.

The staircase opened up to the night air.

Ahilya stepped onto a terrace. She was *above* the temple, she realized. A million stars shone down to give her light. Nakshar had finally flown through the cloud cover, for there was no sign of the storm from earlier.

The terrace was like a secret garden. Rosebushes and topiary writhed and curled, attempting to return after the damage to what must have been their archival design. Ahilya picked her way through the foliage, past nooks and alcoves. She let the fragrant breeze wash over her. The budding garden was so beautiful, the night so peaceful, that for a moment, she forgot why she was here.

She came to a stop down a winding path. About fifty feet away from her, a clearing interrupted the garden. No foliage grew there. Instead, the clearing was pure white stone. A golden dome shimmered above the stone, reaching so high, it seemed like its own building. Ahilya crept closer, moving at an angle, keeping to the expanding bushes.

The golden shimmering came from nearly a dozen layers of deathchambers. Their lights crisscrossed in a complex labyrinth like a dense web. Within the web stood a stone platform about waist-high. Bharavi lay on it, looking diminutive. Her chest rose and fell in deep sleep. Her body glowed with the light of trajection, blue-green shapes twinkling through the translucent robe of her uniform.

And at the edge of the golden light, staring at Bharavi, stood Iravan.

Shadows fell over him, throwing the angles of his face into sharp relief. In the golden light, Ahilya saw his sleeves rolled back like they always were, except now his arms were bare, not a single rudra bead in sight. The absence of the black beads, despite the white of his Senior Architect's uniform, made him look unexpectedly… sinister. Iravan fiddled with something in his hands, but except for that, his body was utterly still.

Ahilya did not know how long he stood there, unmoving, or how long she waited, watching him, but the stars grew deep in the sky and the temperature dropped, leaving her cold.

Then on the stone slab within the web of deathchambers, Bharavi stirred and stretched.

It was as though that was the sign Iravan had been waiting for.

He pocketed whatever had been in his hands and walked into the golden light, through one forcefield into another. Ahilya drew in as close as she could, still hugging the foliage. Bharavi sat up on her stone slab, her radiance astonishing, watching Iravan as he approached. Only one forcefield separated them, but Iravan didn't make to enter it. Instead, he extended a fist to knock and Ahilya realized the last layer was no ordinary forcefield of a deathchamber, but a layer made of glass. He could not get through it. She was looking at a giant deathbox. Death*cage*, Airav had called it.

Iravan nodded to himself. A stone bench waited just outside the glass, evidently for visitors. He sat down on it, his elbows on his knees, his fingers interlocked. Ahilya saw Bharavi's mouth move. Iravan studied her for a long, silent moment.

Then he said something in reply.

Unable to hear them, her stomach clenching in sudden fear, Ahilya watched from the silent shadows.

30

IRAVAN

"Iravan," Bharavi said in her clear, musical voice. "Are you here to release me?"

Yes, he thought, but he couldn't form the word.

His heart grew cold. He watched her as though from a great distance. Irrelevant details came to him. The air smelled of honeyfruit. His hair was damp, grit settled in it. How long had it been since he'd eaten? In the sanctum earlier that morning, while ridding himself of his wheelchair. Had that only been this morning? It seemed so long ago.

"You're still trajecting," he said, at last.

Bharavi glanced down at her arms, where her tattoos moved in strange, unfamiliar shapes.

"I suppose you could call it that," she said, shrugging.

"What would you call it?"

"I don't have a name for it yet."

"Ecstatic trajection? *Super*trajection?"

Bharavi smiled at him across the glass. "If you like."

"There's nothing in there. What are you trajecting?"

She extended an elegant hand. "The jungle."

Iravan drew in a sharp breath. "How's that possible? You're in the *deathcage*."

"I'll tell you if you let me out."

"So, you're trying to escape?" Iravan asked, watching her. "It's not possible, Bha."

"Are you sure, Iravan?" she asked lightly. "Certain you know everything about Ecstasy and about me?"

Iravan stared at her, and she smiled. For a brief second, he forgot the absurdity of the situation. It was like she was mentoring him again, and he was one step behind, trying to guess her mind.

"Why the jungle?" he asked.

"It's where we belong. In the jungle. Not the ski—"

"We die in the jungle," he said. "The earthrages kill us."

Bharavi just laughed, the sound inordinately melodious.

Iravan closed his eyes in a long, slow blink, willing himself to breathe slowly. He looked back at her, and she watched him patiently, so like herself that his resolve almost cracked. Underneath his wavering indifference, the man who had wept next to Ahilya clawed at him, feeling the horror of this moment.

"This power," he said, swallowing. "How long have you been an Ecstatic?"

Bharavi lifted her arms, her skin gleaming blue-green, the patterns growing so complex that he couldn't keep track. "It has grown. I have been wrestling with it for months."

Iravan closed his eyes in shame.

Months.

This was his fault, for not keeping to vigilance. He had thought Bharavi had been easy on him, but in fact *he* had been easy on her. Ahilya's voice washed over on him. *If only you'd been at the watchpost*; and Airav said, *It's time to act like a Senior Architect.*

Laksiya had thought he was too young, too reckless for the job, but he had not been too young. He had just not been good enough. Not *smart* enough.

Iravan opened his eyes to see Bharavi still studying him.

"You battled this power," he said. "And you lost?"

"A poor choice of words, if you only knew what Ecstasy meant, but I gave into it truly when I landed the ashram less than two weeks ago."

"When you landed—" Iravan's interlocked hands clenched. "That was you. You were on watchpost duty before we landed. You called for the landing. Did you manipulate the magnaroot then somehow?"

"I didn't realize that's what I was doing. But the first few experiences are... mystifying. Surely you understand."

"Did you manipulate it when Naila was in there, too?" Iravan asked relentlessly, knowing the answers now but foolishly seeking her denial as though that would help the situation. "Somehow, you stopped the magnaroot from becoming thorny. You trajected the rudra tree, didn't you? Bypassed its impenetrable permissions and forced it to forget that an earthrage was happening at all?"

Bharavi leaned forward on her seat. "I'm sorry you had to carry that burden," she said, and there was genuine regret in her voice. "I couldn't be found out. Not until I could convince everyone this is how things should be, how *architects* should be—not until I had a case."

"And voting to have me Examined would give you that time?"

She gazed at him, her face unreadable.

"I won't deny I voted yes for your Examination. I *called* for it, you know—even though Chaiyya said you needed more rest. But I knew you'd pass, Iravan. If I'd waited—if the council had waited to test you—another day, another week, it would have been too late.

You'd have failed. It would have been you in this deathcage. As it turns out, you have more time to remain undetected."

Iravan's throat tightened. In his heart, he knew she was telling the truth.

"I suppose it doesn't matter now," Bharavi continued. "One slip is all it takes. I was careless. You will be too."

"All those things you said to me in the sanctum. You were talking about yourself."

"I needed to know—if there was a way to control the power—"

"And *is* there?" Iravan asked, his eyes burning into hers. "Have you found control, then?"

"I've found," Bharavi said softly, "acceptance."

When he continued to stare at her, she shrugged again, the gesture graceful.

"It's not something to be controlled, Iravan. It's something to be embraced. I see that now. You'll see too."

Iravan's humorless laugh rang out, disturbing the quiet of the starlit sky.

"So, that's it, then?" he asked, bitterly. "That's my inevitable fate? After all this? After the Exam—after everything? Did it start the same way with you? Did you feel a Resonance too?"

Bharavi shook her head in amusement. "Resonance. Yes, that's quaint."

"What is it?"

"A sign of Ecstasy. But you accept that now, don't you?" For a moment, her shoulders dropped in regret. "I tried to veer you away from it—send you back to Ahilya, when you told me about it after the landing. But you succumbed to it so easily. Do you know why?"

"Don't—"

"Because in your heart you know how right Ecstasy is."

"That's not—"

"It's too late for you now," Bharavi said, leaning back. "You've associated with this Resonance too much. Your ascent is even faster than mine. What you did in the jungle, that was sign enough. And then the library—"

"That was you, then?" Iravan said. He'd worked it out in the last few hours, but hearing her confirm it made the weight in his heart heavier. "That other force that knocked me out?"

Bharavi nodded.

"You helped me," he said, hearing the note of childish hope in his own voice.

"Helped you? I suppose I did, but it was accidental. I defeated an irritating obstruction."

Spiralweed, he thought, feeling the deathbox still in his pocket. "How did you know of the attack in the library?"

Bharavi grinned at him. "I was… *super*trajecting at the time."

"That's why the Maze Architects didn't sense the spiralweed in the Moment. You were holding it back."

"Yes."

"You were protecting the ashram. You still care."

She said nothing, but her indulgent smile spoke volumes. *Believe whatever makes this easier for you.*

Iravan's mouth cracked into an identical twisted smile. "Still couldn't defeat the weed, could you? Despite your supertrajection?"

"I'll admit your help was welcome."

Iravan snorted softly, and for a while they sat in silence, watching each other across the glass. She looked so at peace with herself that something within Iravan's chest leapt in hot envy.

"What about Tariya and the boys?" he said, and at this, his voice choked, some of his restraint slipped.

Bharavi's face grew sad, shadows drawing over it.

"I loved them, didn't I?" she asked softly.

You still do, he thought in anguish, but he whispered, "Very much."

She said nothing, but her mouth trembled. Unreasonably, this indication of grief and indecision escalated his anger. Iravan remembered Ahilya's face as the bark closed in the temple. He had seen Tariya's face in his wife's; he had seen Kush and Arth.

"You said balance was possible," he said harshly. "You said you could do it. Then do it."

"It's not that easy. Manav was right."

"You won't do it for your wife? For your *children*?"

"I'm sorry," she said. "I know you care for them."

"They're my family, too."

"Yes, but balance… I'm not sure it's desirable. I'm sorry, Iravan. You're in for a rough time. You'll try to fight it—I know you will. But sooner or later, you'll give in. You'll see there's no fight at all. You are on your way and there's no going back. And let's face it—you and Ahilya—"

"You know nothing about me and Ahilya," he snarled.

She just shook her head, reminding him of her old self, gentle and exasperated with him.

"We are nothing like you and Tariya," he repeated. "I told you that when we landed."

Bharavi shook her arms out and stood up, appearing tired of the conversation. Iravan sat on his bench, his chest heaving, trying to control his breathing. He watched her as she circled her glass cage, tapping at one narrow pane after another. Her skin grew brighter, the blue-green light beams ricocheting off the panes and the polished stone slab.

"The deathcage will hold," he repeated warily. "You can't traject your way out. You know that."

"We shall see."

"It has held Ecstatics before, Bha."

"Not me. My powers are… untested. I don't know the limits of Ecstasy yet. No one does."

Iravan fell silent, watching as she circled the cage. His heart began to thud in his chest, but it was a low beat; he had exhausted his energy already on this day.

"If I let you out," he said, at last, "what will you do?"

Bharavi whipped around from her corner, her eyes on him. "The truth?"

"The truth."

She raised both her hands. "I'll release the architects from the bindings of the ashram. Everything we've built is… wrong. We need to start anew. Isn't that what you want, too? I know you're tired."

Iravan watched her. His hands were cold in the night air, his face still. A bone-deep fatigue weighed him down. Without getting off his bench, he leaned forward to the closest glass pane and unlocked it. The glass retracted with a *whisk*.

Bharavi watched from her corner, making no sudden moves, but her skin *exploded* with light so Iravan could discern no shapes, no patterns. His eyes watered, but he flicked open the deathbox from his pocket and tossed the spiralweed inside the glass cage.

The spiralweed engorged in a blink as he'd known it would.

Bharavi uttered a howl of rage and agony, but before she could move, Iravan locked the cage again. The glass pane shot back down, severing several whips of spiralweed vines that fell on his side of the deathcage. The dismembered vines crawled toward him like worms, but he sat in layers of nearly a hundred deathchambers and did not traject. The vines grew brown, withering away into dust before they could reach him.

Iravan closed his eyes and buried his head in his hands.

The sounds coming from inside the cage were terrifying.

They went on and on, the thrashing and whipping, Bharavi's enraged screams, her calls asking him to release her, *Iravan, IRAVAN!* And then they changed, into whimpers, into gurgles. The spiralweed was strangling her like it had tried to strangle him in the library, like he'd known it would.

Iravan rocked himself back and forth, not looking up, trapped in this eternal hell.

He did not know if he was crying again.

The sounds of Bharavi dying consumed his mind; every other memory, every thought, vanished; nothing existed except for this horror. He choked, barely able to breathe, this was a nightmare, this was eternal punishment.

It took him a long time to realize the garden was still again.

Very slowly, as though in a dream, he looked back up. The deathcage was dark. A small leaf vibrated on the stone floor, barely visible. The spiralweed had become innocuous again, satiated. It fluttered limply, unable to move.

Bharavi lay slumped in the corner by one of the glass panes.

He must have gotten to his feet. He must have entered the deathcage. The next thing Iravan knew, he was picking up the single source leaf of the spiralweed and trapping it again in the deathbox.

He approached Bharavi's lifeless body.

She looked so tiny.

A million stars reflected in her still brown eyes.

Iravan picked her up in his arms and carried her to the stone slab. He closed her eyes.

Except for the welts around her neck, she might have been sleeping. Except for his self-absorption, she might have still been alive.

For a long moment, he gazed down at her. He tried to absorb the enormity of what he'd done. She would never advise him again. They would never argue.

But Iravan couldn't muster any more tears. He had wept himself dry, holding on to Ahilya, bidding Bharavi farewell. All he felt was a terrible emptiness, a deep desire to sleep and never wake again. He bent down and kissed Bharavi's forehead softly.

Then activating all the locks, Iravan turned and walked away, feeling a hundred years old.

31

AHILYA

On the morning of Bharavi's funeral, Ahilya descended into darkness.

She clutched Arth to her, her eyes blurred with tears. Around her, Maze Architects shuffled and murmured to each other. Someone nudged her, and she turned around to see people clearing the garden path of the reclamation chamber.

Ahilya couldn't see the pallbearers yet, not with the press of bodies, but she had a sudden urge to laugh. Bharavi's funeral was occurring a day after her death, keeping to the traditions of Reikshar from where she had immigrated—and only a few Maze Architects had been able to make it at such short notice, but at least the Senior Architect was receiving a funeral. Oam had gotten nothing; he had been left behind. A sharp pain arose in Ahilya. She suppressed a sob.

And then she caught sight of the four pallbearers carrying Bharavi's body.

Ten-year-old Kush, who had grown taller in the last weeks, and a woman Ahilya didn't know, presumably a native of Bharavi's ashram, carried the rear ends of the pallet. In the front, leading the ceremony, was Tariya, her face glazed with tears. And next to her was Iravan, whose eyes were unseeing even as he marched.

Ahilya clutched Arth to her, choking, trying to inhale, but a hand had seized her lungs; she couldn't get a full breath. The thicket disappeared from in front of her. All the fifty or so assembled Maze Architects melted. She was back on the terrace above the temple, unable to speak, unable to move, condemned to watch as Iravan murdered Bharavi.

She had tried to look away when the spiralweed had strangled Bharavi. She had *wanted* to. Ahilya had moved toward the deathcage, but her legs had collapsed under her. She had sunk to her knees instead, paralyzed in shock, her tongue too heavy to make any sounds. The night had become cold, and Bharavi had screamed, calling out Iravan's name, and Ahilya had watched in horror and fear, complicit in his crime, images of Oam flashing in her head as his vine snapped away from hers.

She embraced Arth closer, and her nephew whined, wriggling in her grasp. Ahead, the procession came to a halt. The pallbearers placed the pallet on an earthy platform.

Iravan stepped forward and began to speak.

Ahilya closed her eyes, fighting nausea. Disjointed words came to her.… "The best friend a man could ask for"… "the kindest mentor"… "reborn in a better age"…

Revulsion and anger so great gripped Ahilya that she had to forcibly remind herself not to crush Arth. The fight nearly eight months before flashed in front of her eyes, the way Iravan had kissed her yesterday, the lies he'd uttered. *Trust me*, he'd said, before he'd proceeded to kill Bharavi. *Trust me*, but he had only wanted to send her away. The taste of him turned to ash in her mouth. Ahilya saw again, all the times she *had* trusted him and the consequences of doing so—the chasm he'd opened in the floor with her and Dhruv, the words he had said in the temple, after Oam. *I saved you. If I hadn't been out in the jungle, you wouldn't have made it back to Nakshar.*

Within the reclamation chamber, Iravan stopped talking. The woman from Reikshar picked up a basket from the floor and threw a few wood chips onto Bharavi's body. Iravan and Kush followed, and Tariya scattered the rest. Cries of surprise echoed around the chamber as showers of white gardenias fell over the assembled from the canopy. Leafy vines grew from the soil, sheathing Bharavi in a gentle embrace. The Senior Architect disappeared into the earth in a final sacrifice to Nakshar.

Tariya began to wail then, an awful heart-wrenching sound that broke Ahilya's heart.

Ahilya moved without knowing. One moment, she was watching her sister crumple, and the next she was by Tariya's side, holding her, wrapping her arms around her. Tariya grabbed her, sobs twisting her body, breathless. Tears filled Ahilya's eyes, too, and Iravan hurried toward them, raw dismay on his face, but a stab of fury flashed through Ahilya, piercing her grief. She clutched Tariya to her, protectively, against Iravan's reach.

He blinked and drew back in confusion, but the next second, Tariya had pulled him into the embrace, too. Iravan wrapped them both in his arms, the boys between them.

Ahilya disengaged immediately, leaving Arth with Tariya. She took a few steps back, her chest heaving up and down, close to hysteria. Iravan's brow creased as he studied her, but at Tariya's sobs, he turned to her.

"She loved you very much," he said abruptly. "It was the one thing she always returned to. You and Kush and Arth. Right to the very end."

Fresh tears ran down Tariya's face. She patted Iravan's cheek—a gesture so like what Bharavi would do—motherly and loving—that Ahilya's stomach clenched in hot fury. Iravan gripped Tariya's hand with both of his, the sorrow in his eyes almost sincere. Ahilya's entire body trembled.

And in that moment, she saw, very clearly for the first time, as she stood there in the clearing reclamation chamber, how her marriage had always been a lie. How she had never known this man who was her husband.

She had excused Iravan, one machination after another, one rationalization after another, determined to see the best in him despite proof to the contrary, despite *advice*, but the last vine had been snipped, and there would be no return to the illusion again. He had lied, betrayed every trust, and Ahilya might as well have traded places with her sister, for something precious had died, and she was now all alone.

A keening sound escaped her. Iravan's face distorted in concern, and he dropped Tariya's hands and reached toward her, but it was more than Ahilya could bear. She uttered a sob, and then she was running past the dispersing architects, her hand to her mouth, her vision blurred.

Ahilya was not aware of where she was going. All she knew was that she had to get away from Iravan. She ran through the ashram, a hatred like she had never known coursing through her. Again and again, she saw him unleash the spiralweed at Bharavi. She saw Bharavi's body spasm. She saw him walk away. His face flashed in front of her eyes, speaking words of duplicitous remorse, the things he had dared to say to Tariya, the things he had dared to say to *her*. *Trust me*, he had said. *Trust me*. She had trusted him and lost it all now, her marriage, her work, her family, and Ahilya ran past trees and startled faces, sobbing relentlessly. She should never have tied her future to Iravan's. She should never have made that bargain. She should have ended it when she could.

Somehow, she found herself back home.

Firemint assaulted her as soon as she entered, *Iravan's* scent. Ahilya grabbed a satchel and snatched her clothes and books, hurling them into the bag. She would go to Tariya's. She would live with her sister for a little while. The boys would need her, *Tariya* would need her. The despair would take her sister soon; there was nothing to compare this event to, no other provocation.

Ahilya reached for her kurtas, her hands brushing over her crimson wedding saree, clutching it, releasing it, when the bark behind her creaked open. She jumped, startled, and there was Iravan.

He strode in, running his hands through his thick salt-and-pepper hair.

"I looked for you," he said, then stopped as his gaze took her in. "What are you doing? Were you going to Tariya's? She won't be home—the nurses have taken her and the boys to the citizens' infirmary to heal. They will allow you to visit but not to stay. Tariya will need treatment and counsel—and they will help her. One of the councilors will speak to her."

Ahilya said nothing. A cold clarity had descended over her; she was suddenly seeing everything for the first time. She reached for the rest of her clothes, and Iravan watched her, pressing the base of his neck, confused. When she continued to remain silent, he shook his head.

"It doesn't matter," he said, beginning to pace in front of her. "I have to set things right. I can't go down that path—I can't—You are my only salvation—I should have known that. Without you—All of this—It came home to me after the—But that's not relevant. This entire time, it's been like I'm in the middle of another earthrage.

My life—the council, being an architect—none of these matter. I don't care about the things you've done—the spiralweed, the smuggling—and the council and its secrets—I don't care anymore. If this tragedy has taught me anything, it's that you are my life, Ahilya. You are my priority—it should have been the obvious path, but I was too blind. It was a mistake from the very beginning—"

Ahilya's heart pounded in her chest. Even now, his words burrowed in her heart, contaminating her clarity. Despite everything, his face was relentlessly handsome, the laugh lines visible, his eyes brooding. *He's a charmer, Ahilya. Stop lying to yourself.*

"What are you trying to say?" she asked bluntly.

Iravan stopped pacing. He turned her away from her packing.

His gaze held hers, and his hands gripped her shoulders.

"I love you. I love you so much, Ahilya. I *need* you. You're the only one who can save me. I know I've been a terrible husband, but I can be better. I can be whoever you want me to be."

For a long moment, Ahilya stayed unmoving. His grip on her shoulders was tight, intimate. His scent was almost overpowering. Very nearly, she leaned into his embrace, but she saw herself from afar, the temptation, the *need* for him like the acutest hunger, the urge to make things right and forgive him. A cold anger washed over her.

Iravan's earnest gaze faltered. He released her but didn't move away.

"You're right," Ahilya said slowly. "It *was* a mistake from the beginning."

Iravan's brow creased. Ahilya took a step back. "I'm leaving," she said. "We're done."

There was a long silence.

They stared at each other.

"I don't understand," Iravan said at last.

"I'm finished," she replied. "Finished with us, finished with this farce. You said it yourself. It was a mistake from the beginning."

Ahilya turned away, awash in the disbelief of her own words. Her vision tunneled, as the gravity of what she'd said settled into her. Her hands shook as she picked up more books. She was moving involuntarily now, just another device from the solar lab. This had been inevitable, and that it was happening, finally happening, left her empty inside.

Iravan's voice became very quiet. "You are saying this now. After everything I just told you. After the way we were—yesterday. Why?"

"You know why."

"Because you think I'm lying? That I'm incapable of change?"

"You did change. That has been the trouble all along. If you did it once, you can do it again."

"But you're still ending this marriage."

"You said your priorities were confounded. I'm making it easier."

"By making *this* decision." He let out a humorless laugh. "Rages, Ahilya. Why now? What has happened?"

That he could ask her this question, that he believed—no, *expected* her to be oblivious, to be ignorant, and had likely taken her forgiveness for granted—Ahilya shook in silent fury, unable to form a reply.

"Why, Ahilya?" he persisted. "Because you no longer want to try? Because you've finally had enough? Because you don't love me anymore?"

She said nothing. Her hands continued to pack as she placed one book after another in a bag.

His shadow moved, a latent aggression to it. Ahilya felt him right behind her, the vibrations of his energy and his anger, rumbling through the house as though he were morphing the architecture. "Which is it, Ahilya?" he asked, his voice hard. "I deserve to know—"

"And I deserve to know things too, Iravan," she said, losing her temper abruptly and whipping around. "But it's not as though you've been open with your secrets—"

"This is unfair. I've told you as much as I can—as much as I'm allowed to—*more*—I gave you things I'm not supposed to—"

Ahilya followed the direction of his eyes, to his rudra bead bracelet dangling from her wrist, to the books she still held, books he had provided her from the architect archives that she had never taken to the library alcove. Her body trembled in wrath. *I saved you*, he'd said. *Trust me*. She dropped the books back on the shelf and moved toward him, her hands clenched into fists.

"*That* is your defense?" she spat, furious. "You want me to be grateful to you? Is that why you brought up the spiralweed right now? Another way to get me to submit?"

Iravan blinked. "No, I misspoke; I didn't say it right. The spiralweed—I meant I don't care about your crime—"

"My crime? How dare you talk about my crimes when yours have been so great? Did you think no one would find out you killed Bharavi?"

Iravan's eyes widened.

His mouth fell open.

"I saw you," Ahilya whispered. "She was going to be excised. She would have returned to Tariya. Is killing people just a habit with you now? First Oam, then Bharavi?"

"Oam was an accident—and Bharavi—"

"Was what? Another accident? Don't bother lying, Iravan. I saw you use the spiralweed. Did you do it so I'd be implicated with you? To ensure my silence?"

"No, you don't understand—"

"You think it'll all be forgiven if you finally tell me you've chosen to place me in a position I should have always been in? Because you tell me I'm *important* to you? Everywhere you go, you destroy so callously—my expedition, Oam's life, Dhruv's experiment, and now this—"

Iravan shook his head furiously, raising an imploring hand toward her. "No, Ahilya, please listen. I did it for her own good. Bharavi wanted this—"

"I watched you," Ahilya shouted. "She was fighting. She was calling out your *name*, Iravan."

"No, you don't understand. Ecstasy—it gives you incredible powers with no regard for the safety of the ashram. And she was deteriorating. I suspected it wouldn't be long before—"

"You killed her because of a *suspicion*? You destroyed Tariya's family—"

"I saved Tariya the pain," Iravan said, his voice raised. "When excision happens, families erode—"

"Why?" she shot back. "Because architects aren't architects anymore? Because they're no longer fucking *special*? Did Tariya ever indicate she loved Bharavi only because of her power?"

"No. No, of course not! But excision cuts away—The families, they don't recover—Love has very little to do with it—"

"*How, Iravan?*"

"Because love is meaningless when a person can't feel, Ahilya," he shouted, goaded beyond endurance. "That's what excision does. Non-architects never fully understand this!"

Stung, Ahilya fell silent. Her cheeks warmed in anger and humiliation. Iravan's words echoed around their home. The foliage in the apartment became prickly: tight, thorny leaves stabbing out of the walls. She saw Iravan crush her rudra bead key before the expedition. Saw him open a hole by her feet, uncaring of her life. *You should be on your knees*, he'd said, *thanking the architects.*

"I'm sorry," he said, forcing his voice into calmness. "I know it's not through any fault of your own."

Ahilya swallowed. Rage and bitterness coursed through her, tightening her chest. She took a deep breath, trying to compose herself. Iravan had always kept his own identity as an architect topmost; of course he would think he would no longer be able to *feel* without the presence of the Moment. Of course he had never thought that non-architects were as sensitive or as complex as architects. He had indicated it before, in so many words time and again, in his explanation of the ragas—*It's a matter of consciousness-sensitivity*, he'd said, words she'd ignored like so many others. But the ones now, they were so telling, so wrong, that revulsion grew in her, choking her. She had been so foolish. His every conversation had been twisted, a trap, a hundred meanings she'd blinded herself to. How could she believe anything anymore? *He's a charmer, Ahilya. Don't take your time, or he will decide for you.* They had finally come to the consequences of his duplicities, and her excuses for him. She had ignored the writing on the wall for too long. No more.

"You have an explanation for everything," Ahilya said quietly. "But you don't see how inadequate it all is."

"It is the truth—"

"Is it? Oam was an accident, and Bharavi's death was for *architect* reasons. You've already cleared your conscience of any misconduct by claiming you saved my life while interfering with my expedition. I can't wait to hear what your explanation is for what you did to Dhruv."

Iravan's expression changed. A muscle in his jaw twitched. Without seeming to know it, he took an aggressive step forward.

"Dhruv?" he asked coldly. "Dhruv broke the law. And I *still* held my silence—"

"Or maybe you designed this somehow from the very start. He told me it was *you* who pushed Kiana into exchanging sungineers the next time the ashrams met, *you* who forced the battery. Did you want him to get transferred? Surely as a councilor, you were aware of a sungineer's limitations, and I know you never liked him."

Iravan's eyes glinted in fury. He stood a handbreadth away. She could hear his agitated breathing. "It was *he* who never liked me, but it seems you're willing to listen to everyone's version of the truth except for mine. To every other account except my own—"

"You haven't shown yourself worthy of trust—"

"Perhaps you wouldn't have brought any of this up," he snarled, speaking over her, "if I had fully acquiesced to you. If I had pretended all along that you were the only important thing in my life, the ashram and the rest of my obligations be damned—"

"Acquiesced to *me*?" Ahilya shouted, incredulous. "This has always been about you and your reputation, your career as an architect, your material bonds—"

"Maybe it would have been better had I openly lied to you," he continued, his eyes flashing. "Agreed with everything you ever said, even if it went against my own principles, against my own logic. But there have been enough deceits in my life without that, and you'll forgive me, Ahilya, if I didn't want to add our marriage to the list."

Ahilya stepped forward, inches away from Iravan, glaring up at him.

"You want the truth, Iravan?" she spat. "This, then, is the truth. All of this with Bharavi and Dhruv and Oam only spared me from keeping the farce of our marriage going. Your manipulations and power tactics, your arrogance as an architect, your secrets and your games, were all indications that you're a terrible husband and will make an even worse father. I'd have decided to leave you even if none of this had happened." She removed his rudra bead bracelet and flung it at his chest. It slid down, and he caught it in his hands.

Iravan flinched once, then stilled.

His eyebrows drew together, but as he stared at her, Ahilya got the impression he was really staring at himself. He remained unmoving for an eternal second, his head dipped down to her, his breathing erratic. Ahilya didn't move, either; she couldn't have even if she'd wanted. They stood there, a few inches apart, their chests rising and falling, their home becoming smaller, more oppressive. A dozen thoughts chased each other in Ahilya's mind. Iravan weeping. The contempt in his eyes in the solar lab. His kiss and the taste of him, how full and empty he'd seemed at the same time.

Finally, Iravan nodded as though in understanding of something.

His voice, when he spoke, was emotionless. "I needed this clarity, Ahilya. Thank you for giving it to me. The house is yours. I'll send someone to collect my things and guide you through our separation."

The bark closed behind him. Ahilya clutched the shelf with a dry sob, her heart pounding in her chest.

32

AHILYA

Ahilya slept poorly that night. In her restless dreams, Iravan came to her, dressed in his spotless white kurta and tapered trousers, his dark skin a shining contrast. He tipped her chin up with a finger to kiss her, but his eyes were hard.

"We were never good for each other," she said to him, full of sadness. "An architect and a non-architect. We should have known from the start."

"We're perfect for each other," he growled, angrier than he'd ever been, more handsome than he'd ever looked. "A murderer and a smuggler. What could be more fitting?"

And he began to laugh, and she laughed with him, hoarsely, piercingly, holding on to him while between them lay the shadow of a child, a family they would never have.

She awoke abruptly, reaching a hand to the other side of the bed.

Of course. He wasn't there.

He hadn't been home in a long time. He wouldn't come back. Ahilya sat up, a leaden weight in her stomach. The bed had narrowed, the living wood large enough only for her. Her mouth moved to speak his name, but they were truly finished now.

Ahilya put her hands over her ears, but she could still hear the awful words. *Love is meaningless when a person can't feel. Non-architects never fully understand. If I had pretended you were the only important thing in my life.* She looked up, breathing heavily, and the leaves in their home rustled, as though he had only just walked out. She could still feel the touch of his lips, from the dream, from two days before, but when she inhaled, she couldn't smell the firemint in their home anymore.

Ahilya rose to her feet, dazed. The apartment was unrecognizable. Their home—*her* home now—had changed overnight. He had removed his presence entirely. The third story was gone. No phosphorescence glimmered on the walls. The ceiling had lowered, oppressive, not intimate. Not even in the seven months of his absence had their house looked so bereft of him. Just as easily as that, he'd cut himself away. Gasping, Ahilya dressed hastily. She had to get away. She had to leave.

Her solarnote on the shelf blinked rapidly, an indication of a significant message, but it could only be the divorce papers. He had already drawn them up, wasting no time in ending their marriage. The thought of reading them choked her. Ahilya waved a hand to the wall, and a doorway opened to one of the main thoroughfares of the ashram. She hurried out, unable to bear the specter of her loss.

Dawn was breaking over Nakshar. Very few people seemed to be awake. Ahilya walked through the city, uncertain where she was headed. Her feet carried her past the dilapidated Architects' Academy, past the broken fig-tree library, past the solar lab, and through the roads leading to the temple. *I'm looking for him*, she realized, when she stopped finally at one of the empty terraces of the ashram. *I'm still looking for him.* She gazed out to the sky and the dark clouds, wishing she could get away from Nakshar altogether. How long had it been since she'd tried to study dust patterns from a terrace much like this? Two weeks, at the most. She could scarcely believe her life had come to this in such a short time. Ahilya wiped her face with a corner of her shawl and turned to see Naila striding toward her.

She stopped short. "Naila," she whispered. "What are you doing here?"

"I came to visit you," the Junior Architect said.

"How did you know—" Ahilya began, but then shook her head. She'd learned architects had their own methods. Did it matter how Naila had found her? "I was just about to leave," she said instead.

"Then may I accompany you?"

Ahilya nodded tightly. For a while, they walked next to each other in an awkward silence. Ahilya did not know what to say; she could hardly summon the energy for thought. The last time she had seen Naila had been in the Academy with him. He... *they* had been making progress. They had *tried. Non-architects never fully understand. Love is meaningless when a person can't feel.* Perhaps she had never known him at all.

"I heard you got information from the yaksha," Naila said. She had been leading the way, keeping to quieter streets. The effects of Bharavi's Ecstasy were rampant. Branches lay across the road, scorched. The earth had cracked, the ground unlevel. Several trees warped on the path, their trunks split in the middle.

"Yes," Ahilya said.

Naila gave her a sidelong glance, and Ahilya remembered that the Junior Architect had meant to accompany her into the jungle before he had... She cleared her throat and told Naila what she and Dhruv had found: the interference in the elephant-yaksha's transmission signal.

The Junior Architect considered this. "How do you explain that?"

"Maybe there's habitation down there for the yakshas, like I said."

"I wonder if it's some kind of jungle plant," Naila mused. "Some species that could block the signal?"

Her response was very much that of an architect. Ahilya shrugged, unable to work up even resentment. "Maybe. But the jungle is recreated constantly. Why would these plants grow in the exact same place after every earthrage? It doesn't make sense."

"Unless they've adapted somehow." Naila bit her lip, then glanced at Ahilya again. "Did you learn anything about the dust patterns?"

Ahilya did not reply. It was no surprise the Junior Architect had thought of the dust patterns now, when they were headed away from a similar terrace where they had once had that discussion. But her question mattered little. Ahilya had discovered nothing useful in the books from the architects' archives. She had thought studying the dust would give her information on how earthrages began in the first place—a feature of the planet's tectonic plates—but all she had found was evidence of multiple epicenters and overlapping storms. Naila had been right all along. The architects had studied the patterns thoroughly; they had found nothing. And now everything was lost to Ahilya with the divorce: her marriage, her study, her purpose.

Naila didn't press the issue. They walked in silence, the sun rising higher. Ahilya pulled her shawl closer. She couldn't feel the warmth of the day. The heat passed right through her.

"I should have come to you," Naila said abruptly. "After the expedition… after Oam…"

Her hands were clenched around the sleeves of her translucent robe. For the first time, Ahilya considered how Naila was, in so many ways, still a child. The burden she carried as an architect, the responsibilities—Ahilya would never know it. Impulsively, she reached for Naila.

"I'm glad you weren't there," she said, pressing the architect's hand. "I would not have lost you, too."

Naila smiled weakly. "If I had been out there with you, we—none of us—would have survived."

Ahilya snatched her hand back. "What are you trying to say?"

"That kind of trajection—I'm not capable of it. Had I gone out there, you would have died. I don't have the skill to do what Iravan-ve did."

Hearing his name was like a stab through the heart. Ahilya suddenly realized Naila had led them to the temple. She took a step back, drawing in a sharp breath.

"Why are we here, Naila?"

"Please—he only wants to talk—"

"Iravan put you up to this," Ahilya said, taking another step back.

Naila raised a pacifying hand. "Please—it's about Bharavi-ve—He said he needed to explain."

Ahilya stopped, shock arresting her movement. Even now, despite everything that had happened, she couldn't help the wave of hurt and betrayal that swept at her. "He told *you* about it?"

"I—I don't know the details. Please—I don't know anything except he wants to explain something about Bharavi-ve. He said it'd be the only way you'd come."

"And he asked *you* to deliver the message instead of coming himself?"

"He didn't think you'd listen," Naila said, and she winced in unexpected mortification. "And I... I owe him for... my misconduct."

The Junior Architect didn't elaborate, but Ahilya had never seen Naila so out of sorts. The woman refused to meet her eyes. She shifted her feet. "Please, Ahilya," Naila mumbled, still staring at the ground. "I—I need to ease my conscience—"

Perhaps another time, Ahilya would have inquired deeper, but she could not bring herself to gather the energy to care. She gave a tight nod, and Naila tapped at one of her rudra bead bracelets.

The bark in front of them slid open. Iravan stood there, evidently waiting. He lowered his hand where a new citizen ring glinted, although Ahilya noticed his rudra bead bracelets and necklaces were still missing. He looked no better than her, as though his night had been just as restless. Dark shadows lingered heavy under his eyes. His face was unshaven, bristles on his cheeks. Ahilya remained frozen. It was too soon. She wasn't ready for this.

"Thank you for coming," he said.

"I wasn't given a choice," she heard herself say.

"I understand if you don't want to talk about it," he continued, his voice quiet. "But you saw something and I want to explain. If you want to leave, I won't stop you."

He waited, unmoving. Ahilya blinked. She nodded again, the words stuck in her throat.

Iravan turned to Naila. "You can report me to Airav now, Junior Architect."

"—Iravan-ve—I don't—"

His eyes glittered in anger. "Please."

Naila hesitated, then gave him a stiff bow. She walked along the curving wall, tapped at her bracelet again, entered a doorway, and disappeared.

Iravan extended a hand, and Ahilya followed as he opened another door. Unlike the path she had sneaked into a couple of days before, this one led into a tinted-glass-lined corridor open to the skies. Iravan walked next to her silently. His gaze remained straight ahead. The distance between them was like an unbreachable chasm, their marriage a corpse buried in the greatest depths. Ahilya's eyes drew to his hands a few inches away, to his energy that surrounded her.

She swallowed. "Where are we going?"

"Are you afraid I'm going to murder you, too, Ahilya?" Iravan asked softly.

She raised her eyes to him, and he looked down at her and sighed.

"This is the sanctum," he said. "The ward where we bring excised architects."

"What are we doing here?"

"When an architect is in danger of Ecstasy, they're made to go through an Examination. If they pass it, they're... free. If they fail—"

"They are excised. I know this."

"Yes, but you don't know what excision does," Iravan said. He stopped in front of one of the glass panes and pressed a dial in the wall. The tint became transparent. He beckoned to her.

Despite herself, Ahilya drew nearer.

The glass looked into a chamber where a woman sat on a chair, rocking herself. Spittle trickled down her lips. Her gaze was unseeing, her hair gray and thin. Ahilya's eyes flickered to Iravan, but he gazed at the woman, his face withdrawn.

"What—" Ahilya began, but then the woman turned.

Her unseeing eyes met Ahilya's through the glass.

And a memory flashed through Ahilya's mind, of the same woman, her head thrown back in healthy laughter, a memory from when Ahilya had been a child and her parents had still lived in Nakshar. Maiya had been a Maze Architect who had become an Ecstatic. Ahilya had thought she'd been transferred after her excision.

Ahilya gasped. "What—Iravan, what is this? What is Maiya doing here?"

He twisted the dials in the glass and the pane became opaque again. Ahilya stumbled behind him as he walked to a patch away from the glass. Iravan trajected, and a wooden bench grew over the grass clearing. Ahilya collapsed on it, her head spinning.

"What—did I just see?" she breathed.

Iravan sat down next to her. He leaned forward to place his elbows on his knees.

"Excision," he said heavily. "It doesn't just cut an architect away from their trajection. It cuts away a part of their consciousness. We take away part of their… personality. Their life force. Whatever that ineffable part is that gives an architect their power. And that's what happened to Maiya."

Horrified, Ahilya watched him. "How can you do this?"

Iravan let out a harsh laugh. "What else is our choice? To let Ecstatic Architects run amok and destroy the ashram? Every Maze Architect knows the risk. They are sworn never to reveal it."

He extended his wrist in front of him. A white bracelet glinted on his dark skin: a healbranch bracelet, appearing to be made of bone.

Ahilya blinked, recognizing it. Iravan had received the healbranch bracelet when he'd become a Maze Architect. Years back, when she had asked about it, his replies had been ambiguous; he'd muttered about rules a Maze Architect had to obey, and Ahilya hadn't pressed. Eventually, in the presence of his many rudra beads, she'd forgotten the healbranch.

Iravan tugged the bracelet with a finger. Thorns grew from it, piercing deep into his wrist, bloodying him, poisoning him, but he didn't wince.

Ahilya had the urge to tell him to stop, to speak no more lest he hurt himself further, but horror churned within her at what he had revealed, and she gazed up at him in disbelief. "Such a huge secret, Iravan?" she whispered. "You keep this from the families of the Maze Architects, too? From their husbands and wives?"

"Nearly all Maze Architects and their spouses know this."

"I didn't."

"This information is shared when..." Iravan trailed off and rubbed his face with his hands.

"When what?"

"When there's a binding commitment between the two people as understood by the council."

"And what is that binding commitment?"

Iravan turned his head to meet her eyes. "A child," he said, softly.

The silence following those words was so heavy that Ahilya could barely breathe.

In her mind's eye, she saw herself around the spouses of the Maze Architects, and how she alone had not known this awful truth; how she had always been an outsider, not because of her profession but because of *this.* Ahilya remembered her argument with Iravan, nearly eight months earlier, when he had tried to convince her to make a baby. It was the argument that had precipitated his punishing silence, that had pushed them down this path; it was one they'd had so many times. Ultimately, it had led them to this moment.

"How enlightened," she said at last. "And what if an architect doesn't want a child?"

"Then they have no business being an architect," Iravan responded, and his voice grew harder. "If a family is something that an architect doesn't want, they are at greater risk of Ecstasy than ever. They'd have no binding material bonds that could withstand the pressures of this occupation—the pressures of the split of Two Visions and of drifting in a space like the Moment. And that is not an acceptable situation."

"So, you force people to bear children, even if they're perfectly happy without them."

"We thought we were happy, Ahilya," he said, and his voice sounded hollow. "We thought we had a lot in common. Look at where we are now."

"A child would not have solved our problems, Iravan."

"Perhaps not," he admitted, sighing. "Not our problems. But for an architect, a child creates an unshakeable material bond. Without that guarantee, without that safeguard, architects cannot progress. They must not."

"*You* did."

"With difficulty," he said, shaking his head. "With being near-perfect in all other conditions, unable to make a mistake. Such a state has been… unforgiving."

Ahilya's mind spun. She had always known arbitrary material conditions mattered to an architect—they were the oldest architect tradition—yet for Iravan to carry such a huge burden all alone—for her to not know this… She couldn't wrap her head around it. Rage, resentment, and guilt coursed through her in equal measure. She felt a deep desire to walk away from this horrible revelation.

"It's an imperfect situation," Iravan said, after some time. "But it's the only way we have. An architect needs to have material bonds, and that is understood as a family. A family with children."

"If it's so important, perhaps you should tell us without the child. Why wait?"

"Being married to an architect is… hard," Iravan said, with a ghost of a smile. "Did you know there was a time when architects married only other architects? That's a part of the secret archives. Many architects succumbed to Ecstasy together, but now every architect is encouraged to marry someone who can't traject. And we wait until the people are pregnant—or until after they've begun adoption proceedings—to share such a secret. It's to give their marriage a chance without the burden of such troubles."

"So, it's more manipulation." Ahilya said softly. "You tell the spouses when they're too far in so there won't be any going back. You leave them no choice."

Iravan's mouth twisted, an ironic smile. "There *is* a choice. People still retain the right to terminate the fetus before consciousness appears. They still retain the right to abandon adoption if they change their mind. And that decision—that's the spouse's alone. The architect gets no say in it. Do you know Reetha?"

Ahilya frowned. "She's a Maze Architect, isn't she? She was pregnant a few years before, but her husband—he left her." She looked up. "I remember you telling me about it. It caused the council a lot of trouble."

Iravan nodded. "Knowing there was a chance that she might be in danger of Ecstasy, and might have to be excised, her husband chose never to have the child at all. The council tried to talk him out of it, but in the end, he chose to end their marriage. And Reetha was transferred."

Horrified, Ahilya wrapped her arms around her belly. "You never told me that."

"It was not my secret to tell," Iravan said. "But this is the question that architects and their spouses struggle with, Ahilya. If you knew there was a possibility that your partner could be destroyed one day in a horrible manner, that they would become so different that they'd not be the same person at all, would you still choose to be with them? Would you start a family and spend your life with them? That entire process can be testing for the marriage. One that Reetha and her husband did not pass. And we didn't either."

"So, Reetha can never have a child?" Ahilya asked. "The ashram lost an architect forever?"

Iravan shook his head. "There are alternatives. Reetha did have another child. The healers assisted her and she was watched carefully for how attached she was to the baby. She is a Maze Architect in Kinshar now but on probation."

Ahilya glanced at him, the angles of his face, his unseeing eyes. "If we'd become pregnant," she said, "you could tell me this, and I would still have retained my choice to have the child after?"

Iravan smiled another twisted smile. "I suppose we don't have to make that decision anymore. But an architect's health is only as good as their family life, and the council keeps a close watch on their marriage. The only reason you and I weren't examined as closely was because I'm a Senior Architect and, well, Bharavi and I made concessions for each other we shouldn't have. But," he added, shrugging, "perhaps those in my position should be examined closer."

For a moment, Ahilya wondered what those concessions were, why if the stakes had been so high, the two Senior Architects had allowed each other to compromise. Then she glanced at him, this man who valued his freedom above all else, imagining how it must have felt to report to someone—even Bharavi—all those times he had spent with his family. How this condition of keeping to material bonds had destroyed their marriage, destroyed *him*. He had chafed against it; of course he had. Ahilya blinked, wondering how she would have reacted if their positions were reversed.

"We have no child," she said. "Yet you're telling me this now."

"I am."

Why? she thought. She was drowning again, caught in the cave-in under the Academy. He reminded her of how they had been when they'd begun courting, how every moment with him had muddled her in some way. She glanced at him, this man she had been married to for so long, this man she still loved so desperately, who was really—in the end—just a stranger.

"Naila will report me," Iravan went on. "That's why I sent her to Airav."

"And you're not afraid of what the council will do?"

He fiddled with his healbranch bracelet, where the thorns had retracted. The bracelet snapped clear into two, the shards dropping into his palm. His wrist still bled—and Ahilya knew the poison had already entered his veins; it would slowly infect him, making him ill until he wasted away—but Iravan wiped the blood away with the cuff of his sleeve carelessly and shrugged. "What *can* they do?"

"They could demote you," she said. "Dismiss you."

"That happened the moment you signed the divorce papers. I was already toeing the line without children, and I'm not fooling Airav about Bharavi. But our divorce and showing you the sanctum right now—they cannot overlook all these offenses. They have likely passed the vote of no confidence against me already."

"And you don't care?"

"Isn't that awful?" Iravan said, smiling his cold smile again. "I don't think I do."

Beyond anything else she'd seen or heard today, the indifference of his voice scared Ahilya. When she spoke, it was more to provoke him into emotion than to hear his response.

"You're not afraid I'll broadcast this to the rest of the ashram?" she blurted.

Iravan glanced at her. "Will you? I don't expect you to keep my secrets—not anymore. I've never been able to control you, anyway.

"But you should know: this knowledge of excision is an architect's greatest shame. No one is more the owner of that shame than a Senior Architect, one who carries out excision. We deal with consciousness in the Moment; we understand its gravity. Yet we do something so heinous to one of our own? If this secret were revealed, we'd lose all credibility. We'd be hunted down for our crime or—if we were lucky—be idolized for our sacrifice. Either would ruin material bonds and drive architects to Ecstasy. Either would be terrible for survival."

His tone sent a chill down her spine. Ahilya was suddenly reminded of her fear with the spiralweed, of technology that could enslave architects.

Iravan gestured at the terrace with a hand. "Nakshar needs Maze Architects, now more than ever before. This knowledge could ruin our culture, erode all the trust architects have."

"So, instead," Ahilya said, her lips trembling, "you tell everyone that excision is dismissal from the temple. You let people think Ecstatics can one day go back to their families?"

Far from provoking him into a reaction, her words merely made Iravan shrug again.

"Theoretically, you can. Chaiyya's entire study is to do exactly that. She has helped rehabilitate several people, and Manav can now speak again when once he couldn't form words after his excision. But it never truly works like you expect it to. That's why Bharavi and I made a pact. If ever one of us was in danger of being excised, the other would do them the mercy and execute them. Ecstatics fight for their lives—that's in their nature, and we knew asking that of each other meant we may have to fight one another. If the murder became public knowledge, we'd be exiled to a different ashram, demoted, imprisoned forever, or perhaps executed ourselves. But," he said, looking at her, "we didn't want our families to ever see us like Maiya. Better to die and be reborn than to live like this."

Ahilya stared at him. "That," she said quietly, "is alarmingly arrogant thinking."

One of Iravan's eyebrows lifted. "As you have told me, Ahilya, I am an arrogant man."

"You speak as though a life can just be erased, that it has no meaning, simply because of rebirth. You are relying far too much on an unknown future to solve the problems of this life. With thinking like that, we could all kill ourselves at the least sign of trouble. We could let go of a dozen Oams, without consequence or guilt. We could absolve ourselves of any and all responsibility."

Iravan shook his head. "You misunderstand me. Rebirth does not give us a blank slate; the desires of our consciousness carry forward within our depth memories, in the form of our actions and intents. Bharavi and I made the pact, knowing it could impact the circumstances of our rebirth. You were right when you said she was scared and angry—but it was not merely when she was fighting for her life. She was scared when she tried to convince me of the goodness of Ecstasy. I'd thought then that her fear was for me—for what she'd have to do to me to fulfill our pact. But surely a part of it was for how any action she'd take would impact her own consciousness. We understood this, but we still chose it—"

"Which makes this interpretation all the more dangerous," Ahilya said. "Where would such a path end? You do not have the ability to traject and you cannot imagine yourself without it, so you kill yourself? Your life changes, so you choose death instead of trying to heal? Imagine the implications for those of us who could *never* traject—imagine what it means for the people in the infirmary, for an ashram to think like this—a whole council—"

"The council doesn't think like this," Iravan said. "This was our choice, Bharavi's and mine, to do what we wanted with our lives after excision. Few make this choice, and it is not encouraged or publicized. Everyone would inquire into the reason behind Ecstatics dropping dead after their Ecstasy was revealed, if it were common practice. The secret of excision would be out immediately. This was not a pact we made lightly—"

"But you made it," Ahilya said. "And you did so without me, our marriage be damned."

Her voice was quiet, without rancor or accusation, but for the first time since the beginning of this conversation, Iravan's gaze fell. He swallowed hard, his fingers curling into fists, releasing, curling again.

"That," he said softly, "was my greatest shame. It was the one thing I needed to tell you but couldn't. For that, as for so many other things, Ahilya, I owe you a deep apology."

Ahilya pulled her shawl closer around her. The breeze was cold despite the hot sun.

His words were sincere, but she could not help the wave of terror and fury that rippled through her. After the incident at the solar lab, she had made her way to the temple; she had been afraid, when Megha had told her about the architect in Ecstasy, that it had been *Iravan* in Ecstasy. What if it had been? What if Iravan had been in Bharavi's place? He had never wanted her to see him like Maiya or Manav, but she was his wife. How dare he allow himself death without her consent, without her knowledge or acceptance? He was hers—he *had been* hers, yet this was the decision he had chosen to make? The betrayal ran deep within her, and Ahilya took a deep breath, trying to calm herself.

"It's only a matter of time before the secret is out," Iravan said, as though he had heard her thought. "The spouses of architects don't make a healbranch vow. Rumors already exist, and the council threatens and cajoles the citizens who do know this secret into silence. Until we have a way to not be reliant on trajection, we cannot widely share the truth; the architects and their spouses, all of us must suffer it—and that's why sungineers are tasked with finding a battery to store trajection. Until that happens, we must propagate our lies so we don't spread our shame."

The weight of all these revelations settled heavy into Ahilya's shoulders.

She curled further into herself.

What had been her duty for all those years of marriage? She had always known about the material bonds of an architect, even if she'd never known the extent. That knowledge had formed a bond and then a prison for her and Iravan. But they had wed *before* he'd become a Maze Architect; they had been in love once. His mysteries had finally become too much, but if she'd known this about excision, would that have changed her actions? Her guilt and anger now—were they fair? Were they *right*? She couldn't think clearly.

"All is not lost to you," she mumbled. "Like Reetha, you could have a child—you could adopt one."

"You mistake me." Iravan sounded tired. "I didn't just want a child, Ahilya. I wanted *our* child. I didn't want to keep secrets from you, and I wish I could say I'd have done things differently had I known where it would bring us. But I don't think it could have been otherwise."

His eyes were trained on the horizon. Ahilya wanted to touch him. She wanted to tell him how she never knew what he was thinking; how he had broken and mended her heart so many times that its shape had changed; how his secrets and his silences were exhausting; how she was pulled and pushed in so many directions. She wanted to tell him how much she loved him.

Ahilya blinked back tears, the unsaid words choking her throat. She couldn't wrap her head around the extent of her loss.

"Dhruv and I," she whispered at last. "When I began the expeditions all those years ago, I started to bring Dhruv plants from the jungle in exchange for his equipment. He felt the pressure to build a battery keenly, and it made him—made us—reckless.

We did it for the council seat, to ward off his transfer and the loss of archeology. But I'm beginning to think neither of us are worthy."

"It's not you. The system is created to favor architects. It forces underhandedness from others." Iravan breathed heavily. "I'm sorry about Dhruv's experiments. For what it's worth."

"We thought we were being careful," she said softly. "When your investigation started, we decided not to place the spiralweed in the lab because that's where you'd be investigating. We left them in my archives. I didn't think..."

"You didn't think I would touch those."

Ahilya shook her head miserably.

"Architects and sungineers have always had their politics," Iravan said slowly. "But at the heart of it, we work together to stay in the skies to survive. That's why I pushed for a battery in recent years. Enslaving architects with a battery has always been a risk; this is why the council must have more architects than sungineers. But between saving ourselves and saving the species? Architect or sungineer, the council agreed. A battery was our only choice. It's the price of survival."

"I should have told you about our deal," Ahilya said. "I didn't think you would understand."

"I suppose," he said, turning to look at her, "we both have a problem with that."

He held her gaze, and Ahilya swallowed. Words circled her mind, spilling almost to her tongue. Her fingers twitched, and she made to reach for him, the pull was too strong—but both their citizen rings chimed softly, and Iravan looked away and the moment was gone.

He tapped at his rudra bead, reading the message that hovered over it. Her heart heavy, Ahilya mimicked his action, then glanced up to see an ironic smile on his face.

"The council is meeting," he said. "I've been called to it."

"So have I," she said, in a low voice.

"There's only one reason they'd summon the both of us."

Ahilya knew what he meant. It would be to discuss the terms of their divorce. She froze, her heart beating rapidly in her chest, unable to move, but Iravan stood up as though it were nothing more than a straightforward occurrence.

"I suppose we go to it, Ahilya," he said quietly, holding out his hand. "End what we started eleven years ago."

She stared at him a long moment. Then Ahilya placed her hand in his and he pulled her to her feet. Iravan turned away, his jaw tightening as his fingers let go. Ahilya followed him out of the courtyard, the touch of him still lingering on her skin.

33

IRAVAN

Outside the sanctum, Iravan generated an elevator that took him and Ahilya to the upper levels of the temple to the council chambers. Ahilya hadn't said a word since the summons. She stood next to him, her head bowed, her hands wrapped around herself, clutching her shawl.

A strange exhilaration rose within Iravan. He was on the precipice of a mountain, daring himself to leap into the abyss. In his mind's eye, the two paths that had haunted him for so long glimmered. He was going to do it—step onto the second path, a path without the bindings of the ashram. He was going to see clearly for the first time. He had ignored that path for so long. No more.

A presence burned at the center of his forehead; it had appeared the instant Ahilya had thrown his rudra bead bracelet at him. Iravan recognized it now. The Resonance. He took a deep breath, clenching and unclenching his fists. He had lost it all, Ahilya, Bharavi, his marriage and his position—but a freedom grew in him with the appearance of the silvery particle. He neither trajected nor entered the Moment, but the Resonance was waiting. He wished for the formalities to be over.

"What should I be expecting?" Ahilya asked softly.

He glanced at her. "Whoever received our papers from the council, they'll try to talk us out of it. There has to be a period of separation, but they might waive that—considering how little time we've spent together in the last few months. Considering how we haven't been intimate lately."

A choked sound escaped Ahilya, midway through a laugh and a sob. "Is it normal for the councilor undergoing the proceedings to be advising their spouse?"

"No," he said. "But you asked, and I know, so I can tell you. A divorce at this level—after so many years of marriage, it's not easy. Architects marry for life. Our divorce will send a bad message. The only way to get through the councilors' arguments is to be sure this is what we want."

"And *is* it what you want, Iravan?" Ahilya whispered, clutching her shawl, not looking at him.

Iravan's eyes widened in shock. The clarity of the second path faltered. He turned to face her.

"Don't you?" he began, but the wall of their elevator creaked open, and Senior Sungineer Kiana stood waiting for them, no doubt to represent the council. Iravan fell silent, his mind reeling.

"Come with me," Kiana said curtly.

Iravan exchanged an apprehensive look with Ahilya. That subtle indication of shared camaraderie took him aback as much as her question had. Her eyes stared into his, and he detected guilt and grief and *fury.* Ahilya tore her gaze away from his and followed Kiana. Iravan found himself walking again as well.

"Where are we going, Kiana?" he asked, his voice hoarse.

"The council chambers—everyone is waiting."

"Everyone?" Ahilya whispered.

"An intervention?" he said grimly at the same time. He grabbed the Senior Sungineer's arm and turned her. "We're not children, Kiana. You don't need to make a production of this. End it here and now, and release us both. As councilor, you have the authority."

Kiana gave him a hard look. "You mean your divorce? You signed it. But, *you*," she said, her gaze taking in Ahilya, "did not."

"You didn't?" Iravan asked, staring at Ahilya. For a moment, rage, hope, and confusion filled his mind, removing the fiery presence of the Resonance from the center of his forehead. The second path disappeared. All he saw was Ahilya on the first.

"I—I don't know anymore," Ahilya stammered.

Her eyes dropped in misery. Iravan took a deep breath.

"I think we need to talk," he said, turning back toward the elevator.

"You do," Kiana said sharply, arresting his movement. "But not right now. Your papers reached the council—and I've been assigned to deal with it. It's not uncommon to feel this after an Examination of Ecstasy or the death of a family member, and Bharavi was close to you both. So, you *will* talk, Ahilya and Iravan, and you *will* figure it out. But right now, you will learn to work together, because the ashram needs you both."

She began walking again. Exchanging another look, Iravan and Ahilya followed her. Iravan noticed what he hadn't before. Kiana no longer carried her cane. Instead, the Senior Sungineer wore her leg brace. Why? The device had always been uncomfortable to Kiana; she had disliked it, only worn it during times of upheaval in the ashram, when the construction was unreliable. Did this have anything to do with the damage Bharavi had wrought?

"What I did," Iravan began, "with Bharavi—"

"We know what you did," Kiana interrupted. "That's architect business. You'll answer to Chaiyya and Airav for that."

Iravan's jaw clenched. Of course. The pact he and Bharavi had made had hardly been an original one. Chaiyya and Airav must have known Iravan would execute Bharavi. It was what Bharavi would have wanted, but Chaiyya was a healer—she had never liked the idea of such pacts. Ahilya's voice echoed in his head: *You speak as though a life can just be erased, that it has no meaning, simply because of rebirth.* How had such a monstrous death impacted Bharavi's consciousness? How had it affected his own? Expert though he was, even Iravan could not know the imprint that action had left in his own depth memory.

"Naila spoke to Airav about your visit to the sanctum," Kiana continued. She studied Ahilya. "I trust you will be silent about what you saw?"

His wife flinched in humiliation, then her chin rose, readying for a fight. Iravan's own anger heightened at Kiana for presuming to speak to Ahilya this way while he stood right there.

"Kiana," he growled. "Why aren't you taking this more seriously? *I* broke the law—several times. You should be dismissing me. Exiling me."

"You're about to find out. This is why the council is meeting now."

"You're inviting *me*?" Ahilya asked. "To an official council meeting?"

"You and Dhruv made some significant discoveries," Kiana answered. "Besides, as Iravan's official nomination for the council seat, you have earned a place in today's meeting."

Ahilya drew back, shocked. Her gaze traveled to Iravan.

Iravan took a deep breath, trying to steady himself. Nominating Ahilya had been his last action as a Senior Architect; he had expected to be dismissed after the sanctum. He'd done it to fulfill his end of the bargain, to give himself a clean slate before he walked the path of clarity, and he'd picked Ahilya because in the end, she was the obvious choice—intelligent, fierce, the kind of woman who could instantly see through an architect's maneuverings. She was what Nakshar needed.

The consideration in her eyes angered him now. He could tell what she was thinking: if this were another game, if he'd said and done these things today to win her back. *Rage you*, he thought. *What do you want? What do you* want? He blinked, unsure if the question was for himself or for Ahilya.

Kiana reached the end of the corridor and tapped at one of her rudra bracelets. The bark slid open to reveal the council chamber.

The room looked much like before, though now the flowers were gone from the walls. A dozen people sat around the round mahogany table, casting each other anxious looks. The councilors sat in their regular spots, but more seats had grown next to them. Dhruv was next to Kiana; two other sungineers on either side of Laksiya. The others were architects: Naila, and two Maze Architects, a woman called Megha and another man, Gaurav, both of whom had been contenders for Iravan's own council seat once. Why were they there? Was the council going to replace him after all? Iravan found that he did not care. Whatever this was, he wanted it to be over.

He made his way to his usual chair. He had expected Ahilya to make for the spare seat next to Dhruv, but she followed him unseeingly. She dropped next to him on Manav's rosewood chair, staring at her hands. Iravan sat down just as heavily. She hadn't signed the papers he had sent to her solarnote. Had she changed her mind after what she'd seen in the sanctum? Did he… *want* that? The Resonance flared in his mind, behind his brows. All he had to do was focus his attention on that burning sensation, and it would merge with him.

Laksiya cleared her throat. "Nakshar faces a problem of survival," she said, without preamble. "The council has called all of you here today because you've noticed threads of the same problem. We can't divulge any more information, so if you want no part of this, then leave now and we won't bother you. But if you choose to stay, then you will have to take a healbranch vow of silence. Make your decision now."

The others began to murmur and shift in their seats. Iravan found it hard to concentrate. He was very aware of Ahilya sitting next to him, her gaze downward in her lap. She filled his senses, her breathing, her scent, her shape. He wanted to reach out and shake her. He wanted to demand what she meant by changing her mind—if she *had* changed her mind. He wanted to kiss her and take her right here on the mahogany table in the council chambers. He wanted to leave her, never see her again.

Iravan swallowed. He extended his wrist like everyone else, barely registering the words of the vow he was making.

The healbranch vines retracted, and the assembled people sat up, once again looking at Laksiya. The Senior Sungineer nodded in satisfaction, then sat down, giving way to Airav.

The bald, bespectacled man rested his elbows on the table, but Iravan saw his hands shake. That, more than anything else so far, pulled him away from his distraction. Airav was the most steadfast man Iravan knew. For him to be perturbed... something terrible had happened.

"For those of you who don't know," Airav began, in his deep rumbling voice, "Senior Architect Iravan was put in charge of the investigation as to why the alarm did not work during the last flight. We have since learned that it was an effect of Senior Architect Bharavi's Ecstasy."

All eyes in the chamber swiveled to Iravan—all except Ahilya, who had gone unnaturally still. How had Airav known? Perhaps despite his skepticism, Airav had conducted his own investigation into the alarm. It would be very much like the man, to portray himself at his harshest yet secretly do his diligence. Iravan noticed now what he hadn't before. None of the councilors wore the healbranch bracelets they had wrought for his investigation. He had been freed.

"During the course of the investigation," Airav continued, "Senior Sungineer Kiana asked the solar lab to find out if the other ashrams had landed at all. As it happens, Dhruv here was able to contact nearly twenty sister ashrams."

Dhruv cleared his throat as everyone's gaze settled on him. "I— Yes, yes I did. Nakshar landed about two weeks ago. But—uh— none of the other ashrams registered a lull at all."

A shocked silence greeted his words. Ahilya's head snapped up; she stared at Dhruv, her mouth falling open.

"That's not possible," Maze Architect Megha said. "Landing is a choice, but the lull itself is a common climatic phenomenon. Magnaroot reacts in a specific manner at the watchpost, and that's true of every ashram. How could the others not have registered it?"

"We know now," Airav said, "that the magnaroot was being manipulated by Senior Architect Bharavi, who was in the throes of Ecstasy."

The architects in the room blanched. Every one of them understood the implications of Airav's words, finally understanding what Iravan had already known. To manipulate the magnaroot in such a manner, Bharavi had trajected the rudra tree itself.

"Do you mean to say," Ahilya said, in a small voice, "that when we went out on my expedition, we were out during *an earthrage*?"

Airav met her gaze. "Yes, Ahilya-ve. That's exactly what I'm saying."

Iravan closed his eyes in a long, slow blink. He had made the connection when Bharavi had confessed her manipulations to him. She had told him as much—she had been trajecting the jungle through the deathcage. How much power had she had? How much had she tried to control herself while landing? If he had only paid more attention to the vigilance he ought to have been performing for her, would she have escaped Ecstasy? Would she be still alive? *You speak as though a life can just be erased, that it has no meaning, simply because of rebirth.*

Ahilya made a gagging sound in her throat. "The—the jungle was birthing itself. We saw that. How could that be, if we were in an earthrage from the very beginning?"

"We don't fully understand Ecstasy, Ahilya-ve. All we know for certain is that it is incredible power, uncontrolled. It is not a far thought to imagine Bharavi trajecting and changing the very nature of the jungle in her Ecstasy. That's likely why you saw it birth."

"This explains why the ashram was so resistant to landing," Naila said, frowning as the other architects nodded. "The ashram plants aren't meant to land during an earthrage. It's only during a lull that we're supposed to land. Despite her trajection, the plants rebelled."

"Why would she do that?" one of the sungineers murmured. "Was she trying to kill us all?"

"She was in Ecstasy," Iravan said coldly, speaking for the first time. "She didn't know what she was doing. She has paid for it already, don't you think?"

Everyone stared at him. Iravan met their gaze, his eyes hard.

Airav cleared his throat. "Bharavi forced us to land, sabotaged the alarm, and trajected the jungle. However, the fact remains that without the false lull, this has now been the longest earthrage in recorded history, topping at two hundred and twenty-four days."

This time, the silence stretched longer. Iravan watched as the unease grew in everyone's faces.

"Exactly what is the concern here?" said the sungineer who had spoken before, a man with shoulder-length hair and thin glasses.

"Are you saying we're not equipped to fly for so long without a rest in the jungle?"

"You noticed it yourself, Umit," Airav said. "You came to Laksiya with observations around how trajection was no longer powering sungineering equipment adequately."

"Why is this happening?" another sungineer said, this a person with curious eyes and the lightest shade of brown skin Iravan had seen in the ashram. "Surely, we should be back at homeostasis. Isn't that what shift duty does?"

"There are a number of reasons," Airav said. "We wasted a lot of trajection with unnecessary landing and taking off. Bharavi's Ecstasy and the damage she wrought weakened us further. But the real reason—and we have confirmed this with our sister ashrams—is that trajection is getting harder. It's what Senior Architect Iravan suspected all along."

Once again, all eyes flickered to Iravan. His knee jerked against his will. In Chaiyya and Airav's gazes he detected the shadow of regret and mortification, but Iravan couldn't bring himself to feel vindication or anger. Instead, absurdly, he felt running through him a sensation he only recognized from his youth: *boredom.* These questions were meaningless when compared to the only question he cared about—the identity of the Resonance.

"You must understand something," Airav continued. "Trajection has not been confirmed to be harder by every architect. But enough people have reported it for it to be a concern for every sister ashram. Ultimately, it is all of a pattern. Earthrages are becoming longer and lulls shorter. And it's affecting our trajection. It is becoming harder for most of us to construct even the simplest mazes."

"I'm sorry," Maze Architect Gaurav said, a man with a clear high voice. "But *are* earthrages truly getting longer? This seems like it has more to do with a difficulty in trajection than anything to do with the rages themselves."

"They *are*," Airav confirmed. "This earthrage is already the longest in our history—"

"But the last few were significantly shorter," Gaurav said.

"It's not an absolute increase," Ahilya said, her voice soft. "Yes, there have been many quick rages, but over time, they've been getting longer. I have the numbers to prove it. Graphs, if you wish to see. These patterns emerge only after decades of study."

Gaurav fell silent, his face thoughtful.

Dhruv leaned forward. "If I may," he said, "I want to understand the practicalities of our situation. Even if the rages are getting longer and trajection harder, shouldn't architects on shift duty allow us to fly?"

"In theory, yes," Airav replied. "But the Maze Architects are tired. Their shifts have become longer, their breaks shorter. We don't have enough architects to sustain this, least of all in our current luxurious architectural design. We're making mistakes—costly mistakes. If we don't find a solution, then soon we'll have many more Ecstatics on our hands."

This time, the silence had a heavier flavor, treacherous and aghast.

It was Ahilya who broke it. "What about the other ashrams? If there's a universal cause for longer earthrages and shorter lulls, then they must be affected too."

"They are," Airav confirmed. "But Nakshar has been hit the worst because of our recent incidents. And I'm afraid there is more yet. Chaiyya and I estimate that we have only twelve weeks before the Disc's trajection becomes so weak that Nakshar will quite literally plummet into the jungle. And it is only a matter of time before that happens to every ashram unless there is a true lull in the earthrage."

To the credit of everyone present, no one uttered a cry at that pronouncement, though several people began wiping their glasses.

Airav let the silence breathe for a few more seconds before he spoke again.

"Perhaps for the second time in our history, we're faced with the collapse of our species in such a sudden manner. The early architects found a way to traject plants to fly. Our challenge is no less significant. Any solution will change the course of our civilization forever. Whatever we decide to do, we need to do it quietly, swiftly, and without spreading panic. If the citizens learn about this, the ashram's plants will react to their consciousness, to their fear, making trajection even harder."

Airav stood up.

"Our course of action, then, is threefold. One, Chaiyya and I will lead the redesign of the ashram. Sacrifices will have to be made in all our lifestyles, and we must make ready the citizens without raising alarm. Two, Kiana and Laksiya will coordinate communication with the other ashrams. All ashrams are hanging by the same vine, even if our hold is the weakest. If we find no solution, then perhaps their architects will.

"And, three, Iravan, you will continue your investigation. Find out why the earthrages are getting longer and why this is affecting our trajection. We need answers."

Airav tapped at one of his rudra bead bracelets. A hologram hovered over it, and he waved a hand. The same hologram reappeared over everyone's citizen rings. Iravan glanced down at his; it was a list of people on various teams. His team shone with three names: Ahilya, Naila, and the sungineer Umit.

Iravan raised his eyebrows. He glanced at Ahilya, but she said nothing. The other councilors rose to their feet, and everyone else followed, gathering toward their leaders.

"Pardon, Airav-ve," Dhruv said as he arose. "I think you're overlooking something important. Why isn't the council exploring how to stop dependence on trajection altogether?"

Ahilya turned to the sungineer and shook her head imperceptibly. Airav looked up from his muttered conversation with Chaiyya.

"Perhaps you didn't hear me about the urgency of the situation," he said mildly.

"I heard," Dhruv said. "But Ahilya and I—well, mostly, *I*—have been working on a solution. On a battery. To reduce reliance on trajection. If she's working with Senior Architect Iravan, then I should be on their team. They'll need a sungineer."

"They have Umit," Kiana said, before Airav could reply. "And I would not spare you, Dhruv. You created a device that might charge itself over long ranges. That's our biggest angle; it's why you're here. We'll need to discuss that with the sungineers of the other ashrams, in case we need to use their energy to sustain Nakshar." The Senior Sungineer glanced at Iravan. "No offense, Iravan, but what I have on my hands is more urgent and immediate."

Dhruv sent a beseeching look toward Ahilya. She shook her head again. Iravan winced, remembering how he had flung away the sungineer's work. *I'd have decided to leave you even if none of this had happened.*

"Allow him, Kiana," he found himself saying. "If he finds anything relevant to your team, I'll send him to you."

Kiana frowned for a long moment, then nodded reluctantly. She, Laksiya, Dhruv, and Umit drew their heads together in urgent conference, no doubt discussing the logistics of this change. Airav's team had already begun, their holograms floating above the mahogany table. Kiana would go to the lab. Iravan studied Ahilya and Naila.

"Where do we go?" he asked.

"The library?" Naila suggested. She still couldn't meet his eyes. A dark, humorless laugh echoed in Iravan's mind.

"No. Not private enough—and it's in no shape after Bharavi's Ecstasy."

"Our—my home," Ahilya said, in a low voice. "We can use that."

Surprised, Iravan nodded. Someone touched his elbow, and he turned to see Kiana there. "Iravan? A word?"

He glanced back at Ahilya. He could see in his wife's eyes—his wife still, and even that thought was mirrored in her—how neither of them had been distracted from their marriage by the things Airav had said.

Ahilya opened her mouth to speak, but Kiana was already leading him away toward a corner of the chamber where the other councilors were waiting.

"We need to talk about your recent transgressions," Laksiya said, her voice cool.

"Does that really matter at a time like this?" he asked.

"It matters more than ever," Chaiyya replied, a deep line creasing her forehead. "You brought a citizen into the sanctum, Iravan. You broke the healbranch vow you took as a Maze Architect. It has pierced you and begun poisoning you, hasn't it? And you don't even *care*. What's to stop you from broadcasting everything we've discussed today to the rest of the ashram?"

"I won't apologize, Chaiyya. I did all of those things knowing the consequences, so either pass a vote of no confidence or let it go."

"You know we can't release you from the council, not right now—"

"Then *let. It. Go*. If you thought I wouldn't keep my mouth shut, you would never have put me in charge of one of the units. What is this truly about?"

"It's about you and Ecstasy," Laksiya snapped. "You're still a danger."

A blaze of anger stabbed at Iravan. "Are you serious?" he hissed. "You tested me not two days ago, and I passed—"

"You turned out ambiguous at best," Laksiya said bluntly. "Under ordinary circumstances, we'd be doing another test right away, continuously, until we had a clear answer."

Iravan opened his mouth to retort, but Chaiyya beat him to a reply.

"We can't afford for you to be in Ecstasy," the Senior Architect said, her voice breaking. "Please, Iravan—not after Bharavi—We need you—You can't leave us to handle this alone—"

Her eyes filled with tears, and Airav put his arm around her, though he said nothing.

Iravan's anger dissipated as soon as it had arisen. "I—Chaiyya—"

His gaze swept over them, the four councilors who had been preserving Nakshar while Bharavi had been consumed by Ecstasy, while Iravan himself had been distracted by his own troubles. Chaiyya was openly crying, but Kiana looked tired, the sparkle gone from her gray eyes. Laksiya's anger was plain on her face, and Airav's hand around Chaiyya's shoulder shook.

"I won't leave you, Chaiyya," Iravan said, tiredly.

"Then come with us," she said, wiping her face. "I will have to slow the poisoning of the healbranch, and there are details about our situation we need to discuss. You are still a Senior Architect and a councilor of Nakshar."

34

AHILYA

Tariya was awake in the infirmary, silent tears trickling down her face, when Ahilya walked in.

Grown in the lowest tier of a giant neem tree, the infirmary had been reduced to a long, narrow hall crammed with healbranch beds. Ahilya remembered how it had once been: a five-story structure with private chambers for different kinds of patients. Now nearly a hundred beds were occupied, bodies rustling under thin linens while nurses walked from one to another, adjusting glass vials and bringing healing potions. Ahilya averted her gaze. The nurses were dressed in their everyday scrubs, but the clothing only reminded her of Oam. Even the conversation with the attendant in the front had been painful. Ahilya had been told that Kush was sent to the temple to speak to a Maze Architect. Her ten-year-old nephew had taken his baby brother with him. Deciding to check on them later, Ahilya strode to Tariya and sat down on the bed beside her sister.

Tariya's beauty had dimmed like a flower closing. Her raven hair was knotted. Her skin appeared ashy. She no longer wore a bindi on her forehead, and on Tariya the absence of the red dot was striking. Ahilya had never kept to the old ways, and Iravan had cared little, but more than anything, this sign of widowhood on her sister startled Ahilya. She withdrew a comb from her pocket, adjusted herself, and silently began brushing Tariya's hair.

Ought she to tell Tariya of what Iravan had said, of what he had done? What purpose would it serve? Besides, now, in the wake of the council meeting, this truth hardly mattered. She brushed her sister's hair, unraveling one knot after another, her mind still gripped by the losses they both had suffered.

She could hear Iravan's voice in her head: *I didn't just want a child, Ahilya. I wanted* our *child.* She saw his jaw clench, saw him pace their apartment, declaring his love, declaring how he would be anyone she wanted him to be. She couldn't fathom what had driven him to say those words. In that instant, Iravan hadn't surrendered, no; he had abased himself out of an arbitrary terror. He had been willing to give her who he was blindly—now they'd both lost each other anyway. Ahilya's eyes grew wet, and she put down the hairbrush.

Tariya dropped her head in her hands. "I miss her so much."

"She—It should not have happened. Bharavi should never have died."

Tariya shook her head, her body shuddering. "There was no other way. She was an Ecstatic. You don't know… what excision does…" Tariya brushed her fingers to her eyes, but as her gaze met Ahilya's, she paused. "You *do* know. How?" Her eyes traveled to Ahilya's stomach. "Are you and Iravan—"

"We're not pregnant," Ahilya said hurriedly.

"But you know?"

Ahilya held her sister's gaze. *It's only a matter of time before the secret is out. The spouses of architects don't make a healbranch vow.* She nodded slowly.

Tariya let out a bitter sound halfway between a laugh and a sob. "So, he did it. He finally did it. Always he rebelled against Bharavi. More than his healbranch vow, it was she who stood in his way of sharing excision's secret. I can see that he wasted no time after her death." Tariya wiped her nose, her voice vicious. "If you know about excision, then you know about their pact."

Anger rippled through Ahilya, leaving her muscles weak. She had already worked it out, that Bharavi would have told Tariya of the pact—the two women had their children; Bharavi had no need for the secret Iravan had been forced to keep. Ahilya took a deep breath, trying to control her rage, but it simmered in her, the horror and anger from the last two days churning to the surface. She had not come there to the infirmary to fight with Tariya, but this blatant admission she could not dismiss.

"You knew," she rasped, unable to keep the accusation out of her voice. "How could you let them do this? You who understand the need for healing. The power of life over death. You who have battled your own despair—how could you let it take them over—that they believed there was no other choice."

"You think I didn't try to stop Bharavi?" Tariya's body shuddered. "This was her decision; there was nothing I could do about it. She didn't want to live in that manner—"

"And you let Iravan make that choice, too. But you didn't think to tell me?"

"Would you have let him go?" Tariya spat. "If their roles were reversed, if it was Iravan who was the Ecstatic, would you have allowed Bharavi to kill him?"

"I would have found another way! I would have torn the ashram asunder to find a different solution! I would *never* have let it come to this."

"There *is* no other way. You think the architects haven't searched for another solution? Bharavi *studied* Ecstasy, Ahilya. She knew how hard, how impossible rehabilitation would be. And you think you'd find the answer?" Tariya began to cry again. She covered her face with her fingers. "All you ever did was fight the architects. You wanted what they had so badly that you never truly saw what you had. And now Bharavi is dead while Iravan is alive. How could any of us tell you this? What would *you* understand of it?"

Ahilya stood up, shaking with anger. Her sister wept, convulsing, her head in her hands. Sobs wracked her body, the shudders painful to watch.

Ahilya's fury left her as soon as it had come.

She dropped back on the bed and held her sister as she cried. Over and over again, she stroked Tariya's head, murmuring to her.

Eventually, Tariya stopped. She pushed Ahilya away and turned on the bed, her back to her.

Ahilya rose slowly. *How could any of us tell you this? What would you understand?*

Iravan had told her. He'd known she'd understand.

What had her responsibility been—her own choices? She had no clear answer, no clear manner in which to think anymore. Her head dizzy, Ahilya walked away from the infirmary, her heart breaking into tiny pieces.

35

AHILYA

Dhruv and Naila were waiting for her outside her home by the time she arrived. Ahilya tapped at her citizen ring, and the leafy wall unfurled to reveal a doorway. The house had shrunk again since dawn, becoming a mere single chamber. Ahilya watched, her cheeks heating, as Dhruv and Naila took in the small circular table in the center, the bed in the corner, the simple kitchen.

"Bit modest for a Senior Architect, isn't it?" Dhruv said, sitting on one of the chairs that grew around the table.

Naila pursed her lips at Dhruv's comment. Ahilya tried to hold her shoulders straight. She busied herself in the kitchen, bringing clay mugs and a jar of water. In her mind, Tariya still sobbed. *How could any of us tell you this? What would you understand?* A knock sounded on the wall they'd entered through, and Ahilya tapped at her citizen ring again. Iravan strode in, filling the small chamber with his energy.

"Thank you, Ahilya," he said, "for the use of your apartment."

She nodded, her throat heavy. Dhruv glanced from her to Iravan. His expression changed, eyes widening in understanding.

His mouth dropped open. He stared at Ahilya but she couldn't meet his gaze. Had everything changed? Did Iravan want to salvage what was left? A few weeks ago, her husband had come to her to reconcile. They went round and round each other, star-crossed, tragic, disastrous. Ahilya's lips twitched in dark irony.

Iravan sat down at the table, opposite Dhruv. As though that were permission, Naila sat down between them. Ahilya followed more slowly, sitting opposite Naila.

"So," Iravan said, glancing at each of them in turn. "Our task is to discover why earthrages are getting longer, why lulls are becoming shorter, and how all of this affects trajection. If we discount everything that was an effect of Bharavi's Ecstasy, what are we left with?"

He gazed at them expectantly. With his considering, rather jaded face, he looked almost like a teacher who knew the answers yet was waiting for his brightest students to arrive at them. Ahilya bit the inside of her cheeks; she had a sudden urge to grin, bordering on hysteria. He seemed so unaffected by what had happened to them, but she knew him too well for that. No matter how composed he looked, Iravan was holding on by a thread, just like she was.

"Well," she said, trying to mirror his tone, "we know there's something down there in the jungle that is blocking trajection. So, that's one thing affecting trajection."

Naila nodded, but Iravan looked at her curiously. "Will you explain that?"

As best as she could, Ahilya explained what she and Dhruv had discovered in the solar lab, but with every word out of her mouth, Dhruv fidgeted in his chair, shaking his head and wiping his glasses as though wanting to interrupt but trying to be polite.

"—implying," Ahilya concluded, "it could potentially be interfering with the ashram's trajection, too—"

"No, I'm sorry—Ahilya, no—It doesn't imply that at all," Dhruv burst out, clearly unable to contain himself any longer.

She glanced at him. "What?"

"I'm saying that everything we discussed in the solar lab is wrong. I don't know what charged the tracker, after all—"

"You said it was the trajection from all the ashrams in flight—"

"Yes, but I've checked it since, and as it happens, it wasn't *trajection* that was charging the tracker. It was—it must be—a whole different kind of energy, some—some *Energy X.*"

Iravan's face grew very still. "What do you mean?"

Dhruv removed his glasses, wiped them on the edge of his kurta, and placed them back on his nose. "About five years ago, I engineered a transmitter-receiver pair. The transmitter became part of the elephant-yaksha's tracker, but the receiver stayed in the lab. I thought I was replicating existing sungineering technology—even though all expeditionary equipment *is* experimental. But as it turns out, neither the receiver nor the tracker functioned off of trajection." Dhruv's plaintive gaze took all of them in. "I don't know what I invented. I don't know what it became."

Naila uttered a soft snort. "Didn't you run any tests when you created it?"

Dhruv let out an exasperated sigh. "Of course I did. And five years ago, all of it seemed to be working off of trajection. Once Ahilya tagged the elephant-yaksha and Nakshar flew away, I didn't pay attention to the receiver because I didn't expect a response from the transmitter. We'd flown too far from the yaksha. When the transmitter began signaling about three weeks ago, I thought it was because we were in range again. But I've run multiple tests since then. And neither the transmitter nor the receiver were being charged by trajection. They were being charged, as I said, by some mysterious Energy X."

Ahilya drew in a sharp breath as something clicked in her mind. "This is why we didn't sense the signal in the lab for all those years. For five years, we had been flying over the elephant-yaksha and the tracker was charging, but somehow, *we* didn't receive a signal until a few weeks ago because the *receiver* was uncharged. It implies there's a common link between the events. Something happened five years ago in Nakshar that happened again about three weeks ago. Something that sourced Energy X."

"Something did," Naila said, excitedly. "Ecstasy."

A silence fell over the small table. Ahilya glanced at Iravan. He seemed not to be breathing, his eyes unfocused on a groove in the wood.

"What are you saying?" Dhruv asked, his voice strange.

"Five years before, there was an Ecstatic Architect in Nakshar," Naila explained. "Senior Architect Manav-ve. And we know Bharavi-ve was in Ecstasy in the last few weeks before we landed. I'll wager anything that if you look at the times for when the tracker charged, it'll coincide with when one of them was trajecting in Ecstasy."

Dhruv's face became thoughtful. "It would explain why the tracker charged itself right before Nakshar was mangled. Bharavi was in Ecstasy then, too. I just assumed it was malfunctioning."

"I don't understand," Ahilya said, glancing at Iravan. "Isn't trajection during Ecstasy the same as normal trajection? Just out of control?"

It was Naila who answered. "It's what we believe, but the only ones who would know for sure are Ecstatics themselves, and all of them have been excised. They're in no condition to tell us anything." The Junior Architect turned to Dhruv. "If your device is picking up on some strange energy that is only available when an architect is in Ecstasy, then perhaps Ecstatic trajection isn't the same as normal trajection. Perhaps it's a completely different energy signature."

"Maybe," Dhruv answered. He removed his glasses and began wiping them again.

"That could help the council, couldn't it?" Naila continued, voice eager. She turned back to Iravan. "It could contribute to better safety measures in the ashram. Dhruv may have invented something that detects Ecstasy."

"He may have invented something that *uses* Ecstasy," Iravan said quietly, studying the sungineer.

Dhruv's eyes looked disturbed behind his glasses. "Maybe. I don't like the implication."

"Neither do I," Iravan agreed.

On both their faces, Ahilya saw the same thought that she had. Technology that used Ecstasy would inevitably create a need for Ecstatic Architects. It would *depend* on architects losing their minds. Naila bit her lip, frowning, evidently realizing all this.

"I think we're getting carried away," Ahilya said into the building silence. "The tracker charged itself in the jungle for the last five years. How could that be if this *Energy X* is the same as Ecstasy?"

"We already know Bharavi-ve was capable of trajecting the jungle," Naila said. "We don't know what Ecstatics are capable of."

"But for five years?"

"It could be the same principle as before," Dhruv said, shaking his head. "The tracker could have been feeding off of Ecstatic trajection from *all* the other cities. We'd have to ask for an account of Ecstatic Architects from every ashram."

"We will never get that," Iravan said. "That's not information the councils of various ashrams share openly. I agree with Ahilya. I think this hypothesis is wrong. If Energy X were truly Ecstatic energy, then you'd need a steady supply of Ecstatics from all the ashrams powering the tracker. But Ecstasy is a rare event. And Ecstatics are immediately excised. This entire theory hinges on Ecstatic trajection being different from normal trajection, and we have no evidence of that."

"Ecstatic energy or not," Ahilya put in, looking from one to another, "that's not our priority. Something down *there* blocked Energy X. And we should be thinking about *that*."

Iravan's face became thoughtful. "You think the same thing blocking Energy X is ruining trajection?"

"It's possible, isn't it?"

"Unless whatever is down there has nothing to do with anything," Dhruv said, "and Energy X is blocking trajection."

"There are too many unknowns," Naila said, in frustration. "We don't even know what *is* down there."

"Yaksha habitation," Ahilya said firmly. "It has to be."

The others gazed at her, but for the first time, Ahilya saw something in their faces that she'd never seen before while claiming this: consideration.

"What kind of habitat could survive the earthrages?" Naila asked, her voice soft.

"Something powerful," Ahilya replied. "Something unbelievably strong. Something that we in our obsession with flight may have forgotten even existed. My theory is that it's architecture humans built a long time before in an early attempt to escape earthrages."

"There's no evidence of *that*," Naila said.

Ahilya swept out a hand. "Our data shows that the elephant-yaksha's tracker stopped recharging each time it went to a single area within the jungle. That is hard evidence. There's something down there."

"But for it to be made by humans? Our ancestors? For it to even be around still? Ashrams began flying nearly a thousand years ago."

"Yes, but flight was not the only method that our ancestors tried," Dhruv intervened. "Our histories tell us there were other attempts made to survive in the jungle."

"Failed attempts," Naila said scornfully. "Abandoned attempts. We already know flight was a miracle—that people had tried different methods, until architects discovered flight. Just because the tracker stopped working doesn't mean it's a habitat down there that survives earthrages. It just means there is something that sungineering cannot get to. And whatever is blocking sungineering could be another trick of evolution—a way the jungle plants evolved over the years somehow. It's a leap to think it's habitat of some kind—"

"It's not a leap; it's deduction," Ahilya said. "Jungle plants wouldn't be able to evolve in such a manner, not in the exact same place, not when there are constant earthrages shattering them apart. The better logic is that whatever is down there is a remnant of archeology. We don't know what materials our ancestors used—once upon a time, they created core trees, embedded them with flight and permissions—something we can no longer replicate. For all we know, they had other means to create a different kind of architecture. Our histories have preserved only what the architects thought was useful—but we know that architects were frightened of the jungle proper, they wanted to be separate from it even when they lived within it. Perhaps it was the non-architects who built something."

"If non-architects built something that could successfully withstand the earthrages, why did they abandon it?" Naila argued. "Why didn't they just stay in the jungle? Why did we fly at all?"

"Perhaps," Dhruv said mildly, "*that* was an architect decision. Maybe the political situation back then was different. It's not like we have indisputable records of anything. Our history is the history of architects. We don't know what happened then between the citizens. Perhaps the habitat was abandoned when flight was discovered, not because of its failure but because flight was a better alternative for a civilization that had always feared the jungle."

"You're blaming the architects again," Naila said, incensed. "If it weren't for us, we'd all have been extinct—"

"We're not blaming anyone," Dhruv answered. "All we are saying is that there's architecture down there that can survive earthrages, presumably created by our ancestors, potentially used by yakshas."

Naila fell silent, but resentment still contorted her features. Ahilya exchanged a glance with Dhruv, who shrugged callously. She could tell even in that one gesture—something had changed in the sungineer, perhaps since Iravan's attack in the solar lab or maybe because of the city's circumstance now. He had stopped caring about appearances, about being on the safe side of the architects. Dhruv had lost something precious and emerged clear on the other side.

Iravan sighed after a moment. "The problem is not just that trajection is becoming harder—regardless of whether something is blocking it or not—but that earthrages are getting longer and lulls shorter. I suppose this brings us back to the question—what causes an earthrage? And how is that connected to trajection?"

Naila stirred. "Pardon me, Iravan-ve," she said, her gaze hovering a couple of inches above his head. "But don't we know this already? An earthrage is an explosion of disrupted consciousness."

"There's more to it," Ahilya muttered, and Dhruv nodded.

"It's a pretty complete theory," Naila said, shaking her head. "A million billion consciousnesses exist on the planet, all of them in conflict with each other, which leads to pressures at a global scale. When the pressure becomes dense, the pressure explodes. That explosion? Earthrages."

"This architectural theory implies that the consciousnesses of all living creatures in the world are connected," Dhruv said skeptically.

"Our consciousnesses *are* connected," Iravan said. "That's what the Moment is. The Moment doesn't just show the possibilities of plants. It shows the possibilities of *every* creature."

"This is why Nakshar's plants are easier to traject closer to the jungle during a lull," Naila said, looking at Dhruv. "When the disruption ends and an earthrage settles into a lull, the consciousnesses of jungle plants and an ashram's plants are in low conflict with each other. They are aligned much more closely. That's essentially what a lull is. And *that* is the connection earthrages have with trajection."

Dhruv's eyes met Ahilya's across the table. She knew what he was thinking. They had both known this theory, but far from being complete, the theory failed to answer some glaring questions. How had earthrages begun in the first place? When had the first one appeared? Had their planet always been besieged by the deadly storms? The architects liked to pretend that earthrages were as old as humankind, but Ahilya had found glimmers in records hinting of a time where there had been no rages at all, when there had been no trajection. The very book Iravan had given her, with the glorious mid-leaf drawing of jungle creatures, had indicated such a time, and nearly forgotten songs and ancient folklore within non-architect circles had hinted at the same.

It was all connected somehow to the erasure of the yakshas, the erasure of non-architects. The interference in the jungle, the histories Ahilya had studied, the early architects' arbitrary terror—somewhere, they were missing information that linked all of this together. She had thought Iravan would have the missing pieces, but her husband—her husband still—only looked thoughtful. He would not keep silent about it, not right now, not when their very survival in the skies was at stake.

"I don't think this theory is as complete as you believe," Ahilya said slowly. "I've been studying earthrages too. And my data does not coincide with your theory."

"What data?" Naila asked.

"Census data. I have a record of the numbers of births and deaths from all of the ashrams. If consciousnesses really did affect earthrages, then why are earthrages becoming longer even though there hasn't been a relative increase in the population of the ashrams?"

"You're talking about consciousness," Naila answered, sounding scandalized. "Such a heavy concept can't be reduced to data points. Each consciousness is expansive, infinite. We can never measure the exact effect a consciousness has on the earthrages, least of all with *numbers*."

"I'm sorry," Dhruv said. "Aren't you a mathematician?"

"Rages, that doesn't mean *numbers*," Naila said, throwing her hands up. "Do you know how rudimentary a tool numbers are? Mathematics is a pursuit of truth!"

Dhruv snorted. He opened his mouth, perhaps to retort, but Ahilya cleared her throat and interrupted before he could speak.

"Look," she said. "Even assuming the architects' theories about earthrages are right—"

"They are," Naila muttered.

"—there's still nothing we can do. Even if there is greater conflict between the combined consciousnesses of life forms on the planet, we can't control it."

"Another dead end," Dhruv said, leaning on the table.

"I have something to offer," Naila said. "But it's a rather technical architectural model."

"By all means," Dhruv said dryly, "please talk down to us."

Naila threw the sungineer a look of deep disgust.

"I've been studying the basic equation of trajection," she said. "Architects have been taught all along that trajection converts a plant's existing state of consciousness into a new state of consciousness, and each trajection releases a raga. But I think there's another byproduct of trajection. I call it Nakshar's Constant."

The Junior Architect took another deep breath.

"I measured Nakshar's Constant. And I think it is a raga too."

"I thought ragas were melodies," Ahilya said, glancing at Iravan.

"They are," he said. "Usually. Or at least that's how architects interpret them. But to be absolutely honest, ragas are more... abstract. They're... an entity that provoke a certain kind of emotion." He frowned. "If Nakshar's Constant is a raga, then architects ought to feel it. They ought to *hear* it."

"Yes, Iravan-ve, but Nakshar's Constant"—a note of frustration entered Naila's voice—"it measures beyond the frequency of other ragas. It's possible we feel it, but it's not surprising that we don't *hear* it. Even architects don't have the sensitivity."

"How sure are you about this?" Ahilya asked.

"I'm positive. I don't know if this is connected to anything we're discussing, but every trajection an architect does, there are two ragas that emerge. One is the base raga, like the flight raga, or the landing raga, or the raga of healing—almost always discernible as a melody. And the other is Nakshar's Constant. Each architect projects this raga every time they traject, and each projection is unique."

"Unique how?" Iravan asked.

"I—I don't know," Naila said. "I can only explain it in metaphors. It's like all the Nakshar's Constants being projected were the color blue, but each architect's emission was its own unique shade of the color."

"And Nakshar's Constant," Dhruv asked, pushing up his glasses. "Is this new?"

"It's as old as trajecting itself. Base ragas dissipate and die off in the act of being produced—they're heard only briefly, and then too only by architects. But Nakshar's Constant is continuous. It doesn't die."

"Maybe Nakshar's Constant is making trajection harder," Dhruv said.

"You're saying," Ahilya murmured, "that *trajection* is the cause for the difficulty with trajection. That embedded within trajection is its own demise?"

"A dangerous theory," Iravan said softly.

"But a good one," Dhruv argued. "If Nakshar's Constant were somehow contributing to the building pressures of consciousness, it would explain why the earthrages have been becoming longer. It's trajection itself that could be causing the pressures on our planet to build."

"Another reason," Iravan said, "for sungineers to do their part and create a battery so we're no longer dependent on trajection."

"As I recall," Dhruv said, his eyes narrowing, "you destroyed my best efforts at doing just that."

"As *I* recall," Iravan said evenly, "your best efforts endangered the ashram."

The two men stared at each other across the table.

Naila's head swiveled from one to another. Ahilya expected Dhruv to break the gaze first, but it was Iravan who looked away, shaking his head wearily. He stood up. Dhruv's lips trembled in a clear desire to say something more, but Iravan spoke first.

"There are too many open questions," he said. "What is this mysterious raga, Nakshar's Constant? What is the block down in the jungle? How is all this making earthrages longer? We have our leads—let's work through them."

The rest of them stood up. Naila gave a hasty bow to Iravan and, surprisingly, one to Ahilya, then ran out through the splitting wall. Dhruv muttered something about returning to the lab to give Kiana a report.

Ahilya and Iravan were suddenly alone. She didn't dare move, not wanting to bring this to Iravan's attention. He stared unseeingly in front of him, his fists resting on the table, but with the others gone, her breathing became faster. She noticed, abruptly, the blinking of her solarnote: the divorce papers, unread, unseen.

"You didn't sign them," Iravan said quietly, reading her as only he could.

"No," she whispered.

He turned to her then, his eyes glinting, whether in passion or anger, she wasn't sure. He closed the gap between them, a handbreadth away, careful not to touch her.

"You've changed your mind? About us?"

"I just... Iravan." Ahilya pressed a hand to her forehead. *How could any of us tell you this? What would you understand?* The guilt grew in her, but she pushed against it, unsure of its fairness. "What you told me in the sanctum, if I'd known before, if you'd shared—" Ahilya looked up. "I understand why you couldn't, I *do*. But we make so many mistakes. We get so angry..."

"Anger is honest, at least," he said, his eyes glittering.

"I'm still furious."

"As am I."

Ahilya swallowed. "But I still care, Iravan. I care so much."

Iravan was unmoving for a long, interminable moment. His jaw clenched and unclenched. She watched him; perhaps she shouldn't have said anything. Perhaps that time was long gone.

"Rages, Ahilya," he finally breathed. "I care too. It's you. It's *us*. Nothing can change that."

Her heart hammered in her throat. Tentatively, Ahilya brushed her fingers against his cheek. He leaned into her touch, closing his eyes as though in pain.

"Do you want to stay here tonight?" she whispered, the words which had been circling her, which she had been too afraid to voice so far.

Iravan opened his eyes. He studied her face.

Then his mouth quirked into a half-smile. "Yes," he said. "Yes, I would like that very much."

36

IRAVAN

His own response took him aback. Ahilya uttered a small, incredulous laugh. She smiled and looked so pleased, so *beautiful*, that for a moment, guilt weighed his heart down at how much he had hurt her. Iravan pressed the back of his head in a sheepish gesture and grinned back.

"I—uh—" He shrugged awkwardly. "I should tell the other councilors what we discussed."

Ahilya didn't say anything, but her smile faltered.

Iravan reached his hands down to press her shoulders. "I'll be back. I promise."

She nodded, her big eyes staring into his. Iravan let go. Waving limply at her, he approached the wall and exited her home. The bark closed behind him, but instead of walking away, Iravan leaned back against the wall. He thunked his head against the bark and closed his eyes.

Her home had changed. He had noticed that instantly on walking in. Was it his home at all anymore? The ashram had removed his presence from the architecture, even if Iravan himself wasn't sure of how he felt. *What am I doing?* he thought, and Bharavi's voice echoed in his head. *Don't you love her anymore?* Did he?

Standing outside in the open air, his head still supported by the leafy wall of Ahilya's home, Iravan searched his heart for the answer. Less than two days before, he had come to Ahilya, begging her to take him back, to *save* him, but after their last fight, he had thought he had made his final decision. He had told her about the sanctum not to change her mind but to make a clean break, cement his last goodbye.

The Resonance danced between his brows, a fiery presence, tempting him to connect with it. Yet in front of it—ahead of the deep, unending presence of the Resonance—flickered Ahilya, smiling at him. He could almost forget about the Resonance if he focused on her.

I love her, he thought. *I love her so much.*

How could he not? She was Ahilya. She was the beacon of everything that was right and true with him; she had always been his guiding star, and when he had lost sight of her—that was when he had lost himself. He belonged, in so many defining ways, to *her*. A fight didn't change that. Nothing would change that.

And yet the Resonance burned in his mind like a candleflame. He was afraid to look at it closely. Bharavi had said it was a sign of Ecstasy. She had been right, of course; he could see that now. He had been in danger of Ecstasy since he'd stumbled into the Resonance during Nakshar's landing. She had said he would fight it. Was this what she'd meant? This contest between choosing Ahilya or choosing Ecstasy? He was too afraid to untangle that thought.

Iravan lifted his head off the wall and took a deep breath. He wound his way slowly down the path leading from Ahilya's small house, but he didn't make his way to the temple. Instead, he walked toward the solar lab.

The lab was busier than ever. Sungineers collected around their bio-nodes, chatting in agitated voices. Holograms floated along the floor, sometimes intersecting with each other, making any meaning illegible. Iravan found Dhruv on the main floor, speaking with the two others from the morning's council meeting. He caught Dhruv's eye, gestured with his head, and strolled away to a quiet window as the taller man trotted up to him.

"Well?" Dhruv asked. "Did you have an epiphany that couldn't wait until our next meeting?"

"Not an epiphany," Iravan replied. "But I do have something for you. A peace offering."

He withdrew a small glass cube from his pocket. The tiny deathbox containing the lone spiralweed leaf sat on his hand, its contours smooth and unmarked. Dhruv stared at it, unmoving. The sungineer didn't reach for it.

"Why?" he asked at last, his bespectacled eyes meeting Iravan's.

"Because the battery is important. Because I think that's the direction in which technology should develop. Because if the tracker is truly feeding off Ecstatic trajection, then it is dangerous."

"You want the tracker in exchange for this, don't you?"

"Yes."

Still, the sungineer didn't take the deathbox. Dhruv removed his glasses, wiped them on the edge of his sleeve, then returned them to his nose.

Iravan waited. He knew speaking now would be a mistake. He counted the seconds, willing himself not to move.

Finally, Dhruv sighed. He withdrew a necklace from his pocket. On its end dangled the chunky tracker that Iravan had seen Ahilya carry during the expedition. "Take it," Dhruv said wearily. "This is likely to be more trouble than it's worth."

The two exchanged the devices. Iravan hefted the locket in his hand. "How can I tell if it's recharging?" he asked.

"It'll begin chiming when it's around Energy X," Dhruv said. He made to leave, but Iravan held out his hand, arresting his movement.

"Wait," he said. "Have you told Kiana about this yet?"

"No."

Iravan said nothing, but his eyes held Dhruv's.

"For fuck's sake, Iravan," Dhruv said. "I won't tell her—if that's what you want."

"It's dangerous. I would keep this to the architects as long as I can. Until I can confirm whether Ecstatic trajection is different from normal trajection—"

"Yes, sure, whatever. I'm sure you have your reasons that *sungineers* shouldn't know about."

Iravan sighed and pocketed the tracker. "Thank you, Dhruv. I think, if circumstances had been different, we could have been… friends."

Dhruv rolled his eyes. "Don't get carried away. I'm doing it for Ahilya, not you. Maybe if you treated her well, you and I would have had a chance at friendship, but she deserves better than you. She always has."

"Someone like you?"

The sungineer cringed. "You know very little about our relationship if you think Ahilya and I could ever be romantic." He turned on his heel and strode away, ending their conversation.

Iravan watched him go. He had not meant his statement to indicate the possibility of romance between his wife and the sungineer—the two had grown up together as siblings; Iravan had known this all along. Still, Dhruv had never liked him. Close with Ahilya as he was, perhaps he had envisioned someone different for her, someone more nurturing, someone who pampered her. Oam flashed in Iravan's mind, the way he had reached out to his wife, the way she had grasped his hand, with Iravan the interloper.

He and Ahilya had never coddled each other; their relationship, and then their marriage, had been built on challenging each other, on becoming *better*, on growing together. Yet the path had grown corrupted without their notice. They had become harder instead of stronger. How had they come to this? Could there be any resolution now? She had asked him to stay, and he had agreed, but the Resonance burned in him, tempting him. How long could he ignore its call?

Lost in thought, Iravan left the solar lab. His feet tracked no destination. Instead, he turned at his whim, past homes and playgrounds, past quiet markets and empty streets. Airav had wasted no time. The ashram that had spanned acres in the sky was contracting. Tall trees grew on every corner, holding multiple crowded apartments in their boughs. Iravan wound his way through narrow lanes and muttering citizens who stood watching the growth. Several people hailed him, but he only waved and hurried on.

He found himself back at the temple within the Ecstatic ward.

No one else was about, and Iravan strode in, unchallenged. He approached Manav's room and spun the dials. The glass cleared, and Manav stared at him, almost at eye level.

Iravan stumbled back, nearly tripping.

The man was inches away, staring at Iravan, staring *through* him. It was like looking into a terrible mirror, their skins almost as dark, their hair just as long. Bharavi shook her head in Iravan's mind. *You are on your way. There's no going back.*

Iravan stared at Manav, forcing himself to truly see him. *Is this my fate? Is this who I will one day become?* He had released Bharavi, a more merciful path than what awaited him. Who would release him? Iravan pressed the dials on the glass and the tint increased.

He stumbled away through the corridor, past the Ecstatic ward, toward an empty courtyard in the sanctum.

A lone bench grew under the sanctum's neem tree. Iravan sat down, shafts of midmorning sunlight warming his skin.

There, embedded in the peace of the ashram he loved so dearly, Iravan closed his eyes and examined the Resonance.

It had dulled to a gentle warmth behind his brows while he had been in the council meeting, and later at Ahilya's home. Now as he watched, it flared under his attention.

I know you, he thought. *What are you?*

The warmth flickered, expanding and contracting behind his eyes like wings flapping. Iravan took a deep breath. Gently, he let his attention draw closer.

The Resonance grew warmer.

He retreated.

The warmth subsided.

He drew closer again, and once more the Resonance flared, burning hot yet not uncomfortable. The two paths opened in his mind. He saw himself standing at the inevitable fork, suspended in animation as he struggled to choose.

I've found, Bharavi said to him, *acceptance.*

And Iravan chose the second path.

He touched the Resonance.

His vision split in the manner of trajection—no, it enhanced. He saw himself sitting there, alone on the bench underneath the neem tree, and above him the sky moved, the sun descending into the night sky into the morning sun into the night sky. Time trickled around him, one drop into another, one state becoming another, but he was eternal. He heard the grass grow, the *shrrrkk* sharpness of the sound, a part of the melody he heard. He saw the dew collect, the pool of water reflecting his own infinite states of being.

And in what had once been his second vision, he saw himself in the blackness of the non-Moment.

The darkness was no longer terrifying. It was a welcome oblivion, as though by acknowledging it, *he* had brought in the light. Iravan wandered in the folds of the familiar dark, his belly dropping like he was suspended in a vacuum. The blackness stretched infinite in all directions, but what was direction? There was no conception of time and space in this dimension, this *Deepness*. He *thought*, and the Moment appeared in front of him, a globule of lights like a dewdrop that had trapped all the stars.

Above him, the sun set and rose many times.

The song of the Resonance echoed within his heart.

And Ahilya burst through his mind, her smile faltering as he told her he was going away, as he promised he would return.

Iravan wrenched himself out of the Deepness abruptly.

He was still sitting on the bench under the neem tree, but dusk had fallen. How many dusks? How long? The two paths opened in his mind again; he stood at the fork. He had taken a step down the second path, but he still had a choice. He knew there would come a time when the fork disappeared, when choosing a path would be irrevocable, a decision he couldn't undo.

Iravan jumped up, panic racing through him, and ran along Nakshar, through the winding streets and the muddy paths until he reached Ahilya's home. He didn't knock; he banged on the wall with his fist. Leaves trembled on the ivy, sending echoes of his panic inside the structure. The bark split open. Iravan hurried in to see Ahilya sitting at the table, several notebooks spread out in front of her, a finger just releasing her citizen ring.

"What happened?" she asked, pushing back her chair.

"How long was I gone?"

"A few hours—since this morning. Why, what do you mean?"

Iravan covered his face with a trembling hand and stumbled toward the table. A few hours. That was all. A part of him knew the horror in the relief he felt—he had disappeared for *a few hours*, and hadn't known, but it could have been worse, it could have been much worse. He had pulled himself out because of a fleeting memory of a promise. What if he had ignored it? How long would he have lost himself in the Resonance? Was that what lay on the other path? Not clarity but a deeper loss of *himself*?

He stood hunched over the table, his fists on the wood, deep breaths shaking his body.

"Iravan, what happened?" Ahilya asked, standing up.

"Did—did anything—Is Nakshar all right? There wasn't another Ecstatic attack like Bharavi's, w-was there?"

"No, of course not. Why are you asking that?"

Iravan shook his head, unable to answer. In a way, the connection with the Resonance had been similar to the merging of his Two Visions except, somehow, *freer.* Instead of losing his visions, his sight had opened to more dimensions, seen a truer version of reality. Was he losing his mind? *Sooner or later, you'll give in*, Bharavi said. *And let's face it—you and Ahilya. You and Ahilya*—He pushed away from the table. Ahilya had approached him, her beautiful eyes clouded with concern, her hand retracting like she had thought to touch him but had been unsure of it.

Iravan grabbed her wrist before she could pull away completely.

"What do you want, Ahilya?" he said angrily, reeling from everything that had happened.

Her eyes went wide, startled. "I want you to be happy. I want *us* to be happy. I want you to kiss me."

Surprise lanced through Iravan, shaking him out of the memory of the Resonance. Of those three demands, he chose the one he *could* fulfill. He pulled her closer, bent his head, and brushed his lips against hers.

Her breathing was shallow, and she pressed her mouth to his, her arms coming up to encircle his waist. Iravan cradled her face, deepening his kiss before he knew what he was doing. His teeth grazed over her lips, and he bit her, softly first, then harder. Ahilya moaned deep in her throat, her hands running through his hair, and for a moment, Iravan forgot everything else. All of his rage and confusion and fear poured out of him; he lifted her up, her body pressed against his, her legs wrapped around his waist, and he kissed her hungrily.

Gasping, Ahilya pulled away. She stared at him, her eyes wide.

"I—" Iravan began, starting to release her. "Ahilya—I'm—"

She leaned forward and kissed him again. Iravan hitched her higher and backed up toward the corner where her bed was. He waved a hand to widen the bed and stumbled into it, abruptly sitting on it. Her legs were still wrapped around him; she tugged at his kurta, and Iravan yanked it off, over his head. She pulled hers off too, shucking off her trousers, undoing the drawstring around his, removing both of their clothes. Then she was pushing him back on the bed and straddling him.

"Ahilya," he growled, the heat gathering in him.

"No," she said. "Don't speak."

Her hands fluttered over his chest, reaching lower. She leaned down to kiss him again, and her hair tickled his neck. His hands cupped her lush curves, and he squeezed. Ahilya gasped again, and she pulled him into her, and she felt so *right*, so familiar, like the sweetest nectar, that Iravan groaned, his breathing ragged; the both of them moved faster, holding on to each other, and Ahilya's grip in his hair was almost painful as she rode him and he moved deeper. Iravan spasmed and shuddered and she did too—

Then she collapsed onto him, her chest heaving, both their bodies sweaty.

They remained unmoving for a long time.

Ahilya disengaged slowly. She made to get up, off the bed, but Iravan reached for her. She froze, then settled back into his shoulder. Their fingers entangled, in and out. For the first time in nearly eight months, some of his tension receded.

She broke the silence first. "Iravan," she said softly. "I—We didn't—My cycle…my month's blood—" Ahilya took a deep breath, her chest rising under his arm. "It's not why I asked for this—but if we were to make a baby—it was… the right time."

His hand stilled in hers, and she lifted herself up to look into his eyes, but it was not Ahilya he saw. Iravan saw the faces of their children, a girl who looked like Ahilya, and a boy with his midnight-dark skin. The image flickered for a second, and an ache grew in him, so strong, so deep, that for a second Iravan couldn't breathe. He thought of his fight with Ahilya all those months before. He thought of Bharavi saying *You were holding on to your material reality while exercising the Ecstatic powers of trajection.* And Iravan thought of the Resonance that had reappeared in his mind, that had never truly left, even during his act of intimacy. His fingers twitched uneasily.

"What do you want, Ahilya?" he asked, but this time there was no anger in his question. He watched as a dozen expressions flew over her face, confusion and anger and regret.

"I want our marriage back," she said. "What do *you* want?"

Iravan's eyes drifted from hers to the ceiling, where sungineering globes emitted their soft yellow light, and where there was still no phosphorescence. "I want to do what's right."

"And what is that?"

"I'm not sure anymore."

The Resonance glimmered again in his head, and Iravan pressed a hand to his forehead to suppress it. The two paths had reappeared. Would they never cease to haunt him? He looked back at Ahilya, but she had quieted, her face withdrawn. It would not do. If balance were possible, he would achieve it—he would not become like Bharavi. He could not.

Iravan nudged her closer. "We never talked about that time in the jungle."

"There wasn't anything more to say," she muttered.

"I shouldn't have—The way I—" Iravan grimaced. "I'm sorry, Ahilya. I shouldn't have hijacked your mission."

The corner of her lips lifted slightly. "As everyone is reminding me, I only survived because of you, Iravan-*ve*."

"No," he said at once, sitting up. "Not you. Please, not you."

Iravan wasn't sure what he was denying, her excuses for him or her use of the respectful suffix, but her words wrought a thorn through his heart. He shook his head again, and Ahilya nodded slowly, as though understanding what he himself could not. She sat up too and stroked his jaw with her hand, her thumb running along his cheek. Iravan leaned into her, this comfort she was giving him that he did not deserve.

"You were so fearless in the jungle," he said. "It was the first time I went back in there since my own Junior Architect training; did you know that?"

Ahilya nodded, but she didn't remove her hand from his cheek, and she didn't say anything.

"Isn't that ridiculous?" Iravan continued, with a sarcastic laugh. "A Senior Architect oblivious of the jungle? We have forgotten so many of our roots. Each time you went on an expedition, the Junior Architect you took with you reported to the council about the nature of the jungle, but we only saw the jungle as part of the topography.

We never looked at it as something to learn from. You've been right all along. We only evade the earthrages. We don't really survive them. And being out there again—Ahilya, I was scared. I was so scared. But you were fearless. You were amazing. I should have told you that before."

He closed his own hand over hers. Ahilya shifted her weight. She settled herself along his lap, sitting atop him, facing him, gazing into his eyes.

"I love you," they blurted out at the same time, and Iravan saw his own surprise and delight reflected in her. He pulled her closer and kissed her again, holding back his hunger, trying to pour into his kiss all his devotion instead.

When she pulled away this time, her eyes sparkled. "I *was* afraid in the jungle," she said, laughing a little. "But not of the jungle. I was afraid of you, of you finding out about the spiralweed I was going to smuggle in." Ahilya swept a shaky hand through her hair, her breathing slightly ragged. "We were in the middle of an earthrage, Iravan. I should have been terrified. I guess I didn't know enough to be scared."

Goosepimples covered her arms, and she rubbed them. Iravan twisted to reach down to the floor, where their discarded clothes lay in a pile. The both of them pulled their kurtas over themselves, then arranged themselves cross-legged.

"I should have insisted we return," he said.

"I wouldn't have listened."

"Then I should have convinced you," he replied. "I knew something was wrong the minute we entered the jungle and I heard the jungle raga. A raga is a residue of trajection, Ahilya, but I could hear it *before* I had begun trajecting the jungle at all, which shouldn't have been possible. I should have guessed it was an Ecstatic, even if I couldn't have known it was Bharavi." Iravan got off the bed.

He pulled his trousers on and rolled the sleeves of his kurta back again. "You were right about the council's priorities. You were right about the jungle. I wonder how much else you were right about."

Ahilya rose too, pulling on her own trousers and settling her kurta. She ran a hand through her hair, detangling the knots. "Would you consider that I am right about the habitat?"

Iravan shook his head. "I don't want to sound like an architect, but I think Naila is right. How could anything survive the rages?"

"You're missing the evidence. There *is* something down there."

"But architecture?" Iravan asked. "What could the early architects have trajected that could survive—"

"We don't know what materials they had, what they could have used. And it needn't be architects at all; you're only thinking of architecture in terms of trajection—"

"It's the only way I know to think about it," he said, making a face. "And for architecture to be that complex, the trajection involved would have to be—"

And Iravan froze mid-sentence.

His mouth fell open, and he stared at Ahilya unseeingly. Sudden understanding exploded in his mind as pieces connected together. The charging of the tracker. The signal being blocked. The expedition and the terror he'd felt in the jungle.

"Iravan?" Ahilya asked, frowning.

He looked at her, his body trembling with abrupt excitement. It was as though seeds had begun to grow where once there had only been fallow land.

"Ahilya," he said slowly, trying to be methodical. "I think you're right. I think there has been complex architecture down there from the very beginning. But I think I'm right, too. I think trajection had something to do with it."

"What do you mean?" she asked sharply. "Have you remembered

something about our history? Of someone capable of building it?"

"Not someone," Iravan breathed. "Some*thing*."

He threw his arm out toward the window, where they could see a few stars glimmering in the dusky sky. He saw Ahilya's comprehension in the widening of her eyes.

"The yakshas?" she said, but she didn't laugh as he'd expected her to. Her face grew considering and Iravan watched her silently. If there was anyone in the world who would understand, anyone who could corroborate his hunch, it was Ahilya.

"Iravan—" she said slowly. "It's an interesting theory, but the yakshas are passive creatures. They can't traject. They can't even sense us. I've never noticed anything even remotely architect-like about them, and you said yourself how you didn't even detect consciousness from the elephant-yaksha. Is there more about them in the architects' archives that I don't know?"

"No. No—you know it all now—whatever I do. But Ahilya, what I felt in the jungle with the elephant-yaksha—" Iravan began to pace her small apartment, his legs eating up the distance, so every few steps, he had to turn around. "Consciousness exists on a scale of sentience and awareness. We thought human beings existed at the highest level as the most sentient creatures, but what if the yakshas exist at an even higher state? You can only sense an equal or lower level of consciousness in the Moment—maybe that's why I didn't sense the elephant-yaksha. I couldn't have if its consciousness is *greater* than mine."

Ahilya's mouth dropped open. She sat down heavily on the bed, staring at him. He stopped pacing and turned to her.

"The missing piece," she whispered. "'*Deathlike, the yakshas' consciousness is unbreachable. Unnatural creatures who must be avoided. Trajection is unviable; destruction, inevitable. For greater a consciousness, greater the danger.*'"

The words sounded like a quote, vaguely familiar to Iravan, but before he could ask, Ahilya had stood up and her eyes were shining.

"Iravan, I think you're right. The architects *feared* the yakshas always—that much is clear, but it was never clear why. Maybe they feared the yakshas because they were higher beings capable of trajection? Maybe this information was deliberately left out from the records?"

"If they truly can traject, then it's clear to see why," Iravan said darkly. "Architects would not have liked the… the *competition*. There are secret archives even I do not know about in ashrams like Katresh. Rages, you must think me a fool to be so certain of our histories before, when I knew all of this—to be so willingly obtuse when I know how they keep things even from me—"

But Ahilya shook her head, dismissing his admission with a hand. From her expression, he could tell her mind had raced ahead already.

"It wouldn't be about competition," she said. "Maybe the architects didn't broadcast this information because the yakshas were dangerous somehow. Maybe erasing their danger, pretending they didn't exist, was better than the alternative—admitting they were superior in some way—especially if the architects could do nothing about them—"

Iravan frowned. The Resonance glimmered in his mind, silvery and mercurial, pounding behind his eyes. He could feel it coming now, the inevitable realization. "Dangerous how?"

"Dangerous to the planet," she said, throwing her arm out. "I know the prevailing theory says that the earthrages are caused by the disruption of consciousnesses at a global level—"

"You never agreed with it—"

"I said there was more to it. And maybe there is. Perhaps I was measuring the wrong consciousness all along. I think that's why my census data didn't show any correlation. I was measuring humans, but if I could study the yakshas some more, I'd find out exactly why the rages are getting longer. Especially if they are at a higher consciousness level than we are—maybe something is happening with *them*. Maybe somehow *they* cause the earthrages."

Iravan nodded slowly. "That aligns with the existing theory," he said. "Our consciousnesses are too tiny to affect anything. Citizens can't even affect plants without trajection, and even architects must work hard in the Moment. For a consciousness to affect something at a global level, it has to be incredibly advanced; it has to have *gravity*. But trajection has an effect, Ahilya—it is related very deeply to our very bodies. Yakshas don't glow like architects do when an architect trajects, and you just said there was nothing architect-like about them—"

"I've only ever seen a yaksha during a lull," she said, shaking her head. "They wouldn't *need* to traject during a lull. They'd only need to traject during an earthrage to survive it. And for all we know, their trajection markings could be like curls in their tusks, or stripes in their coats—or," she said, her eyes widening, "rings around their irises—like the elephant-yaksha—like I'd already noticed..."

She shook her head again, wonder in her eyes.

"It would explain so much," she said. "That thing blocking the signal down there—that point in the map where the tracker disappeared—that has to be yaksha habitat, and it is architecture the yakshas *trajected*. If they truly are superior to human beings, then the architecture they create must be *unbelievably* complex. Of course no technology of ours would penetrate it."

Her head snapped up and she shrugged, the gesture embarrassed.

"You weren't the only one being obtuse," she said. "I always thought it was non-plant architecture, something the humans left behind—non-architects. But maybe it *is* trajection-related after all—just not made by *human* architects. It's why we didn't stay in the jungle. Flight occurred to escape from the yakshas, these creatures that were superior to us..."

She trailed off and grew still, her eyes unseeing before her. Iravan stared at her, the sheer beauty of her, the fierce intelligence, a master at work. How could he ever have thought her incapable of the council? He had dropped the seeds, but she had built an entire explanation out of it, as though waiting for the chance. He forced himself away from the burning Resonance, forced himself to see her, the only thing that mattered. The two paths blinked at him; he saw himself take a step—

Then Ahilya caught his gaze and shook herself. "This is the farthest I've come," she said, laughing softly. "I could build several hypotheses just off this alone, even if I'd have to rearrange my assumptions. If I had proof of some kind, it would change everything."

"You *do* have proof," Iravan said quietly. "It's been staring at us from the very beginning."

She tilted her head, curious, and Iravan made a gesture with his hand.

"Spiralweed," he said. He had considered it, on and off, as he'd thought of how the plant had reacted to him in the library and to Bharavi in the deathcage, similar but not the same. "Spiralweed evolved to feed off trajection, but there are no trajecting ashrams down there. Then how did it evolve to do that over so many earthrages? How did it survive in the jungle? It would need trajection—and it is trajection the yakshas supply."

"And that's how the elephant-tracker charged itself so mysteriously," she said, nodding. "It wasn't mysterious—we've been blind. The tracker was being charged by the elephant-yaksha—" But Ahilya cut herself off, a frown drawing on her face. "No, that won't work. The tracker charged during Bharavi's Ecstasy, too. It's not as though there was a yaksha *in* Nakshar."

"No," Iravan said slowly. "There wasn't... But there was something else. Five years before..."

He turned away from Ahilya and looked out of the window into the dark sky, thinking...

He had considered this the minute Dhruv had spoken about Energy X. Naila had innocently pointed it out, minutes after, but though her words had been thoughtless, her logic had followed Iravan's own. The last Ecstatic Nakshar had produced before Bharavi had been Manav, five years earlier. But like Bharavi, Manav's Ecstasy had remained undiscovered for a while. Dhruv must have created the tracker for the elephant-yaksha around then, when Manav was likely experimenting with his new powers. The sungineer hadn't known his tracker was being charged with Energy X; he had assumed it was running on trajection, like everything else in the ashram.

But Energy X was *Ecstatic* trajection.

And Ecstatic trajection was *different* from trajection.

As much as he didn't want the others to know, as much as he had tried to pivot away from this during the discussion, Iravan knew this to be the truth. He had experienced it, and Bharavi had confirmed it for him. He had been trajecting Ecstatically in the jungle when he'd created magnaroot armors for himself, Ahilya, and Oam. That's why their citizen rings hadn't responded; *those* devices only responded to trajection. As for the elephant-yaksha's tracker... There was only one way Ecstatic trajection could charge the tracker in the jungle through all those years... only one reason why the tracker during their escape from the jungle had continued chiming even though their citizen rings hadn't...

Iravan's hand trembled as he withdrew the device Dhruv had given him from his pocket.

Then he turned around to fill his gaze with Ahilya.

"Don't leave me," he whispered.

Ahilya took a step toward him. "Iravan—"

He dove into the silvery Resonance.

He tumbled into the Deepness, spinning through the blackness, his stomach dropping. His skin lit up blue-green. His legs buckled, but Ahilya was there, holding him up, looking into his eyes, saying, "Are you—"; yet he saw her only as a dim memory of what had been, of all the many Ahilyas she could have been and the many Iravans he was.

The energy of Ecstasy flowed through his veins like a river current. Iravan gathered it to him in the manner of a deep inhalation. He spun in the Deepness until he saw the globule of the Moment suspended like a water droplet in the darkness, stars glimmering inside it. A light emerged from him in the Deepness, bright golden, and Iravan focused it, a thin, *thin* ray, shooting it into the globule of the Moment, aimed at the jungle down in the earthrage.

And the locket in his hand began chiming, charging.

His Ecstatic trajection was charging the tracker.

The elephant-yaksha had done the same thing.

Those creatures could traject Ecstatically; not trajection but *super*trajection.

"Ahilya," Iravan whispered, and all the infinite Ahilyas in his mind leaned toward him in concern, their faces shining with love.

Have you found control, then? he asked Bharavi, and she laughed at him. *I've found acceptance. I've found acceptance. I've found—*

The Resonance wrenched from him, appearing in his second vision, its silvery wings mirroring his golden light in the Deepness.

And for the first time, Iravan accepted it for what it was: a siren that had been calling out to him for years, for lifetimes, echoing through time, waiting for him to acknowledge it.

The Resonance reacted to his acknowledgement. Its silvery molten flaps whooshed out of the Deepness, and he saw instead the architect behind that call—

A gigantic falcon-yaksha flying toward him, its wings spanning nearly a hundred feet, its black eyes glinting in uncontrollable fury at how long Iravan had made it wait, how many eons, how many births—

And Iravan saw himself mirrored in the falcon's mind, saw the creature's intent; it would kill them all in its pursuit of him, it had found him at last, hidden behind layers of flying foliage—

The falcon-yaksha dove from the twilit sky with the force of a storm. Iravan jerked back, and all the Ahilyas resolved into *his* Ahilya, and she was holding him up as he stumbled on the floor, only just completing her sentence: "—all right?"

The next instant, Nakshar rocked with the impact of collision. The world tilted, the ground split open under them, and Ahilya was thrown off him.

Iravan screamed.

37

AHILYA

Ahilya slid along the tilted floor of her home into the endless sky.

She had no time to scream; one second, she had been leaning over Iravan, and the next, the darkness yawned below, calling out to her. She rolled, caught a glimpse of Iravan, blue-green, still in the house, open sky. Her fingers scrabbled for purchase, digging into the mud, ripping nails.

She screamed then, terror clawing at her throat.

Her scream cut off with a grunt.

A vine encircled her waist. Ahilya twisted to see Iravan nearly fifty feet away, braced against the wall of their crumbling home. A whole section of the house had fallen off. Iravan stood in what had been the kitchen, vines banding his waist. He was like a blue-green spider caught in a corner, tight against the wall, foliage tethering him like webbing.

He snapped in and out of her vision as he pulled her up, and then she was next to him, tied to him. His skin was blinding blue, and she saw—for the first time—that his tattoos resembled not flowing vines but glinting wings.

"I-Iravan?" she breathed.

"Hold on," he said grimly. He gripped her to him, an arm around her waist, his hold painful. The wall behind them opened like a tunnel.

The next instant, the both of them shot through it.

Ahilya had no sense of up or down. They were flying through the tunnel, or falling perhaps. Green flashed by her eyes. Mud flew around them, she smelt wet earth, but none of the flakes hit her. Iravan had encased them somehow in a protective bubble that the green, earthy tunnel could not touch.

The tunnel opened; a hint of twilight.

The two of them burst through it, the force of their momentum shooting them into the night sky.

And below her, Ahilya glimpsed Nakshar disintegrate into fire and chaos.

It was a moment's glimpse, but it was enough. A section of the ashram broke apart in slow motion, the very section they had been in. It cracked like chalk, and Ahilya watched in horror as part of the city plummeted toward the jungle. Bodies hurtled out, terror in their gestures, limbs flinging, then disappeared into the darkness. She couldn't hear the screams; the wind of passage filled her ears, but tears overcame her vision—where was Tariya, where were the boys?—Ahilya pressed her face against Iravan's chest; and then they were shooting through another tunnel again, abruptly coming to rest on solid ground.

Ahilya's knees buckled. She emptied her stomach, but Iravan didn't let go of her. He grasped her to him, his chilling gaze going beyond her. She turned and her heart climbed her throat.

There in the night sky, flapping its gigantic wings, was a monstrous yaksha shaped like a falcon.

For a brief moment, sheer wonder overtook Ahilya's fear.

The falcon-yaksha was the most beautiful creature she had ever seen. Its glossy wings, spanning nearly a hundred feet, gleamed silver and gray. Its pitch-black eyes glinted malevolently. Startled, Ahilya noticed the same strange ringed pattern in its eyes she had seen in the elephant-yaksha a few weeks before. She tried to make sense of it, but the yaksha opened its golden hooked beak and screamed, a high-pitched yarp. The sound sent fresh thrills of terror running through her. She ducked her head, her gaze catching torn rosebushes and scattered leaves. Iravan had brought her to the terrace garden above the temple. The terrace was flat; they must have emerged from a hole in the floor, through the tunnel Iravan had trajected.

About twenty Maze Architects in various states of dishevelment stood between Ahilya and the yaksha, blood and earth streaking their faces. Their robes were frayed and tattered. Their dark skins gleamed with the light of trajection. A hundred bamboo stems shot up around the architects, like jagged spears aimed toward the creature.

"No!" she shouted, and Iravan shouted it too.

The bamboo stems exploded before they could reach the falcon. Shards scoured the air, embedding themselves in soft bodies. Maze Architects dropped like flies, the blue-green light dying out of them.

"NO!" Iravan screamed again, and the falcon-yaksha tilted its head as though it could hear him. "Stay here," her husband growled, and then he was sprinting across the terrace, glowing like a blue star, blinding.

Ahilya didn't realize she had risen to her feet, but she was running too as earth exploded around her. Chunks of rock flew at her. Dust obscured her vision, but she followed the shape of Iravan's white kurta, slipping and sliding, leaping over holes opening in the ground.

A boulder smashed into her, knocking her off her feet.

Ahilya flew at an angle and landed with a painful thud. Dizziness swept over her. Something wet dripped down the side of her face. Blood. She tried to stand, but she was trapped. Vines grew over her, holding her down like ropes. It was healbranch; she tried to shake it off, but the vines tightened around her chest and her wrists. They held her down; they were choking her.

Dust and tears obscured her vision, but she saw past them: Iravan standing in front of the falcon-yaksha, a lone figure in white, his skin gleaming a brilliant teal.

Ahilya's breath squeezed out of her. Her eyes watered. "E-vuhn," she choked, trying to form his name.

And he heard.

Somehow, miraculously, he heard.

Iravan turned as though in a dream. He extended a hand toward her, took a step forward, his back to the flapping falcon-yaksha.

The yaksha uttered a bloodcurdling scream of pain and outrage. The cords around Ahilya's throat tightened. Iravan took another faltering step to her. It seemed to happen very slowly.

The yaksha reached down, its talons snatching at Iravan. Its wings flapped once, twice.

Then the creature was gone, disappeared into the night sky.

Blackness enveloped Ahilya.

38

AHILYA

She was back in an earthrage. The ground roiled under her, and Oam died again. In her dreams, Iravan came to her. "Don't leave..." he said. "Don't leave me." Over and over, the same words. She jerked, trying to catch them; if only she could catch them, it would all be better. Bharavi exploded into blue-green light, and Dhruv slept on the floor by her, glasses askew. Ahilya reached, but his body crumbled into ashes as soon as she touched him. She screamed, and Iravan returned, swallowing her scream with his kiss, pulling back to say again, "Don't leave me."

She awoke from a lonely haunted place to raised voices.

"—need to ask her—"

"—only one with expertise—"

Tariya and Dhruv's voices answered, murmuring insistently. Ahilya blinked, and lights resolved. Sungineering glowglobes twinkled in a low, earthy ceiling. She tried to sit up, but healbranch vines looped around her wrists and chest. Her breath came out panicked; she was choking, the vine was going to kill her. She struggled, gasping, trying to pull the white vines off, but her arms were bound in splints; she couldn't move.

And then Dhruv was there, hurrying toward her, sitting down on the floor, and stroking her hair. "Easy," he said. "Easy. You're all right. You're safe."

He braced her as she tried to sit up. Ahilya's throat felt like sandpaper. She scrabbled for the jug Dhruv was picking up, but he batted her feeble attempts away. He poured the water into a small cup and held it out to her. Ahilya drank thirstily, sloshing water over herself, one cup, then another and another. Dhruv watched, his eyes bloodshot behind his glasses.

"What—" she began, but her voice came out softer than a whisper. She wasn't sure she had spoken at all. Her throat burned. Tears pooled in her eyes and fell down her cheek.

"You need to slow down," Dhruv said, gently wiping away her tears with the edge of his sleeve. "You were badly hurt. You broke your arm, you might have a concussion, and you were nearly strangled."

"Ta-ya... boys..."

"They're safe. Tariya has gone to get something to eat. She'll be back soon."

"Ee-ah-vuhn..."

"You need to rest." Dhruv put down the jug he was holding and removed his glasses. "It's only been two weeks since the attack. You still need to heal."

Two weeks.

"*Iravan...*" she rasped, more insistently.

The sungineer studied her, his face grave and weary. Tears filled Ahilya's vision; she began to sob, her throat throbbing. Panic drowned her lungs.

"He's alive," Dhruv said hurriedly. "Ahilya, please, Iravan is alive, all right? He's alive."

Ahilya stared at him, searching his face for a lie, but Dhruv would not lie to her—not about this.

"Please," he said, his voice breaking. "Just lay back."

Some of the pressure in Ahilya's lungs released. *He's alive.* She obeyed, and Dhruv drifted out of her vision.

She didn't know how much time had passed, but the next time she woke, she was alone. Ahilya sat up slowly. Her every muscle ached. Her right arm was in a cast of bark, but she could move. She touched the ridges along her throat. The skin was bruised but the bumps were receding.

Standing up took a long time. Ahilya had to clutch the wall next to her to pull herself up. She was in a small chamber. If she'd stood in the center and extended her arms, she'd have touched opposite walls. Ahilya willed the bark to part, and it creaked open to a narrow corridor.

She stumbled through it, confused. The corridor, lit by tiny glowglobes, led into a balcony. Ahilya lurched toward the railing, looking down. Blue-green light sparkled below in what appeared to be a tiny courtyard. Trajecting lights. The Architects' Disc. She was in Nakshar's temple. Nakshar had survived. But the shape… this shape… She was up so high.

Ahilya's heart started to race again. Vertigo gripped her. The temple looked like a gigantic beehive, a hundred narrow corridors leading away from the central railings into darkness. When she squinted, she could see other shapes leaning on the railings in the lower levels. It seemed all of Nakshar's citizens had been brought to the temple. Her mind reeled; this design resembled the landing architecture so many weeks earlier. Iravan's landing architecture. Had there been another lull? Were they finally landing? Where was Iravan? Why hadn't he come to her?

Hurried footsteps sounded behind her, and Dhruv emerged from the dark corridor.

"Oh, thank rages," the sungineer said. "I wondered where you were. How are you feeling?"

"Thirsty," she said. Dhruv was carrying more water, and this time, he let her take the jug from his hands and drink.

"How long?" she asked when she was finished.

"Three weeks on the whole," he replied, accepting the jug back. "You've been under sedation to heal, and you're recovering. That's good. Tariya and I were worried. She'll be back soon. She's been helping on the infirmary floor." Dhruv studied her face. "Do you remember much?"

"Nakshar… disintegrating." A sob grew in Ahilya's throat, and she swallowed it back painfully. "Tell me… what happened."

"There was an attack," Dhruv said slowly. "A yaksha attack—this bird-yaksha—"

Ahilya shook her head. She remembered it, but her mind could not accept this. Yakshas did not attack. They were not predators.

"The creature was huge," Dhruv went on. "And, well… we don't know very much. The yaksha came out of nowhere, and the next moment, the ashram was breaking apart. The rudra tree survived, as did most of the temple, but it was a near thing. All the citizens—the *surviving* citizens—they've been brought here. *This* is Nakshar now." He swept a hand out the railing, toward the honeycomb they were in.

The bile rose in Ahilya's throat. In her mind's eye, she saw a piece of Nakshar fall away again, bodies hurtling into the night sky.

Dhruv answered her unspoken question. "We lost too much. The library, so many homes, much of the solar lab—it's all gone. I was in the temple when it happened, but so many sungineers—they're—" Tears filled his eyes. He started to tremble.

Ahilya grasped his arm, and he engulfed her in a hug, careful of her cast. She patted his back, disoriented, unable to help him, unable to speak. When he pulled away after a minute, his eyes still shone with tears but his voice was more composed.

"You should return to your chamber," he said. "You need to rest. Recover and rest. It's up to the sungineers and the architects now. There's nothing you can do."

Ahilya shook her head. He was trying to dismiss her. She needed to know why. She pressed his arm and searched his face. "What aren't you telling me?"

Dhruv wiped his eyes. "Nothing. We're flying under critical conditions now. Everything is rationed. We won't last very long, but Reikshar is flying toward us. We… we don't know if it will arrive in time. Kiana, Laksiya, and I… we're trying something with the spiralweed—"

"Spiralweed," Ahilya said, her eyes widening. "You told them about it."

"I didn't have a choice. We're staring annihilation in the face now, Ahilya. We've lost so much, and the citizens are panicked. All that fear, all that confusion—I chose to tell Kiana about the battery, and she and the others in the council chose to tell the citizens; to give them some hope. The city responds to people's desire, and if I—*we*—hadn't made the decision, we wouldn't be able to sustain even this." He waved a limp hand at the temple—at Nakshar—and dropped it. "The spiralweed is a desperate attempt for a battery, even for a short-term battery—just enough until Reikshar reaches us. But we haven't tested our prototype yet. It's—it's not looking good."

Ahilya swallowed, and nodded; it was the right decision, but Dhruv did not meet her gaze. She pointed at the courtyard below them. "I have to get down there. It's where Iravan is, isn't he? What's the fastest way?"

"I…"

"He must be unhurt and working, or he would have been right next to me. You said—" Ahilya's voice faltered. "You said he was alive. He is, isn't he?"

"The yaksha—he was fighting it—trajecting at it. But the others saw—he..." Dhruv took a deep breath. "The yaksha took him away. I'm sorry. He's as good as dead."

"No."

"Ahilya, please, I know this is hard—"

"You said he was alive. You said so."

"I—" Dhruv reached for his glasses, but Ahilya arrested his movement with her hand.

"How do you know he is alive, Dhruv?"

The sungineer gave her a long look, his mouth drawing down in sadness. Then he reached into his pocket and withdrew what looked like the elephant-yaksha's tracker.

"Iravan came to me before all this happened. We made an exchange, the spiralweed for the yaksha-tracker, but I'd made a backdoor earlier to the device, and I gave him a replica connected to this one. *His* tracker—it's been sending a signal. It's recharging where he is—"

She pressed his arm. "How do you know he's *alive*? How do you know it's not just the tracker recharging because of Energy X?"

"The tracker still tracks," Dhruv said miserably. "It's recording data, just like the tracker on the elephant-yaksha did. Energy X is what powers it and recharges it, but there are circuits inside the tracker that capture information, and I've received vital signs from them. He's—he's alive, Ahilya, but there is no way we can go to him, not with Nakshar like this."

"And Energy X is charging your receiver somehow?"

"Yes. I know what you're thinking—that Energy X is Ecstatic energy, but I don't think there's any architect in Ecstasy right now—"

Dhruv disengaged her grip on him. "The councilors have been waiting for you to wake. They only left you alone so far because Tariya threatened she'd reveal information on some secret pact."

"I'm awake now. Let's go."

"Ahilya, listen to me. I know why you want to talk to them. It's not about the city, is it? Before you go and ask for something stupid, please know this—Nakshar is running on critical energy. The city has no trajection to fly, let alone chase after Iravan. We're bobbing in the sky, waiting for Reikshar to catch up to us. We're ready to collapse into the earthrage ourselves. Iravan is—gone."

"I—"

"And there's no telling when his signal will die," he went on. "What if the yaksha goes back to its habitat in the jungle where we get no signal? What if somehow this receiver"—he waved the tracker in his hand—"stops working because our mysterious supply of Energy X runs out? There's no certainty. He's—You have to let him go."

"You can take me to the council," Ahilya said. "Or I will find my own way. But it'll be faster if you help me. Please, Dhruv. *Please.*"

For a long moment, he stared at her. She thought that he would leave, ask her to figure it out herself. But then the sungineer withdrew a solarnote from his pocket and swiped through some images. "Maybe this will change your mind," he mumbled. "Your scans from the infirmary."

Ahilya stared at the glassy screen and was immediately nauseous. "I'm… This is…"

"Yes. You're pregnant." Dhruv took the tablet back. He didn't congratulate her.

Ahilya pressed a hand to her stomach, dizzy. No wonder Dhruv had been so cagey, so relentless that she return to recover. Ahilya had known pregnancy was a possibility when she and Iravan had been intimate; it had been the perfect time, her body had been ripe for it, but for it to betray her now, at this moment—

She staggered a little and held tightly to the railing. Her eyes closed and she breathed rapidly, hearing her own panic resounding in her ears. *I want to be a father*, Iravan had said. *Why is that so hard to believe?* Tears trickled down her closed eyes, unbidden, and she wiped them away hurriedly. *I want you to be happy. I want our marriage back.*

"Let me take you back to your room—" Dhruv began.

But Ahilya opened her eyes and dashed the tears away with a furious hand. "No," she said, surprised to hear how calm her voice sounded. "No, Dhruv, take me down there to the councilors. I have news that will help them."

The sungineer stared at her, unmoving for a second. Then his shoulders slumped in defeat. Perhaps he could see her stubbornness; he knew her well enough to know she would not back down. Dhruv turned toward the corridor they had come through. He tapped at his citizen ring and the bark wall split open. An elevator took them down in silence through the temple's levels.

They emerged directly in the small courtyard at the bottom. Ahilya stumbled behind Dhruv, her mouth dropping open, her heart sinking in dismay. The rudra tree was shorter than she was, barely a sapling. Its leaves had darkened at the edges, scorched. The Architects' Disc was no longer a Disc. Instead, one portion of the courtyard was cordoned off, a thin, leafy barricade rising from the floor. Blue-green light flickered behind it.

Dhruv headed to the other end of the courtyard, and Ahilya followed slowly. Never had the temple looked so cavernous or Nakshar so small. From down there, she couldn't make out the hollows or railings in the structure at all. How many citizens had survived? How had the council decided who would live where? She swallowed and looked ahead, trying to focus on the one thing she wanted, the one thing she *could* still change.

Far from the splendor of the council chambers, Nakshar's council now sat on a circular bench, a small sungineering heater in the center. They looked a weary, bedraggled bunch, the two remaining Senior Architects and Sungineers, and their apprentices from the last emergency meeting. Ahilya's stomach clenched. She had never liked the council, but she had never wanted them brought down this way. Whispered voices carried over, then Kiana noticed Dhruv, and all of them fell silent.

Airav straightened. "Ahilya-ve. It's good to see you. How is your arm?"

The others shuffled on the circular bench, making way for her and Dhruv. Ahilya climbed over and sat down, facing them. Dhruv squeezed in beside her.

"You've been waiting for me," she said.

Chaiyya glanced at Airav, but the bald, serious man had eyes only for Ahilya.

"Yes," he said. "You're the expert on yakshas. You—This attack—" Airav sighed. "You must know by now the situation we face. We need explanations that we can relay to the other ashrams. If yakshas are suddenly attacking us, then the skies are no longer safe, and the jungle is… well, the jungle has never been safe. Ahilya-ve, it's probably no exaggeration to say that we are staring at an end to our species. Anything you can tell us will be helpful."

"I have information that can help," Ahilya said slowly. "Something that might sustain the ashram for a long time. Something that might even provide a new source of energy."

Chaiyya sat up, her eyes wide. Kiana glanced at Dhruv, who was staring at his hands. Laksiya uttered a soft snort of skepticism. The others, Megha, Umit, and Reya, slapped each other on the backs, making sounds of relief. Only Airav remained quiet.

"We're listening," he said carefully.

Ahilya studied them, their sober faces full of nervousness and anticipation. She wouldn't feel her pregnancy yet, but her stomach spasmed as though in warning. *Don't leave me*, Iravan said, and she knew the smart thing, the safe thing, the *logical* thing, would be to help the ashram now in its time of need. Dhruv still stared at his hands. He had known what she was going to do, of course. It was why he had been reluctant to tell her anything.

"I'll give this information to you if you promise to go after Iravan," Ahilya said.

Silence greeted her words. Dhruv shifted next to her. Airav's lips lifted in a humorless smile; he alone of the councilors had perhaps guessed at her intention.

"That's impossible," Laksiya said flatly. "We don't have the energy."

"You'll make the energy," Ahilya said, but she didn't look at the sungineer. She took in Airav and Chaiyya, the two Senior Architects, with her gaze. "Iravan is out there somewhere. We have a location on him. He can't be far, not if we can track him. This is his design, isn't it? The way the ashram is right now? *His* landing architecture that you're relying on?"

"It's not that easy—" Kiana began.

"We don't have the resources," Chaiyya said. "Ahilya, I'm sorry—I really am—but the ashram is our priority—"

"He's one of you. He's alive. You're content to just abandon him?"

"It's not so clear-cut. As councilors, we have to think of the greater good—"

"Then think of the greater good," Ahilya implored, leaning forward. "Think of what you will lose if I don't give you my information. Find a way to bring him back or we have nothing more to discuss." She stood up. Her head spun; she hadn't eaten in so very long.

"You would hold the entire ashram hostage?" Airav asked softly, speaking finally. "Your sister? Your nephews? All these lives? Our ashrams and the others? "

"Your oldest tradition is an architect's need for material bonds," Ahilya replied coolly. "Perhaps that thinking is finally reaping its true fruits."

The Senior Architect didn't blink. Ahilya turned and climbed over the bench and walked away. She heard Dhruv mutter something to the councilors, then he joined her and they both sat down cross-legged on the floor of the courtyard, their eyes on the ring of the councilors.

Ahilya started to shake. She clutched her belly with her free arm and leaned forward, heaving, trying to catch a breath. What had she done? Had she truly given such an ultimatum? What if they didn't agree? Could she hold herself to her words? And what about the child that was growing in her? To make such a decision and put herself in danger now…

Out of the corner of her eye she saw Dhruv's boots nudge the grass. He was furious, she knew. *He's a charmer, Ahilya. He's a charmer.* All their agreements and deals and experiments seemed so laughable now. Their ambitions to the council, their attempts to change the world—Hysteria built in Ahilya's mind. Her cast itched. *You would hold the entire ashram hostage?*

"I'm sorry," she whispered, trying to cut out the noise in her head.

Dhruv didn't reply. She was almost grateful for his silence. Nothing he could say would change what she'd done. Nothing could justify the choice that she'd made.

"You've lost your mind," Dhruv muttered at last. "There's safety here for you and your child. They'd make you a councilor just for the information you give them. Rages, if we survive this, then with Iravan, Bharavi, and Manav gone, they could make *both* of us councilors. The mandatory five-year timeline for the council seat would no longer apply, not when the total councilors number only four. We could have everything we ever wanted. *You* could have everything you wanted."

"Not everything."

"Not Iravan, you mean?"

She made no reply to that. "Will they do it?" she asked instead. "Find a way?"

Dhruv removed his glasses and pinched the bridge of his nose with two fingers. "There *is* a way. They need to test the prototype battery that Kiana and I have built. They've been vacillating because of its potential dangers, but you've just forced them to take that step."

Ahilya watched the councilors in the distance, their hunched postures, their whispered arguments. Several times, one or the other leaned over to look at her, then returned to their whispering. *Potential dangers*, Dhruv had said; but the greatest danger of a battery was its potential to enslave architects. Was that what the council was discussing now? What survival and civilization would look like if they took that step? She looked away, her stomach roiling. She could not believe this was the choice she had made; a part of her wished to get up and take back her ultimatum, now before it was too late; before she led them down a path that would only mean their eventual destruction. But Ahilya sat unmoving on the grass, Iravan's voice in her head, saying, *Don't leave me.*

"Do you remember when we were children?" Dhruv said, still massaging his forehead. "That one time when Nakshar was landing and everyone was told to return to their homes to be safe? You were seven, and I was ten, and you wanted to go to the temple to your parents. Tariya and I were babysitting you, but you were such a brat that Tariya finally left to her friends' home just to get away. But I, fool boy that I was, indulged your tantrum."

Dhruv had led her by the hand, his other fist clutched around an old-fashioned sungineering lamp as they roamed the darkness, searching the ashram's architecture for the temple. When Nakshar had landed, the two had been caught in the foliage, cocooned in rock and bark. A search party of Maze Architects had finally found them.

"I think about that so often," Dhruv went on, his voice muffled as he continued to press his forehead. "I got into so much trouble, and your Maze Architect parents threatened to exile my whole family because of the danger I put you in. They would have done it too, but you told them if I disappeared, you would run away to the jungle. You were *seven*—there was no way you could have done that—but they must have known you'd do something rash. You protected me despite the trouble you got into yourself."

"I'd still do anything for you," Ahilya murmured.

"Not for me," Dhruv said. "For *you*. You protected me because I was *yours* to protect, everything else be damned. You really would let the world plummet to protect those who are yours. That used to be me when we were children. And Tariya and the boys have always had that consideration. But Iravan supersedes us all now."

"He's my husband."

The sungineer shook his head. "It's why you became an archeologist. You could have been a sungineer or a mathematician or anything else. But you needed something that was yours—wholly, fully, truly yours. Something that couldn't be touched by anything or anyone else. And so, you found the deadest field in the world."

Ahilya watched the councilors. Kiana and Laksiya were silent, but Chaiyya was shaking her head, pressing Airav's arm, evidently begging him to reconsider.

"I never did like him, you know?" Dhruv went on, and Ahilya knew he was talking about Iravan. "Even when you first started courting him. He was arrogant and high-handed and so damned aware of his own charm that he used it ruthlessly like a weapon. But he did one thing with you that no one has. He didn't enable your selfishness."

Ahilya's eyes met Dhruv's. She couldn't think of a single thing to say.

"Do you think," Dhruv asked softly, "he'd want you to do what you're doing right now?"

They stared at each other. She knew he was right—about Iravan, about *her*. A chill went through Ahilya. Iravan against the world. That's what her choices had come down to. That, in the end, was the price of survival. *Don't leave me*, he had said, but he would have asked her to stay had he known this. *He* would have stayed to protect Nakshar, given the same choices; done what was right, overcome the pull of his bonds to her for his bonds to the ashram, no matter how much it hurt.

But she couldn't. *She* couldn't.

Dhruv patted her hand with his. "You two deserve each other."

His words were like a slap on her face. Ahilya grew cold. She rose to her feet mechanically as Airav waved at them. Dhruv joined her, and they approached the bench and sat down again, neither of them speaking.

"We'll do it," Airav said without preamble. "Do you want us to make a healbranch promise?"

"No," Ahilya whispered. "I trust you."

"Then tell us your information. And if it's sound, we'll find a way to take you to Iravan."

Ahilya didn't dare glance at Dhruv. Guilt weighed her down, shaking her resolve. Quietly, her voice dull, she told them everything she and her husband had worked out right before the attack, about the yakshas being sentient beings, about their habitat in the jungle, about the real reason behind the earthrages. They listened, spellbound, as she told them how she and Iravan had connected the missing pieces within the architects' records, how they had decoded the historical fear of the jungle, how they'd thought proof lay in the evolution of spiralweed. When Ahilya reached the part about yakshas trajecting, Chaïyya let out a startled exclamation.

"It makes sense," the Senior Architect breathed, her hand around her pregnant belly. "The suddenness of the attack, and why the third quadrant was destroyed. This was why none of our battle trajection worked against the creature."

"How is this possible?" Kiana asked. "Yakshas have *never* attacked humans before. What could prompt this, even if we are to believe they can traject?"

"It's not trajection," Ahilya said wearily. Iravan had been silent only about one thing while navigating the conversation, but Ahilya had worked it out for herself. "It's Energy X. It's the same as Ecstatic trajection. Dhruv has already engineered something that uses Ecstasy. You want an alternate source of energy to replace trajection? Find a way to harness a yaksha. That's why the elephant-yaksha's tracker remained charged for the last five years. This is probably why Iravan's tracker right now is working. The falcon-yaksha must be trajecting Ecstatically. For us to be able to pick up the signal—the falcon and Iravan, they must be close enough to reach."

The others turned their gaze to Dhruv. He didn't meet their eyes, but his shoulders trembled.

"The yakshas are neither predator nor prey," Ahilya said. "At least, they haven't been, before—even the histories agree to that.

But something triggered the falcon-yaksha to attack. I don't know what, but its eyes had a pattern I've only noticed once before on the elephant-yaksha during the last expedition. I can draw it for you, but I suspect that those patterns work the same as an architect's tattoos. They only appear when the yaksha is trajecting. This is all I know—I swear it. And now it's your turn to fulfill your end of the bargain."

"We can never get close enough to a yaksha if this is true," Laksiya said, turning to Chaiyya. "How does this help us?"

"It's still information we can relay to the others," Chaiyya replied. "Not everyone's situation is as desperate as ours."

"But the implications of this," Gaurav said, leaning in. "If we're not the only trajectors in the world... if our histories are so incomplete, what else is being kept from us?"

"I think you're all forgetting the ethical implications," Kiana said quietly. "Are we suggesting we want to drain a harmless creature and enslave it for our own existence?"

"It's hardly harmless—"

"This is exactly why normal citizens don't like us—"

Someone touched Ahilya's shoulder. Airav had risen and approached her. He extended his hand, and she stood up and left the arguments of the council. Airav and Dhruv followed her. Ahilya still couldn't meet Dhruv's gaze, and Airav seemed lost in thought. The three walked silently until they reached the shrunken rudra tree.

Then the Senior Architect turned to her. "I can't claim to understand your thinking. But you have helped, and I will honor our agreement."

"You'll take the ashram to Iravan, then?" Ahilya asked, hope rising in her chest.

"No. But I will send *you* to him."

She frowned, glanced at Dhruv, then back again at the Senior Architect. "How?"

"You'll see. But it behooves me to tell you this, Ahilya-ve," the Senior Architect said. "This attempt is suicidal. You will most likely crash into the earthrage. We don't know if our idea will work, or if the architecture will last long enough for you to track Iravan down. You don't rightly even know where he is, and Dhruv has told me that Iravan's tracker could die any moment. You'll be flying out in the dark alone, and even if you find Iravan, how do you intend to rescue him if the falcon-yaksha can traject Ecstatically?"

Ahilya made no reply. Her arm beneath the cast twinged. Her stomach churned. She thought of the fetus forming in her body. It had no consciousness yet, a mere mass of cells. But Iravan was alive. *He* was *alive*.

"I see," Airav said. "And therefore, I must ask you. Are you sure you want to attempt this? You have no obligation to anyone—not even to Iravan—to risk your life in such a manner. You are a citizen, Ahilya-ve, and you are to be protected, not imperiled, least of all in your condition. I must emphasize that there is very little chance of success."

"As much a chance of success as you have with my information," she said.

"I suppose so." Airav turned to Dhruv, as though he had known already his words would have no effect. "If you wouldn't mind, please get your battery ready. Ahilya-ve, I suggest you say your goodbyes. The elevator will take you to the temple's terrace. I'll see you there in half an hour."

"You're sending her *now*?" Dhruv asked, stunned.

"There's no reason to wait," Airav said. He started to walk away, back to the councilors, but Ahilya touched his arm and he looked up, surprised.

"I'm sorry," she said.

Senior Architect Airav tilted his head, studying her from behind his glasses. A weak smile grew on his features. "You know, Ahilya-ve, I don't think you are. But you seem to be doing what you think is right. And that's all any of us can do."

Ahilya's hand fell away. She nodded, her throat thick again.

"Now, please," Airav said, gesturing gently. "Do as I say. It's time."

39

AHILYA

Tariya didn't try to stop her. She only said, her voice very quiet, "You're leaving me too."

Ahilya's tongue felt heavy. She swallowed, trying to dislodge the pain in her throat, trying to lessen the guilt in her stomach, but she could not lie to her sister, not now, not after everything that had happened. She *was* leaving; she was taking herself away from Tariya the way their parents had, the way Bharavi had been taken away. The despair grew in her sister's big eyes, hidden behind a veil of indifference and anger. Tariya would not say any more, but she would spiral deeper into her sadness. Ahilya knew this, and the thought choked her now.

"I need to do this," she whispered. "For Iravan. For myself. Please."

Tariya said nothing. She simply turned away, her shoulders slumped, her body shuddering, and Ahilya recognized the weakness of her own words. Iravan was likely dead; she had told Tariya what had happened, how he had been snatched away, how low the chances were of finding him. Ahilya could almost hear her sister's thought, the sick vindication. In the end, everyone had left Tariya, and Ahilya was now going to be one of them, however she justified it. Tariya would not believe anything else—and in this moment, Ahilya had no words to refute her.

She kissed a sleeping Arth and Kush, hugged an unmoving Tariya, then walked away from the infirmary floor before her nerve failed her. A satchel filled with some food and water, identical to the bag she took on her expedition, weighed her shoulders down.

Dhruv's words consumed her mind. Was that what she forced people to do? Enable her own selfishness? Airav must have known she wouldn't back down. The Senior Architect had barely argued; he had almost *expected* her to do what she had. Ahilya held her cast close, her throat burning with thick shame. The elevator ascended through the silent, dying ashram.

She stepped off at Nakshar's only rooftop terrace. Wind buffeted her at once, blowing her hair back and chilling her to the bone. Small and circular, the terrace was shaped like a cave, open to the skies on a side but covered everywhere else with hard bark. Thick gray clouds slipped in through the skyward side and cut away. A fading sun glistened behind the mist. Vertigo gripped Ahilya. She swayed on her feet, terrified. For a long second, she was unable to move, her breath panicked. What was she doing? She wasn't a hero. She was nobody. But then Dhruv waved her over from a corner, and it was too late to change her mind.

The sungineer was tinkering with the forcefield of a solid glass deathbox within which a tiny spiralweed leaf fluttered, green and bulbous. As she approached, Dhruv pointed to a pile of sungineering equipment without looking at her. "Got some things for you."

Ahilya knelt and sifted through his equipment: a wrist-compass, two twines of rope, folding shovels, machetes, a telescope, a brand-new solarnote, and—she saw—the duplicate elephant-yaksha tracker in the form of a necklace. Her throat thickened with emotion. The tracker's surface was like glass. It chimed softly, and a red dot blinked far into the dark east, away from the setting sun. Iravan.

"Thank you," she whispered as she slipped the necklace around her neck and the equipment into her satchel.

The elevator bark she had come through split open and Airav emerged. He removed some of his rudra bead bracelets and necklaces as he approached her.

"I'm no architect," she said as he made to hand the beads over.

"These contain emergency permissions," Airav said. "To navigate your aircraft and to manipulate the plants inside. If everything works well with the battery, these ought to work concurrently with the craft, as though you were in a miniature Nakshar."

Ahilya accepted the beads, but their weight was uncomfortable, like wearing someone else's clothes. Not even Iravan's beads had felt so heavy. She had once been envious of Naila; she had wanted beads like these as a councilor, but she didn't deserve them. The weight in her stomach grew leaden. Silently, she tucked the jewelry under her kurta, where it was less conspicuous.

Senior Architect Airav nodded, then waved a hand. Blue-green vines grew over his skin as he trajected. A healbranch chair grew over the grass, right next to Dhruv. Airav watched it grow, then pushed his glasses up in a movement of decision. He approached it and sat down abruptly on the chair. Wordlessly, Dhruv connected circuits of optical fibers from the deathbox to Airav's ankles and wrists and forehead, and back to some unfamiliar equipment. Airav winced but did not ask the sungineer to stop.

"If you please, Ahilya-ve," he said instead, "could you seat yourself on the battery, facing us?" He pointed toward the edge, where the clouds whipped in to take a bite out of the terrace.

Ahilya noticed only then that a small white box waited a couple of feet from the edge. Thin, glassy optical fibers connected it to the spiralweed deathbox like shining worms.

"What will happen?" she asked, unmoving.

"I'm going to create a nest for you. The plants I'm using are... intelligent, some of the most precious we have remaining. But this pod won't be connected to the rudra tree. This means you won't be able to fly—but you *will* glide, and the rudra beads will control navigation. You will have to be specific with your desires. The more abstract your desire, the fewer chances there are of success."

"What do you mean?"

"Give the pod instructions," Airav said. "Say *I want*, and follow Iravan's tracking signal. The orb will obey."

"Can I change the architecture?"

"I advise you don't try," Airav said dryly. "The design is fragile and unsupported by a core tree. You have no idea how the plants will react. The pod should open, close, and land as you give it instructions, but don't tell it what you need it to do. Say what *you* want, and the design will fulfill it in its own best manner. The battery"—Airav glanced at Dhruv—"ought to hold trajection, and it will hopefully sustain the pod's architecture as though there were an architect in there with you. But don't use any sungineering equipment unless you absolutely have to. That will consume trajection."

"How long will the battery last?" Ahilya asked.

"I suppose it depends on how much Dhruv drains me."

"We don't know the correlation," Dhruv muttered as he twisted the dials of the deathbox. A golden forcefield blossomed, inches away from Airav's chair yet not touching him. "It needn't be about how much I drain you. Rages, we're dealing with unknowns, and we're conducting desperate human trials. It could last a few days or a few hours or a few seconds or it might not work at all. Are you sure you want to do this, Airav?"

"Yes."

"Why are you doing this?" Ahilya asked Airav quietly.

"Your conditions—"

"No. Why are *you* doing this?"

"Perhaps I should sacrifice a Maze Architect instead? No, Ahilya-ve, that's not how a Senior Architect behaves." Airav considered her. "Besides, I owe a debt of trust to your husband. Iravan is not here to collect, so you will have to do. You should know, Iravan saved Nakshar on multiple occasions. He loved this ashram, more than most councilors I have known, more than his own native city. I hope your actions today do not destroy it."

"And what will happen to you?"

The Senior Architect raised his brows. "Does it matter now?"

"I suppose not." Ahilya stole a glance at Dhruv, but her oldest friend in the world was not looking at her. His back had stiffened. What had she thought? That Dhruv would endorse her choices? That he would hug her goodbye? He had already said goodbye in the little speech he'd made. It was as final as anything could be.

Sickened with herself, Ahilya turned away miserably and approached the battery. Wind tugged at her from behind, billowing through her jacket and kurta, but heat radiated off the equipment. The second she sat down, thick, twisty branches began to grow from around the battery and looped over her like a harness, holding her in place, cradling her cast. Other branches grew from the sides, interlocking like a nest. Some of the wind cut out, but she could still see the two men through the gaps in the foliage. Airav's skin glowed blue-green with the light of trajection.

"Brace yourself," Dhruv called out.

"Ready!" Airav shouted.

Dhruv flipped the dials in the deathbox. At once, the spiralweed within the forcefield began to expand, its single bubbly leaf engorging. Airav closed his eyes, his chest pumping up and down. Dhruv flicked more switches, and the battery underneath Ahilya warmed, cooled, then warmed again. The nest crisscrossed faster, thickening.

Through the gaps in the branches, Ahilya saw Airav's entire body buck in his chair. His eyes flew open unseeingly and he began to scream—except no sound came out. The tattoos on his skin grew dark like burn welts, scarring like Iravan's had so long before. Dhruv started to swear, trying to restrain Airav's seizing body. She was killing Airav, this wasn't right, she had to stop this—

Her view cut off.

The nest had thickened. Overlapping branches reached above Ahilya and tied themselves. It was like she was back in the earthrage, except instead of Iravan, it was Airav who was dying. She couldn't see anything beyond the branches, though she could hear Dhruv shout.

She needed a window. Sobbing, Ahilya focused her attention and gasped, "I-I w-want t-to see."

The branches in front of her thinned slightly. Airav was still bucking, and the spiralweed within the deathbox was monstrous, its bubbly leaves cracking the glass, but Dhruv waved his arm at Ahilya. She couldn't tell what he was screaming, but she could see the shape of the word. It was now or never, what did she want, what did she *want*?

"Fly," she whispered.

The orb she was in tilted. Her vision skewed. Breath wrenched out of her as the orb tipped over the edge of the ashram, but the harness held her. Her heart climbed her throat. Her stomach plummeted. The wind *scree*d at her. The rudra beads warmed against her skin, and Ahilya screamed against her will. This wasn't going to work. They'd failed. She'd killed Airav and herself—

The next moment, the nest jerked as though something had yanked at it from the top.

The branches creaked ominously, nearly bending under the pressure, but the orb stabilized. Ahilya pictured it floating in the air like a dust mote. Nakshar blinked at her, already so far away, a giant wooden oblong bobbing in the sky. The clouds rushed past her and then Nakshar was gone.

Ahilya's rapid breathing resounded in her ears.

A terrifying sense of loneliness washed over her.

She was alone now—completely alone; she might be the only creature alive in the world.

Then the nest tightened, blocking out her view, plunging her into darkness. The only light came from the bright red dot blinking from her chest. Ahilya withdrew the chiming tracker locket. Unaided in the nest, she smelt, of all things, firemint and eucalyptus. Iravan's scents. Ahilya touched the red dot, tears silently streaming down her face.

Don't leave me, Iravan whispered in her mind.

I'm coming, she answered.

40

AHILYA

The next few hours were the longest of her life. Each creak of the bark, each shift of the wind startled Ahilya. The branches had closed on their own again, cutting off her view. Ahilya did not try to open them. She did not know how much energy she would waste in doing so. The pod floated on steadily, too slowly, while her heart beat frantically, but she was too afraid to command it any speed. She had tried to count the minutes, tried to calculate how fast she was moving, but the winds of the earthrage buffeted her, sometimes too fast, sometimes slow enough not to be noticed. There was no real feeling of advancement, and tiredness weighed her down. Once or twice, she nodded off, then awoke gasping out Iravan's name.

She must have dozed off. The next thing Ahilya knew, her entire body was shuddering.

Her eyes flew open. The *pod* was shuddering.

Red beams from the tracker locket bounced around, flashing on one spot then another within the orb. Branches tore and whipped away from the construct even as more grew to replace them. "Stabilize," Ahilya cried, her voice hoarse. "Stabilize, *stabilize*!"

The nest continued to quiver as though in a storm. Branches disintegrated into dust on her lap. Grit entered her mouth; she smelled wet earth. Ahilya coughed and snatched at her rudra beads, hoping for something.

"Stabilize!" she tried again, wildly shaking the rudra beads. "I want you to become stronger. Harder. *Balance yourself.*"

The nest shook like a leaf in the wind, a jarring, heart-shaking sensation. Ahilya's teeth clacked together and she bit her tongue. Hot blood filled her mouth, and she spat it out, horrified. More branches ripped from the pod, darkness outside, a wisp of clouds. Then her vision skewed completely as the nest *flipped.*

Ahilya gagged, her stomach churning, blood rushing to her head, hair lashing across her face. The harness held, but the pod plunged toward the earthrage.

Stabilize, she begged frantically, unable to form the words as the orb plummeted. *Fly. Float. Glide. Do SOMETHING. Please!*

A roaring filled her ears, either her blood or the earthrage below—the same earthrage where she'd lost Oam, where she'd likely lost Iravan. Tears leaked down her face as she fell headfirst. Ahilya closed her eyes and gritted her teeth, but her insides jangled as the nest dove like a comet. Her hand clutched the tracker locket in her fist, and she thought, *I'm sorry. I'm so sorry.* She was helpless. She couldn't traject, she couldn't speak, she couldn't do anything.

The pod flipped in the air again, upright; Ahilya's hair whipped around her like in a windstorm, the tracker's chiming grown louder. Burning bile gurgled in her throat. She choked, opened her eyes, and saw through the branches—dust, earth, great clods of debris, flashing and cutting away. She was *in* the blast zone of the earthrage. She covered her head with an arm, sank her face toward her knees, and gasped out in desperation, "Protect me!" Beyond the terrifying sounds, an unearthly cry echoed, like a bird screaming, and—

The orb smashed into the jungle.

It rolled, its branches exploding even as more grew to replace them. Ahilya's head spun. Fear gripped her heart. She couldn't move; was this death, some kind of horrible awareness, what was happening, what was *happening*? Her ears rang; she opened her mouth to retch but nothing came out. Outside the pod, the earthrage roared like a furious creature in pain.

She sat there, still harnessed to the orb, her breath wheezing, cold sweat drenching her, body trembling. The battery underneath her grew cold.

Finally, Ahilya opened her eyes to unmoving darkness.

The pod had stopped rolling.

She was upright.

She lowered her arm, and her fingers scrambled at the wooden harness.

"Release me," she whispered. The branches retracted from around her chest and waist.

As though her words had been a signal, the pod itself began to dissolve. One second, she was in a shattered orb made of branches; the next, the ruined branches burst, fizzling and scattering around her into nothingness.

Ahilya lurched to her feet, fell, and stood again, her knees shaking. She blinked, but green sparkles blurred her vision. She took a deep, shaky breath, almost a sob. She could see nothing ahead of her, just a dim green light that fuzzed into green dust, the more she stared at it.

She shouldered her satchel and wrapped her free hand around the tracker locket. It no longer blinked or chimed. Heart in her throat, Ahilya stumbled toward the glittering green light.

41

AHILYA

At first, she couldn't see anything through the haze of sparkling green dust. She was surely breathing the dust in, but the air smelled fresh, clean, almost too cool for comfort, as though the humidity of the jungle and the dirt from the earthrage could not affect this place. Yet even as she thought this, the temperature grew warmer. The goosepimples on her arms receded. Ahilya swallowed, her mouth dry, as this realization hit her.

She stopped a few feet away from the remains of the orb. Behind her, the bone-white sungineering battery glinted in the green light. She didn't want to leave it behind—this last remnant of Nakshar, of *Dhruv*—but it was useless to her; she couldn't do anything with it.

Despite that, moving away was difficult.

With every step she took, Ahilya glanced back.

Soon, she couldn't see anything but the glittering green dust. Swallowing the lump in her throat, she stretched her hands forward, blindly.

Ten feet in, the dust vanished.

It didn't dissipate slowly; it *vanished.*

And Ahilya stared.

Her mind couldn't comprehend what she was looking at. Her knees buckled and she staggered to the ground, staring up. She supposed it was architecture, but it was nothing like she had ever seen, ever *imagined.*

Shafts of blue-green light shone and glittered in every direction, like angled and reflected rays of trajection, except it wasn't light—those shafts were *plants.* The shafts undulated and changed even as she watched, perhaps *because* she watched. She caught a flicker of leaf; she blinked, and it was gone, returned to being a part of the… structure. Out of the corner of her eyes she glimpsed a woody stem, but it rippled as she whipped her head around, and it was mesmerizing light again.

The light was *watching* her, just as she was watching it.

And then the blue-green light coalesced.

The shafts glinted to resemble pillars.

Ahilya's breath came out in short bursts. Her hand clutched at the ground; it felt like solid earth, like grass, but she looked and the ground shimmered like a pool of green water. Her senses contradicted one other, touch different from sight different from smell, and she smelled suddenly the scents of *Nakshar*, lush moss and healbranch and the rudra tree.

Ahilya closed her eyes, hyperventilating.

How could plants be imbued with trajection light? Plants weren't architects; they weren't complex beings. Her hands came up to grip her tracker locket. Slowly, very slowly, she opened her eyes. She focused on the tracker locket and nothing else. Her mind lurched back to what she had come to do, to *Iravan.*

The red dot had disappeared.

The chiming had stopped.

She had noticed it before, but her mind registered the implication only now. Her heart skipped a beat. Why wasn't the tracker working? Had Energy X stopped? Or maybe it was this place? But there was only one area in the jungle where any sungineering signal died, only one area which the earthrages could not touch.

The yaksha habitat.

Her entire body trembled, releasing her terror, as her mind wrapped around this realization. Never could she have imagined the habitat to look like this—whatever *this* was. How had her orb landed there? How had she been so lucky?

She closed her eyes and she could hear all of their voices: Dhruv telling her she was selfish; Tariya asking her to stop with her childish pursuits; Iravan telling her so long before how no such thing as a yaksha habitat existed. Under her knees, the ground felt solid, like earth, but when she glanced at it, it shimmered again.

Ahilya took a deep breath and placed her palm on the glassy ground. *Get up*, she thought. *You're an archeologist. Do your job.* Trembling, she pushed herself to her feet and stood up.

Her hand fumbled at her satchel to reach for her solarnote and sketch what she saw, but she stopped before she could unlatch her bag. Her other arm was in a cast. Besides, the solarnote would not work. No sungineering equipment would. She would have to commit it to memory—

Incongruous hysterical laughter bubbled out of her.

She didn't need to commit it to memory. She wasn't going back. The only way was forward.

Ahilya took another step, and the glassy ground under her coalesced into a circle and began to rise. "No," she gasped, the beginning of vertigo gripping her, and the circle stopped. It lowered and shimmered. Almost, she thought, the ground was *considering* her.

Then slowly, tentatively, in the manner of doing something new, the ground converted into a gentle ascending staircase, each step as large as a field.

Ahilya climbed the first step, her bamboo boots tapping against the grass as though it really were glass. Before she took more than a couple of steps, the staircase *rippled*, and the stairs became human-sized, then a gentle ramp. Her climb became faster; she received a distinct sense of the ground being *pleased*, but that was bizarre; it wasn't a living thing…

It *was* a living thing.

It was grass, no matter how little it resembled the grass she knew.

These plants here were sentient. Perhaps each of them was as sentient as the rudra tree.

She gulped and continued climbing, shafts of light intersecting and undulating around her. She had no sense of distance; the view didn't change at all, like the plants here were trying not to alarm her. She tried to count how many steps, but the numbers fell away from her mind. Goosepimples covered her neck. She was used to living architecture, but architecture that could *think* and *feel*? Architecture that could anticipate her before she'd fully known her own desire? It seemed benign now, but what if it turned hostile? She clutched the locket tight.

The grass flickered and turned green, resembling Nakshar's variety. She knew it was for her benefit.

"No," she whispered again. "You can be you."

Hysterical laughter built in her head; she was talking to *grass*, but was this any different from yelling commands to Airav's pod? Nakshar's pod held trajecting energy in the battery; that's what had made her flight possible, but this—

Perhaps the very ground here held Ecstatic energy. Perhaps Ecstasy ran through the plants here, just like trajection ran through the plants in Nakshar. She had no way of knowing what such concentration of Ecstatic energy could do. Could it imbibe plants with *personality*?

Ahilya reached the top and paused. She turned around and her breath caught in her chest.

She had no idea how high she was, but glittering green dust surrounded her again. She felt like she hadn't climbed at all. She wished suddenly to see beyond the dust, and something pulled at her eyes, the green dust vanished, and—

The earthrage stared at her, filling her vision.

Ahilya stumbled back, terrified. An unearthly face screamed at her from beyond the habitat. The earthrage surged, filling her mind, bark ripping off trees like flayed skin, hollowed darkness like eyes being torn. She scrambled back unseeingly, tripping over her own feet, *the face*, the earthrage had a *face*, and—

The sparkling green dust returned, covering the image of the earthrage, glorious green peaceful dust as far as she could see.

Ahilya stifled a sob. Her heart pounded in her chest.

She turned around again, but her back prickled like she was opening herself to a predator, and she thought, *It* is *a predator. That is what the earthrages have always been.* The ground grew under her heel, nudging her. Warily, Ahilya began to walk forward on a shimmering landing.

A long while after—or perhaps too soon—she became aware of another sensation.

Her heart fluttered, then her ears reacted. It sounded like music, rhythmic and melodic, except more profound, somehow meaningful in a familiar way, like a language she had once known but could no longer speak. Iravan's voice came to her from a lifetime before. *By-products of trajection. Interpreted as melodies. Indiscernible to non-architects.*

Raga.

For the first time in her life, Ahilya heard a true raga.

Almost as soon as she recognized it, the raga settled in her, like a layer of clothing she no longer could feel, like water she had drunk that had *become* her. It receded to the back of her mind; and she could not remember its tune.

She did not know how long she walked.

The view remained unchanged. The raga of the habitat warmed her from within, and green dust glimmered in front, guiding her through her blindness.

Then the green dust vanished again.

She stood in a small copse, thin trees standing tall, grass sprouting under her. Neither the grass nor the trees were any kind she knew, yet a sense of familiarity imbued them. Shafts of blue-green light still surrounded the edges. The copse smelled of eucalyptus and firemint. For a brief second, it reminded her of Nakshar, of the very copse she and Iravan had made love in, the very copse they had fought in. She blinked, and something grew clearer in the center of the clearing. A body on its back, spread-eagled. Iravan.

Ahilya's heart froze.

Sobbing, she tottered to the body—to *Iravan*—and dropped to her knees. He lay there, head to one side, eyes closed, his chest unmoving. She touched his cheek, pushed back his tangled hair, her mind going in circles, *be alive, be alive, please.* Ahilya pressed her lips to his, but she couldn't feel him breathing. She placed her ear on his chest but couldn't hear a heartbeat. In desperation, she flung out everything from her satchel, grabbed the healbranch seed, pressed it to his skin, but nothing happened.

"Help," she sobbed. "Help, please, whatever you are out here."

Nothing happened.

She scrambled back to Iravan, pinched his nose closed, tried to breathe into his mouth like Oam had told her once. She pumped his heart with the heel of her hand, broke, and breathed into him again. Minutes passed, and Ahilya sobbed, trying to continue, trying to get her husband to breathe.

Finally, she staggered back with a voiceless cry, head pounding, silent tears trickling down her cheeks. There was nothing she could do. He was gone.

He was gone.

Her mind went numb. An eerie calmness took her over. Her tears stopped abruptly. Ahilya crawled over to Iravan. She cradled his head in her lap and stroked his cheek again and again. It was over. It was over. She had come here for nothing. They had lost each other before they had begun.

She sat there, engulfed in shock so great that her hand kept stroking his warm cheek. There was nothing to do, nowhere to go—

His cheek. It was warm.

Ahilya's eyes flew open. She stared at Iravan still cradled on her lap, his chest unmoving, his body not appearing to breathe. Her hands ran over his arms, fingers, his neck and chest. He was warm all over. How?

The next few heartbeats were the worst of Ahilya's life. She stared at Iravan, afraid to blink, afraid to move, afraid to think.

After what seemed like eons, she saw his chest rise.

The movement lasted an eternity.

He stilled again.

She watched, rubbing her eyes, another eternity.

And his chest fell.

He was breathing, but

s l o w l y.

Each breath lasted a lifetime.

He was asleep.

He was *alive.*

All her strength drained out of her with this realization. Ahilya settled Iravan back to the grass, the way he had been. She removed a roll of linen from the mess of her things. Then, covering himself and her, Ahilya adjusted herself on the ground and began a vigil over her husband.

42

IRAVAN

Behind him, Nakshar disintegrated into storm and chaos. "Stay here," Iravan snarled at Ahilya. He sprinted across Nakshar's terrace toward the falcon-yaksha. His vision had expanded into two as soon as he had touched the Resonance and entered the Deepness. He saw the monstrous bird in front of him, its gigantic silvery wings cutting out the sky.

Overlapping the second vision, however, past the blackness of the Deepness, Iravan *was* the bird.

He saw from behind its eyes, saw himself running, and all of the creature's relief and outrage poured into him like a crashing storm.

He slid to a stop in front of the bird, held up his hands, and gathered the energy of Ecstatic trajection to him like an inhalation. The falcon yarped, the bizarre patterns in its eyes bright—

Beyond the Deepness, Iravan and the yaksha mirrored each other, rippling within silver-molten mercury. The reality of Nakshar's terrace muted to a faint buzz in the background.

And for the first time, Iravan saw his own consciousness.

He was in a maze; he knew that instantly.

He *was* the maze.

That realization took him aback.

The puzzle was exquisite in its simplicity.

It shimmered and settled; no puzzle, after all, just a simple route.

He moved in the manner of taking a step, except it was not true movement, only a memory of an unconscious habit. Still, the path glittered and took shape. He stood at the base of a mountain; its peak, his destination.

Iravan stepped forward, and plunged into—

Nidhirv bolted awake, stifling a scream. Next to him, his husband rumbled, still in deep sleep. Nothing except an earthrage could wake—the name eluded him for a heart-stopping second—Vishwam.

His husband's name was Vishwam. They had married only yesterday. Tomorrow, Nidhirv would take his place with the others of his ilk. He would *become* one of them, an architect. They had timed it perfectly, the moment of birth, when the fetus Karinita was carrying would be ripe for consciousness. Nidhirv had visited her yesterday for the first time, spoken to her and assured her of success. He had sounded confident, but awake now, he could feel his own nervousness. This was to be his first time. The ceremony could not go wrong, not for Karinita, nor for him.

He rearranged the covers he had pulled off his husband and arose from their cot. Nidhirv stepped on light feet and left their mudbrick cottage. Night cloaked the jungle. No one was about the ashram except for sentinel architects. He rubbed his cold arms and stopped as he saw his skin. It had been… *darker* than this, hadn't it? He had been taller, too. Vishwam had warned him the ceremony could be disorienting, but the ceremony hadn't truly begun.

Nervous, Nidhirv walked toward the edge of his little ashram, where a waist-high hedge gently nudged the jungle away. He peered into the darkness. The sounds washed over him, trees rustling, cicadas chirping. Some of his tension receded. The jungle could always calm him. He and Vishwam would go into the foliage tomorrow after the ceremony. They would spend a few nights in meditation and in love. They would wander the jungle, keeping away from the wild creatures, but perhaps they would see a yaksha, a being to be revered and admired, a being to learn from. The thought of it warmed Nidhirv. A smile tugged on his lips.

When the earthrage came a few hours later—his first earthrage as a participating architect—Nidhirv clasped Vishwam's hand. Along with the other architects, the two men merged their beings with the cosmos. Identical blue-green tattoos grew on their skin in the shape of a spiral. Plants grew, covering the ashram in a dome. The jungle roared in agony and trees whiplashed beyond the ashram. Nidhirv's hand shook as he glimpsed beyond the vision, beyond the melody, where the separation sounded like a scream—

The scream of birth, Vishwam had said, *a scream essential to life*, but Nidhirv choked as the ceremony continued. A few minutes later, when the jungle came to rest and the earthrage ended, the fetus Karinita was carrying bore consciousness. They had done it. They had brought about birth.

Nidhirv would always remember that first time. The memory

of the scream stayed with him through the years, through age and the colors of life, through the darkness when Vishwam died, and through the light of initiating architects for their own ceremonies.

When death finally came to Nidhirv, he lay on a cot, surrounded by his sons and daughters. They were unrelated by blood, but *his* nonetheless, for he was an architect and they were too. His family drifted in and out of his filmy gaze, and Nidhirv wished he could see the sky; he had never truly seen it; the jungle covered everything. He breathed deeply and saw, from behind a gaze that seemed so familiar, a vision of flight. Nidhirv exhaled his last breath; he thought his last thought. *There, friend. I will find you—*

And through the dim haze of a latent current reality, floated a voice…

a familiar voice calling out a word… a *name*

his name.

Iravan.

He turned and saw a woman, beautiful and in pain, blood trickling down her forehead, vines holding her down. Behind her, the architects of Nakshar fell to their knees, thorns and spikes stabbing through them. Blood trickled down the woman's face, and vines grew around her neck, strangling her. Her hand reached toward him, and in her eyes he saw

endless love

Iravan lifted his own hand, took a faltering step. A shadow fell—

And he was back again within the maze of his own consciousness, staring up at the mountain that was his destination. He glanced behind and the base seemed leagues away. With that one step, he had climbed so high. He stepped forward and—

Askavetra parted the leaves, using her hands.

In a corner of her mind, she knew what she was doing was wrong. To be an architect meant to choose life and the ashram, to choose family and society and material bonds. It was the oldest wisdom. Yet here she was, out in the jungle, in a blatant betrayal of their code. All architects were told to keep away from the yakshas, yet she was deep in the jungle, inches away from the tiger-yaksha.

She approached carefully, and the tiger-yaksha watched her, its striped tail swinging lazily behind it. Askavetra reached as close as she dared and then waited.

Even though the elders had forbidden interaction with the yakshas, she had always felt a companionship with the creatures. Her own mother had once told her stories of architects who had been abducted by the creatures and had never returned. But those were only stories, right?

The tiger watched her for so long that Askavetra grew cold. Then the yaksha padded forward. It was almost of a height with her, and she was the tallest woman in their ashram. The creature bent down and nuzzled her neck. She laughed despite herself and embraced it. The tiger purred in its throat, a sound that sent warmth through her belly.

They played in the jungle a long time, tumbling and running, hiding and discovering. The yaksha made the plants move just like architects did, of course. But when Askavetra touched the Moment, the yaksha growled threateningly.

She stopped at once, chastised. They had told her in the ashram to practice her skills as an architect, but touching the Moment agitated the yakshas. She had known it. She should not have tested it now.

The tiger padded to her, its yellow eyes dark, circling patterns within them. It crouched as though to pounce. Askavetra gasped, stumbling back, and the yaksha leapt to the branch above her and disappeared. She ran back to the ashram then.

Too afraid to approach a yaksha again, Askavetra told no one about her adventure, not through the years when the architects worried about the frequency of the rages, not through the times when all the ashrams convened to discuss survival in the jungle.

Yet when death embraced her, Askavetra's last vision was that of a yaksha flying in an unfamiliar sky, lonesome and in pain; she sought it but it was too late. Another earthrage came, and she became—

Him.

He was *he* again, although those limits were fleeting; they had always been themselves.

In that space between the two steps, he saw all of the sister ashrams on the brink of plummeting into the earthrage. He saw her, the strangely familiar woman, lying behind a giant bark oblong in the sky. He watched her thrash wildly and thought, *Wake up, and remind me*

of who I am.

She jerked up—

On the mountain path, Iravan planted both feet on the ground. He had left his origin far behind, but ahead the peak awaited; another kind of origin, he knew.

Another step,
another life/ves
innumerable

In the space between, he saw the woman, but she was inside an orb now, and the orb plunged toward destruction. He moved reflexively, and the falcon dropped from the sky.

In its clutches, he saw himself, a body limp in his own talons, head back and eyes closed, asleep. He had been flying in circles, almost as though waiting, knowing, and now he swooped down, and he felt its—his—rage at these choices. His free talon snatched her orb from the falling sky and released it into a shimmer of green dust.

On the mountain, Iravan reached a crossroads.

Two paths unfolded, leading in opposite directions.

One path was littered with more lives, yet unlived, unification but a forgotten concern for whomever he became next. The other path led to his choices. *Him. Iravan.*

There was joy and fury on the first path, desire and fear, love and life, Ahilya.

On the other, there was *clarity*.

Iravan froze in agony, poised at the crossroads.

43
AHILYA

There were rules to the strangeness of the habitat, Ahilya learned. Rules she neither knew nor understood but which were consistent nevertheless.

At first, she sat watching over Iravan, her muscles tense in anticipation. If the falcon-yaksha had brought him there, then perhaps it would come back. The machete trembled in her hand, a slim defense against what was really a gigantic magical creature.

But nothing happened for… she did not know how long. Time was meaningless here. It could have been minutes or days or years. Iravan did not wake, and the copse did not change. She tried her sungineering devices, but they didn't work. She tried to rouse him, but when she pulled his eyelids open, his pupils were rolled back. Whatever this sleep was, it was not natural. She ate most of her food, though she wasn't hungry; she drank all of her water, though thirst didn't trouble her. In restless desperation, she *watched* the sentient grass, but when she looked too closely, it merely waved in and out of its light-shifting form, becoming nothing more than the sparkling green dust.

That green dust was everywhere.

The dust was related to Ecstatic trajection somehow, she knew. The architecture had chosen to present itself to her as a copse—the very copse she and Iravan had once fought in—most likely to provide her with familiarity. It was anticipating her, of course. Somehow, it had tapped into her memory and desire. It must have a system like Nakshar's archival designs, something like the rudra tree—but any thought of Nakshar weighed Ahilya down with guilt. *You're perfect for each other*, Dhruv said; and Tariya stared at her, *You're leaving me too.* Ahilya buried her head in her hands, shaking while the memories consumed her.

She spoke her regrets out loud, to her husband.

Once or twice, she cried.

But Iravan did not wake.

And Ahilya did not sleep.

She had tried, but her body didn't seem to need it. Instead, she was left with her doomed mind in a unique state of torture.

Once, driven by restlessness, she unwound the rope that Dhruv had given her. She tied one end to Iravan's waist and the other to her own. Then, kissing Iravan's lips, she set out into the green dust. She wandered for a thousand steps, until she asked for a way out. Then the dust dissipated.

Beyond it, the unearthly face screamed, snapping and attacking.

It was the earthrage, ubiquitous and pervasive.

Ahilya stumbled back, tripping over her own feet. Flecks of dust flew at her; a thousand branches ground together like bones gnashing. Her stomach seized and wind pulled her hair in all directions. She gripped her rope and tugged herself back until she was surrounded by the green dust again.

"There's no way out," she reported to Iravan. "As long as we're in this dust, we're safe, but beyond there is only death, there is only the earthrage, no matter what direction I go in."

Iravan remained still, breathing his slow breaths. He was warm to the touch, much warmer than he had been when she'd first found him, almost as warm as her own skin. She studied him, the angles of his dark, handsome face, the way his thick salt-and-pepper hair fell over his forehead. She caressed his cheek and it was smooth under her fingers—

"Why don't you need a shave?" she asked him. "And why don't I need food or water or sleep?"

His chest rose in a deep inhale. The day she had discovered him, she had not noticed his breathing or felt his warmth, but now it seemed that his chest rose and fell in time with her own. Either her body had adapted somehow to this place or his condition had changed.

"I think the dust is trajecting *us*," she said, answering her own question. "I think it's somehow manipulating my senses, trajecting our very bodies."

It made sense to her. She had been hurt in her orb's crash, but there were no signs of injury. Her bark cast had broken of its own accord, disappeared into dust, and Ahilya could use her arm again. Iravan must have been hurt too, but his body was unscarred except for the dark welts he had gained in the expedition so many weeks before. Those had become a part of him since their escape from the jungle. There didn't seem to be an escape now. Had there been an escape for Nakshar? Were Tariya and the boys and Dhruv alive?

"I tried again," she told Iravan. "To look for a way out. But a hundred steps in, the earthrage appeared again. I think time stands still in this copse, my love, but the earthrage is inches away, outside the dust. I don't think the dust can fight it for very long. I don't think we have more time. I haven't seen a single yaksha. Perhaps they sense this place is deteriorating. Perhaps it's time for us to leave too."

Iravan exhaled, unmoving. His dark skin glowed faintly blue-green. Ahilya watched him, unsurprised. He had always been bathed in the light of trajection since she had found him there in the copse. Her sight had merely adjusted to it now.

"Some of Airav's rudra beads broke today," she said one time. Necklaces had shattered, the black beads falling to the ground. Ahilya had searched for them but had found none in the strange grass. "I think it's a sign. Something terrible has happened to the rudra tree. To Nakshar. Something I am to blame for."

She had condemned them all to death with her decision. *You would hold the entire ashram hostage?* She had killed Dhruv and Tariya, Kush and Arth. She had killed herself and her child, all the citizens of Nakshar.

"If you were really here," Ahilya said, stroking Iravan's hair, "you would tell me I should have stayed back. I'd argue, and we'd fight, but in the dark, you'd tell me you wanted me to be safe, and I'd tell you the same. And you'd shake your head and say there could never be a victor between us, and I would tell you that none of it was ever really a game."

Iravan's eyes flickered behind closed lids.

He slept his deep sleep.

"I wonder if this is how we'll die," she said, softly, touching his lips. "You were right—our civilization could never live here. If we did, would we even be humans anymore? Perhaps the architecture creates us just as much as we create it. And this—we have had no part in this, surely. This habitat is dying. I only walked fifty steps before I saw the earthrage today."

Iravan's fingers curled and moved a fraction.

She watched as he breathed deeply again.

Her guilt had replaced her heart, beating against her chest. She stroked his cheek, ran her hands through his hair.

"We've made so many mistakes. But you must know how much I love you. You must see how bad we are for each other. Who else would be here but the two of us? This was always our destiny. We were always each other's completion, each other's ruin."

Iravan swallowed in his sleep. His curled fingers relaxed as he breathed out.

"Maybe we ought to have let go of each other when we had the chance," she whispered. "Maybe I should never have come here. But maybe that was never possible with us. If you would wake, we could find a way out. Don't you think you should wake now? Isn't it time, my love?"

His eyes flickered.

He swallowed again, and then his breathing changed into a rhythm of wakefulness.

Iravan opened his dark, almost-black eyes, full of awareness and purpose, as though he had never really been sleeping. He gazed back at her.

She had known this would happen. Of course she had. Her senses had adapted to his rhythms. She'd spoken, and he had listened.

Iravan pushed himself up to a seat. She moved away, scuttling back, not daring to touch him anymore lest she break the spell.

"Ahilya," he said, and his voice was clear.

"I'm here," she breathed.

44

IRAVAN

Iravan filled his gaze with her. She sat inches away but didn't touch him, although he was sure she had been running her hands through his hair only an instant before.

Afraid, he didn't make a move either.

Instead, he stared at her before he disappeared, before *she* did.

He waited on the crossroads of the mountain path; he could see himself standing there in eternal agony. Was this vision another life? Had he lived this already? Was he… *he*?

Ahilya's long, wavy hair rippled to her waist, undone. Her terra-cotta skin glowed with vitality and health. And those big eyes, beautiful and bottomless, watched him with wariness and intelligence. She wore rudra beads on both her wrists now, several of them; more peeked out from below her kurta, over her neck.

"Is this now?" he whispered at last.

She tilted her head. "Yes," she said, wonderingly. She sounded like she had known the answer but not the question. "Yes, I think this is now."

"Are you real?"

"Are *you*?" she replied.

He seized her and kissed her then. Under her grip, he felt his own solidity. She smelled of jasmines and sandalwood, and as he inhaled, his own lungs expanded, took shape, *became*.

She kissed him back with an abandon he had never known from her before. Something had happened to her, a silent metamorphosis. She was Ahilya, more herself than ever before, and so, more *his*; his Ahilya, finally.

They unclothed each other, but it wasn't in lust; it was in discovery. Their hands wandered everywhere, squeezing every muscle, touching every inch of skin. Iravan watched his fingers run through her hair, watched as they caught in the tangles. A weight of presence, of *materiality*, descended over him under her touch. It was as though his senses had relearned their purpose; the gravity of this body, *his* body, had reasserted itself. The two came toward each other together; there was no rush, this was *now*, as much as anything could be.

When they broke apart, Ahilya was gasping, as was he, both out of breath. That alone seemed so bizarre, so natural, that a strange peace settled inside of Iravan in the recognition of the idea that this was *right* and as it should be. His forehead touched hers. Her shoulders trembled under his hands.

"Iravan," Ahilya whispered against his lips. "I think the architecture has been watching us."

"No," he said. "Not watching us. Nothing as base as that. This is something… different."

An urge to laugh grew within him. Ahilya had never been modest, not when it came to their intimacy, and he had hardly been reluctant when the mood took him over. The copse almost resembled the very one they had stripped each other in hastily, right before they'd had their bitter fight.

Perhaps she was thinking of the same thing, the absurdity of returning to a place that looked so much like the one so many months past. Ahilya inhaled deeply. "What do we do now?" Her voice didn't quiver. She sounded… amused.

Iravan reached for his clothes, but his eyes fell on his skin, registering its color for the first time. He stared at his arms and his legs, down at his chest. In the sparkling dust of this place, he had not noticed before, but his skin glowed with the blue-green light of trajection—of Ecstasy.

Within his first vision, Ahilya stared back at him. She had already put her clothes back on. Her sleeves were rolled back as his had been so often, a more comfortable manner for the rudra beads on her arms.

In his second vision of Ecstasy, Iravan hovered in the darkness of the Deepness. He summoned the Moment, and it appeared, a dewdrop-like globule containing an infinity of stars. Already he could feel comfort in the Deepness as though he had been exploring it his entire life. Had his visions been split without his notice?

"You've been glowing all this while," Ahilya confirmed quietly.

"How long?" he asked, still naked.

She made a sound in her throat, half-disbelief, half-amusement, like his question made no sense. "Since the last time we were together in Nakshar. Do you remember anything?"

"Too much," he replied. Very slowly, Iravan pulled on his own kurta and trousers. The familiarity of his second vision within the Deepness was almost eerie. "I remember us in Nakshar. The ashram tearing apart. And the… falcon-yaksha. What happened to the ashram?"

She tilted her head, considering her answer. Then, her gaze steady on him, clearly watching for his reaction, she told him about the scorched and shrunken rudra tree, about the deal she had made with

Airav, about her flight through the earthrage and the consequences of that action. "They could all be dead by now," she said softly. "There's no way to know. Or perhaps Reikshar made it to them in time. I hope it did."

"They're not dead," he said. "I saw them—all of the sister ashrams, struggling. They have only days left. Hours, for some of them."

She didn't ask him how he knew. She almost looked indifferent to his news. Ahilya had always been stubborn, always been brave—far more than he could be, but she had never been ruthless. *All this has remade you*, he thought, *into something terrible and wonderful at the same time.* "You came looking for me," he said quietly.

"You told me not to leave you."

"I asked you to stay back."

"Yes," Ahilya answered, her gaze on his. "And I chose to ignore that."

Iravan smiled despite himself.

She pulled one of his sleeves back, her fingers feather-light on his arm. "Your trajection tattoos back in Nakshar… they were different. Not the vines and leaves of normal architects. They looked like… *wings.* Why did they change?"

Iravan stood there, staring at the glimmers on his dark skin, but he stood at the crossroads to the mountain peak too. And with Ahilya's question, a deep rumbling grew on the mountain path like the beginnings of an avalanche.

"They're connected to the yaksha somehow," he said.

"This whole place is, I imagine," she replied dryly. "And yet I haven't seen a single one."

"They're here—very close. I don't think they wish to be seen yet."

Ahilya's glance was curious. "You know so much suddenly. Is this because of Ecstasy?"

He swallowed. "Yes. I think so. I have memories now—of a time long before, of lives lived before. And what I know of trajection…" He took a deep breath. "Beyond the Moment lies a place called the Deepness. I can summon the Moment there—almost as though it were a suspended drop of water within a never-space. I know where every star is within the Moment, where every possibility is. I think this intimate knowledge of the Moment… it is a feature of Ecstasy."

"Then we can never return to Nakshar?"

"No—I don't think I can."

Neither his admission of Ecstasy nor the idea of abandoning the ashram seemed to faze Ahilya. She nodded; she had known this already, and his words had been mere confirmation. A deep wellspring of love bubbled within Iravan, filling his heart. In the back of his mind, he remembered Vishwam and Radha and Taruin, all the husbands and wives and partners he had ever had; they flickered like the green dust he stood in. Almost all had been born with the ability to traject. Had any of them been as remarkable as Ahilya?

She didn't notice his wonder. Instead, her hands continued to pull his sleeves back to study his arms, to where his skin was lightest. "This isn't like Bharavi's Ecstasy."

"They've never truly understood Ecstasy in the ashrams. They put an end to Ecstatics before it got too far."

"But there must be measures. Limits. Some indicators to the power."

"The most irrefutable indication is if an architect breaks the known and studied limits of trajection."

"Which are?"

"Innumerable. They're observations of impossibility, studied and revisited, and thus understood as a tenet. Like changing permissions that are nurtured within core trees. Like being powerful enough to manipulate plants against the combined trajection of the Maze Architects. Like being able to traject a higher being."

Ahilya nodded, still studying his arm. "That explains how you healed. You must have used Ecstasy on yourself. You trajected yourself, a higher being."

"Yes. There's a physical connection between our bodies and trajection. Something that causes the trajection tattoos and residual scars, something that can cause incineration of veins if an architect overdoes it. Chaiyya has been studying this field for years, but I think the true answers lie in Ecstasy. I think that's how Bharavi healed herself."

Iravan thought back to what—in the chaos of that terrible night—had not occurred to him. He had swung the branch at Bharavi with enough force to smash her head in, yet not only had she survived, she had been fully in her senses on waking. And before... she must have broken through her own healbranch bracelet and the vows she'd made as a Maze Architect, in order to land Nakshar in the jungle during the earthrage. He himself had recovered from his broken healbranch vow; even with Chaiyya's intervention, it should have affected him deeply, making him sick after he'd broken it, yet he had felt no consequence from it before he'd arrived at the habitat, as though Ecstasy had given him self-healing as a passive ability.

Ahilya looked thoughtful. "If Bharavi broke these limits, can you?"

Iravan frowned. "I—I don't know. Why? What do you mean?"

"This place—" Ahilya waved a hand and displaced some of the green dust that had crept along the copse. "It's falling apart, the dust diminishing, but surely, it responds to the trajection of the yakshas. If Ecstatic trajection is the same as theirs, and I think it is, then maybe you can traject here somehow—"

"I wouldn't *know* how."

"It can't be very different from trajection itself. Maybe the principles are the same?"

"Or maybe they're completely different. After all, trajection is not the same as Energy X. Dhruv said they have different energy signatures."

"We'll never know until you try, right?"

"I—Ahilya—" Iravan grabbed her hands and bent over them as though in prayer. "I'm scared," he admitted softly.

She lifted his chin so he met her eyes. "Why? There's no architecture here to destroy with Ecstasy. It's the perfect place to try."

He hesitated. Poised at the crossroads of the mountain path, he knew any decision now would propel him in one direction or another. He could see clearly, what his journey would look like on either path. Ahilya on the first path, a life no matter how short, rich with experiences and emotion; and after death, many more lives.

But on the other path, *answers*.

Once he took a step, it would be irreversible.

This time, the fork would not reappear.

"It's not about the destruction," he said, swallowing. "I think this path of Ecstasy will—Ahilya, I think it'll change us—you and me—in some way. There won't be any going back."

She drew back at that. "Then we stay here in this copse. We wait until it vanishes. We stay together until we're reborn."

He stared at her. "You would do that? For me?"

"Not for you. For me." She smiled slightly, a sardonic smile, like in a private joke. "But is that what you want?"

Iravan imagined it, a life lived in the thicket, waiting for death. Could he do that? Could he embrace fate so easily while the ashrams fell and their own destruction was inevitable? His eyes returned to hers, beautiful, amazing, challenging Ahilya. "No," he admitted at last. "It's not what I want."

She smiled; she had known this, of course.

Iravan sighed. "All right. Let me try."

Ahilya moved away, gathering everything that had been scattered around the copse, the sungineering equipment, the solarnote, an identical tracker locket to the one around his neck. She stuffed all of it into her satchel, then approached him, holding two ends of the rope. She began to tie one end around his waist. "Just to be safe," she muttered.

Iravan watched her, saying nothing. He examined his overlapping visions. Like with trajection, in the first he saw Ahilya as he would normally, winding the rope around her waist, tightening the knots with deft fingers. In his second vision he saw the now-familiar dark of an Ecstatic's Deepness.

And yet—

He realized—

He was on the crossroads on the mountain path in *neither* of those visions.

There were *three* visions.

There was a third place like a constant backdrop to the other two.

In this third place, he had seen the maze of his own consciousness. Here, he had watched from behind the falcon-yaksha's eyes; he had seen his own consciousness; he had lived and died a thousand times; more. This… *vastness*, this… this *Etherium*—it existed beyond the Moment and the Deepness, glimmering and burning behind his brows. Suddenly, Iravan could separate all the times he had been taken over by it. All those weeks before, when he had fought the magnaroot in the jungle during the earthrage, he had seen the Moment not as a motionless reality but a raging storm. In the library, when he'd nearly died—he'd floated in a never-space and watched Nakshar, watched the earthrage, and seen beyond it to a terrifying vision of a shattering being. Right before the attack on the ashram, when he had seen the falcon-yaksha, when he had *become* it—

All that had occurred within the third vision of the Etherium.

Standing there in the surreal copse, Iravan trembled from head to toe. The truth of this knowledge slammed into him. On the mountain, he saw himself lift a foot and set it down on the path toward clarity.

The shock of it sent a chill through his spine.

The first path disappeared, taking away the promise of Ahilya and all his unlived lives.

He gasped—this was a path to death, then, ultimate, irreversible death; no more lives in the future, now truly a final end.

Unaware of the choice he had made, Ahilya finished tying the rope around him. She coiled the other end around herself so they could move but not separate.

Very carefully, Iravan released the Deepness.

He jerked as his two visions collapsed. He stood in the copse fully, watching his wife tie intricate knots on the rope. The Etherium faded to a blur like he was seeing it from a great distance. He stumbled on it, forward and upward, to the mountain peak.

Shuddering, Iravan felt for the Deepness in his mind again. It sprang up, right next to the Moment, two caverns instead of one; the Moment filled with pinpricks of stars, and the Deepness with forceful blackness.

There was, he realized, a way to move from the Moment into the Deepness and vice versa, a thin conduit of nothingness that connected the two caverns.

Yet the Etherium, despite its wavering imagery, remained ever-present, almost a superimposed image behind the two caverns. Was the third vision a space that existed *beyond* any kind of trajection—Ecstasy or otherwise? Could non-trajectors sense the Etherium too, then? Did he have control there? He barely understood the Deepness, and the Etherium was more, so much more.

Ahilya approached him, offering her hand.

He engulfed it in his. "Don't let go."

Gripping her tight, Iravan dove into the yawning black cavern of the Deepness. He summoned the Moment—by thinking about it. Simultaneously, he gathered the energy of Ecstasy to him. A thin golden current of light emerged from his dust mote. He guided it into the Moment, aiming it for where he knew the stars of the green dust existed. The golden jet struck and—

In front of the two of them, the sparkling green dust froze, unmoving.

The two stood in a glimmering world of frozen particles.

"It's never done that," Ahilya breathed, fascinated.

She reached a hand to touch the closest sparkles but her hand went through the frozen dust. Iravan imitated her and flinched back. He could *feel* the particles, warm and somehow pulsing, alive. He exchanged a nervous glance with Ahilya.

"What *is* this?" she asked.

"I think—it's like the yakshas. It exists at a higher state of consciousness than human beings, so architects would never have noticed it. But this dust is *everywhere*. Everywhere in the Moment."

Iravan swallowed, imagining the star-studded universe of the Moment far more cluttered and complex than he had ever known it to be. In the second vision, the Moment glittered like a globule, his stream of golden light pouring into it.

"Can you do anything with it?" she asked, her voice low.

Iravan shifted the dust with his hand. The frozen particles moved where he placed them, but nothing else happened.

"Huh," Ahilya said. "Maybe try a principle of trajection?"

"It won't work. When architects traject, they connect constellation lines between stars—" Iravan cut himself off, his eyes widening.

He touched the frozen green dust in front of him, and memory spiked within him. The frozen dust reminded him of the luminous stars within the universe of the Moment, but each star there was a plant's possible state of being. Could this dust be... *pure* possibility, independent of an attached consciousness?

On the mountain path, he saw himself lurch forward and upward to painful clarity.

In the copse, Iravan connected one particle to another with invisible constellation lines. The dust glittered, then solidified into a simple wall, the first true structure of this bizarre habitat.

Ahilya lifted his arm. His constant glow had remained the same, except instead of the vines of trajection or the wings of supertrajection, strange spirals now glowed and disappeared.

"I don't think I'm as good an Ecstatic Architect as I was a normal one," he said.

"Not necessarily a bad thing," she answered fervently. "But it looks like you can manipulate this dust. Maybe make pathways, not walls?"

Iravan nodded. Both arms in front of him, he began to shape the dust, connecting one to another almost in the manner of connecting constellation lines. Here, he was a real-life mote and the green sparkles were stars.

Structures started to form around them, arches and pillars and galleries along the perimeter. The copse transformed into an intricate hall. With each new form the green dust took, Iravan moved faster up the mountainous path of clarity in the Etherium.

He could feel it; understanding was imminent.

The tattoos on his skin grew more vivid. As though he had always known it, the markings of an architect suddenly made perfect sense.

When he had trajected all his life before, vines had grown on his skin because he had only trajected the possibilities of plants.

With this trajection, he shifted pure possibility, and so his tattoos spiraled like dust coalescing. The subject of trajection determined the imprint on the architect. Why had they never considered that before? What did it mean for the winged tattoos, then? Had he been trajecting the falcon-yaksha somehow? But if the yakshas were architects, perhaps he was the one *being* trajected? Perhaps he and the yaksha had trajected each other *simultaneously*. What, then, *was* trajection?

He jerked as a weight pulled at him.

Iravan glanced down at his waist where he'd felt the rope tug, then looked behind him to Ahilya. She supported herself against a pillar, staring beyond him to the vast complex he had created. Her eyes rose to the top, where a shimmering green ceiling grew in the shape of a dome.

On the mountainous path, Iravan sprinted now, rocks tumbling, shards of earth chipping as he reached ever closer to understanding. He shifted the dust, and the floor under Ahilya rippled, bringing her close to him again.

"How are you doing this?" she asked.

"Ecstasy—it's similar in many ways to trajection," he said, excitement rising in his voice. "But all of this—Ecstasy and trajection—it's always been a method midway between an idea and an action. It's as though I were asking the dust a question and it created all of this to answer me. I'm *communicating* with it, Ahilya. In the ashrams, they have a simplistic understanding of what trajection is—mere plant manipulation. But I suppose true trajection is more akin to communication. Through constellation lines, we suggest a form to the stars of the Moment, and the plants fulfill it in the ashram's architecture. And that's what I'm doing now."

"If you can communicate with it, then you can change it," she said. "We could save the ashrams. We could save ourselves."

A jolt of excitement rushed through Iravan. "We're very nearly there," he said. "Hold on."

He joined his hands, then broke the hold. A circular descending ramp unearthed itself by their feet, the dust settling. Iravan gripped Ahilya's hand and led the way down. On the mountain path, he raced toward the peak, to his clarity and destination.

45

AHILYA

Ahilya followed Iravan down the earthy ramp. His hand felt warm in hers, too warm, like he was on fire. She thought abstractedly of his waking in this strange place. If it weren't for the blue-green light that sparkled through the foliage, the architecture could have been Nakshar. If it weren't for his unnatural warmth, Iravan could have been *her* Iravan.

She gripped him tighter. *He's still mine*, she thought. This place had changed him, made him a part of itself in some insidious way, but hadn't she changed too? Her senses seemed more alert yet somehow quiescent. The green dust swirled around her, and she took a deep breath, aware it was dissipating. Beyond its limits, the earthrage roared. The storm was coming for them, and her heart beat rapidly in sudden terror. Ahilya discerned at the edge of her awareness a building panic, but it was gone in a blink, almost like a memory of a significant dream, tucked behind the diminishing security of this place. She and Iravan climbed down the last section of the ramp, hand in hand. They gazed at where they had emerged, spellbound.

The staircase ended in a tunnel, its ceilings so low that the earthy top almost brushed Iravan's head. The walls were too narrow to walk side-by-side anymore, and the light was dimmer. They waited at the foot of the staircase, letting their eyes adjust. Ahilya could almost make out something on the walls, moving, shifting…

Her eyes adjusted the instant her mind articulated the thought.

Carvings.

She exchanged a nervous look with Iravan, then preceded him into the tunnel.

Intricate carvings, all lines and spiral patterns, covered the tunnel walls, hewn directly into the rock. As Ahilya approached, the carvings shifted like displaced ink. Curiosity and wonder blossomed in the same part of her mind where panic fluttered. The lines and spirals on the rock undulated, reminding Ahilya of the holograms in the solar lab, reminding her of the book Iravan had given her. Pain grew at the thought of Dhruv and Nakshar, then receded to a corner, keeping company with her nervousness and panic.

"Are *you* doing this?" she whispered.

"I—I think so," Iravan replied, just as softly.

"But you didn't physically build this now."

"I didn't have to before, either. I'm still learning. I—I asked for understanding right now, for a solution to what is happening to me. These carvings must be the dust's answer."

"But these images don't make any sense."

"I—I don't know what else to try."

Ahilya gently disengaged from him. She reached her fingers forward tentatively.

The moment she touched the rock, the carvings began to resolve.

Images of trees grew out of the lines, a garden, woods, then an entire jungle.

More lines settled into tiny human beings, a hundred thousand of them, heads, shoulders, eyes, a whole civilization growing in the jungle on the wall.

The pictures ran deeper into the dimly lit tunnel.

Exchanging another glance with Iravan, Ahilya began to follow. Behind her she heard his careful tread.

The light shifted on the carvings the deeper they went, as though the sun were rising and setting over and over again. *It's passage of time*, Ahilya thought. *That's what the dust is trying to tell us.* The people changed, more and more of them within the wall's jungle. Babies were born, they grew older, they lived, they died. The jungle flourished, still and calm, almost unnaturally so, and animals within it cavorted and hunted. Ahilya recognized the shapes of the strange creatures, elephants and tigers and other such lost beings.

"I-Iravan," she stuttered. "I think these pictures depict our history. The history of our civilization."

Her husband's eyes grew wide. He nodded mutely, illuminated by his own light, a mere step behind her.

"I think," she said, as the people began to tame the jungle. "I think this was a time before trajection, before earthrages themselves. A time before yakshas at all. When our ancestors lived in the jungle, in ashrams that weren't dependent on architects."

Her heart raced in her chest. Her mind seemed unable to comprehend this. There *had* been a time before earthrages, then. She had been right all along. All the histories she had ever read had erased this era, but if the dust's projection was true, then earthrages had been an unnatural phenomenon. What could have caused those storms? Surely, not the yakshas like she and Iravan had thought; there were no yakshas depicted. Ahilya moved forward faster, almost jogging in her haste, her hand on the wall.

She stopped as the images changed.

Under the miniature people within the pictures, the jungle suddenly roiled.

The people scrambled, ran, died. Trees and branches broke, impaling bodies, whipping heads away. Dust balloons blew over the earth, smashing into little huts.

"Here," she whispered. "The first earthrage. But why did it begin? What *caused* it?"

From one picture to the next, the jungle creatures changed, became monstrous. There seemed to be no transition; in one image, the creatures were their old selves; in the next, they were transformed. A tiger, but not a true tiger—instead a massive yaksha shaped like one, a purposefulness to its stance. An elephant, but not a true elephant, instead a yaksha—looking so like the one she had tagged but for the intelligence on its face that was almost human. Rings glinted around the creatures' eyes in an indication of Ecstatic trajection.

"They—evolved from true jungle creatures," Ahilya said softly. The light of realization shone bright in her head. "I think it was the earthrages that precipitated their change. But it wasn't evolution—not in the slow way of evolving. It was… a spark. An instant transformation. Rages, I never believed that was possible. Then that picture in the book was right. It wasn't a slow maturation. The architect histories are right about this."

Iravan's fingers scrabbled for hers. She squeezed his hand but didn't stop moving.

"If these animals morphed into yakshas that could traject," Ahilya murmured, "then it must be around the same time that *we* learned trajection."

On the wall, the pictures confirmed her theory. Instead of being crushed by the trees, some people began to control the foliage, spinning blue-green webs of stars. Far away from the humans, the yakshas disappeared, hidden by the foliage, mere shapes in the background.

Iravan made a choking sound in his throat. "Our history. Our—*my*—true history. The first people to traject."

"I think the earthrages *gave* humans their trajection somehow," Ahilya replied, recalling the discussion the both of them had with Dhruv and Naila so long ago around her kitchen table. "We talked about that in Nakshar—that trajection and the earthrages are inherently related. Maybe it was a balance in nature. The earthrages gave us their storms but also gave architects their powers."

"Architects," Iravan murmured. "And the yakshas."

Ahilya nodded vaguely but kept moving. She stopped at another picture. One face stood out among the architects, a young girl, appearing no older than ten, as though the artist who was sculpting the rock had decided to pay attention to her face. The girl spun a hundred stars together, unleashed her constellation lines, and more foliage grew in the jungle. Around her, the shapes of non-architects cheered.

"This girl," Ahilya said. "Iravan, her trajection—"

"It's too complex," he breathed back. "I don't think I could do it now."

The girl appeared younger than most beginner architects. Yet that trajection… In the moving pictures, Ahilya detected a complexity of patterns on the girl's skin that she'd never seen on an architect.

Iravan nudged her and she moved along again. More architects appeared on the walls, their skins blue-green. Again, there was a single clear face, this time a man. Ahilya tightened her hold on Iravan as they hastened through the tunnel.

More walled ashrams grew on the walls. The jungle churned, more and more frequent, yet always a single face appeared clearest, sometimes a woman, sometimes a man, other times undefined.

Light shifted, and Ahilya knew she was seeing another passage of time. The rages grew, and more architects appeared, spinning webs out of stars; more civilians, attending to matters of civilization within the ashrams.

Ahilya glanced at Iravan. "I think there is confirmation here of what we studied in Nakshar. For as long as there have been earthrages, they have been growing in length and frequency. A consistent pattern but not a linear one."

He said nothing, just gripped her hand harder.

Ahilya turned back to the wall, keeping pace with the forming pictures. Her heart beat a tattoo in her chest. Somewhere, she knew she ought to be recording this experience for posterity, but the thought was distant; she could barely keep up with the wonder of this instant.

In the next picture, a small group of architects surrounded a sapling. The same image grew across the wall, a thousand saplings in a thousand different parts of the jungle. Core trees, being embedded with ancient permissions. Among one group stood out a face, a short man, something eerily familiar about him.

Yet now, for the first time, smaller groups diverged from the architects and their walled ashrams, and headed back into the jungle.

About a dozen teams, consisting of architects and civilians, turned their backs on the ashrams, anger and rebellion in their postures. They paused and dust shimmered where they stopped. Ahilya gripped her husband's arm.

"What does it mean?" Iravan asked.

"It's a moment of choice," Ahilya replied, her heart beating fast. "These new groups headed into the jungle to find an alternative method to survive. Iravan, I was right. These must be the groups that attempted to find a way to *live* in the jungle, *before* flight was discovered. They must have created the habitats."

His eyes grew wide. "Are you saying there could be others in the jungle right now? A whole other race of humans descended from these people?"

"No." Ahilya pointed to where the creators of the habitat had stopped. Earthrages came and went. The dust shimmered, its circumference painfully constricting until only one bubble of shimmers existed, contracting over time. "Constant earthrages ate away at the habitats. It's what is happening to ours here, the last of its kind. Humans ultimately only survived in the groups that embedded the core trees. And if I'm right, then the next few images will show—"

They hastened forward a few steps, then paused in shock.

It couldn't be any clearer.

Flight.

Foliage surrounded the saplings of the core trees. Each sapling grew tall, magnificent, embracing a hundred people in its boughs. They watched as nearly a thousand core trees drifted upward into the sky, carrying hundreds of people, while others smashed and fell to the destructive jungle. This here was their history. This here, truly, was how they had ascended to the skies.

Ahilya glanced at Iravan and saw tears shining in his eyes. "Why did so many more architects choose to fly instead of attempting to create habitats in the jungle?" she asked. "Surely, the habitats had a greater degree of success. They had the technology to build them. Flight was a miracle, a risk. It was unknown. Could they have known the habitats would fail? Were they hedging their bets with flight?"

"No," Iravan said, his voice hollow. "No, Ahilya, architects were forbidden from going into the jungle once. The group that went into it—the ones who built the habitats—they rebelled against the ashrams to do it. The creators of the habitat, they were architects and citizens... Flight was no hedging of bets. It was a political decision."

"What kind of a political decision?"

"One that had to do with Ecstasy." Iravan moved forward slowly and touched the rocky wall.

Instantly, the image focused on a single flying ashram.

Within it, the same man appeared, who had been trajecting into a core tree with other architects in the jungle before. He was short and familiar, though Ahilya could not say where the familiarity came from—the image was pure lines and angles, too abstract, only a hint of a man at all.

Iravan touched it and the man was replaced by a young girl.

The ashram changed too, becoming bigger, leafier.

Ahilya glanced at her husband, confused.

This time, Iravan led the march down the wall, drawing her along. The focus shifted from the ashrams to a single person. The young girl in the picture became a man, another man, then two women in succession, while the ashram grew and changed. It was as though this person were a fixed point, a hundred, no five hundred transformations, as civilization in flight grew around them—

And then the picture resolved, and there was no ambiguity.

It was a man again, a tall man, the shadows falling on him in such a way that Ahilya got the distinct impression that his skin was dark. He stood in the shade of a core tree, and a Disc revolved in the tree's highest boughs. The man stared at something, patterns on his skin changing. She would have recognized his stance in a crowd of a million people.

Ahilya turned to Iravan. "This is you," she said quietly.

"They're *all* me," he said, his voice hollow in the tunnel. "Each of those clear faces. We just saw my personal history. An architect from the very first time there were any architects at all, from the very first time there was *trajection*."

Ahilya nodded slowly. Rebirth was a fact of life. Dead bodies nourished the ashram, became plant matter, which in turn became food that sustained and created citizens; and consciousness moved from one state to the next. No one truly remembered their past lives, but what did it matter? Iravan had been all those people before, but he was Iravan now. He was *hers*. The panic in her mind fluttered harder, like a trapped bird. She clasped both of his warm hands in hers, watching him carefully.

Iravan trajected, the patterns on his dark skin winding like spirals.

The dimness of the tunnel lifted.

Light blossomed on the entire wall this time.

And Ahilya saw—circling the tapestry of pictures—a falcon-yaksha soaring in the wall's skies.

The yaksha's wings grew with the passage of time, pain in its flight. It soared above Iravan's past, above the other men and women he had been; it soared in an endless infinite loop, until—grown monstrous—it flapped right above the image of Iravan himself as he stood in what could only be Nakshar's temple, staring after Ahilya as she left for her expedition.

She turned to her husband slowly, a chill in her heart. "What does this mean?"

Iravan touched the falcon-yaksha in the rock, tears in his eyes. "The Resonance. It was a call. A call I had been too blind to see, to *feel*. The falcon has been trajecting for years, for centuries, ever since it formed, ever since *I* formed. And in its trajection, it released an… an undying residue, a constant *raga*… the Resonance."

"Nakshar's Constant," Ahilya said, understanding. "A raga that doesn't dissipate. That releases each time an architect trajects, unique to the architect."

"Yes," Iravan said. "A unique call. A unique shade of blue. Nakshar's Constant, Resonance, the Raga of Awakening. Call it what you will, but it is the same. Each architect releases it every time they traject, and it's a call to a yaksha, *their* yaksha. And each yaksha releases it as well, except we have always been too afraid to hear our yaksha's call."

Ahilya's heart thudded in her chest. "Iravan, Nakshar's Constant emerges out of architects—not out of yakshas—"

"They're architects too, Ahilya. You saw those carvings on the wall. The jungle creatures morphed into yakshas the same time as human beings snapped to become architects. Trajection must have developed in both species at the same time."

"But—"

"This is why no one else could sense the Resonance. It was a unique call, emitted by the falcon for *me*. And I ignored it. I ignored it for so many lifetimes." Iravan bowed his head, great breaths heaving his body.

Ahilya placed a hand on his back, her heart sinking in an unnamed terror. "Why would the yakshas and the architects be connected this way? You're suggesting a relationship of lifetimes. Even if there had been a time when architects and yakshas had been symbiotic, that relationship wouldn't last across such a period of destruction. Not between a particular human and yaksha. That would indicate a much deeper correlation, something *beyond* our wildest theories."

Iravan's shoulders shuddered. The light of trajection on his skin sparked brighter in anger. "There *is* a deeper correlation, and we knew it. The early architects—whoever *I* was back then—Askavetra and Mohini and the others—they—*I*—knew it. It's why interaction with the yakshas was once forbidden—and so the jungle itself was forbidden. Eventually, we forgot about the yakshas altogether. All records were erased, along with records of the rebel groups."

Ahilya's stomach clenched. "Why forbid this knowledge of the yakshas? Why take the risk of flight simply to avoid the yakshas, when survival was at stake?"

"Because it was *their* survival that was at stake," he said angrily.

"*Their* way of life. Their trajection. Trajection itself was never meant to be. It was a mistaken resource. It was a false step in the dark."

"Iravan—trajection developed as a defense against the earthrages—"

Blue unfurled like an angry flame deep within his black eyes. "You saw these cave pictures, Ahilya. That little girl was spinning complex mazes that even a Senior Architect doesn't have the capability for now. A small group of architects once embedded a core tree with permissions, and now we need whole Discs of Maze Architects just to fly an ashram. We aren't capable of that kind of trajection because trajection hasn't just been getting harder for the last few months; it has *always been getting harder*, since its inception. We always assumed we lost a few tricks, but the truth is that within trajection lives the seed of its own decay."

Ahilya's heart hammered in her throat. She could sense it, the moment of inevitable painful understanding, imminent upon them.

"If we weren't meant to be trajectors," she asked, "then why did we develop the ability? Why did we evolve to have it?"

"There can only be one reason," Iravan said, his hand curling into a fist. "We evolved to have trajection so we may find *Ecstasy.* Just like the yakshas naturally did. They never trajected, Ahilya—they always *supertrajected.* Trajection was meant to be a path toward Ecstasy. That little girl we saw—I was her, but because I never reached Ecstasy, trajection became harder through all my lifetimes, like pressure building. I guarantee that every architect who has felt trajection getting harder ignored Ecstasy in their own past lives. And the ones who found Ecstasy finally—well, we excised them, didn't we?"

Ahilya stared at him, unable to speak. The horror of what he was saying sank into her. Tears filled her eyes.

Iravan slammed his fist against the wall. "This is why, no matter what we try, architects have always been in danger of Ecstasy.

That's why the rules of trajection are so arbitrary. Because Ecstasy was always our final destination. Ecstasy was meant to be our true state. But we excised ourselves when we got too close."

Ahilya's mind reeled. All the architects that had ever been excised, all those lives that had been sacrificed—

She saw Maiya again, sitting on her chair, drool dripping down her mouth.

She saw Bharavi, strangled by the spiralweed.

And she saw Iravan, begging her to take him back, promising to be whoever she wanted him to be.

Her voice trembled when she spoke. "Ecstasy is unbridled power. Why would the architects deny themselves that power by limiting themselves? Especially if they knew all this?"

"Because Ecstasy changes you," Iravan said, staring at the wall. "Bharavi tried to tell me. She said she would destroy everything we'd built; she said there would be no going back. Perhaps she landed the ashram because she meant to unite with her own yaksha. She asked me what I'd lost, and she meant my yaksha—perhaps she had been hoping for me to say it. She told me to follow my own moral intuition, and she was right. When you climb the path to clarity, *everything* becomes clear—including your greatest shame."

The glowing light of Ecstasy reached his eyes, like fire igniting. He stood there, his shoulders heaving, tears falling down his face. Ahilya stroked his back, tears trickling down her face as well. She wished she had never left the copse with its glimmering dust.

"What knowledge could be so terrible," she whispered, "that architects would choose excision over it? That they would deny themselves the true power of Ecstasy? Deny themselves a deeper connection with their own yaksha?"

Iravan engulfed her hand in his once again, the heat from him enveloping her—

"Let's find out," he said grimly, and trajected.

The tunnel exploded in silence.

Ahilya gasped, startled, as the rock disintegrated around her into soft green dust, filling her vision. She didn't know how long—it was a deep breath—

The dust sparkled, then *vanished*.

They were submerged in deep darkness, the first true darkness of this strange habitat. Iravan's light muted to a twilight glow. Ahilya blinked and squinted. She could make out shapes in the yawning shadows. Grass crunched underneath her feet.

"What did you do?" she whispered.

"I brought us to clarity," he said quietly.

"Where are we?"

He didn't answer, but his hand tightened over hers in assurance.

"Iravan, this darkness..." Ahilya said, swallowing. "You could make light."

She felt more than saw his head shake. "It's best not to disturb them, I think."

Ahilya frowned, not understanding. Her sight adjusted to Iravan's dim light, and shadows grew, like great hills around them—

They were not alone.

Eyes glinted out of the darkness, monstrous great eyes, yellow and green and red.

Yakshas.

Ahilya's mouth went dry. Her heart pounded so hard against her chest, she thought it might rupture.

Iravan strode forward into the dark, sensing his own path.

Ahilya kept close to him, trembling against her wont, as snarls filled the darkness. She had ventured out to study yakshas before, but this—to know they were truly architects, trajectors of the highest kind—complex beings—She couldn't stop shaking.

Something breathed by her ear, a heavy presence. Once, she saw a tusk, with what looked like a sungineering tracker attached to it; another time, a jagged set of teeth.

Ahilya gripped Iravan's bicep, and he put his arm around her but carried on, oblivious to the snarls that filled the dark. She imagined them walking through an endless cavern full of gigantic sleeping yakshas, although she could see nothing but the grass under her, illuminated one step at a time. The path sloped up; they began climbing. Ahilya kept her eyes in front of her. She focused on Iravan's touch, tried not to bolt as much as her body told her to—

Iravan stopped.

His light grew a touch brighter.

They'd reached a flat mound of grass. Silver glinted, and then a rustling came to Ahilya. Wings unfurled, then shook out, and Iravan grew brighter. Ahilya squinted. Less than twenty feet away, perched on a rocky outcrop—

The gigantic falcon-yaksha.

Despite being prepared for it, the creature's size took Ahilya aback.

The bird towered over them like a great building. It ruffled its silvery-gray shoulders, then unfurled its majestic wings. The yaksha looked down at the two of them, its eyes glinting black, rings forming in the pupils.

Ahilya froze.

It was going to traject.

"Iravan," she began in terror.

Light burst on Iravan's skin, the patterns of spirals merging with delicate winged patterns.

The yaksha cried, a high, chilling sound.

On the short path toward the creature, a vortex of blinding blue-green light erupted from the grass. It shot into the sky, seemingly without beginning or end.

"Stay here," Iravan said, and let go of her. He marched forward, his eyes on the bird. On the other side, the bird, a mere shadow in the dark, scuttled to the vortex of light as well.

"No," Ahilya gasped, and lurched to follow him, but she was unable to move. Vines had grown from the floor, tying around her legs.

"It'll be all right," Iravan said. "It will be all right, my love."

"Iravan, NO!"

Behind Ahilya, snarls broke out as her shouts and the vortex awoke the slumbering yakshas. Iravan and the falcon approached the swirling blue-green light.

Iravan fumbled at the rope around his waist that connected her to him. Ahilya groped inside her satchel. She grabbed her machete and slashed at the vines trapping her legs.

"Iravan, *DON'T*," she shouted. "You don't know what will happen!"

He had almost undone the knots; he was only a few feet away from the vortex.

"*IRAVAN*," Ahilya screamed, slashing faster, but he ignored her and strode forward purposefully.

He was nearly at the vortex. He fumbled with the last knot; the tension of the rope released.

Ahilya snapped the last vine off, kicked its remains, and sprinted forward. She reached out a hand for his kurta to pull Iravan away. The falcon yarped, its eyes glinting—

Flames climbed Ahilya's extended hand, burning from the inside—

She screamed in agony, lost her balance, and slammed into Iravan.

They tumbled together into the blue-green light.

46

IRAVAN

The instant Iravan saw the falcon perched on the rocky outcrop, the Resonance appeared in the Deepness.

It was the falcon-yaksha, of course, knowable in his second vision only through its raga. Perhaps to the falcon, Iravan appeared like an abstract version of Nakshar's Constant. They hovered warily, as though they were seeing each other for the first time in Nakshar's temple.

Iravan smiled and saw his own certainty reflected on the mirrored silvery surface of the Resonance. This was why the dust had brought them there. He had asked for clarity of *himself*, finally the right question, and the dust had opened up a path to the yakshas, to *his* yaksha.

His shoulders released their tension. His breath slowed. A great inevitability built within him, a sense of rightness deeper than any he had ever felt before. *I've lost myself!* he had screamed to Bharavi in Nakshar's sanctum. *I've found*, she replied, *acceptance.*

This here, finally, would be acceptance.

Within the Deepness, Iravan generated his golden stream of

light aimed into the Moment, and the Resonance mirrored him, generating its own silver jet; the both of them found each other's stars, and they trajected simultaneously. A blinding vortex of blue-green light erupted from the grass and shot into the sky, created with their combined Ecstatic trajection of each other. The falcon-yaksha cried, flitting toward the vortex.

Iravan let go of Ahilya's hand.

He scrambled to the mountain peak within the Etherium, almost at the top.

Dimly, he heard Ahilya's voice as he strode forward. He thought he said, *It will be all right, my love*, but the thought was distracted. He undid the knots on the rope in his first vision, even as he reached ever closer to the peak in the Etherium. The Resonance fluttered in the Deepness, right next to him; and a silence built in the back of his mind, a presence; he knew it was the falcon-yaksha, living within a pocket of his own awareness; then—

Ahilya slammed into him—

The combined Ecstatic trajection of himself and the Resonance grew complete—

He pulled himself to the peak, surveyed the landscape—

And as all three visions coalesced into one, Iravan finally saw themselves in their true form.

47
IRAVAN

They were immortal once.

They had lived for millennia.

Consciousness had been a game, easy to manipulate.

They descended, took *form*, in the manner of a child playing with a new toy.

They separated and scattered their minds, in the manner of a river breaking its tributaries.

A beast, a plant, a mountain, an ocean; these were the same—a mere sheath to hold them, an affair with *substance*, before unity occurred as it always did.

A million million years with other immortals of their kind; that was their sublime existence.

Communication was thought, it was *being*.

They were so evolved that the very idea of language was primitive. They were so ancient that the very idea of death was amusing.

Tied to the planet, they had been *created* with the memory of their own death; they had shifted through little deaths, taken new forms. Complete with their immortal essence, they had always been *themselves*. What was time to such a being? It meant nothing.

And then they discerned…

Something within such meaningless time.

A moment of catastrophe when the dimension of their existence would disappear, when the planet would melt into the sun; a million short years, in what was a mere blink to them.

Terror spread. The terror of non-being, of *in*-existence.

This would not be death. This would be *erasure*.

It could not be changed; it could not be controlled. They had only ever controlled their own consciousness, after all.

A solution rippled through their kind, a radical answer.

Mutilating the earth would be the cost of survival, but it was a small price to pay; it would not be *their* payment. There would be no return from what they intended, but it would be a life, and life was always preferable to death.

And so, they changed again, this time in finality; to become creatures of fewer dimensions, limited in perception, reduced in lifespans but immortal still; they transformed, into something lesser, yes, but at least they would be themselves.

Shatter.

The agony was surprising; excruciating.

Shatter.

They hadn't accounted for this separation. They… *they*?

S-H-A-T-T-E-R.

And the earth shattered with them.

48

IRAVAN

Iravan screamed and screamed, unable to stop.

In the vortex, he fell blindly, the truth of clarity splitting his mind. In the Deepness, his stream of golden light winked out; darkness surrounded him wherever he spun. The mountain collapsed under his feet in the Etherium; he was buried alive in an avalanche of rock.

He had seen his origin, the face of the earthrage.

The being that caused the earthrage now—once upon a time, he had been a being like it.

This separation, this aching loneliness that had burned within him all his lives, the cataclysms that had plagued the planet for millennia—

Once upon a time, he had wrought it too.

They had wrought it.

They had been creatures of infinite power, tied to the planet, yet they had willingly fractured themselves. Iravan had never known himself; the yaksha had spiraled through a lost existence, unheeded, in agony. They had forgotten the storms they'd perpetuated, forgotten what they'd done, forgotten themselves.

How could they have *forgotten*?

Shock and horror raged through him in all his visions. In his bones he felt the pain of tearing himself apart, the pain of the planet. It ate at him like teeth gnawing his insides. This was worse than excision; this was worse than death. They hadn't merely sliced away a part of themselves; they had reached inside with broken fingernails and clawed their very being out, smiling as they did so. They'd rained down destruction, unleashed the earthrages, *broken* the world, and done it knowingly, in blind arrogance.

Iravan could see it, all the million deaths, all the ashrams crashing down as thousands of people screamed, trying to escape. He saw the architects that had been excised, drooling in their chairs; he saw Nakshar even now awaiting its doom in resigned terror. He, *they*, had thought to trade their immortality for a perception of longer life, but they'd only ruptured the planet in an attempt to flee its obliteration. They had destroyed everyone else for their own survival.

They were monsters.

And another monster like them was going to break the earth again.

No more, he thought. *We end this.*

As though that thought were a command, the Etherium changed. The avalanche of rock transformed into a maze of stars.

Iravan stared.

The Moment. The Etherium was showing him a specific place in the Moment. The rift where the earthrage was occurring.

Iravan recognized this place; he had seen it before—back in the jungle, during Ahilya's expedition, when he'd tried to hold together the magnaroot nest. He had seen the Moment as a raging storm, intent on annihilation—*this* was what he had seen—*this* spot, the rift where the being behind the earthrage had pushed against the Moment to rupture it.

The Etherium had shown him what to do to end the storm. Iravan had not understood then.

He understood now.

The Etherium evolved again with his understanding, showing him one step at a time, like a vision of guidance.

A maze appeared in it—the most complex labyrinth Iravan had ever seen, a million billion constellation lines intersecting in intricate patterns he could barely fathom. A maze that used the Resonance, used himself, used the sheer possibility of the green dust somehow.

This was what he needed to build to end the earthrage.

NOW, he thought, an order to himself.

Iravan and the Resonance dove into the Moment from the Deepness. He approached the stars at the rift, wielding his constellation lines. Powered somehow by the Resonance, his constellation lines had never been as strong, as elastic. He intersected them with the stars of the pure green dust in the Moment, steadied himself; the constellation lines pulled at him, wanting to be released—

Iravan spun through the Moment, unleashing them, whirling in and around the stars by the rift—

The lines shimmered—

And *shattered.*

Iravan staggered back, his dust mote careening through the Moment with the force of recoil. His constellation lines burned at the edges, charred. Pain radiated through him; the Resonance *screamed*, a high-pitched whine.

Frantic, Iravan tried again. He returned to the point of rupture in the Moment. Exerting his will, he generated more constellation lines, layered them in the dust, but the Resonance was tiring next to him, unable to give him more power. His constellation lines vibrated, weaker.

The face of the earthrage mocked him.

<*YOU CANNOT STOP US*>, it said. <*YOU ARE BROKEN.*>

You will become broken too, Iravan thought, anguish in his heart. He gathered his constellation lines to him, hunting for grooves in the stars to embed them.

<*WE ARE STRONGER. WE WILL REMEMBER.*>

That is your arrogance, Iravan replied. *It was our arrogance, too.*

He rammed his constellation lines into the stars, even as the being behind the earthrage pushed. His lines shattered again, before he had truly begun.

Iravan gasped, nausea rising. The Resonance dulled, its silvery flaps slower. The Moment was not its true place; the universe constricted the Resonance. The falcon belonged in the Deepness, for Ecstasy was its natural state. To be here, assisting him—the falcon-yaksha was weakening, forced into a cage where its powers were limited. They could not do this forever.

Stop, Iravan thought desperately at the rift. *You will forget yourselves. You do not know the pain.*

<*YOU DO NOT KNOW*>, the being said, <*ERASURE.*>

Please—

<*YOU CANNOT AVERT US.*>

Iravan had no more warning.

The being attacked.

One instant, the Etherium was showing him what he must do to end the earthrage; the next, it reflected his own consciousness. A small maze of stars which were Iravan's own possibilities, connected through constellation lines that his choices had wrought.

Iravan stopped in the Moment, shock arresting him.

In his third vision, the Etherium flickered, and he saw that the being was right.

He was broken.

They were broken.

His own consciousness and that of the falcon-yaksha consumed the Etherium—but there were no complete mazes here, no clean lines.

Instead, the constellation lines were weak. Iravan had built those with his choices through several unknown lifetimes, through *incompletion.*

He had a second's glimpse of the cosmic being enter his own consciousness, and—

The reality of Iravan's own existence unraveled as the cosmic creature attacked him with the might of the earthrage. Stars winked out in his consciousness.

In his second vision, Iravan hovered as a dust mote in the Moment, paralyzed in shock. In his first vision, he floated in the vortex, eyes glassy, mouth open in slow horror. He couldn't move, he couldn't think, he couldn't do anything.

The being ripped him apart.

Iravan's mind

EXPLODED

Scattered images came to him
the rudra tree

Nakshar

the scent of sandalwood

The being crashed through the lines, unraveling his connections.

Possibilities collapsed from his future

fatherhood

happiness

Ahilya's smile

Iravan screamed then, trying to hold on to shreds of himself, even as the creature *erased* him, but there was only

n o t h i n g n e s s

A last scattered thought came to him through a blur.

He should have stayed in the copse of green dust with Ahilya.

49

AHILYA

She watched Iravan unravel.

Ahilya had tumbled into the vortex and seen everything as though the vortex were a series of bio-nodes with sungineering holograms hovering around her. She had seen the wisps of wind that were cosmic creatures of an amazing kind, seen Iravan's anguish when he'd learned of his own origins, seen the rift of stars where the Moment had been weakened.

Now she watched the cosmic creature break her husband apart.

In the vortex, he floated next to her, blue-green light all around them. His mouth was open in a silent scream. His eyes were glazed. Tears flowed down his cheeks. The gigantic falcon-yaksha was motionless too, its silvery wings around the two of them in an embrace.

Frantic, Ahilya clutched Iravan, shaking him.

He did not respond.

In one of those images in the vortex, she saw the ashrams plummet, running low on trajection. Tariya clutched her children to her, weeping. Dhruv frantically swept at his bio-node. Nakshar had only hours. Hours before it crashed.

What could she do? *What could she do?*

Ahilya saw then how small she was. All along, she had thought to make the world better, to find a different way of survival, to matter. She had been mistaken. She had no power of trajection, no Ecstasy, no ally in a companion yaksha. Even Iravan was helpless.

Blackness spread from his pupils to his irises and his corneas.

It was killing him.

It was *erasing* him so he would never have existed.

The earthrages would erase them all, if not now, then eventually.

Stay with me, she thought in terror and anguish. *Stay with me.*

The darkness pooled out of Iravan's eyes like tears.

Nakshar fell from the skies.

What can I do? Please, show me, tell me, what I can do?

Iravan *flickered.*

Behind her, the yaksha spasmed too; she saw it mirrored in the vortex.

Iravan had moments before he disappeared, before every memory of him was gone. She saw the face of the earthrage, furious, mighty, desperate; it would not end, not before a million deaths, not before Nakshar was destroyed.

No, she thought in sudden fury. *He is mine. They are mine. You cannot have them.*

And in despair, Ahilya cupped Iravan's face with her hands, pressed her forehead to his, and poured all of her will and desire and being into one thought.

I will not let this happen.

The images in the vortex changed.

Superimposed on the stars of Iravan's consciousness was her *own* consciousness—its maze complex and complete.

The cosmic creature hesitated, curious at her interference.

Then it pushed against her.

Ahilya screamed. She had never experienced such pain. Her flesh sloughed off her skin, burning. Her bones cracked. Thorns grew inside her brain, and her muscles crushed under her. It was too much, she would not be able to bear it, death would be better—

Again and again, the creature attacked.

The blackness receded from Iravan's eyes; he blinked and shook his head in shock; he could see her pain, she knew—

Fire incinerated her veins. Ahilya saw Oam die again. Nakshar disintegrated, and Tariya said, *What would you understand of this?* Bharavi exploded into light, dying, while Dhruv patted her hand; *You two deserve each other.* The images grew over the vortex so she lay witness to all her shame, all her hurt, an open wound, condemned to watch this forever.

And in that moment of poised torture, Ahilya understood.

The creature could not erase her like it had attempted with Iravan. It could only inflict pain. Unlike Iravan, she had not split to form a yaksha. She had not broken.

Iravan could not touch the creature.

But she could.

As long as her will was strong, as long as she had *desire*, her existence was inevitable.

Holding the line, her own consciousness forming a protection for Iravan and the world, Ahilya screamed, in agony and release, forming a shield in the Moment.

The cosmic being could do its worst.

She would not break.

50
IRAVAN

Ahilya would hold the earthrage back alone, in eternity, in agony. Horrified, Iravan knew this.

Within the Etherium, his collapsing consciousness was replaced by hers—unflinching, exquisite, flawless.

He froze, amazed at her beauty, *wanting*. He felt every part of her, her breath, her heartbeat, her memories. He had never seen such wholeness; he could never have imagined it. Tears filled Iravan's eyes as *love* blossomed in her Moment like the raga of completion. He saw himself as she saw him, flawed yet somehow *perfect*.

He knew what he had to do; the Etherium was showing him yet again.

He was an architect.

He had to build himself.

A billion constellation lines emerged from him, and he unleashed them with the force of a storm, interlacing between his own stars and those of the falcon in the Moment, spinning in and out endlessly, remaking himself as best he could, copying Ahilya's consciousness. Old lines split apart, but he locked the stars with new ones, expanding his possibilities, giving himself, *themselves*, one final chance to do better, to be better. His body lurched and changed; his mind exploded into a million shards, then returned to shape, this time uniting with the yaksha; the falcon was a part of him; they had once been one being.

Mazes snapped together, took on their flavor.

The lines glittered. A raga sounded, the raga of harmony. Iravan's body reknit itself, healing, unlike anything he'd been before; stronger, magnificent, perfectly poised.

His mind *EXPANDED*.

His skin exploded into blue—

The falcon-yaksha grew in might and strength—

Their consciousnesses reforged; a union occurred that had awaited lifetimes. He—*they*—

Became

In the Etherium, Ahilya's consciousness sparkled, holding strong against the creature.

Let's end this, Iravan said, finally knowing what had to be done.

Together, she replied, understanding.

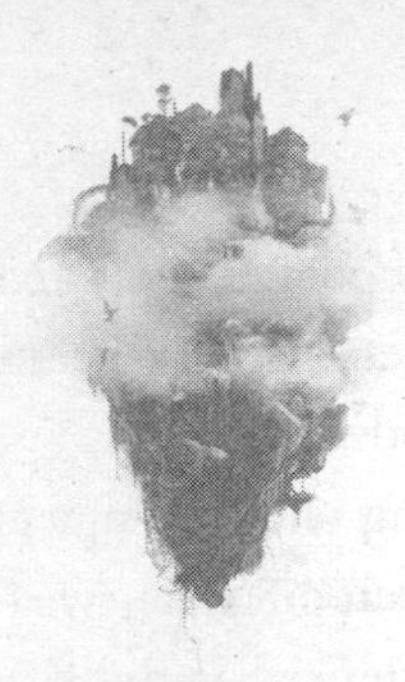

51
TOGETHER

They approached the creature with one will.

Embedded in different visions, a part of different worlds, Ahilya and Iravan floated in the vortex, holding each other, able to see *everything*, sharing a consciousness.

The Resonance generated its silvery stream of light in Iravan's second vision. He spun his golden ray, and it collided with the Resonance's jet of power, the streams thickening instead of canceling each other out. He grasped the rope of combined light in the Deepness, then flung himself into the Moment.

The combined light transformed into sparkling hair-thin constellation lines as soon as he moved from the Deepness to the Moment. The green dust of possibility swirled around him, and Iravan intersected his lines with the dust again, readying himself. Woven out of his two split selves, coated with pure possibility, the constellation lines were unbreakable this time.

Ahilya smiled. With Iravan by her side, her agony had become a buzz in the back of her mind. Why had she fought it before? The pain was hers; she would not let the creature own it. *Have you considered*, Tariya had said to her, *you're stronger when you want the same things?* Finally, she and Iravan wanted the same thing. She knew what she had to do.

The rift at the Moment shuddered, a raging hurricane of stars as Iravan flew in and out of gaps, weaving his indestructible constellation lines, building what the Etherium had shown him before: a labyrinth of a billion twists that circled to where they began, a hundred impossible stairs that looped unto themselves, countless false egresses that would seduce the being deeper into the maze and imprison it.

Iravan had failed before when he had tried it alone. He would not fail now.

For *Ahilya* converted pure possibility into reality.

She focused her desire as Iravan built his maze. She pinpointed her will so the green dust he had used to intersect his lines with converged toward a single possibility of success. Iravan spun, using all his skill, all his Ecstatic power, all Ahilya's command of the dust.

Now, Ahilya! he said.

And Ahilya caught the exquisite web he had spun, in the manner of holding it between her fingers. She enforced the unfragmented desire of her total consciousness, with everything she had been, everything she was, all that she ever would be. She drove Iravan's maze toward the rift where she had been the shield; she focused on a singular possibility—*for them to endure.*

The lines throbbed, and Iravan roared, raging, trying to hold on to his pattern—

Ahilya screamed, pushing against the rift, willing the maze into existence—

The planet shuddered, one last heave of the earthrage, of a consciousness attempting to fragment—<*NO*>, the being screamed, enraged—

Then—

The constellation lines snapped into place.

A gargantuan web of stars spanned the infinite Moment, trapping the splitting being at the rift.

All over the planet, the earthrage rumbled in its last throes, dust ballooning, then settling, trees growing instead of shattering. The ashrams bobbed in the sky, shuddering, as the trajection of a thousand architects relaxed, became easier.

In the vortex, Iravan took a deep breath, and the yaksha yarped, a sound of blissful joy.

Ahilya smiled as her pain disappeared.

The vortex collapsed.

The Moment winked out.

The Etherium cleared.

Ahilya and Iravan floated down to the grass, like two leaves swirling.

52

AHILYA

She had not been asleep, yet Ahilya stirred into what could only be described as wakefulness.

She blinked, and green filled her vision. She was lying on dewy grass.

Slowly, Ahilya sat up. A stream of clear water sluiced past her, gurgling and rushing to disappear behind a thick red beech. Ahilya stretched toward it and caught a glimpse of herself.

She had thought she had burned in the vortex, but her skin was still the exact shade it had been. Her eyes were the same brown, thick lashes framing them. Her eyebrows arched slightly, sardonic, in this examination of herself. Ahilya's long black hair rippled to her waist, windswept, undone. The satchel was still strapped around her shoulder, and the normalcy of the bag took her aback, as though the events in the vortex had been a dream, occurring in a different reality. Ahilya blinked, and cupped her hands to taste the water; it was sweet like nectar. She drank thirstily; she couldn't remember the last time she'd drunk water.

When she'd had her fill, she glanced around her. She was in

a garden, wild yet deliberate. It birthed in front of her eyes, but not in the riotous manner of the jungle after an earthrage. Every branch that grew on a tree was careful. Every tendril that tied itself to another seemed designed. Wildflowers bloomed in a profusion of colors, yet the colors were coordinated, pinks merging with lilacs, blues contrasting with golds.

Through the whispering of the foliage vibrated a melody—no, a raga. It grew in her heart, like life springing. A stirring rippled in her belly, flowed through her limbs, tingled in her fingers and toes. For a very long time, Ahilya remained still, letting the sounds wash over her.

Finally, she arose and turned her gaze away from the garden to look behind her.

And she saw him.

Iravan.

He sat less than twenty feet away on the highest steps of a grassy staircase. His thick hair was ruffled, his kurta rumpled and tattered. He had rolled up his sleeves again—what was left of them—and he stared at his bare arms, at the blue-green patterns that grew on his skin like restless vines. The falcon-yaksha lay curled behind him on the stair's landing, its head tucked under one of its massive silvery wings. Behind them, moss-covered rock opened into a jagged window. Thick tree trunks stood past the window, leaves waving gently in the breeze.

Ahilya took a step forward.

Iravan looked up.

His eyes shone with blue-green light, obscuring the white sclera, overtaking his once-black irises. He stared at her with that unearthly gaze, the angles of his face as though hewn out of the very rock he sat on.

Iravan had never looked as wild nor as majestic. He stared at her a long moment, and she paused, stared back, uncertain of her welcome.

His face broke into a smile.

"Ahilya," he said, and it was *his* voice, no matter how different he looked.

He made to stand up, but Ahilya ran up the stairs. She stopped as she neared him, and he shifted to make space. Ahilya sat down beside him.

For a while, they just looked at each other. Closer, she could see the patterns of his skin weren't mere vines. Spirals twined over him, reached up to his neck, glimmered lightly on his face.

"I'm building," Iravan said simply.

He waved a hand around them. Arches and pillars grew out of the bark, solidifying. Curtains of vines crept down from the ceiling, braiding to create veils and shady nooks. On the grassy floor, pathways ran between the wildflowers, as though the place were anticipating a large party of people and was intent on giving them a warm welcome.

Ahilya turned back to Iravan. He hadn't looked away to the garden. His unearthly eyes rested on hers, yet despite that formidable gaze, he seemed nervous.

"Your eyes," she said.

"I think—" he said, raising a hand to his face. "I think it'll fade. But it's too soon… since the union."

"The union," she repeated. "Between you and the falcon?"

"Between me," he replied, "and me."

Ahilya nodded slowly. She had seen something in the vortex. Snatches of the vision returned to her, of formless air fragmenting into two; of a star-studded universe like Iravan dying; of another universe where she and Iravan had forged a wondrous labyrinth.

"I saw all that," Ahilya said. "How?"

"I'm not sure," he said, his voice heavy. "I don't understand it all. But I think when you entered the vortex, you somehow linked with my Etherium."

"Your… Etherium."

"A third vision. Beyond the two split visions of trajection or the two expanded visions of Ecstasy. I think you have it too."

Ahilya frowned, trying to picture what he meant. "The mind's eye, you mean?"

"No, a different dimension that lies far beyond the mind's eye. A place of guidance." Iravan shook his head. "It's difficult to explain. I don't understand it myself."

Ahilya closed her eyes. Images beckoned her, of Iravan's glowing eyes, of the vortex, of the cave where they'd seen those carvings. Yet beyond that she discerned *something*, a presence that was watching her even as she watched it, focused and burning behind her brows. She had never once paid attention to it, but now that Iravan had pointed it out, she knew the presence had always been around her, within her.

"The other yakshas," she said, opening her eyes, alarmed at sensing the Etherium. "Where are they?"

"Somewhere around the habitat. Or perhaps back into the jungle now that…"

"Now that we've ended the earthrage."

"Yes."

Ahilya shook her head. "I've spent my life studying them—and to know that they've been here all along… so many of them." Her breath came out in a shudder. "I suppose they are immortal."

Iravan nodded solemnly. "In a way, yes. I have died and been born so many times, but the falcon has retained its shape and its memory. No matter the passage of time, it will always remember me."

Ahilya swallowed. She had considered it—the agelessness of the yakshas, the minute she had seen them snap from jungle creatures on the carvings. Yet the fact of it—the falcon resting behind her now, the elephant-yaksha she had tagged, all those creatures she had examined and studied so closely… That they had all been around since the very first earthrages… Awed tears filled her eyes. She couldn't comprehend the enormity of this revelation. The yakshas were the most ancient creatures in the world. What she would not give to see the passage of life through their sight.

She turned to Iravan and squeezed his hand, but tiny glasslike tears shone in his blue-green eyes. "What is it?" she asked.

"The yakshas," he said quietly. "They are immortal and they remember, but I think—I suspect—we have done great damage to many already."

"How so?"

"Through excision," Iravan said. "I can't be sure, but I think that's what excision does. It cuts an architect away from their yaksha, from the source of their connection to trajection and Ecstasy, and from their Nakshar's Constant. I imagine it drives the creature insane—perhaps even makes it mortal somehow. Perhaps the yaksha forgets its architect, the same way an architect no longer can perceive the Constant." He took a deep, ragged breath, as though struggling with a great burden, then stilled again.

Ahilya did not speak. What could she say? Iravan had felt guilty about excising Manav before, but now, when he knew the whole truth of his action, an action he and the others had been forced to do through generations of lies? Her own history had been erased, but for Iravan to learn of *his* history now—the shame and consequence of it—nothing she said could alleviate his guilt.

He seemed to be following the same line of thought. When he spoke, his voice was calm, though she could still detect an undercurrent of fury. "Architects are taught about earthrages," he said. "They learn that earthrages are caused by a disruption of consciousness. But the true extent of that theory… it is not fully known. If it were, it would devastate us."

"You mean that thing… that being," Ahilya said softly. The Etherium had shown it to her as a formless wisp of air. She had felt its desperation in its attack. She had known desperation like that once. "It is not the yakshas that cause the earthrages like we'd thought."

"No. It is a cosmic creature. I don't have a term for it yet. For the kind of thing I… *we*… used to be."

His hand gripped hers. The other hand clenched into a fist on his knee. Behind them, the falcon ruffled its feathers and uttered a growl in its throat. Vibrations rippled through Ahilya like the aftershocks of an earthrage.

After a long moment, Iravan released his hold on her fingers. He smoothed his hand, caressing hers in apology.

"When a cosmic being like that splits," he said, "the disruption to consciousness occurs at a planetary level. Those beings were connected to the planet in some intrinsic way. That is why we have trajection. Each time one of those creatures splits, an earthrage begins. And it only ends when they're successful, when they embed their broken consciousness in… in an available vessel. In humans who are subsequently born with the ability to traject," he said pointing at himself. "And animals that snap to become yakshas." He gestured at the falcon, which seemed to have gone back to sleep.

"You are implying that every earthrage we've ever had, a new architect was born in some ashram or another."

"An architect born, and a yaksha formed. But given how wild creatures don't exist in the jungle anymore… perhaps that's something you can answer?"

Ahilya considered this. "Perhaps the yakshas formed in the most recent earthrages are not yakshas at all but something else altogether. I'd have to study the split to know how many forms the two halves of a being can take."

Iravan pressed her hand. "I suspect the yakshas—all the ones you've studied, and all the ones we saw before the vortex—those must be the counterpart creatures of the original architects. The *first* architects. Yet more and more of those cosmic beings have been splitting, into architects and some unknown form. A new earthrage begins on the heels of the last, without a break. Perhaps multiple beings split at the same time. It might be why the rages have been getting longer and the lulls shorter. We were lucky that we had to stop only one of the creatures—although it is only a matter of time before the being we trapped breaks through our barrier or another one attempts the split."

Ahilya nodded. She had already worked it out. It corroborated the census data she had once studied. More and more people had been born with the ability to traject. If earthrages created architects, it only made sense. And if multiple beings split at the same time... Could that explain the many epicenters of a single storm?

"That being I saw," she said, confirming, "that wasn't you."

"No. But it was of the same species like me. Like *us.*" He nodded back toward the falcon. "A yaksha and an architect are fragments of the cosmic being, but a being is greater than its parts. We lost something in the process of splitting that no amount of union can repair. Despite our union, we are incomplete."

Ahilya stared at him. The cosmic creature had appeared nothing more than a wisp of air to her, but its split had seemed like the world breaking. Rocks had shattered in her mind, and a chilling scream had echoed over the planet. It was what had happened to Iravan, to what he and his yaksha had once been. How had they survived the pain of that for so many lifetimes? The guilt?

"You are still you," she whispered, almost afraid of what he'd say. "Aren't you?"

Iravan smiled. "Yes. I am still me. More so than I've ever been."

"And the union?" Ahilya asked, studying his face, those unearthly eyes. "How do you feel?"

Iravan's shoulders moved uncomfortably. "It feels like I've… grown… a limb where once there had only been a phantom. I can see the Resonance in the Deepness. And I feel a silence in the back of my mind. I know both of those are the falcon, but we'll have to learn to communicate with each other. Fragments as we both are, the bird has as much its own consciousness as I have mine."

They sat silently, their fingers weaving in and out of each other's. Around them, the garden grew in rasps and creaks. *There could be life here*, Ahilya thought. Birds and animals and people, just like there were in the ashrams above. This could be the haven that she'd always sought in her research, a place for humankind to live again. A weight of sadness filled her chest. She swallowed, trying to loosen it.

"When we were in the caves," she said after some time, "you said Ecstasy brought clarity. Is this what you meant, about the yakshas and these cosmic beings?"

"More than that," Iravan said. "I meant clarity about my history. Ahilya, the ancient architects always knew yakshas were their own selves—their other halves—they knew this from the very beginning. There was a time when the yakshas were revered, when architects released the cosmic beings into birth deliberately to sustain trajection, and sought the yakshas after, perhaps to unite with them. That was a time when Ecstasy was desirable. Yet Ecstasy was a reminder that we split, that *we* created the earthrages. If a society of architects chose Ecstasy, there'd be no going back—and so, eventually, architects began to fear the jungle. They erased the yakshas and buried this knowledge, perhaps in a part of the histories that they kept secret even from their own kind. I don't know what brought the change about, but I can understand it. Architects would have had to live with the knowledge of their guilt and shame—and more, they would have to recompense for what they had done after they became Ecstatics."

Ahilya glanced at him. "What do you mean? Recompense how? Why?"

Iravan took a deep breath. "Ecstasy—it changes you. Bharavi tried to tell me, but it is only now that I understand—now that I feel this burning desire in me so clearly. Inherent to Ecstasy is the union with the yaksha, and inherent to the union is the desire to make up for lifetimes of mistakes."

Iravan raised a slow hand to his chest.

"I can feel it," he whispered, staring. "The desire to make amends weighs on me, heavy on my heart. If architects throughout had allowed Ecstasy, they would have had to make up for everything they had once done; they would almost have had no choice. It was better to outlaw Ecstasy altogether—to build material bonds and limits and arbitrary rules, and forbid the jungle and forget the yakshas. It was better to be worshipped by those who couldn't traject instead of admitting to them how we had destroyed their world. That secret—that is my shameful history."

"But you built the labyrinth. You stopped the earthrage."

Iravan shook his head, dropping his hand. "No, Ahilya. *You* stopped the earthrage. *You* were the template to fix me. You were the shield that could touch the creature. You brought the will and the desire and the form. I merely had the means, but you—and those like you without the ability to traject—you hold the power to stop earthrages and take away trajection altogether, for all future to come. It's why the architects feared your kind. It's why they erased you. What we did today—somewhere out there is a fetus that will gain consciousness, but it won't have the ability to traject. It will be… whole unto itself. Like you. That is not the kind of thing the architects would have liked. Only a very small section of architects sought to find the truth."

"Those rebel groups we saw in the caves," Ahilya whispered, understanding.

"Yes. A group of architects and citizens. I think they chose to build the habitat and tried to stop the earthrages. They knew that the rages couldn't be stopped by architects alone—or by complete beings who cannot traject. They needed to work together, one to build, the other to push the labyrinth into reality. But they were a splinter group. Most architects chose to fly. Rather than face their truths, they escaped into the skies. In the end, the increasing earthrages killed the rebels, too." Iravan's hands trembled once, then stilled. "I was one of them. One of those who chose power and flight instead of truth and completion. Again and again and again."

Tears thickened her throat. Ahilya couldn't think of a single appropriate thing to say. If Iravan was right, then everything their civilization had built itself on, all the decisions the ashrams took—they were all based on a lie. She had been right, but she couldn't feel vindication. A heavy sadness grew in the place where anger had once lived. Her lingering resentments against the architects faded like fog in sunlight.

She broke the gaze and looked back at the garden Iravan had built. It had bloomed in the last few minutes. More streams of water had appeared, and Iravan had constructed several waterfalls gently trickling down the rocks. Ahilya smelt the moisture and life in the air.

"It's beautiful," she said. She could feel him smile though she couldn't bear to look at him, not with the tears threatening to spill down her cheeks. "You've built this place for others, too."

"Yes. I..." Iravan choked on his own repressed tears. "I don't belong to an ashram anymore. Not like this. Not with who I've finally become. But my purpose has never been clearer. To find a way to tell the other ashrams about the truth I've learned, to release the architects from the fear of Ecstasy, and to—"

"End every earthrage," Ahilya whispered.

"Yes. With your help."

Ahilya shook her head. "Those beings were trying to escape erasure. You would stop them from doing so? Is that right, Iravan? When once you funneled them into birth yourself?"

"What else is our choice? To let them split? To let them break our planet?"

"So, it is us against them?"

"I've been so lost, Ahilya. I would not wish it upon those beings. It is... harrowing."

"I've been erased, my love. It is harrowing too."

Iravan said nothing, but his brow furrowed. Carefully, Ahilya disentangled her fingers from his. Iravan froze, but she raised her hand to his cheek and stroked it. "You said leaving that dusty little copse would change us. You were right."

He closed his own hand over hers, gazing at her with those blue-green eyes. "It doesn't have to change *us*. It doesn't have to change you and me."

Ahilya said nothing, but a choked sob escaped her.

"In the vortex," Iravan continued, "there was a moment where—I was broken, the falcon and I, *we* were broken. We knew we must unite and complete ourselves, but we didn't know how." Iravan took another deep ragged breath. "You showed me how. You saved us."

Behind them, the falcon ruffled its feathers. One wing lifted slightly, and Ahilya glimpsed a gigantic black eye, unringed. She thought she detected grudging gratitude from the bird. She glanced back at Iravan and only felt awe and humility from him.

Tears burned in her throat. He was making this difficult. Of course he was.

"What else did you see?" she whispered.

His gaze locked on to hers. "Your reality. Ahilya, you're… pregnant."

She made no reply to that. Iravan's grip tightened on her hand, almost painful.

"You knew this," he breathed. "Why didn't you tell me?"

"Would you have left the copse and made the choices you did?"

"So you forced the choice on me by keeping me ignorant?" A growl laced his words. "Ahilya, it was not your decision to make alone! You don't know what that vortex did to you. You don't know—"

"We ended the earthrage. I saved you. You said this yourself."

Iravan trembled in anger. She snaked her other arm around her belly, remembering all the arguments the two of them had so long before, remembering how he had lived with that fear as an architect; the decision that she could take about any child they had, alone, without his participation.

Perhaps he was thinking of the same thing, for his grip loosened and he took another deep breath to calm himself. "I can never go back to Nakshar. Not like this. Not yet."

"Then the ashram survived," she said. She had seen it in the… Etherium, of course, but until Iravan nodded, she hadn't known how much she had been waiting for his confirmation.

He watched her a long moment, his eyes growing brighter.

She could feel it coming, the moment of inevitability.

"You're leaving me," he said quietly. "You're saying goodbye."

"I'm trying very hard not to," she said, uttering a humorless laugh. He didn't smile, so she looked back into his eyes. She thought of Dhruv and Tariya and Arth and Kush, and the things she had made Airav do. Iravan against the world. That was the choice she had made. She needed to answer for it. "There are others who need me now," she said. "To whom I owe explanations. I've… done what I could for you."

"I *want* you," Iravan said. "Isn't that better than need?"

"Yes," she said sadly. "It is. It really is."

They sat in silence, fingers still entangled. Behind them, the yaksha rumbled softly and shook its feathers. An explosion of jasmines covered the walls, running like a wave from one end of the garden to another. The scent was intoxicating; and she breathed it in, its fresh, sultry heat. He was doing this, of course. Perhaps he didn't know he was.

"You were the best of them," Iravan said abruptly. "Of all the lives and all the many partners I've had—you made completion possible." He stared straight ahead past the garden that filled with jasmines. "Our civilization is embedded with the need for material bonds. It's passed down to us as the greatest wisdom, because architects weren't supposed to be Ecstatic. I lived a hundred, a *thousand* lives with that wisdom, but I couldn't have found the falcon in any of those. In no other life did I have someone who pushed me to find myself like you did. You…" He turned to her then, his blue-green eyes gazing into her. "You made *me* possible. And I will never stop owing you for that."

Tears trickled down Ahilya's cheeks. It was more than she could bear. Her heart pounded in her chest. She stood up before she could change her mind.

The yaksha ruffled its wings and stretched, sudden shade falling on Iravan and Ahilya. The creature's wings extended high above her. Individual feathers shone like mercury.

Iravan stood up slowly. His jaw clenched, but she knew it was not in anger. He was holding back tears. He walked over to the front, and the giant falcon gazed down at him with its glittering black eyes. Her husband stared back with his ethereal blue-green ones; the yaksha yarped, an imperious and haughty lift to its beak, but as Iravan raised a hand, the yaksha bent its sharp beak and let Iravan stroke it.

Iravan strode back to Ahilya. He knelt, making a step with his hands.

Ahilya walked forward, placed a hand on his shoulder, and he boosted her up so she sat astride the falcon. The yaksha rustled under her, and she breathed deeply. The creature felt alien, its glistening feathers cool under her skin. It smelled of earth and smoke, truly a creature of the jungle.

Iravan vaulted over behind her, and the scent of firemint overpowered Ahilya.

She gripped feathers with both her hands, and he closed his own over hers. His legs wrapped around hers, the breathing ragged in his chest—

The yaksha uttered a scream. It strode toward the opening in the wall. Trees separated in front of them, through Ecstatic trajection. The bird opened its wings, and—

It launched itself into the air.

Ahilya gasped and laughter escaped her. Iravan laughed too, a roar of surprised delight, and the flight pushed her back into him; they cleared the trees and ascended into the blue sky. Land fell away as the falcon climbed higher, its wings beating twice before it began to glide. The sungineering locket around her neck began to chime. Iravan's locket pressed into her shoulder, both the halves signaling to each other, using the power of Ecstasy.

Wind rushed at her, making her eyes water. The jungle below was a vision of green and brown, dust still ballooning as the last waves of the earthrage settled. A single oasis of calm lay amidst the green—the epicenter of their feat, the habitat. Dust balloons radiated out from it, and Ahilya thought abstractedly of how she had thought to study these very patterns so long before, standing on Nakshar's terrace. There was still so much left to understand about those cataclysms, a study like she could never have imagined even existed.

Eventually, a shape became visible in the sky.

Clouds obscured it, but there was no mistaking the giant hovering oblong structure. Nakshar.

Iravan didn't make straight for it. Instead, he nudged the yaksha to glide around the city. Nakshar whipped in and out of clouds, in front of them and then to their left. The ashram was ellipsoidal on one side, and—Ahilya gasped—attached to another flat city on the other. Ashrams traded with each other all the time, but she had never seen anything like this before. Reikshar had evidently come to Nakshar's rescue.

They drew closer. The patterns on Iravan's arms changed, and leaves grew around them, extended from the ashram. The falcon moved in a haze of cover. Ahilya couldn't see anything except snatches of bark and sky. Moisture pricked her face. Tears.

The falcon landed with a gentle thump. Iravan trajected, and the leaf cover lessened. Ahilya flung one leg around so she was sitting sideways on the falcon. She stared at her husband, and he stared back. The blue-green light had leached out of Iravan's eyes. He looked like he always had, his salt-and-pepper hair slightly too long, his almost-black eyes drawn in sorrow. Ahilya wanted to say something; there was so much to clarify, so much she wanted him to understand, that this was not in punishment, it was in necessity.

Iravan's mouth turned slightly up. He understood. Of course he did.

He leaned forward and brushed his lips against hers, in a whisper of a kiss.

"Perhaps this is not goodbye," she murmured.

"You are my family," Iravan growled. "And you carry the possibility of my child. It is *never* goodbye."

Then his hands encircled her waist, and he lifted her up and lowered her down to the ground that rose to gather her. Ahilya stepped back, away from the falcon.

The bird flapped its wings, once, twice—

Iravan raised a hand in farewell—

And then they were gone.

For a long time, Ahilya remained standing on the strip of green Iravan had trajected. She couldn't see him or the falcon, but her hand clasped the sungineering locket hard. Only when the locket went cold and silent did Ahilya turn away from the open sky and begin walking towards the city proper.

There were questions, of course.

The citizens of Reikshar didn't recognize her, but that was hardly surprising. Nakshar had merged with the other ashram, and people from Reikshar had welcomed the citizens of Nakshar as their own. Someone brought her back to the temple, and there was a flurry of activity while Ahilya sat silently in front of the rudra tree sapling, waiting for a councilor and what they had in mind for her actions with Airav. She had been gone less than a week, she learned; they thought that her attempt at finding Iravan had failed, that she had hovered in her orb for a few days and returned. Some people stared at her, muttered about her recklessness, about her heroism. Ahilya waited, not bothering to correct them, her hands curled around her satchel.

It was Chaiyya who finally came to her. The Senior Architect trajected, and healbranch grew around Ahilya, wrapping her arms and legs. For long minutes, Chaiyya examined her. Then she sat back in bemusement, no doubt wondering how Ahilya's wounds had healed if her clothes looked so ragged.

Ahilya broke the silence. "You survived. When I left, you'd said Nakshar had only days."

The Senior Architect nodded tiredly. "Reikshar came to us a few hours ago, but we survived the days before that because of... well, because of you."

Ahilya drew back, surprised.

"The battery you forced us to use," Chaiyya said. "Its counterpart here generated enough power to sustain the ashram until Reikshar made it to us."

"Airav," Ahilya asked. "How is he?"

Chaiyya pressed a hand to her waist. She had days perhaps until her delivery. "Airav hasn't trajected since then. There are costs to the battery, though we don't yet know if his situation is temporary. He's conscious but hasn't yet been able to enter the Moment. I'm trying to heal him."

"I'm sorry," Ahilya said softly.

"I know." Chaiyya didn't look angry, only weary. "And I should tell you—news of Airav's condition has spread. People already knew we were working on the battery and especially now that we used it—well, the Maze Architects know of what happened to Airav."

Ahilya stared at her. "You told everyone?"

"We had to. The Maze Architects had already noticed his absence. They did not see him in the Moment or on the Disc, and we had to make a statement to them to assuage their fears. We have told them that they needn't fear the sungineering battery—that yakshas can traject Ecstatically and we intend to use that for our purpose. Without that assurance, they will fear the use of a battery for their own enslavement—"

"I understand the dangers—"

"Then you should understand your role in it," Chaiyya said. "They may come to you, Maze Architects and Junior Architects, seeking to know more. You are the expert on yakshas, and your involvement in the battery is now well known. Ahilya, I know you and the council have had their differences—"

"I won't say anything that will make matters worse, Chaiyya. You have my word."

Chaiyya nodded, then hesitated.

"There's more?" Ahilya urged.

"What you did. Forcing us to make the choice… the flight all alone to look for Iravan…"

"I accept my punishment. I wouldn't change my actions."

"No—you misunderstand. Iravan is gone, Bharavi is gone, and Airav can't traject anymore. That leaves Kiana, Laksiya, and I in the council."

Ahilya waited, unsure of where the Senior Architect was going.

"I'm offering you a position as Nakshar's councilor," Chaiyya said heavily.

Shocked, Ahilya stared at the woman, for a sign of a trap or manipulation, but Chaiyya only looked tired.

"I'm not an architect," Ahilya said, at last. "Nor a sungineer."

"No, you're an archeologist. We've accepted Iravan's nomination. Your assistance during the investigation, the information you shared about the yakshas, and frankly, your daring… Perhaps these are what we need now. The others all agreed. Do you accept?"

For a heartbeat, Ahilya remained speechless. Here it was, everything she had worked for from the very beginning, the opportunity to make a real difference to the society of Nakshar.

Yet there was more to this than Chaiyya was saying. "Dhruv invented the battery," Ahilya said slowly. "Did Kiana not nominate him?"

"Senior Sungineer Kiana made no nomination of her own. Instead, she seconded Iravan's nomination of you." Chaiyya took a deep breath loaded with meaning. "I cannot fault her reasoning," she added softly. "Dhruv's battery destroys an architect, but *your* information might help the architects. You know the secret of excision already, you know what an architect sacrifices, you were married to a Senior Architect. None of the other candidates came close to any of these qualities. They were out of the running long before, and we decided unanimously, once Kiana seconded your position."

Ahilya studied the woman. It wasn't a fair decision, she knew. At the heart of it, they had decided based on who was the better choice for the architects.

And yet there was more there. What Chaiyya said now—the logic behind choosing Ahilya—it was the public reason, no doubt. Another sungineer on the council—especially one who had created the battery—would only create more fear for the architects who were questioning their own safety in light of this new invention.

But why not select a Maze Architect, then? Why choose someone like Ahilya who had a history of antagonism toward the trajectors? The council always had more architects than non-architects—Iravan had told her it was necessary. Yet with herself, Laksiya, and Kiana on it, that critical number would be switched. Why would Chaiyya take this step, knowing what the implications of such an imbalance would be?

No, this had something to do with the citizens, something Ahilya wasn't being told.

She tore her gaze away from Chaiyya and studied the temple, how citizens still lingered by the pillars and walls, how several stared at her, speaking behind their palms. Ahilya was used to whispers about her, but now in their faces she discerned not contempt but admiration, even awe.

Nakshar had come close to its own destruction, only days past. Dhruv had told Ahilya that the council had chosen to inform the citizens about the attempts at a battery. They had done it, under duress, so the combined fears of the non-architects did not work against the trajection of the Disc and plummet the already-fragile ashram into the earthrage. But had the citizens awoken to their own importance, their own status, because of it? Ahilya's absence had not gone unnoticed. Perhaps people had talked—and by strongarming the council, she had set a precedent.

The councilors needed her now. They needed a citizen to side with them—someone who was neither a sungineer nor an architect but still somehow associated with both—yet it was not this alone. Matters were only going to become more fragile in the ashram, with the invention of the battery and the awakening of the non-architects. Chaiyya was looking for a scapegoat to sacrifice, for when things went awry. Ahilya had forced Airav to use a battery; she had smuggled in the spiralweed; she had put Iravan first before the lives of any of the citizens. If she slipped now, she would become the whipping girl for all the citizen groups: architects, non-architects, sungineers.

Her eyes widened as the truth of this hit her. She stared at Chaiyya and for the first time saw not a simple maternal woman but a keen politician who had undoubtedly thought of every angle before offering Ahilya the councilorship.

"Do you accept?" Chaiyya asked again, meeting her gaze.

Ahilya thought of the implications of those words, the burdens she had to carry, the future she would build. She thought of the traps and the machinations, her hostilities with the council, and the manner in which Iravan had lost himself within this very role.

"I accept," she breathed.

Chaiyya arose ponderously. "Good. You'll take your vows at our first meeting as soon as we land. We haven't formally announced it yet, but the earthrage has ended—the sungineers of Reikshar and Nakshar have both confirmed so. It will be a few hours before the citizen rings begin chiming, but when they do, I will expect you at the temple again. See to your sister in the infirmary if you need to, and I'll send Maze Architect Naila to escort you back here when it's time." Chaiyya paused, her gaze piercing. "Brace yourself, Ahilya," she added softly. "Being a councilor isn't easy."

She gestured, and Ahilya stood up, her mind reeling with the path she had set herself on. Her feet took her not farther into the temple toward the new infirmary but back out into Reikshar. There would be apologies and explanations to make—to both Tariya and to Dhruv—but her thoughts were too chaotic; Ahilya had to think it over, the consequences of telling people everything she had learnt in the caves, about the true nature of Ecstasy or the architects' connection with the yakshas. She had to calculate her timing, her new position.

Past the congregated citizens of both the ashrams, Ahilya finally found herself alone on a terrace bordering Nakshar with Reikshar. The citizen rings had not begun chiming yet, but she could see the change in the architecture already, the manner in which both the ashrams had decided to merge into a single unit to mimic the model Iravan had designed so long before to conserve trajection energy.

If it weren't for the scent of pine and cedar that Reikshar favored over Nakshar's leafier varieties, she would not have known she was in another ashram. If it weren't for the underlying melody, one she recognized as the landing raga susurrating through the foliage, slightly off-key from what she was used to, she would not have known this wasn't truly home.

The hedge had grown waist-high, sharp brambles poking out from it as it extended higher into a dome. Ahilya's wrists felt heavy with Airav's rudra bead bracelets—and a stray wondrous thought came to her—she would soon have her own beads, her due now as a councilor.

She didn't tap the bracelets to change the bush's permissions. Instead, she stared at the bobbing shape she had spotted from one of the pathways. Her fingers toyed with the telescope in her ragged satchel. Her throat grew heavy with the tracker locket, reminding her of the choice she had made in returning to Nakshar, the choice she had left behind.

The bush continued to grow, nearly to her chest. Soon, the brambles would block her view. The tracker locket around her neck began chiming again, ever so softly, muffled by the thick fabric of her kurta.

Her heart pounding, Ahilya raised the telescope to her eyes and aimed it straight ahead. The bobbing shape focused into a faraway falcon, its wings spanning a hundred feet. Atop the creature sat a figure, his white kurta gleaming in the blue sky, his windswept hair a tangle. Iravan raised a hand, and she caught the glint of a smile.

Ahilya laughed—

Raised her own—

Then the brambles closed, knitting themselves together.

The smile still playing on her face, Ahilya turned and walked away from the terrace. Jasmines erupted along the grass, leading her way back to the temple.

GLOSSARY

- ARCHITECTS' ACADEMY: A place outside the temple where architects go to learn trajection. Non-architects are not privy to this place.
- ARCHITECTS' DISC: A Disc circling the rudra tree where Maze Architects perform trajection to construct the city and keep it in flight. Non-architects are not privy to this place.
- ASHRAM: An airborne city.
- BASIC EQUATION, THE: A commonly understood mathematical equation that measures the loss and conversion of energy during trajection: Plant's old state of consciousness + trajection = a corresponding dissipating raga.
- DEATHBOX: A sungineering device made of glass that creates a pocket Moment.
- DEATHCAGE: A gigantic deathbox that can potentially contain people within it.
- DEATHCHAMBER: A sungineering invention comprising forcefields that create a pocket Moment. Unlike deathboxes or deathcages, deathchambers have no physical boundaries of glass, thus allowing one to walk in and out of them unobstructed.
- DISC ARCHITECT: An architect charged specifically with

working on the Architects' Disc. Usually Maze Architects or Senior Architects.

- Earthrages: Cataclysmic storms that destroy the surface of the jungle planet constantly and unpredictably.
- Ecstasy: A state of uncontrollable power for an architect, which is extremely dangerous.
- Examination of Ecstasy: An Examination that only those architects suspected of Ecstasy are called to. Undergoing it can be harrowing. Failing it results in excision. Passing it can still be traumatic.
- Excision: The cutting away of an architect from their trajection. Only done to Ecstatic Architects.
- Healbranch: A plant grown in Nakshar that provides immunity to everyone.
- Junior Architect: A person who can traject and is one level below Maze Architects and two levels below Senior Architects. Their uniform comprises a long green kurta and narrow green trousers. A formal translucent robe is belted over those for official ceremonies.
- Maze Architect: A person who can traject and is one level above Junior Architects and one level below Senior Architects. Their uniform comprises a long brown kurta and narrow brown trousers. A formal translucent robe is belted over those for official ceremonies.
- Moment, The: An extradimensional reality only available to architects, where they are able to see the consciousness of plants.
- Raga: A melody that is discernible only to architects. A byproduct of trajection.
- Rudra Tree: Nakshar's core tree that is embedded with flight permissions from ancient times that allow the city to fly.

- Rudra Beads: Dark black beads that are created from the rudra tree, and are embedded with both trajection and sungineering technology. The greater the number of beads, the more responsibility a person has. Each bead contains specific permissions, and several beads make rudra bead necklaces, bracelets and rings.
- Sanctum: A place within the temple where architects go to heal. Non-architects are not privy to this place.
- Senior Architect: The most senior position an architect can aspire to. A level above Maze Architect. All Senior Architects automatically become councilors, and it is awarded very rarely after a very critical process. The uniform comprises a long white kurta and narrow white trousers. A formal translucent robe is belted over those for official ceremonies.
- Senior Sungineer: The most senior position a sungineer can aspire to. All Senior Sungineers automatically become councilors, and it is awarded very rarely after a critical process.
- Spiralweed: Contraband. An illegal plant in most cities.
- Sungineers: Engineers who harness trajection to build everyday devices.
- Temple: A city's core that houses councilor chambers, the sanctum, the Architects' Disc and other such privileged and protected spaces. No one may come in without permission from the councilors.
- Trajection: The power that architects use that allows them to manipulate plants in order to build.
- Two Visions: The way an architect can split their sight. The first vision allows them to see normally with their eyes, and the second allows them to drift in the dimension of the Moment.
- Yakshas: Gigantic jungle creatures that live in isolation. Little is known of them.

ACKNOWLEDGMENTS

You'd think when you've finished writing a whole book, the acknowledgment section would come easy—but wow, that is so not the case. Books are nebulous things, coming into reality from half-formed thoughts and daydreaming; and the publishing industry is ruthless, with many systemic messes. For this to become a thing I can touch and smell and hold and feel… it is nothing short of magic.

There is a temptation—especially with your very first book—to thank everyone who had even the slightest to do with bringing you to this point; from your English teachers who graded your essays with joy and pushed books into your hands, to the stranger who didn't laugh when you shyly mentioned you wanted to be an author.

So ah!—is this ever going to be an incomplete, arbitrary list… and if I miss you out, it is not because I am not grateful. Just maybe tired and overwhelmed as I write this, hah!

Thank you, first and foremost, to my wonderful team at Titan: my editor George Sandison whose communication, gentle navigation of the story to make it its best, and vision for the book made me see my own work differently—something I never thought I'd be able to do through so many re-reads. I cherish your feedback immensely.

Thanks to my copyeditor Richard Shealy for untangling commas and the finer details of sentence structures, and being so communicative through the process; to my marketing team Katherine Carroll, Kabriya Coghlan, Lydia Gittins, Hannah Scudamore, and all of the extended Titan family. After a brutal experience in the initial stages of The Rages Trilogy, being welcomed and cared for by you was like coming home. You reignited joy in the debut experience when I was fairly certain I was entering into all this pretty jaded.

Thank you to my fabulous cover artist Leo Nicholls, and the Titan art team; especially Julia Lloyd for all the gorgeous art (did you, dear reader, catch that coolness in the interior art of Chapter 51, by the way?), and all of the things that made Iravan and Ahilya, and the world of The Rages Trilogy feel so alive. Thanks to Adrian McLaughlin for typesetting magic—when I tell you that it was one of my largest concerns, how some formatting would be rendered—ah, but I needn't have worried at all. Thanks to the PRH sales team who worked so hard behind the scenes to get this book into the hands of booksellers and readers. Thank you to the wonderful team at Recorded Books, who got the audiobook out—and oh my goodness, is it ever surreal to hear your book read out like that, what a trip! It feels so goddamn real, in a whole different way!

Deep gratitude to the BookEnds Literary Agency, and especially to Naomi Davis, my dear friend and brilliant agent. I will never forget how you were so excited about this book when it was nothing but a seed, and I was but a stranger, back when we met at a con. Look at how far we've come, huh? I cannot thank you enough for your passion for my career, for taking me at my own estimation and always believing in me—and for standing by me through events that are certainly no part of an ordinary debut experience. We weathered it all, and here we are on the other side, and we are a badass team, you and I.

So much gratitude to the many, many people who have taught me about the industry. It would be impossible to name everyone, but I would be remiss if I didn't mention two groups. The Writing Excuses crew, whose podcasts I'd listen to every morning driving to work in those very, very early days when I was drafting this book, before I even had an agent—you folks reminded me of why I loved writing when I truly needed it. When I look back, those podcasts really shine as a starting moment for The Rages Trilogy and my own career as a writer. Thanks also to SFF Powerhouse, who kept me company through the ups and downs of life in the last few years—Chelsea Mueller, Gabriela Romero Lacruz, Rachel Fikes, Sue Lynn Tan, and all my other wonderful agent sibs on the server. You are all so generous for sharing your expertise freely, and you've taught me about community in this very topsy-turvy, lonesome industry. I could not be more grateful.

Several people also read the early drafts of this book, and tremendous gratitude to them all, especially my excellent beta readers: Cheyanne Lepka, David Esarey, Léon Othenin-Girard, and Francesca Gabrielle Hurtado, whose constant love for the story through the years gave me enduring faith in my own work when doubts crept in. You are all rockstars, and you answered the inanest of queries with patience and calm, and helped me reverse-outline my character motivations when I sent you late-night Discord messages, saying, "Wait, would Ahilya or Iravan really do that?" I see you, my friends.

This would be an incomplete list if I did not thank the book community who showed up, especially during my deep moment of crisis in 2021 when it felt like *The Surviving Sky* was not going to see the light of day, because of Publishing Mess™. Look what we did together! You made *The Surviving Sky* the little book that could. You're wonderful!

Thank you, thank you, thank you, to the good folks at Fantasy Hive UK for helping with the cover reveal, and being among the first few to reach out and offer support—even back when I didn't truly cotton on to how much I needed it. Thank you, Shazzie at Fantasy Book Critic for your constant cheerleading of the book and the characters, and making me truly believe that yes, Representation Matters—I was *delighted* to see you pick up on all the Hindu philosophy stuff; thank you, Rogier Capri who was the first champion of *The Surviving Sky* online—I still remember being shocked when I saw you saying you anticipated my book so much all those years ago when there was no buzz around it at all. Deep, deep gratitude to all the booksellers, bookbloggers, bookstagrammers, and Tiktokers who have shared their love for this book. Truly, in my deepest moments of doubt, your support for *The Surviving Sky*, and for Ahilya and Iravan, kept me going.

Thanks also to my dear writing friends—authors who I love and admire so much, and honestly, I still pinch myself—what is this reality where I can call you friends? Fake news! You reached out with your support, and I will always remember your kindness—Tasha Suri, Shannon Chakraborty, Anna Stephens, Essa Hansen, Andrea Stewart, EJ Beaton, Melissa Caruso, Marshall Ryan Maresca, Sunyi Dean, Hannah Long, Fran Wilde, and oh god, I know I am just forgetting some names—I'm sorry! Deep thanks to all of the wonderful people who blurbed this book. How so many and so amazing, each of you? I am blush! You should know, I read your blurbs many times, especially when I was writing the sequels—your words mattered so much. Thank you for taking the time out of your schedules to read early copies of this book.

Thank you to my parents and brother who grew me up on books.

Look ma and pa and Kateek—I haz written words. Those days of bringing me back stacks of heavy tomes from your school library everyday; or taking me to the public library that was so far away from home; or posting my childish essays out to the local magazines and bragging to your friends, "My daughter/sister wrote this"… they got me here. Your daughter/sister wrote *this*. (Insert cool sunglass emoji.)

Many thanks to you, reader, to whom this book is dedicated. I thought long and hard about the dedication, and it seemed the only appropriate one for this book, my first one out in the world. After all, ever since I was a dreamy kid chewing on a pencil and thinking up plotless stories, I had you at the back of my mind. Now I get to meet you through my words, and it is such a privilege. I hope you stick around for the rest of Ahilya and Iravan's journey. I promise it is going to be good.

And finally—I deliberately kept this for the end, because I don't know if I will *ever* have the right words, and I *know* how inadequate these words are—thank you to my dear, loving family. To my husband, Tate—you are the treasure of my life, the best person I know, and none of this would have been remotely possible without you. If I tried to list the ways you have contributed to not just this story, but my whole writing career, I'd fill up another book.

And to my Rohan, my beautiful, brilliant darling. You were along for so much of the journey, weren't you? I wrote through when *you* were an idea, through the pregnancy and nursing sessions through maternity leave and then the end of it. I wrangled publishing woes with you right by my side, and burst into tears of overwhelm when both good and bad things happened while cuddling you; and you just stuck by me, giving me so much love. I hope one day when you're old enough to read these books, you enjoy them, and are proud of your mom. I love you more than anything else in the world.

ABOUT THE AUTHOR

Kritika H. Rao is a science-fiction and fantasy writer, who has lived in India, Australia, Canada and The Sultanate of Oman. Kritika's stories are influenced by her lived experiences, and often explore themes of consciousness, self vs. the world, and identity. When she is not writing, she is probably making lists. She drops in and out of social media; you might catch her on Twitter, TikTok, or Instagram @KritikaHRao. Visit her online at www.kritikahrao.com.